THE WORKS OF

HENRY VAN DYKE

AVALON EDITION

VOLUME XIV

❦

MESSAGES AND PERSUASIONS

I

Christ among the Lowly
From a painting by L. Lhermitte in the
possession of the Metropolitan Museum of Art, New York

*Behold I bring you good tidings of great joy
which shall be to all people.*—LUKE 2:10

THE GOSPEL FOR AN AGE OF DOUBT

AND

THE GOSPEL FOR A WORLD OF SIN

BY

HENRY VAN DYKE

NEW YORK

1921

PREFACE

THE two books in this volume came directly out of the experience and work of a man trying, however imperfectly, to help other men through the service of the Christian ministry.

The light which Christ had given me in the conflict with intellectual doubt, the aid and comfort which his Cross had brought me in the inward and outward fight with evil, I wished to pass on to other men.

How closely limited this power of "passing on" is, how little our systems and theories in religion can do for others, how truly every man must "come and see" for himself what Christ can do for him, I know now even better than I felt then. Writing to-day I might press some arguments and conclusions less absolutely than I did twenty years ago. But my central conviction that the light and hope and deliverance of the world are in the gospel of a person, and that Jesus Christ is that person, and that to know him as the Son of God is immortality, —this conviction remains unchanged. Why change the form in which it was uttered?

PREFACE

After all the volume makes no claim to be a system of theology; it is only the partial record of a working, struggling faith. The spirit in which it was written is that of the apostle John, in his first epistle: "That which we have heard, which we have seen with our eyes, which we have looked upon, and our hands have handled, of the Word of life, . . . declare we unto you, that ye also may have fellowship with us."

The first book, *The Gospel for an Age of Doubt*, consists of lectures given on the Lyman Beecher Foundation at Yale University in 1896. The divinity students to whom they were addressed appealed to me less as budding theologians than as young men with a life to live and a work to do in the modern world, in their own age, in their own way. The question, "How to make sermons," was far less important for them than the question, "What to preach." For if they did not have a real gospel,—good news,—there was no call for them to be ministers. They would better be carpenters or mechanics or farmers,—more useful!

Now that age,—the close of the nineteenth century,—was one of doubt. Not of atheism, nor of positive disbelief, you understand, but of universal questioning, hesitation to believe in anything spiritual, and consequent uncertainty and sadness. The only good news that I could find in such an age was the answer of Jesus to the questionings and needs of the souls of men, which physical science had neither stilled nor satisfied. This was the gospel which had brought help to me in a battle with doubt whose darkness I did not care to recall. This was the gospel I wished to persuade my brothers to receive and preach,—the gospel of a person for persons,—the gospel of Jesus, bringer of that eternal light which is the life of men.

The second book in this volume, *The Gospel for a World of Sin*, consists of lectures and university sermons delivered at Harvard, Princeton, and other colleges in 1897 and 1898. I felt, more and more, (and friends deepened this feeling by their frank criticism,) that the first lectures were incomplete. They dealt chiefly with the difficulties which religion presents to the mind, and not enough with those burdens which the sense of sin lays upon the heart. Most men, at some time, are doubters. But all men are sinners, and that is what makes them restless and unhappy. The mystery of evil,— the saving power of the Cross,—to leave these out is to miss the full meaning of the gospel.

But I have not tried to define that vital truth

PREFACE

which is known to theologians as the doctrine
of the atonement. No definition is sufficient.
It is beyond words. It is the crowning act of
the human life of God. It is the unsearchable
glory of divine self-sacrifice.

In these dark days that follow the dark war,
we see from the valley of vision the light of
the cross on the hill. If God could not suffer
he would be far from man. Christ giving himself for the world is the wisdom, power, and
love of the Eternal to everyone that believeth.

HENRY VAN DYKE.

AVALON, December 8, 1920.

CONTENTS

BOOK I
THE GOSPEL FOR AN AGE OF DOUBT

BOOK II
THE GOSPEL FOR A WORLD OF SIN

CONTENTS

BOOK I

THE GOSPEL FOR AN AGE OF DOUBT

I

AN AGE OF DOUBT

THERE is one point in which all men resemble each other: it is that they are all different. But their differences are not fixed and immutable. They are variable and progressive. Types of character survive or perish, like the forms of animal life.

Thus it comes to pass that underneath all the diversities of individual life, we may discern vaguely the features of a *Zeitgeist*, a spirit of the time. Generations differ almost as much as the men who compose them. There is a personal equation in every age.

To know this is a necessity for the preacher. Even as the physician must apprehend the idiosyncrasy of his patient, and the teacher must recognize the quality of his pupil, so must the preacher be in touch with his age.

In endeavouring to arrive at this knowledge, contact with the world is of the first consequence. For one who desires to make men and women what they ought to be, nothing can take the place of an acquaintance with men and women as they are.

3

AN AGE OF DOUBT

One means of obtaining this acquaintance is through literature,—not that highly specialized and more or less technical variety of literature which is produced expressly for certain classes of readers, but literature in the broader sense, including contemporary history and criticism, poetry and fiction, popular philosophy and diluted science. This kind of literature is the expression of the *Zeitgeist*. It is at once a product, and a cause, of the temperament of the age. In it we see not only what certain men have written by way of comment on the movement of the times, but also what a great many men are reading while they move. It expresses, and it creates, a spirit, an attitude of mind. "I do not imagine," says Paul Bourget, "that I am announcing an altogether novel truth in affirming that literature is one of the elements of the ethical life,—the most important perhaps; for in the decline, more and more evident, of traditional and local influences, the book is taking its place as the great initiator."

A course in modern novels and poetry might well be made a part of every scheme of preparation for the ministry. The preacher who does not know what his people are reading does not know his people. He will miss the significance of the current talk of society, and even of the

daily comments of the newspapers, (a cheap substitute for conversation,) unless he has the key
to it in the tone of popular literature. It is
from this source that I have drawn many of the
illustrations for this lecture. If they appear unfamiliar or out of place in a theological semi-
nary, I can only say that they seem to me none
the less, but perhaps the more, significant and
valuable on that account. For I think that one
of the causes by which, as John Foster wrote
seventy years ago, "Evangelical Religion has
been rendered unacceptable to persons of cultivated taste," has been a certain ill-disguised
contempt on the part of persons of orthodox
opinions for what they are pleased to call,
"mere *belles-lettres*." The preacher who wishes
to speak to this age must read many books in
order that he may be in a position to make the
best use of what Sir Walter Scott called "the
one Book." He must keep himself in touch
with modern life by studying modern literature, which is one of its essential factors.

I

As soon as we step out of the theological circle into the broad field of general reading we see
that we are living in an age of doubt. [1896.]
I do not mean to say that this is the only

5

feature in the physiognomy of the age. It has many other aspects, from any one of which we might pick a name. From the material side, we might call it an age of progress; from the intellectual side, an age of science; from the medical side, an age of hysteria; from the political side, an age of democracy; from the commercial side, an age of advertisement; from the social side, an age of publicomania. But looking at it from the spiritual side, which is the preacher's point of view, and considering that interior life to which every proclamation of a gospel must be addressed, beyond a doubt it stands confessed as a doubting age.

There is a profound and wide-spread unsettlement of soul in regard to fundamental truths of religion, and also in regard to the nature and existence of the so-called spiritual faculties by which alone these truths can be perceived. In its popular manifestations, this unsettlement takes the form of uncertainty rather than of denial, of unbelief rather than of disbelief, of general scepticism rather than of specific infidelity.

It is not merely that particular doctrines, such as the inspiration of the Bible, or the future punishment of the wicked, are attacked and denied. The preacher who concentrates his attention at these points will fail to realize the gravity of the situation. It is not that a spirit of bitter and mocking atheism, such as Bishop Butler described at the close of the last century, has led people of discernment to set up religion "as a principal subject of mirth and ridicule, as it were by way of reprisal for its having so long interrupted the pleasures of the world." The preacher who takes that view of the case now will be at least seventy years too late. He will fail to understand the serious and pathetic temper of the age.

The questioning spirit of to-day is severe but not bitter, restless but not frivolous; it takes itself very seriously and applies its methods of criticism, of analysis, of dissolution, with a sad courtesy of demeanour, to the deepest and most vital truths of religion, the being of God, the reality of the soul, the possibility of a future life. Everywhere it comes, and everywhere it asks for a reason, in the shape of a positive and scientific demonstration. When one is given, it asks for another, and when another is given, it asks for the reason of the reason. The laws of evidence, the principles of judgment, the witness of history, the testimony of consciousness, —all are called in question. The answers which have been given by religion to the most difficult

7

and pressing problems of man's inner life are declared to be unsatisfactory and without foundation. The question remains unsolved. Is it insoluble?

The age stands in doubt. Its coat-of-arms is an interrogation point rampant, above three bishops dormant, and its motto is *Query?*

II

If we inquire the cause of this general scepticism in regard to religion, the common answer from all sides would probably attribute it to the progress of science. I do not feel satisfied with this answer. At least I should wish to qualify it in such a way as to give it a very different meaning from that which is implied in the current phrase "the conflict between science and religion."

Science, in itself considered, the orderly and reasoned knowledge of the phenomenal universe of things and events, ought not to be, and has not been, hostile to religion, simply because it does not and cannot enter into the same sphere. The great advance which has been made in the observation and classification of sensible facts, and in the induction of so-called general laws under which those facts may be arranged for purposes of study, has not even touched the

8

two questions upon the answer to which the reality and nature of religion depend: first, the possible existence of other facts which physical science cannot observe and classify; and second, the probable explanation of these facts.

What has happened is just this. The field in which faith has to work has been altered, and enormously broadened. But the work remains the same. The question is whether faith has enough vital energy to face and accomplish it. For example, the material out of which to construct an argument from the evidences of final cause in nature has been incalculably increased by the discoveries of the last seventy years in regard to natural selection and the origin of species. The idea of final cause has not been touched. Only the region which it must illuminate has been vastly enlarged. It remains to be seen whether faith can supply the illuminating power. Already we have the promise of an answer in many books, by masters of science and philosophy, who show that the theory of evolution demands for its completion the recognition of the spiritual nature of man and the belief in an intelligent and personal God.

The spread of scepticism is often attributed to the growth of our conception of the physical magnitude of the universe. The bewildering

number and distances of the stars, the gigan-
tic masses of matter in motion, and the tremendous sweep of the forces which drive our tiny
earth along like a grain of dust in an orderly
whirlwind, are supposed to have overwhelmed
and stunned the power of spiritual belief in
man. The account seems to me incorrect and
unconvincing. Precisely the same argument was
used by Job and Isaiah and the Psalmists to
lead to a conclusion of faith. The striking dis-
proportion between the littleness of man and
the greatness of the stars was to them a demonstration of the necessity of religion to solve the
equation. They saw in the heavens the glory
of God. And if man to-day knows vastly more
of the heavens, does not that put him in position to receive a larger and loftier vision of the
glory?

We observe, moreover, that it is just in those
departments of science where the knowledge of
the magnitude and splendid order of the physical universe is most clear and exact, namely, in
astronomy and mathematics, that we find the
most illustrious men of science who have not
been sceptics but sincere and steadfast believers in the Christian religion. Kepler and New-
ton were men of faith. The most brilliant
galaxy of mathematicians ever assembled at one

time and place was at the University of Cambridge in the latter half of the nineteenth century. Of these "Sir W. Thomson, Sir George Stokes, Professors Tait, Adams, Clerk-Maxwell, and Cayley—not to mention a number of lesser lights, such as Routh, Todhunter, Ferrers, etc. —were all avowed Christians." Surely it needs no further proof to show that the pursuit of pure science does not necessarily tend to scepticism.

No, we must look more closely and distinguish more clearly in order to discover in the scientific activities of the age a cause of the prevailing doubt. And if we do this I think we shall find it in the fallacy of that kind of science which mistakes itself for omniscience.

"What we see is the pretence of certain sciences to represent in themselves all human knowledge. And as outside of knowledge there is no longer, in the eyes of science thus curtailed, any means for man to come in contact with the realities, we see the pretence advanced by some that all reality and all life should be reduced to that which they have verified. Outside of this there are only dreams and illusions. This is indeed too much. It is no longer science, but scientific absolutism."

"The history of the natural sciences," said

11

Du Bois-Reymond in 1877, "is the veritable history of mankind." "The world," says another, "is made of atoms and ether, and there is no room for ghosts." M. Berthelot, in the preface to his *Origines de l'alchimie*, claims that "the world to-day is without mysteries"; meaning thereby, I suppose, that there is nothing in existence, from the crystallization of a diamond to the character of a saint, which cannot be investigated and explained by means of a crucible, a blow-pipe, a microscope, and a few other tools.

This is simply begging the question of a spiritual world in the negative. It is a stupefying assumption. It is a claim to solve the problems of the inner life by suppressing them. This claim is not in any sense necessary to the existence of science, nor to any degree supported by the work which it has actually accomplished. But it is made with a calm assurance which imposes powerfully upon the popular mind; and, being made in the name of science, it carries with it an appearance of authority borrowed from the great service which science has rendered to humanity by its discoveries in the sphere of the visible.

The result of this *petitio principii* in the minds of those who accept it fully and carry it out to its logical conclusion, is a definite system of metaphysical negation which goes under the various names of Naturalism, Positivism, Empiricism, and Agnosticism. Its result in the minds of those who accept it is the development of a sceptical temper. Its result in the minds of those who are unconsciously affected by it, through those profound instincts of sympathy and involuntary imitation which influence all men, is an attitude,—more or less sincere, more or less consistent and continuous, —an attitude of doubt.

The spirit of the age tacitly divides all the various beliefs which are held among men into two classes. Those which are supported by scientific proof must be accepted. Those which are not thus supported either must be rejected, or may safely and properly be disregarded.

III

Now this general scepticism, in all its shades and degrees, is reflected in current literature. Never was literary art more versatile and successful than in the present age. Never have its laws been more widely understood and its fascinations more potently exercised. Never has it evoked more magical and charming forms to float above an abyss of nothingness.

AN AGE OF DOUBT

In the lay sermons and essays of Huxley and Tyndall and Frederic Harrison and W. K. Clifford, scepticism appears militant and trenchant. These knights-errant of Doubting Castle are brilliantly equipped as men of war; and even when they fall foul of each other, as they often do, the ground of the conflict is an accusation of infidelity to the principles of unbelief, and its object is to drive the adversary back into a more complete and consistent negation.

In the vivid and picturesque historical studies of Renan and Froude, scepticism is at once ironical and idealistic, destructive and dogmatic. In the penetrative and intelligent critiques of Scherer and Morley, it adheres with proud but illogical persistence to the ethical consequences of the faith with which logic has broken: like a son disinherited, but resolved to maintain the right of possession by the strong arm.

In the novels of unflinching and unblushing naturalism,—like those of Zola and Maupassant and the later works of Thomas Hardy, scepticism speaks with a harsh and menacing accent of the emptiness of all life and the futility of all endeavour. In the psychological romances of Flaubert and Bourget and Spielhagen, George Eliot and Mrs. Humphry Ward, it holds the mirror up to human nature to disclose a face darkened with inconsolable regret for lost dreams. Far apart as *Madame Bovary* and *Cosmopolis, Problematische Naturen* and *Middlemarch* and *Robert Elsmere* may be in many of their features, do they not wear the same expression,—the melancholy of disillusion?

Fiction in its more superficial form, dealing only with the manners and customs of the social drama, and relying for its interest mainly upon local colour and the charm of incident narrated with vivacity and grace, betrays its scepticism by a serene, unconscious disregard of the part which religion plays in real life. In how many of the lighter novels of the day do we find any recognition, even between the lines, of the influence which the idea of God or its absence, the practice of prayer or its neglect, actually exercise upon the character and conduct of men? Take, for example, Du Maurier's *Trilby*, as the type of a clever book carelessly written for the public of a passing moment. It is incredibly credulous in regard to the dramatic possibilities of hypnotism. It is pitifully inadequate in its conception of the actual potencies of religion; and it uses Christianity chiefly as a subject for caricature.

Poetry has always been the most direct and

15

intimate utterance of the human heart. And
it is in poetry that we hear to-day the voice
of scepticism most clearly, "making abundant
music around an elementary nihilism, now
stripped naked." Listen to its sonorous chant-
ings as they come from France in the verse of
Leconte de Lisle, celebrating the sombre ritual
of human automata before the altar of the unknown and almighty tyrant, who agitates them
endlessly for his own amusement. Listen to
its delicate and decadent lyrics, as Charles
Baudelaire sings his defeat in life and his thirst
for annihilation.

> "*Morne esprit, autrefois amoureux de la lutte,*
> *L'Espoir dont l'éperon attisait ton ardeur*
> *Ne veut plus t'enfourcher. Couche-toi sans pudeur,*
> *Vieux cheval dont le pied à chaque obstacle butte.*
>
> *Résigne-toi, mon cœur, dors ton sommeil de brute.*
>
> *Et le Temps m'engloutit minute par minute*
> *Comme la neige immense un corps pris de roideur :*
> *Je contemple d'en haut le globe en sa rondeur*
> *Et je n'y cherche plus l'abri d'une cahute !*
>
> *Avalanche, veux tu m'emporter dans ta chute ?*"

Turn to England and hear its musical confession in the cool, sad tones of Matthew

AN AGE OF DOUBT

Arnold, no enemy of faith, but her disenchanted lover.

> *"Forgive me, masters of the mind,*
> *At whose behest I long ago*
> *So much unlearned, so much resigned—*
> *I come not here to be your foe;*
> *I seek these anchorites not in ruth,*
> *To curse and to deny your truth;*
>
> *Not as their friend, or child, I speak*
> *But as on some far northern strand,*
> *Thinking of his own gods, a Greek,*
> *In pity and mournful awe might stand*
> *Before a fallen Runic stone,—*
> *For both were faiths, and both are gone."*

There is a poem by Tennyson (who never broke with faith, though he felt the strain of doubt), in which he describes with intense dramatic sympathy the finality of scepticism in the human soul. It is called "Despair." There is another poem, called "Sea Dreams," in which he gives a vision of the rising tide of doubt as it threatens to undermine and overwhelm the beliefs of the past. The woman is telling her husband the dream which came to her in the night as she watched by their sick child.

> *"But round the North, a light,*
> *A belt, it seem'd, of luminous vapour, lay,*

AN AGE OF DOUBT

And ever in it a low musical note
Swell'd up and died; and, as it swell'd, a ridge
Of breaker issued from the belt, and still
Grew with the growing note, and when the note
Had reach'd a thunderous fulness, on those cliffs
Broke, mixt with awful light (the same as that
Living within the belt) whereby she saw
That all those lines of cliffs were cliffs no more,
But huge cathedral fronts of every age,
Grave, florid, stern, as far as eye could see,
One after one: and then the great ridge drew,
Lessening to the lessening music, back,
And passed into the belt and swell'd again
Slowly to music: ever when it broke
The statues, king, or saint, or founder, fell;
Then from the gaps and chasms of ruin left
Came men and women in dark clusters round,
Some crying, 'Set them up! they shall not fall!'
And others, 'Let them lie, for they have fall'n.'
And still they strove and wrangled: . . .
*   . . . and ever as their shrieks*
Ran highest up the gamut, that great wave
Returning, while none mark'd it, on the crowd
Broke, mixt with awful light, and show'd their eyes
Glaring, and passionate looks, and swept away
The men of flesh and blood, and men of stone,
To the waste deeps together."

It was only a dream, but how many souls
have felt the vague sadness, the haunting, helpless pity and fear of a like vision, looking out
upon the landscape of man's inner life, and see-

ing the ancient landmarks slowly melted or swiftly swept away, the shrines of memory shaken and removed, the fair images of immortal desire and aspiration dissolving and disappearing in the onward waves, silently creeping, or surging with mysterious and inarticulate music out of the waste deep of doubt,—

"*The unplumbed, salt, estranging sea.*"

Who can think of the sharp anguish and dull grief that have fallen upon innumerable hearts, through the loss of their most precious faith; who can think of the gray, formless, ever-moving, yet immovable flood of mordant gloom that has covered so many once bright fields of human hope, so many once peaceful homes of human trust and confidence,—who can think of these things, even though his own standpoint be still untouched, his own faith-dwelling founded upon a rock far above the tide, without a sorrowful perturbation of spirit and a deep, inward sense of compassionate distress and dread? We stand upon the shore, but we stand beside the sea. And we look out upon it, as Émile Littré sadly wrote, like the women of Troy, whom the Roman poet pictured gazing at its mighty currents and engulfing waves:

"*Pontum adspectabant flentes.*"

IV

It is with no unsympathetic and condemning spirit, that I have tried to draw this picture of the sceptical age in which we live. Its faults, its perils, are mine and yours. So far as current scepticism has its source in evil, it flows from faults of which we all partake,—the pride of intellect, the haste of judgment, the preference of the seen to the unseen, the impatience of ignorance, and the disloyalty of reason to conscience.

But this is not the point of view from which we speak. Doubt, as we are thinking of it, is not a crime, but a malady. And if we are to have any hope or power of staying its progress and healing its ravages, we must not only be sympathetic in our understanding of it, but we must also look through it, earnestly and patiently, to see whether there are not some favourable symptoms, some signs of enduring vitality, some promises of returning health and strength in the spirit of the age.

Of these it seems to me that there are three, so evident and so important, that we ought not to overlook them. First, the acknowledged discontent and pain of unbelief; second, the practical recoil of some of the finest minds from the void of absolute scepticism; third, the persistent desire of many doubting spirits to serve mankind by love, self-sacrifice, and ethical endeavour. In other words, I would read the lesson of encouragement in the sufferings of doubt, in the doubts of doubt, and in the splendid moral inconsistencies of doubt.

Begin, then, with pain, which is not only a warning of disease, but also a sign of life. The pessimism which goes hand in hand with scepticism is a cry of suffering.

It seemed at one time as if the course of modern scepticism was to be free from sadness, a painless malady. At the beginning of the century the tone of infidelity was jubilant and triumphant. Percy Bysshe Shelley walked into the inn at Montanvert and wrote his name in the visitors' book, adding "democrat, philanthropist, atheist,"—as if it were a record of victory and a title of glory. This cheerful type of scepticism still survives, here and there, in a few men who insist that the process of disenchantment is pleasant and joyous, and that the optimism which belonged to faith may remain while the faith itself disappears. It is like the smile of the Cheshire cat, in the child's story-book, which broadened and brightened while the cat faded, until finally the animal was gone and nothing but the smile was left.

But for the most part modern doubt shows a sad and pain-drawn face, heavy with grief and dark with apprehension. There is an illustration of this change in the life of George Eliot. In her girlhood she passed suddenly, by an unconditional surrender, out of a warm faith in Evangelical Christianity into the coldest kind of rational scepticism. She writes of the dull, and now forgotten, book which wrought this change, Charles Hennell's *Inquiry concerning the Origin of Christianity*, with strange and almost fantastic merriment: "Mr. Hennell ought to be one of the happiest of men that he has done such a life's work. I am sure if I had written such a book I should be invulnerable to all the arrows of all the gods and goddesses. The book is full of wit to me. It gives me that exquisite kind of laughter which comes from the gratification of the reasoning faculties." But the arrows which she despised struck home, ere life was ended, to her own heart.

"I remember," writes Mr. F. W. H. Myers, "how at Cambridge I walked with her once in the Fellows' Garden of Trinity, on an evening of rainy May, and she, stirred somewhat beyond her wont, and taking as her text the three

words which have been used so often as the
inspiring trumpet-calls of men,—the words God,
Immortality, Duty,—pronounced, with terrible
earnestness, how inconceivable was the first,
how unbelievable was the second, and how
peremptory and absolute the third. Never,
perhaps, had sterner accents affirmed the sovereignty of impersonal and unrecompensing
law. I listened and night fell; her grave, ma-
jestic countenance turned towards me like a
Sibyl's in the gloom; it was as though she with-
drew from my grasp, one by one, the two scrolls
of promise, and left me the third scroll only,
awful with inevitable fate."

An inevitable fate, seen through the gloom
of falling night,—that indeed is the aspect of
life which the literature of doubt displays to
us. A gray shadow of melancholy spreads over
the questioning, uncertain, disillusioned age;
languid sighs of weariness breathe from its
salons and palaces. Bitter discontent mutters
in its workshops and tenements. "Never, I
believe," says Paul Desjardins, "have men
been more universally sad than in the present
time." And then he adds, with keen insight,
"Our misery lies in feeling that we are less men
than we were sixty years ago." Human life
has been unspeakably impoverished and nar-

rowed by the loss of faith. Comedy has become tragic, and tragedy has grown mean and sordid. Men have lost the sound of a Divine voice in the story of their existence and learned to listen to it as

> "*a tale*
> *Told by an idiot, full of sound and fury*
> *Signifying nothing.*"

Love itself, the great purifier and ennobler, has been transformed in the subtle analysis of sexual passion, from the sea-born Venus, pure and radiant with immortal youth, to a dirt-engendered goddess, concealing her secret ugliness with illusory and artificial charms, and presiding with malignant power over the lower currents of man's being,—a veritable Cloacina of human life.

The thought of "the grandeur and misery of man," as Pascal conceived it, was painful but elevating. The conception of the insignificance and misery of man as scepticism presents it, is painful and dispiriting. Born of blind force and unconscious matter, quickened by some mysterious cruelty to a consciousness of his own origin and a foreboding of his inexplicable and fruitless destiny, he "drees his weird," between two fathomless abysses of gloom, as one who is indeed weary and heavy-laden. The

24

music with which he accompanies his march towards the blank and dismal bourn, rolls and clashes through the literature of every land with deep and mournful discords, as if man had at last invented that strange organ of expression which a satirist has called "the *Misérophon*."

"This philosophy," says Stendhal, commenting upon the last reflections of his hero in *Rouge et Noir*, "was perhaps true, but it was of such a nature as to make one long for death." And then the critic from whom I have quoted these words, adds his own commentary. "Do you perceive, at the close of this work, the most complete which the author has left, the breaking of the tragic dawn of pessimism? It rises, this dawn of blood and tears, and, like the clearness of a new-born day, it overspreads with crimson hues the loftiest spirits of our age, those whose thoughts are at the summit, those to whom the eyes of the men of to-morrow lift themselves,—religiously. I am come in this series of psychological studies to the fifth and last of the personages whom I propose to analyse. I have examined a poet, Baudelaire; a historian, Renan; a romancer, Flaubert; a philosopher, Taine; I have just examined one of these composite artists in whom the critic and the imaginative writer are closely united; and I have found in these five Frenchmen of such importance, the same philosophy of disgust with the universal nothingness."

If we turn to Russia, which has given us some of the most brilliant and influential, though undisciplined, writers of modern fiction, do we not hear, in an accent harsher and more formidable, the same conclusions, the same cries of nausea over the inextricable confusion and vain efforts of human life? If we turn to England, do we not see the same cloud of melancholy, less threatening, less angry, but no less dark, rising from the chasm which doubt has made between man's inner life and the world as scientific positivism pictures it? How mournful is the voice in which W. K. Clifford proclaims, "The Great Companion is dead!" How dark with silent, passionate grief is that lonely wood in which "Robert Elsmere" feels himself going blind to the dearest visions of his former faith. How black the air in which "Jude the Obscure" breathes out the last throbbings of his insurgent heart in curses upon his sordid and desperate fate! Let a poet speak the last word of doubt,—the epitaph of *The City of Dreadful Night*. The portentous figure of "Melancholia" sits enthroned above her vast metropolis.

AN AGE OF DOUBT

"The moving Moon and stars from east to west
Circle before her in the sea of air;
Shadows and gleams glide round her solemn rest.
Her subjects often gaze up to her there:
The strong to drink new strength of iron endurance,
The weak, new terrors; all, renewed assurance
And confirmation of the old despair."

But why despair, unless indeed because man, in his very nature and inmost essence, is framed for an immortal hope? No other creature is filled with disgust and anger by the mere recognition of its own environment and destiny. This strange issue of a purely physical evolution in a profound revolt against itself is incredibly miraculous. Can a vast universe of atoms and ether, unfolding out of darkness into darkness, produce at some point in its progress, and that point apparently the highest, a feeling of profound disappointment with its partially discovered processes and resentful grief at its dimly foreseen end? To believe this would require a monstrous credulity!

Atheism does not touch this difficulty. Agnosticism evades it. There are but two solutions which really face the facts. One is the black, unspeakable creed that the source of all things is an unknown, mocking, malignant Power, whose last and most cruel jest is the misery of disenchanted man. The other is the hopeful creed that the very pain which man suffers when his spiritual nature is denied, is proof that it exists, and part of the discipline by which a truthful, loving God would lead man to himself. Let the world judge which is the more reasonable faith. But for our part, while we cling to the creed of hope, let us not fail to "cleave ever to the sunnier side of doubt," and see in the very shadow that it casts the evidence of a light behind and above it. Let us learn the meaning of that noble word of St. Augustine: *Thou hast made us for Thyself, and unquiet is our heart until it rests in Thee.*

The inquietude of the heart which doubt has robbed of its faith in God, is an evidence that scepticism is a malady, not a normal state. The sadness of our times under the pressure of positive unbelief and negative uncertainty has in it the promise and potency of a return to health and happiness. Already we can see, if we look with clear eyes, the signs of what I have dared to call "the reaction out of the heart of a doubting age towards the Christianity of Christ and the faith in Immortal Love."

Pagan poets, full of melancholy beauty and vague regret for lost ideals, poets of decadence and despondence, the age has born, to sing its

28

grief and gloom. But its two great singers, Tennyson and Browning, strike a clearer note of returning faith and hope. Pessimists like Hartmann work back unconsciously, from the vague remoteness of pantheism, far in the direction, at least, of a theistic view of the universe. His later books—*Religionsphilosophie* and *Selbstersetzung des Christenthums*—breathe a different spirit from his *Philosophie des Unbewussten*. A statesman, like Signor Crispi, does not hesitate to cut loose from his former atheistic connections and declare that "the belief in God is the fundamental basis of the healthy life of the people, while atheism puts in it the germ of an irreparable decay." The French critic, M. Edouard Rod, declares that "only religion can regulate at the same time human thought and human action." Mr. Benjamin Kidd, from the side of English sociology, assures us that "since man became a social creature, the development of his intellectual character has become subordinate to the development of his religious character," and concludes that religion affords the only permanent sanction for progress. A famous biologist, Romanes, who once professed the most absolute rejection of revealed religion, thinks his way soberly back from the painful void to a position where he confesses that "it is reasonable to be a Christian believer," and dies in the full communion of the church.

All along the line, we see men who once thought it necessary or desirable to abandon forever the soul's abode of faith in the unseen, returning by many and devious ways from the far country of doubt, driven by homesickness and hunger to seek some path which shall at least bring them in sight of a Father's house.

And meanwhile we hear the conscience, the ethical instinct of mankind, asserting itself with splendid courage and patience, even in those who have as yet found no sure ground for it to stand upon. There is a sublime contradiction between the positivist's view of man as "the hero of a lamentable drama played in an obscure corner of the universe, in virtue of blind laws, before an indifferent nature, and with annihilation for its denouement," and the doctrine that it is his supreme duty to sacrifice himself for the good of humanity. Yet many of the sceptical thinkers of the age do not stumble at the contradiction. They hold fast to love and justice and moral enthusiasm even though they suspect that they themselves are the products of a nature which is blind and dumb and heartless and stupid. Never have the obligations of self-restraint, and helpfulness, and equity, and universal brotherhood been preached more fervently than by some of the English agnostics.

In France a new crusade has risen; a crusade which seeks to gather into its hosts men of all creeds and men of none, and which proclaims as its object the recovery of the sacred places of man's spiritual life, the holy land in which virtue shines forever by its own light, and the higher impulses of our nature are inspired, invincible, and immortal. On its banner M. Paul Desjardins writes the word of Tolstoi, "*Il faut avoir une âme;* it is necessary to have a soul," and declares that the crusaders will follow it wherever it leads them. "For my part," he cries, "I shall not blush certainly to acknowledge as sole master the Christ preached by the doctors. I shall not recoil if my premisses force me to believe, at last, as Pascal believed."

In our own land such a crusade does not yet appear to be necessary. The disintegration of faith under the secret processes of general scepticism has not yet gone far enough to make the peril of religion evident, or to cause a new marshalling of hosts to recover and defend the forsaken shrines of man's spiritual life. When

31

the process which is now subtly working in so many departments of our literature has gone farther, it may be needful to call for such a crusade. If so, I believe it will come. I believe that the leaders of thought, the artists, the poets of the future, when they stand face to face with the manifest results of negation and disillusion, which really destroy the very sphere in which alone art and poetry can live, will rise to meet the peril, and proclaim anew with one voice the watchword, "It is necessary to have a soul! And though a man gain the whole world, if his soul is lost, it shall profit him nothing." But meanwhile, before we come to that point of spiritual impoverishment where we must imitate the organized and avowed effort to recover that which has been lost, we see a new crusade of another kind: a powerful movement of moral enthusiasm, of self-sacrifice, of altruism, even among those who profess to be out of sympathy with Christianity, which is a sign of promise, because it reveals a force that cries out for Christian faith to guide and direct it.

Never was there a time when the fine aspirations of the young manhood and young womanhood of our country needed a more inspiring and direct Christian leadership. The indications of this need lie open to our sight on every side. Here is a company of refined and educated people going down to make a college settlement among the poor and ignorant, to help them and lift them up. They declare that it is not a religious movement, that there is to be no preaching connected with it, that the only faith which it is to embody is faith in humanity. They choose a leader who has only that faith. But they find, under his guidance, that the movement will not move, that the work cannot be done, that it faints and fails because it lacks the spring of moral inspiration which can come only from a divine and spiritual faith. And they are forced to seek a new leader who, although he is not a preacher, yet carries within his heart that power of religious conviction, that force of devotion to the will of God, that faith in the living and supreme Christ, which is in fact the centre of Christianity. All around the circle of human doubt and despair, where men and women are going out to enlighten and uplift and comfort and strengthen their fellowmen under the perplexities and burdens of life, we hear the cry for a gospel. All through the noblest aspirations and efforts and hopes of our age of doubt, we feel the longing, and we hear the demand, for a new inspiration of Christian faith.

AN AGE OF DOUBT

These are the signs of the times. We must take note of them, we must labour and pray to understand their true significance, if we are to say anything to our fellow-men which shall be worth our saying and their hearing.

Renan made a strange remark not long before his death: "I fear that the work of the Twentieth Century will consist in taking out of the waste-basket a multitude of excellent ideas which the Nineteenth Century has heedlessly thrown into it." The sceptic's fear is the believer's hope. Once more the fields are white unto the harvest. The time is ripe; ripe in the sorrow of scepticism, ripe in the return of aspiration, ripe in the enthusiasm of humanity, for a renaissance of the spiritual life.

Already the horizon brightens with the tokens of this renaissance. There is a new interest in religion as the most living of all topics. There is a new sense of its vital meaning for the whole life of man. There is a new determination to apply it all around the circle of human responsibilities and test its value everywhere. There is a new cry for a Christ who shall fulfil the hopes of all the ages. There is a new love waiting for him, a new devotion ready to follow his call. Doubt, in its nobler aspect,—honest, unwilling, morally earnest doubt,—has been a

AN AGE OF DOUBT

John the Baptist to prepare the way for his coming. The men of to-day are saying, as certain Greeks said to apostles of old, "Sirs, we would see Jesus." The disciple who can lead the questioning spirits to him, is the man who has the Gospel for an Age of Doubt.

II

THE GOSPEL OF A PERSON

THE prevalence and the quality of modern
doubt, with its discontent and sadness, its
misgivings and reactions, its moral inconsistencies and fine enthusiasms, bring the preacher
who is alive and in earnest, face to face with
the most important question of his life. What
can I do, what ought I to do, to meet the
strange, urgent, complicated needs of such a
time as this?

First of all, as a man,—and every preacher
ought to be a man, though not every man is
bound to be a preacher—as a man, it is necessary to lead a clean, upright, steadfast, useful
life, lifted above all selfishness, and especially
above that form of religious selfishness which
is the besetting peril of those who feel themselves rich in faith in the midst of a generation
that has been made poor by unbelief. Never
has there been a time when character and conduct counted for more than they do to-day.
A life on a high level, yet full of helpful, heal-

ing sympathy for all life on its lowest levels,
is the first debt which we owe to our fellow-
men in this age.

But beyond this, is there not something personal and specific which the conditions of the
present demand from us, as men who have not
only the common duty of living, but also the
peculiar vocation of speaking directly and constantly to the inner life of our brothers?

The moment we look at the problem in this
light, we see that there are various lines of activity open to us, and along all of these lines
men are making promises and prophecies of usefulness and success. The cures which are suggested for the malady of the age are many and
diverse. Of some of them we need speak only
in passing, to recognize that for us, at least,
they are unsuitable.

Herr Max Nordau, for example, in his curious
and chaotic book, *Degeneration*, diagnoses the
sickness of modern times as the result, not of
a loss of faith, but of a fatal increase of nervous
irritability produced by the strain of an intricate civilization. He declares that the malady must run its course, but that in time it
will be healed by the restorative force of
"*misoneism*, that instinctive, invincible aver-
sion to progress and its difficulties that Lom-

broso has studied so much and to which he has given this name."

The name is certainly not a pretty one, nor do I think that, after the first feeling of pleasure in learning to pronounce a newly imported word has passed, the contemplation of its meaning will afford us any profound sense of satisfaction or hope. The picture of mankind as a magnified Jemmy Button, returning from his temporary residence in England to his native *Terra del Fuego*, and flinging away his gloves and patent-leather shoes, to relapse into a peaceful and contented barbarism, is not inspiring. Who is there that would care to devote his life to the hastening of such a result? Who but the veriest quack, himself affected by the hysteria of the age, would think of curing the convulsions of St. Vitus' dance in an overstrained humanity by throwing the patient into the stupor of typhoid fever?

Another and very different method of dealing with the malady of the times is suggested by those who believe that Science itself, in the immense future advance which is predicted for it, will supply the antidote for the scepticism which has accompanied its previous course. New discoveries will be made which will support the proposition: *Il faut avoir une âme.*

New arguments will be constructed which will give us a scientific demonstration of the unseen universe and the future life. It is in this spirit that Mr. F. W. H. Myers calls attention to the phenomena of mesmerism and hypnotism and telepathy, and suggests that the need of the age is a more cordial and general interest in the investigations of the Society of Psychical Research. I do not think, for one, that these investigations are to be slighted or despised. They may be of great value. But it is difficult to believe that this is the source to which the preacher is to look either for his inspiration or his message. For, in the first place, it is highly improbable that science is about to make any such astonishing advance, either in methods or results, as some men anticipate. The best authorities admit this, and warn us that there are "limitations in the nature of the universe which must circumscribe the achievements of speculative research." Mr. Myers himself makes the same admission, and says that so far as our discoveries are confined to the physical side of things, there is no ground whatever for sanguine hope. Moreover, in the second place, whatever work may be done in this direction must be accomplished, not by preachers, but by scientists. The average preacher has

39

no particular vocation, and no adequate qual-
ification, for the task. Neither by temperament nor by training is he fitted to judge of
these matters. Now and then you will find a
rare exception; but as a rule nothing could
be of less value than the scientific sermons of
preachers who have only a bowing acquaintance with science. If the cure of modern scepticism is to be accomplished by the further
progress of physical investigation, at least we
must confess that this enterprise is not for us.

But there are two other ways of dealing with
current doubt which demand closer attention.
One of them is the philosophic method of a
reductio ad absurdum. The logic of rationalism
is applied to its own premises in order to show
that they are unfounded and unverifiable. The
result of this attack, as it has been made with
a relentless and masterly hand by Mr. Arthur
James Balfour in his *Defence of Philosophic
Doubt*, is to exhibit the startling fact that "the
universe as represented to us by science is
wholly unimaginable, and that our conception
of it is what in theology would be termed purely
anthropomorphic." The evidence for the existence of a world composed of atoms and ether
is no more conclusive, the account which science
gives of their nature and qualities is no more

40

coherent, than the evidence and account which faith gives of a world created by a personal God and inhabited by immortal souls. Pure agnosticism is thus forced into the service of Christianity and used to destroy all *a priori* objections to it. Giant Doubt is brought low by turning his own weapons against himself, even as Benaiah, the son of Jehoiada, slew the Egyptian "with his own spear." [1]

The value of this service of philosophy is considerable. The Christian preacher ought not to be ignorant of its actual results, for they are such as to encourage him in preserving his independence against the tyrannous claims of positivism; nor unfamiliar with its methods, for they are fitted to train and discipline his mind by hard exercise and exact work. But it must be remembered that only a mighty man of valour, one who, like Benaiah, ranks above the host, and above the thirty captains of the host, can hope to play a leading part in this enterprise of "carrying the war into Africa." It must be remembered also that the reduction of scientific naturalism to an absurdity falls far short of the establishment of religious faith as a verity. Grateful for all that philosophy can do, and is doing, to clear the way, the preacher

[1] 1 Chron. 11 : 23.

must have a principle, an impulse, a line of action which will carry him beyond the negative result of making unbelief doubtful, to the positive result of making belief credible.

At this point our attention is called to another way of dealing with current scepticism, —the dogmatic method, which relies for the defence of faith upon the construction of a complete and consistent system of doctrine in regard to God and man, the present world and the future life. Faith, in other words, is to be established by fortification, surrounded and entrenched with banquette and parapet, scarp and ditch and counterscarp of iron-worded proof, defended on every side by solid syllogisms, and impregnable against all assaults of unbelief. It is foolish not to recognize the great work which has been done along this line by wise and strong men in the past. Those who affect to despise it and make light of it, are simply ignorant of some of the loftiest achievements of the human intellect. The works of Augustine and Anselm and Thomas Aquinas, of John Calvin and Richard Hooker and John Owen, of Ralph Cudworth and William Chillingworth, of Richard Baxter and Samuel Clarke and Joseph Butler, of Jonathan Edwards and Charles Hodge and W. G. T. Shedd, are massive works. They impose a sense of wonder upon every thoughtful observer.

But concerning the attempt to conquer modern doubt by a system of dogmatic theology, certain things must be remembered. The conditions of warfare change from age to age. The vast fortresses of solid stone whose possession was once regarded as the security of nations, are not ranked so high as they were a hundred years ago. The earthwork, the rifled cannon, the iron-clad ship, the torpedo, have wrought great changes. Deductive logic is just as strong as it ever was, but somehow or other men are not as much impressed by it. Induction is the method of to-day: and that is a subtle, evasive, mobile method. It cannot be shut in by a ring of fortresses. Already the dogmatic systems in which the inductive method is ignored or subordinated (whether made long ago, or constructed yesterday on ancient models) are out of date. They are good for the men who are within them, but on the outside world they have no more effect than Windsor Castle would have in protecting England from a foreign invasion.

We feel sure that theology, in time, must and will vindicate its claim to be considered as an essential factor in the intellectual life of man, by adapting itself to the changed conditions, and producing even mightier works by the new methods than those which it produced by the old. Already we see the promise of a renaissance of dogmatics in such books as Mulford's *The Republic of God*, Harris' *The Self-Revelation of God*, Orr's *The Christian View of God and the World*, and Fairbairn's *The Place of Christ in Modern Theology*. But we must remember that even those who anticipate and predict this reconstruction of the old truth on the new lines most enthusiastically, recognize that it must be a long and difficult task, and that the man who is to be a master-builder must have a magnificent equipment. How exhilarating at the first sight, but at the second sight how overwhelming and discouraging, are the demands of the age upon him who would fain be an epoch-making theologian, as they are stated, for example, in Mr. Balfour's *Foundations of Belief*, or in Dr. George A. Gordon's inspiring book *The Christ of To-day*. Truly it appears that such a man must realize the supposition of St. Paul: he must speak with the tongues of men and of angels, and have the gift of prophecy, and understand all mysteries and all knowledge. Who is sufficient for these things? It will take a long time for the best of us to learn all this. Perhaps the most of us

44

may never go so far. Meantime we need something divinely simple and true that we can preach at once, directly, joyfully, fervently to the heart of the age.

We look out upon the world and we see that some men have had such a gospel without being in any sense finished and systematic theologians. St. Paul and St. Peter and St. John had it. St. Chrysostom and St. Francis of Assisi and Savonarola had it. John Wesley and George Whitfield had it. In different ages and under different conditions these preachers had the primal message which moves men to believe. And in our own age, under our own conditions, a like message has been proclaimed with power. Père Lacordaire preached such a message in Notre Dame, and Canon Liddon in St. Paul's, to listening thousands. Phillips Brooks made it thrill like a celestial music through the young manhood of America; and Dwight L. Moody has spoken it with vigorous directness in every great city that knows the English tongue. In many things, in ecclesiastical relation, in theological statement, in dress, in manner, in language, these preachers are unlike. One thing only is the same in all of them, and that is the source of their power. Their central message, the core of their preaching, is the personal gospel of Jesus of Nazareth, the Son of God and Saviour of mankind. This, in its simplest form; this, in its clearest expression; this presentation of a person to persons in order that they may first know, and then love and trust and follow him—this is pre-eminently the gospel for an age of doubt.

I

The adaptation of our central message, thus conceived and thus expressed, to meet the peculiar needs of a time of general scepticism, is the theme of this lecture. I do not say that this is the whole of Christianity. I do not say that when the preacher has delivered this message in this form he has fulfilled all of his duties. He may have to bear testimony against errors of thought and vices of conduct; he is certainly bound to give encouragement and guidance to new efforts of virtue and new enterprises of benevolence in every field. But his first and greatest duty, the discharge of which is to give him influence over doubting hearts and strength for all his other work, is simply to preach Christ.

This gospel meets the needs of the present time because it is the gospel of a fact.

Personality is a fact. Indeed we may say that it is the aboriginal fact; the source of all perception; the starting-point of all thought; the informing and moulding principle of all language. "All human observation implies that the mind, the 'I,' is a thing in itself, a fixed point in a world of change, of which world of change its own organs form a part. It is the same, yesterday, to-day, and to-morrow. It was what it is, when its organs were of a different shape and consisted of different matter from their present shape and matter. It will be what it is, when they have gone through other changes."

This fact of a rational, free, conscious, persistent self is the foundation of all sensation and of all reflection; it is the basis of physics as well as of metaphysics. By contrast it gives us our first notion of matter; by resistance, our first notion of force; by operation, our first notion of causality. It is a necessary assumption even in the philosophies of agnosticism, positivism, and materialism. They cannot move a step without it.

"They reckon ill who leave me out."

To deny personality is to deny the possibility of any kind of knowledge and reduce the universe to a blank.

Moreover, it is not only true that the recognition of our own personality lies at the root of perception and reasoning. It is also true that contact with other personalities, conscious, intelligent, free, and persistent like ourselves, is the gateway through which we reach the reality of all external things. To a solitary mind the outward world may be only a dream. But the moment two minds come into contact and communication, it becomes at least a permanent possibility of sensation. By comparison and contrast with the sensations and experiences of others, we verify our own. If it were not for this the whole universe would dissolve around us like the baseless fabric of a vision. The subtle analysis of modern science, transforming the apparently solid elements into invisible atoms, and these atoms into vortex rings in the impalpable and immeasurable ether, throws us back, more and more, upon personality, subjective and objective, as the only thing that remains sure and immutable.

Persons, then, are the most real and substantial objects of our knowledge. They touch us at more points, they affect us in more ways and with greater intensity, they fit more closely into the faculties and powers of our own being, than anything else in the universe. A person who has influenced us or our fellow-men leaves a more profound, positive, permanent, and real impression than any other fact whatsoever. We live as persons in a world of persons, far more truly than we live in a world of phenomena or laws or ideas.

Now, in an age that is characterized, as some German writer has said, by "a hunger for facts," the gospel of a person, if it is rightly apprehended and preached, ought to have peculiar power because it is a factual gospel. We can come to those who are under the benumbing spell of universal doubt and say: Here is a fact, a personality, real and imperishable. It is not merely a doctrine that was believed in Palestine eighteen hundred years ago. It is some one who was born and lived among men. It is not merely a theory of God and the soul and the future life that sprang up in the East in the first century and has strangely spread itself over the world. This religion is historical in every sense of the word, as the actual fulfilment of an ancient hope, and the starting-point of a new life.

The person of Jesus Christ stands solid in the history of man. He is indeed more substantial, more abiding, in human apprehension, than any form of matter, or any mode of force. The conceptions of earth and air and fire and water change and melt around him, as the clouds melt and change around an everlasting mountain peak. All attempts to resolve him into a myth, a legend, an idea,—and hundreds of such attempts have been made,—have drifted over the enduring reality of his character and left not a rack behind. The result of all criticism, the final verdict of enlightened common-sense, is that Christ is historical. He is such a person as men could not have imagined if they would, and would not have imagined if they could. He is neither Greek myth, nor Hebrew legend. The artist capable of fashioning him did not exist, nor could he have found the materials. A non-existent Christianity did not spring out of the air and create a Christ. A real Christ appeared in the world and created Christianity. This is what we mean by the gospel of a fact.

II

And here we come at once into sight of the second quality of this gospel which is peculiarly fitted to meet the needs of a doubting age.

If it be true that a person is a fact, it is no less true that a person is a force. The world moves by personality. All the great currents of history have flowed from persons. Organization is powerful; but no organization has ever accomplished anything until a person has stood at the centre of it and filled it with his thought, with his life. Truth is mighty and must prevail. But it never does prevail actually until it gets itself embodied, incarnated, in a personality. Christianity has an organization. Christianity has a doctrine. But the force of Christianity, that which made it move and lent it power to move the world, is the Person at the heart of it, who gives vitality to the organization and reality to the doctrine. All the abstract truths of Christianity might have come into the world in another form,—nay, the substance of these truths did actually come into the world, dimly and partially through the fragmentary religions of the nations, more clearly and with increasing, prophetic light through the inspired Scriptures of the Hebrews; but still the world would not stir, still the truth could not make itself felt as a universal force in the life of humanity until

"*The Word had breath, and wrought*
With human hands the creed of creeds,
In loveliness of perfect deeds,
More strong than all poetic thought."

I think we must get back, in our conception of Christianity and in our preaching of it, to this primary position. The origin of its power was, and continued to be, and still is, the Person Christ.

This was the secret of his ministry. He himself was the central word of his own preaching. He offered himself to the world as the solution of its difficulties and the source of a new life. He asked men simply to believe in him, to love him, to follow him. He called the self-righteous to humble themselves to his correction, the sinful to confide in his forgiveness, the doubting to trust his assurance, and the believing to accept his guidance into fuller light. To those who became his disciples he gave doctrine and instruction in many things. But to those who were not yet his disciples, to the world, he offered first of all himself, not a doctrine, not a plan of life, but a living Person. This was the substance of his first sermon when he stood up in the synagogue at Nazareth and having read from the Book of Isaiah the prophecy of the Great Liberator, declared unto the people "This day is this Scripture fulfilled in your ears."[1] This was the attraction of his universal invitation, "Come unto me, all ye that labour and are heavy laden and I will give you rest."[2] This was the heart of his summary

[1] St. Luke 4 : 16–21. [2] St. Matt. 11 : 28.

of his completed work when he said, "I, if I be lifted up from the earth, will draw all men unto me." [1]

We are not considering, at this moment, the tremendous implications of such a personal self-assertion, unparalleled, I believe, in the founder of any other religion. We pass by for the present that famous and inevitable alternative, *Aut Christus Deus, aut homo non bonus est*. The point, now, is simply this. As a matter of history, setting aside all question of the divine inspiration and authority of the Gospels, taking them merely as a trustworthy report of a certain sequence of events, it is plain that the force which started the religion of Jesus was the person Jesus. Christ was his own Christianity. Christ was the core of his own gospel.

Read on through the other books of the New Testament, the Acts and the Epistles, and you will see that they are just the record of the operation of this force in life and literature. It was this that sent the apostles out into the world, reluctantly and hesitatingly at first, then joyfully and triumphantly, as men driven by an irresistible impulse. It was the manifestation of Christ that converted them,[2] the love of Christ that constrained them,[3] the power of

[1] St. John 12 : 32.   [2] Gal. 1 : 16.   [3] 2 Cor. 5 : 14.

THE GOSPEL OF A PERSON

Christ that impelled them.[1] He was their certainty[2] and their strength.[3] He was their peace [4]
and their hope.[5] For Christ they laboured and
suffered;[6] in Christ they gloried;[7] for Christ's
sake they lived and died.[8] They felt and they
declared that the life that was in them was his
life.[9] They were confident that they could do
all things through Christ which strengthened
them.[10] The offices of the Church—apostle,
bishop, deacon, evangelist,—call them by what
names you will—were simply forms of service
to him as Master;[11] the doctrines of the Church
were simply unfoldings of what she had received
from him as Teacher;[12] the worship of the
Church, as distinguished from that of the Jewish
Synagogue and the Heathen Temple, was the
adoration of Christ as Lord.[13]

Now it was precisely this relation of the early
Church, in her organization and doctrine and
worship, to the person Christ, held fast in her
memory as identical with the real Jesus who
was born in Bethlehem and crucified on Calvary,
conceived in her faith as still living and present
with his disciples,—it was this personal anima-

[1] 2 Cor. 12 : 9. [2] 2 Tim. 1 : 12. [3] 2 Tim. 2 : 1.
[4] Eph. 2 : 14. [5] Col. 1 : 27. [6] Phil. 3 : 8–10.
[7] Gal. 6 : 14. [8] 2 Cor. 4 : 5, 11. [9] Gal. 2 : 20.
[10] Phil. 4 : 13. [11] Eph. 4 : 8–12.
[12] 1 Cor. 11 : 1, 23; 15 : 3. [13] Phil. 2 : 11; 1 Cor. 12 : 3.

54

tion of the Church by Christ that gave her influence over men. Contrary to all human probability, against the prejudice of the Hebrews who abhorred the name of a crucified man, against the prejudice of the Greeks and Romans who despised the name of a common Jew, she made her way, not by concealing, but by exalting and glorifying, the name of Jesus Christ. Indeed, it seems as if her career of conquest was actually delayed until that name was taken up and written upon her banners. It was in Antioch, where the disciples were first called Christians,[1] that the missionary enterprise of the Church began, and it was from that centre, with that title, that she went out to her triumph.

The name of Christ was magical; not as a secret incantation, but as the sign of a real person, known and loved. It enlightened and healed and quickened the heart of an age which, like our own, was dark and sorrowful and heavy with doubt. It was the charm which drew men to Christianity out of the abstractions of philosophy, and the confusions of idolatry darkened with a thousand personifications but empty of all true personality. The music of that name rang through all the temple of the Church, and

[1] Acts 11 : 26; 13 : 1-3.

to its harmonies her walls were builded. The acknowledgment of that name was the mark of Christian discipleship. To confess that "Jesus is the Christ" was the way to enter the Church. The symbolism of that name was the mark of Christian worship. The central rites of the Church were baptism into Christ and communion with Christ. Fidelity to his name was the crown of Christian martyrdom. Unnumbered multitudes of men and women and children went down to death because they would not deny the Christ. Whatever the early Church was and did, beyond a doubt her character and her activity were but the resultant of the personal influence that flowed from Jesus Christ.

When we turn to follow the history of Christianity through the later centuries down to the present time, we see that the same thing is true. The temporal power of the Bishop of Rome doubtless grew out of the union of the Church with the Empire. The immense wealth and secular authority of ecclesiastics may be traced to social and political causes. But the inward, vitalizing, self-propagating power of Christianity as a religion has always come from the person of Jesus who stands at the heart of it. The attraction of its hymns and psalms and spiritual songs, the beauty of its holy days and solemn ceremonies, were derived from him who is the central figure in praise and prayer. The renaissance of Christian Art sprang from the desire to picture to the imagination the visible, adorable form and face of him whom speculative theology had so often concealed or obscured. The penetrating and abiding fragrance of Christian literature resides in those books, like *The Imitation of Christ*, in which the sweetness of his character is embalmed forever. The potency of Christian preaching comes from, and is measured by, the clearness of the light which it throws upon the personality of Jesus. Read the roll of those in every age whom the world has acknowledged as the best Christians, kings and warriors and philosophers, martyrs and heroes and labourers in every noble cause, the purest and the highest of mankind, and you will see that the test by which they are judged, the mark by which they are recognized, is likeness and loyalty to the personal Christ. Then turn to the work which the Church is doing to-day in the lowest and darkest fields of human life, among the submerged classes of our great cities, among the sunken races of heathendom, and you cannot deny that the force of that work to enlighten and uplift, still depends upon the simplicity and reality with which it reveals the person of Jesus to the hearts of men. Christianity as a missionary religion would be fatally crippled if you took out of it the familiar story of Jesus and his love.

"Mr. Darwin," says Admiral Sir James Sullivan, "had often expressed to me his conviction that it was utterly useless to send missionaries to such a set of savages as the Fuegians, probably the very lowest of the human race. I had always replied that I did not believe any human beings existed too low to comprehend the simple message of the Gospel of Christ. After many years he wrote to me that the recent account of the mission showed that he had been wrong and I right . . . and he requested me to forward to the Society an enclosed cheque for £5, as a testimony of his interest in their good work."

Observe, we are not constructing an argument. We are only tracing a force,—the force that flows from the person of Jesus Christ. The more closely, the more powerfully we can feel it in ourselves and in others, the more confidently we can come to a doubting age and say: Here is this force, intense, persistent, far-reaching. It has moved all kinds of men, from the highest to the lowest. What do you make of it? What will you do with it? Is it not the only thing that can lift and move you out of your doubt? For scepticism is just the inertia of the soul which stands poised between contrary and mutually destructive theories. From that state of impotence there is but one deliverance, and that is by force, the force of life embodied in a person.

III

But the force which proceeds from the person of Jesus is not mere power, blind and purposeless. It moves always in a certain direction. It carries with itself an evidence of things not seen, a substance of things hoped for.

An aura of wonder and mystery surrounded Jesus of Nazareth in his earthly life. All who came in contact with him felt it; in love, if they desired to believe; in repulsion, if they hated to believe. In his presence, faith in the invisible, in the soul, in the future life, in God, revived and unfolded with new bloom and colour. In his presence hypocrisy was silenced and afraid, but sincere piety found a voice and prayed. This effluence of his character breathes from the whole record of his life. It was not merely what he said to men about the eternal verities that convinced them. It was something in himself, an atmosphere surrounding him, and a silent radiance shining from him, that made it easier for them to believe in their own spiritual nature and in the Divine existence and presence. He drew out of their fallen and neglected hearts, by some celestial attraction, spontaneous, gentle, irresistible, a new faith and hope and love. Where he came a spiritual springtide flowed over the landscape of the inner life.

Faith was not imposed on doubting hearts by an external and mechanical process. It grew in the warmth that streamed from him. It was not merely that men were at their best in his company, except, indeed, those who were at their worst through sullen resistance and malignant alarm at his power. It was that men were conscious of something far better than their best, a transcendent force, an influence from the immeasurable heights above them. And to withstand it they must sink below themselves, make new falsehoods and new negations to bind them down, grapple themselves more closely to the base, the earthly, the sensual. But if they yielded to that influence, it lifted and moved their thoughts inevitably upward. It was not merely what he told them of his own sight of spiritual things. It was what they saw reflected in his face and form of that loftier, wider outlook. He was like one standing on a high peak, reporting of the sunrise to men in the dark valley. They heard his words. But they saw also upon his countenance the glow of dawn, and gleaming all about him the incommunicable splendours of a new day.

This was the effect of the personality of Jesus, as he stood amid the shadows and uncertainties of human life; an effect strangely overlooked and ignored, often even beclouded and hidden, in much that has been written about him by theologians and historians. I do not dream that I can put it into words. But I know that it can be felt as a reality in the Gospels. And I turn back to one who saw him face to face, one who touched his hand and leaned upon his bosom, for the expression of the soul-uplifting wonder of the person of Christ: *The Word was made flesh and dwelt among us, and we beheld His glory, the glory as of the only-begotten of the Father, full of grace and truth.*[1]

Nor has this effect vanished from the world with the removal of the bodily presence of Jesus. It still flows from the picture of his life which is preserved in the Gospels, from the image of his character as it is formed in the minds of

[1] St. John 1 : 14.

61

men. Eliminate, if you please, what is called the miraculous element. Make what allowance you will for the enthusiasm of his disciples. There still remains that enthusiasm itself to be reckoned with, an enthusiasm which was kindled by him alone. There still remains the figure of the person of Christ, who never can be expressed in terms of matter and force, who never can be explained by natural and historical causes, who carries us by his own inherent mystery into the presence of the spiritual, the divine, the supernatural.

Something of this spiritual light comes from every human personality, even the lowliest, in so far as it refuses to be summed up in terms of sense perception, in so far as it gives evidence, by its affections and hopes and fears, of elements in man that are not of the dust. But in Christ this light is transcendent and unique, because he manifestly surpasses the ordinary attainments of humanity, because he cannot be accounted for by the laws of heredity and environment. The more closely we apply these laws, the more clearly he shines out above them.

"The learned men of our day," says M. Pierre Loti in his book, *La Galilée*, "have endeavoured to find a human explication of his mission, but they have not yet reached it. . . . Around him, none the less, there still glows a radiance of beams which cannot be comprehended."

Historically he appears alone, as no great man has ever appeared before or since. Heroes, teachers, and leaders of men have always been seen as central stars in larger constellations, surrounded by lesser but kindred lights. Plato shines in conjunction with Socrates and Aristotle; Cæsar with Pompey and Crassus; Luther with Melanchthon and Calvin; Shakespeare with Beaumont and Fletcher and Ben Jonson; Napoleon surrounded with his brilliant staff of marshals and diplomats; Wordsworth among the mild glories of the Lake poets. In every case, if you search the neighbourhood of a great name, you will find not a blank sky, but an encircling galaxy. But Jesus Christ stands in an immense solitude. Among the prophets who predicted him, among the apostles who testified of him, there is none worthy to be compared or conjoined with him. It is as if the heavens were swept bare of stars; and suddenly, unexpected, unaccompanied, the light of lights appears alone, in supreme isolation.

Nor is there anything in his antecedents, in his surroundings, to explain his appearance and radiance. There was nothing in the soil of the narrow Jewish race to produce such an embodiment of pure and universal love. There was nothing in the atmosphere of that corrupt and sensual age to beget or foster such a character of stainless and complete virtue. Nor was his own life,—I say it reverently,— judged by purely human and natural laws, calculated to result in such an evident perfection as all men have wonderingly recognized in him. The highest type of human piety, the excellence of a beautiful soul, has never been reached among men without repentance and self-abasement. But Jesus never repented, never abased himself in shame and sorrow before God, never asked for pardon and mercy. Alone, among his followers who kneel at his command to confess their unworthiness and implore forgiveness, he stands upright and lifts a cloudless face to heaven in the inexplicable glory of piety without penitence. Moral perfection of this kind is not only without a parallel; it is also without an approach. Men have never attained to it, and there is no way for them to climb thither. We can only look up to that perfection, serene, sinless, unsurpassable, and feel that here we are in sight of something which cannot be expressed except by saying that it is the glory of eternal spirit embodied in a person.

THE GOSPEL OF A PERSON

IV

But the force which resides in the person of Jesus is not exhausted in the production of this profound impression of its own spiritual and transcendent nature. It goes beyond this result of a vivid sense of the reality of the unseen. It has in itself a purifying, cleansing power, a delivering, uplifting, sanctifying power. The Gospel of Christ is the gospel of a person who saves men from sin. And herein it comes very close to the heart of a doubting age.

The great and wonderful fact of this experience, which can neither be questioned nor fully explained, is not involved in the theological speculations which have gathered about it. The person of Jesus stands out clear and simple as a powerful Saviour of sinful men and women. In his presence, the publican and the harlot felt their hearts dissolve with unutterable rapture of forgiveness. At his word, the heavy-laden were mysteriously loosed from the imponderable burden of past transgression. He suffered with sinners, and even while he suffered he delivered them from the sharpest of all pains,—the pain of conscious and unpardoned evil. He died for sinners, according to his own word; and ever since, his cross has been the sign of rescue for humanity. Whatever may be the nature of that sublime transaction upon Calvary; whatever the name by which men call it,—Atonement, Sacrifice, Redemption, Propitiation; whatever relations it may have to the eternal moral law and to the Divine righteousness,—its relation to the human heart is luminous and beautiful. It does take away sin. Kneeling at that holy altar, the soul at once remembers most vividly, and confesses most humbly, and loses most entirely, all her guilt. A sense of profound, unutterable relief, a sacred quietude, diffuses itself through all the recesses of the troubled spirit. Looking unto Christ crucified, we receive an assurance of sin forgiven, which goes deeper than thought can fathom, and far deeper than words can measure.

> *"We may not know, we cannot tell*   .
> *What pains he had to bear,*
> *But we believe it was for us*
> *He hung and suffered there.*
>
> *He died that we might be forgiven,*
> *He died to make us good;*
> *That we might go at last to heaven,*
> *Saved by his precious blood."*

This is not theory, this is not philosophy, this is not theology. It is veritable fact. The person Jesus, living with men, dying for men,

has actually brought this gift of pardon for
the past and hope for the future, into the heart
of mankind. And from pure love of him—a
love which is first of all and most of all a sense
of gratitude for this immeasurable service—
have blossomed, often out of the very abysses
of sin and degradation, the saintliest and sub-
limest lives that the world has ever seen.

Now this, as I know from experience, is the
gospel for doubting men, the gospel of a Person
who is a fact and a force, an evidence of the unseen, and a Saviour from sin. Will we preach
it? Then one thing is necessary for us, a thing
which might not be necessary, perhaps, if our
message were of another kind.

All knowledge, of the world, of human nature, of books, will be helpful and tributary;
all gifts, of clear thought, of powerful speech,
of prudent action, will be valuable and should
be cultivated; but one thing will be absolutely
and forever indispensable.

If we are to preach Christ we must know
Christ, and know him in such a sense that we
can say with St. Paul that we are determined
not to know anything save Jesus Christ and
him crucified.[1] We must study him in the

[1] I Cor. 2 : 2.

record of his life until his character is more real and vivid to us than that of brother or friend. We must imagine him with ardent soul, until his figure glows before our inward sight, and his words sound in our ears as a living voice. We must love with his love, and sorrow with his grief, and rejoice with his joy, and offer ourselves with his sacrifice, so truly, so intensely that we can say, as St. Paul said, that we are crucified by his cross and risen in his resurrection.[1] We must trace the power of his life in the lives of our fellow-men, following and realizing his triumphs in souls redeemed and sins forgiven, until we know the rapture that thrilled the breast of St. Bernard, St. Francis, Thomas à Kempis, Samuel Rutherford, Robert McCheyne; the chivalrous loyalty that animated Henry Havelock, Charles Kingsley, Frederick Robertson, Charles Gordon; the deep devotion that strengthened David Brainerd, Henry Martyn, Coleridge Patteson. We must become the brothers of these men through brotherhood with Christ. We must kindle our hearts in communion with him, by meditation, by prayer, and by service, which is the best kind of prayer. No day must pass in which we do not do something distinctly in Jesus' name, for Jesus' sake.

---

[1] Gal. 2 : 20.

THE GOSPEL OF A PERSON

We must go where he would go if he were on earth. We must try to do what he would do if he were still among men. And so, by our failure as well as by our effort, by the very contrast between our incompleteness and his perfection, the image of our Companion and our saving Lord will grow radiant and distinct within us. We shall know that potent attraction which his person has exercised upon the hearts of men, and feel in our breast that overmastering sense of loyalty to him which alone can draw us to follow him through life and death.

"If Jesus Christ is a man,—
And only a man,—I say
That of all mankind I cleave to him,
And to him will I cleave alway.

If Jesus Christ is a God,—
And the only God,—I swear
I will follow him through heaven and hell,
The earth, the sea, and the air." [1]

[1] Richard Watson Gilder, "Song of a Heathen, sojourning in Galilee, A. D. 32."

III

THE UNVEILING OF THE FATHER

IN the famous fifteenth chapter of *The Decline and Fall of the Roman Empire,* Gibbon,
who was but a superficial sceptic though a profound historian, introduces an account of the
rise and spread of the Christian Religion. He
attributes its remarkable triumph over the
established religions of the earth to a series of
causes which he ironically describes as secondary, and uniformly treats as primary. He
exhibits them as in themselves sufficient to
explain the peculiarly favourable reception of
the Christian faith in the world, and sets aside
the question of a possible divine origin as unnecessary. With serene self-satisfaction he
traces the rapid growth of the Christian Church
to the five following causes: I. *The Zeal of
the Christians,* derived from the Jews,—but
purified from that narrow and unsocial spirit
which, instead of inviting, had deterred the
Gentiles from embracing the law of Moses.
II. *The Doctrine of a Future Life,* improved
by every additional circumstance which could

give weight and efficacy to that important truth. III. *The Miraculous Powers* ascribed to the primitive Church. IV. *The Pure and Austere Morals* of the Christians. V. *The Union and Discipline of the Christian Republic,* which gradually formed an increasing and independent state in the heart of the Roman empire.

Now this is a brilliant example of the kind of work which was done by the shallow and complacent scepticism of a century ago. But the moment we subject it to the more searching analysis of the scepticism of the present age, it dissolves into a thin and incoherent absurdity. For it is evident that, so far from giving an explanation of the growth of Christianity, Gibbon is simply describing some of the phenomena which accompanied that growth. What, for example, is "the zeal of the Christians" but an unilluminating name for a contagious and irresistible enthusiasm which spread through the world in connection with faith in Christ? What is "the union and discipline of the Christian republic" but a description, without explanation, of the organic unfolding of a new, mysterious principle of fellowship? These alleged "causes," more closely examined, are in fact the very things that require to be accounted

71

for. Instead of clearing up the mystery, they increase it.

By a singular fatality of language, the sceptical historian has embodied in the statement of his position the demonstration of its insufficiency. In each of his causes, and in the relation that subsists between them, he has practically suggested a difficulty which demands another and a higher solution of the whole problem. Examine his words carefully.

By what means, human or divine, was the zeal of the Christians "purified from the narrow and unsocial spirit of the Jews"? The natural history of sects and schisms teaches us that their invariable tendency is to intensify rather than to eliminate bigotry and exclusiveness. Through what influence was the doctrine of a future life "improved by every additional circumstance that could give it weight and efficacy"? The inevitable course of its human development under the guidance of abstract philosophy has been towards vagueness, coldness, and uncertainty; under the guidance of concrete superstition, towards puerility and crass sensualism. On what grounds were miraculous powers ascribed to the early Church? They must have been ascribed truly or falsely. If truly, there must have been some basis of fact for them to rest upon. If falsely, the Christians themselves were either ignorant, or cognizant, of the falsehood. Take the former supposition, and you present yourself with the inexplicable theory that what Pliny the Younger called *superstitio prava immodica*, and imagined would be easily and certainly extirpated, was able to hold its own against all the assaults of learning and philosophy. Take the latter supposition, and you are forced to the incredible assumption that a conscious deception was the fountain of highest and strongest moral force that the world has ever felt. How then did the "pure and austere morals of the Christians" come into existence? From a lie, or from a truth? If from a truth, what was the nature of that truth, in what form was it expressed, and how did it win credence? And, finally, how did "the Christian republic" succeed in maintaining and increasing itself as an independent state in the heart of the Roman empire? Every other attempt to do this particular thing, by secret philosophic doctrine, or by open political organisation, failed, and was violently crushed by imperial power, or silently dissolved by imperial statesmanship. How was it that this one invisible fellowship, this one visible organization, lived, and spread, and stood out at last, serene, complete, and magnificent, when the time-worn ruins of the empire crumbled around it?

The answer to these questions is found in the person of Christ. This is not a matter of choice. It is a matter of necessity. For if he was, as all candid observers will admit, the originator and animator of Christianity, then to stop short of him in our inquiry as to the causes of its existence and progress is to stop half-way, as if one should account for the flow of the Nile, after the fashion of the ancient geographers, by attributing it to the melting of the snows on the Mountains of the Moon.

Christ stands above and behind the Church, and all these secondary causes which have been enumerated to account for her growth and power flow directly from him. He it was who purified and humanized the zeal of Christians, so that they emerged from the narrowest of races to preach the broadest and most universal of all religions. He it was who cleared and enlarged their view of immortality, so that it became at once important and efficacious, the only doctrine of a future life that has exercised a direct and uplifting influence upon the present life. He it was who endowed the Church with whatever powers she possessed. He it was

74

who cleansed and ennobled her moral ideals and gave her the only pattern and rule of virtue which has been universally acknowledged as self-consistent, satisfactory, and supreme. He it was who cemented her union and strengthened her discipline to such an indestructible solidarity, that the tie which bound the individual soul to him was regarded as superior to all earthly relations, and the fellowship which that common tie created, surpassed and survived all fellowships of race, of culture, of nationality.

These are simple historical facts. In stating them we make no assumptions and propound no theories. It is not necessary to take anything for granted or to adopt any particular theological or philosophical system, in order to see clearly and beyond the possibility of mistake that all the force and influence of Christianity in the world have, as a matter of fact, flowed directly from Jesus Christ and from the faith which he has inspired in the hearts of men.

The one question of supreme importance, then, if we would understand what Christianity really means, is, Who is this person who stands at the centre of it and fills it with life and strength? What did the first Christians see in him that made them believe in him so absolutely and implicitly and gave them power to do such mighty works? What has the church seen in him through the ages that has bound her to him as her living Lord and Master? And what are we to see in him if he is to be in deed and in truth the theme of our gospel? *"What think ye of Christ?"*

This question is vital and inevitable. If we are to have a Christianity which is real and historical, we must get into line with history. If we are to have behind us the power which comes from actual achievements of our gospel in the world, we must understand the relation which it has always held to the person of Christ. If we are to be in any sense the followers of the first Christians, and to share the joy and peace and power of their religion, we must take the view which they took, of Jesus of Nazareth.

I

We are not to suppose that faith in Christ began with a clear and definite conception of his divinity. On the contrary, it is evident from the whole gospel record that the belief that Christ was divine gradually developed and unfolded in the minds of those who knew and loved and trusted him. The idea of an incarnation was foreign to the Hebrew mind. There was no race in the world that held so strongly to the thought that God was solitary, unsearchable, and incommunicable. They believed that even his true name could not be pronounced by human lips, and that it was impossible for human eyes really to behold his glory. And the very strength of this ancestral faith of theirs, standing as it must have done directly in the way of belief in an incarnation, is an evidence of the tremendous power and unquestionable reality of the experience which forced the disciples, by slow degrees, to believe firmly and unhesitatingly in the divinity of Christ.

The process by which this result was accomplished lies open to our thought in the New Testament. We must go back to the point indicated in the second lecture. It was the impression made upon the disciples by Christ's own manifestation of himself, his character, his actions, and his words, evidently consistent and unique, which led them at last to see in him the divine object of faith and worship. He was not a mere man. That was evident and undeniable. He was higher than men; holier than men; he possessed an excellence and a power which made them feel in his presence that he was more than they were. What then was he? There were but two directions in which their faith could move. The alternative was sharply set before the disciples on that memorable day at Cæsarea Philippi, when Christ asked them first, "Whom do men say that I, the Son of man, am?" and then, "But whom say ye that I am?" There were but two lines open to them. One was the line of popular superstition, which led them back into the past to see in Christ only the ghost of John the Baptist, or Elias, or one of the prophets come to life again. The other was the new line of Christian faith which led them forward to see in Jesus "the Christ, the Son of the living God." [1]

It is evident that the disciples did not know at first what was meant by the Christhood, the Messiahship, the fulfilment of all ancient prophecy and sacred ritual in Jesus. But they learned the lesson as they kept company with him. They heard him speak with an authority which none of the prophets had ever claimed. Recognizing a divine inspiration in the Old Testament Scriptures, he distinctly set himself above them as the bringer of a new and better revelation. He accomplished, interpreted, and revised them. "Ye have heard how it hath been said by them of old time"— by whom? By the lawgivers and prophets and

[1] St. Matt. 16 : 13-16.

78

psalmists whom Christ recognized as his own forerunners and foretellers. "But *I say* unto you, love your enemies, bless them that curse you, and pray for them that despitefully use you." [1]

Suppose that this were all; suppose that the Sermon on the Mount were the whole of the New Testament, what should we behold in it? Not merely the revelation of a morality more pure and perfect than any other the human heart has conceived, proceeding from the lips of an unlearned Nazarene peasant of the first century, but the absolutely overwhelming sight of a believing Hebrew placing himself above the rule of his own faith, a humble teacher asserting supreme authority over all human conduct, a moral reformer discarding all other foundations, and saying, "Every one that heareth these sayings of mine and doeth them, I will liken him unto a wise man which built his house upon a rock." [2] Nine and forty times, in the brief and fragmentary record of the discourses of Jesus, recurs this solemn phrase with which he authenticates the truth: *Verily, I say unto you.* And every time that the disciples heard it they must have gotten a new idea of what it meant to be the Christ.

[1] St. Matt. 5 : 43, 44.   [2] St. Matt. 7 : 24.

THE UNVEILING OF THE FATHER

Think also of the significance which the favourite Messianic title used by Jesus to describe himself must have had to their minds. He called himself "the Son of man." [1] Why? Was it merely because he was human? If that was all, surely it would not need to be asserted and emphasised again and again. Imagine any other man, the highest and the holiest, insisting upon the reality of his human life, dwelling upon it, repeating the assertion of it over and over. But this title was, in fact, the claim to a peculiar and supreme relation to the human race. Christ was not *a* son of man, but *the* Son of man, one who, in the luminous words of Irenæus, *recapitulavit in se ipso longam hominum expositionem.* And as such he assumed on earth and in his prevision of heaven a position which no mere man could rightly take. "The Son of man hath power on earth to forgive sins." [2] "The Son of man is Lord also of the Sabbath." [3] "When the Son of man shall come in his glory, and all the holy angels with him, then shall he sit upon the throne of his glory; and before him shall be gathered all nations, and he shall separate them one

---

[1] In St. Matthew, 30 times; in St. Luke, 25 times; in St. Mark, 14 times.
[2] St. Matt. 9 : 6.   [3] St. Mark 2 : 28.

80

from another, as a shepherd divideth the sheep from the goats."[1]

Consider what this implied. It was a declaration that Jesus expected, and was willing, to take into his own hands the task of discriminating between the good and the bad in the unsearchable confusions and complexities of the human heart, and of determining, without hesitation, without misgiving, without redress, the final destinies of the untold myriads of men; "an office," it has been well said, "involving such spiritual insight, such discernment of the thoughts and intents of the heart of each one of the millions at his feet, such awful, unshared supremacy in the moral world, that the imagination recoils in sheer agony from the task of seriously contemplating the assumption of these duties by any created intelligence." When the disciples heard their Master declare that he would fulfil this office of Judge of the World, they must have begun to feel what it meant to be the Christ.

Nor do I suppose that they realized at first the full intention of that second phrase in which their view of Jesus was expressed. *The Son of the living God,*—that also was an idea to be gradually apprehended and unfolded. And think

[1] St. Matt. 25 : 31, 32.

81

what light must have fallen upon it from the conduct of Jesus as they followed him from day to day. The more closely they knew him, the more deeply they felt his sinless purity and sovereign virtue. There was a certainty, an independence, a freedom from all effort and from all restraint in his goodness, such as no other good man has ever shown. He had the deepest knowledge of the evil of sin, yet no shadow or stain of it fell upon his own soul. He was on terms of closest intimacy—an intimacy such as no saint ever dared to assume—with God. He conversed with the Father in a friendship which was utterly without fear or penitence or misgiving.

Now when the disciples saw this, it must have put them upon deep thoughts, and the guidance to these thoughts was given by Christ's own words about himself. He put himself side by side with the Divine activity. "My Father worketh hitherto and I work."[1] The Jews who heard him say this, sought to kill him, because he had not only broken the Sabbath, but said also that God was his Father, making himself equal with God. And if the Jews thought this, what did his own disciples think? He claimed a Divine origin and mission: "I came forth from the Father";[2] "My Father

[1] St. John 5 : 17.   [2] St. John 16 : 28.

sent me."[1] He claimed a Divine knowledge and fellowship: "No man knoweth the Father save the Son";[2] "O righteous Father, the world hath not known Thee, but I have known Thee."[3] He claimed to unveil the Father's being in himself: "He that hath seen me hath seen the Father. I am in the Father and the Father in me."[4]

To what conclusion must such conduct and such words as these lead the disciples in their interpretation of the true meaning of the title "the Son of God"? A conclusion which Jesus himself, if he was as wise and good as all men admit, must inevitably have foreseen. A conclusion which he himself, if he had been only a holy man, better than his disciples but of the same nature, would certainly have guarded against and prevented at any cost. A conclusion which is expressed in the attitude of Thomas, kneeling at the feet of Christ and crying, "My Lord and my God."[5] A conclusion which is finally and definitively embodied in the action of the apostles going out into the world to disciple all nations, and to baptize them "into the name of the Father, and of the Son, and of the Holy Ghost."[6]

---

[1] St. John 12 : 49.   [2] St. Matt. 11 : 27.   [3] St. John 17 : 25.
[4] St. John 14 : 9, 11.   [5] St. John 20 : 28.   [6] St. Matt. 28 : 19.

83

II

There cannot be any question as to the state of mind which this action implied. It was the deep conviction, not necessarily reasoned out and formulated, but lying at the very root of conduct, that Jesus Christ the Son was the unveiling of his Father God, and that the Holy Spirit who came upon the disciples was the Spirit of the Father and the Son. The part which the resurrection played in the clarifying and confirming of this conviction was important. But we must not misunderstand the meaning of the resurrection. It was not in any sense a new and different revelation of God, imagined or actually received. Whatever the form in which Jesus appeared to the disciples during the forty days that followed his death, he was recognized as the same Jesus; and the one effect of his appearance was simply to confirm and deepen the truth of what he had said and done while he was with them. And with this confirmation the truth took shape and substance as an active and enduring power in human faith and life and worship.

There is no more room for doubt that the early Christians saw in Christ a personal revelation of God, than that the friends and followers of Abraham Lincoln regarded him as a good and loyal American citizen of the white race. And even if we could find no direct and definite statement of either of these views, the evidence that men held them could be clearly and certainly read in the facts of history.

Divine honours were paid to Christ in the primitive Church. The first common prayer of the disciples, when they were assembled to choose an apostle in the place of the traitor Judas, was addressed to Christ.[1] The Christians were distinguished both from the Jews and from the heathen as those who called upon the name of the Lord Jesus Christ.[2] The dying martyr Stephen showed what was meant by this phrase in his prayer, "Lord Jesus, receive my spirit."[3] Saul of Tarsus, when he was convinced by that strange experience on the road to Damascus that Jesus was not an impostor, but the Christ, at once addressed him in prayer, "Lord, what wilt thou have me to do?"[4] And Ananias, who received Saul into the Church, asked guidance and direction from the same Lord.[5] Peter baptized the multitudes on the day of Pentecost in the name of Jesus Christ.[6] John wrote of prayer to the Son of God as a

[1] Acts 1 : 24. [2] Acts 9 : 21; 1 Cor. 1 : 2. [3] Acts 7 : 59.
[4] Acts 9 : 6. [5] Acts 9 : 13. [6] Acts 2 : 38.

familiar ground of confidence in Christian experience.[1] The apostolic benediction was: "The grace of our Lord Jesus Christ, and the love of God, and the communion of the Holy Ghost be with you all."[2] The whole current of adoration and devotion in the New Testament leads up naturally and without surprise to the magnificent words of St. Paul, in which he speaks of "Christ, who is over all, God blessed forever."[3]

It should be frankly recognized that the first Christians assigned a certain subordination to the Son in relation to the Father; but it must be admitted with equal candour that this subordination was not in any sense a separation, and that it really implied and involved a unity between them which made it possible and natural and inevitable for the disciples to pay an adoration to the Son with the Father, which, if it had been offered to, or claimed by, the greatest and best of the apostles, would have been instantly repudiated by the whole Church as not only absurd but radically blasphemous.

It is easy to trace the worship of Christ in the later development of Christianity. There are two sources of evidence: the Christian hymns and liturgies; the heathen attacks and the apologies which they evoked.

[1] 1 John 5 : 13–15.   [2] 2 Cor. 13 : 14.   [3] Rom. 9 : 5.

THE UNVEILING OF THE FATHER

The earliest hymns of the Greek Church, the "Thanksgiving at lamplighting," "Shepherd of tender youth," "The Bridegroom cometh," the "Hymn to Christ after Silence," celebrate the praise of the Lord Jesus. Syriac poetry, through its great poet, Ephrem Syrus, takes up the same strain of adoration to the Son of God, and its undying music may still be heard among the mountains of Armenia where the unspeakable Turk is exterminating a whole race for loyalty to the name of Christ. Latin hymnody, from its earliest origin in translations from the Greek like the *Gloria in Excelsis* and the *Te Deum*, through its splendid unfolding in the poetry of Hilary of Poictiers, Ambrose of Milan, and Gregory the Great, to its sweet culmination in the two Bernards, of Clairvaux and of Cluny, repeats the same burden:

> *"O Jesus, Thou the glory art*
> *Of angel worlds above;*
> *Thy name is music to my heart,*
> *Enchanting it with love."*

In every land and language, in German, in French, in English, the most precious hymns of the Church are fragrant with the name of Christ.

The early liturgies bear the same testimony to the pre-eminence of the Lord Jesus in the doxologies and supplications of Christian faith.

THE UNVEILING OF THE FATHER

The Apostolical Constitutions,[1] the liturgy of St. James,[2] the liturgy of St. Mark,[3] the liturgy of St. Adæus and St. Maris,[4] unquestionably preserve the spirit of the early Christian worship; and they all are witnesses to the fact that the Christians prayed directly to Christ. Indeed, it lies upon the very surface of history that the growth of Christianity, as manifested in a spreading worship, was not simply the increase of those who were willing to adore God on the authority of Christ. It was distinctly and essentially the diffusion of an inward force which impelled men to blend the name of Christ with the name of God in their prayers, and to worship the Son with the Father. The beautiful Prayer of St. Chrysostom, which closes the Litany and the Morning and Evening Prayers of the Protestant Episcopal Church, is addressed to Christ, "who dost promise that when two or three are gathered together in Thy name, Thou wilt grant their requests."[5] There is not in the world to-day a single great liturgy, Greek,

[1] *Apost. Const.*, Book VIII., chap. vii.
[2] *The Divine Liturgy of St. James*, iii.: "Sovereign Lord Jesus Christ, O Word of God," etc.
[3] *The Divine Liturgy of the Holy Apostle and Evangelist Mark*, v., xxii., etc.
[4] *Liturgy of the Blessed Apostles, composed by St. Adæus and St. Maris*, xiv.
[5] St. Matt. 18 : 20.

Roman, Armenian, French, German, Scotch, or English, which does not contain ascriptions of divine glory, and petitions for divine grace, addressed to Jesus Christ.

Heathen writers of very early date assure us that this was the practice of Christians from the beginning. The younger Pliny reported to the Emperor Trajan that the people called Christians were accustomed to assemble before daybreak and "sing a hymn of praise responsively to Christ, as it were to God." In the public trials that followed there was never any denial of this statement. It was admitted alike by those who apostatized under the pressure of persecution and by those who remained faithful to the name of Christ. The Emperor Hadrian wrote to Servian that of the population of Alexandria "some worshipped Serapis, and others Christ." Lucian, the pagan satirist, says in his biography of Peregrinus Proteus: "The Christians are still worshipping that great man who was crucified in Palestine."

In all the apologies for the Christian religion which were put forth during the persecutions under Hadrian, and his successors Antoninus Pius and Marcus Aurelius, there was no attempt to refute the universal charge that the Christians worshipped Christ. As if to confirm this evidence by one of those indications which are all the more significant because they are so slight and so clearly unpremeditated there still exists a rude caricature, scratched by some careless hand upon the walls of the Palatine Palace in Rome not later than the beginning of the third century, representing a human figure with an ass's head hanging upon a cross, while a man stands before it in the attitude of worship. Underneath is this ill-spelled inscription,—

"Alexamenos adore his God."

Thus the songs and prayers of believers, the accusations of persecutors, the sneers of sceptics, and the coarse jests of mockers all join in proving beyond a doubt that the primitive Christians paid divine honour to the Lord Jesus. I do not see how any man can be in touch with Christianity as a living form of worship in the world, unless he knows the reality and appreciates the force of this unquestionable fact.

III

Nor will it be possible to understand the intellectual and moral teachings of the Christian religion, as they are recorded in the New Testament, unless we put ourselves at the focal point from which, as a matter of history, these teachings were first conceived and then unfolded. This point was the vision of an unveiling of the being and mind of God in Christ. It was not merely that Jesus said certain things about God which men had not known, or had forgotten. It was that they saw in the coming of Christ a personal revelation of the Divine Being. And this revelation touched and transformed every possible sphere of thought and feeling in regard to the problems of religion. The personality of God was made distinct and luminous, not only by the recognition of an eternal Fatherhood in his nature, but by the light of the knowledge of his glory shining in the face of a person.[1] The righteousness of God was disclosed in a new aspect by the thought that he had sent his own Son in the likeness of sinful flesh, and for sin to condemn sin in the flesh.[2] The goodness of God was confirmed and made sufficient for all possible human needs by the conviction that he who spared not his own Son, but freely delivered him up for us all, would also with him freely give us all things.[3] The saving will and power of God were apprehended through the vision of him in Christ reconciling the world to himself.[4]

[1] 2 Cor. 4 : 6.   [2] Rom. 8 : 3.   [3] Rom. 8 : 32.
[4] 2 Cor. 5 : 19.

THE UNVEILING OF THE FATHER

The everlasting and inseparable love of God became the sure ground of hope only when it was seen embodied in Christ Jesus our Lord.[1] The true meaning of filial obedience to God and of union with God was interpreted in the light of conformity to the image of his Son.[2] And the immense significance of immortality was comprehended in the possession of a life hid with Christ in God.[3]

Now the window through which men caught sight of these truths was, and could have been, nothing else than faith in a real incarnation of God in Christ. The personal, moral, sympathetic view of God which distinguished the early Church was seen only through that opening. She saw the Divine Being beaming with a new radiance, she saw the wide landscape of human duty and destiny illuminated and transfigured, she saw a new heaven and a new earth, when she saw in Christ all the fulness of the Godhead dwelling bodily. And it was in the strength and enthusiasm of this vision, that she concentrated all her moral and intellectual energies on the one point of keeping that window open, and maintaining against direct assault and secret dissolution the real and personal Deity of Christ.

[1] Rom. 8 : 39.   [2] Rom. 8 : 29.   [3] Col. 3 : 3.

THE UNVEILING OF THE FATHER

IV

I am careful to put the statement in this form because I believe that it alone corresponds with the facts, and because it is only by getting our minds into this position that we can hope to understand the course, the meaning, and the force of Christian doctrine. The early Christians looked at God through Christ: they did not look at Christ through a preconceived idea and a logical definition of God. The true development of theology, to put the matter plainly, was not abstract, it was personal and practical. The doctrine of the Trinity came into being to meet an imperative necessity. That necessity was the defence of the actual worship of Christ, the actual trust in Christ as the Unveiler of the Father, which already existed at the heart of Christianity. It was recognized instinctively that the loss of this trust, the silencing of this worship, meant the death of Christianity by heart-failure. Every speculation which threatened this result, every theory of human nature or of divine nature which seemed to separate the personality of Christ from the personality of God, was regarded by the Church as dangerous and hostile. Every attempted statement of theological dogma which appeared to obscure or to imperil the reality and the validity of the revelation of the Father in the Son, was resented, and a counter statement of theological dogma was framed to meet it. This was the intellectual conflict of Christianity in the first centuries: a struggle for life centring about the actual Deity of Christ.

As we trace the progress of this conflict, its vital importance emerges more and more clearly. Often, I suppose, we cannot help feeling a sense of sympathy with the earnest purpose and the personal character of those men who were called heretics. Often we are conscious of a certain distrust for the metaphysical and exegetical arguments, and of a grave repugnance for the physical and political methods which were used by the orthodox to enforce their definitions. Athanasius was not an altogether lovely person. Some of the early Church Councils were almost as disorderly and reckless as some of the regiments that have fought in various wars to defend the cause of human liberty and justice. But the question is not one of the manner of defence or attack. It is a question of the reality and significance of the cause attacked and defended. And here we see that Athanasius with all his faults was on the right side, and

THE UNVEILING OF THE FATHER

Arius with all his virtues was on the wrong side. Through all the confusion of metaphysical dispute about the exact meaning of substance and subsistence, nature and personality, ideal existence and real existence,—terms which must change their significance as the methods of human philosophy change, and must always represent imperfectly a mystery which is for us unsearchable and indefinable,—through all this confusion one fact shines out clear and distinct. The unveiling of the Father in Christ was, and continued to be, and still is, the Palladium of Christianity. All who have surrendered it, for whatever reason, have been dispersed and scattered. All who have defended it, in whatever method, have been held fast in the unity of the faith and of the knowledge of the Son of God, provided they were willing to live up to its consequences.[1]

This point of view must condition the attitude of our minds towards the doctrine of the Trinity. No Christian man can be hostile or indifferent to it when he remembers its history. It may have been too much elaborated by minds over-curious in metaphysical distinctions. It may have been put in a position of undue preeminence by theologians whose energies were

[1] Eph. 4 : 13.

all absorbed in its construction and in the contemplation of the work of their own reason in the service of Christianity. But in spite of all excesses and errors, it stands as an enduring monument of the loyalty of the faith to its central conviction. In all its forms, from the sharply tri-personal Trinity of Athanasius, to the essentially tri-modal Trinity of Augustine, the great service which it has rendered is not abstract nor philosophical. It is practical. It has protected the conviction that the real nature of God is revealed in Christ; it has justified the consciousness that the Spirit of Christ, animating the Christian life, is the Spirit of God; it has preserved the sense of real communion with God in Christ which is the nerve of Christian worship.

But the doctrine of the Trinity is not the gospel, nor is it the foundation of the gospel. It cannot be preached as a saving message to the souls of men, except in that form in which we find it in Phillips Brooks' noble *Sermon for Trinity Sunday*, and Dr. George A. Gordon's powerful discourse on *The Trinity the Ground of Humanity*. It is the effort to apprehend a relation of the Being of God to the conscious experience of man; a truth exhibited in the course of revelation and recognized in its mysterious unfolding both before and after all efforts to symbolize it in theological language; in brief, it is the reaching out of the human mind, conscious of its limitations and conditions, towards a vision and worship of the Father in the Son through the Spirit. The doctrine of the Trinity is not the Palladium. It is the defence. In its broad outlines it seems to me necessary and satisfactory. No other answer to the profound questions which inevitably arise out of the contact between the idea of God, and the experience of real life in all its manifoldness, appears to me half so reasonable or complete as that which asserts that "the various fundamental forms of society on the earth, the essential relationships of humanity, have their Archetype, their Eternal Pattern and Causal Source, in the nature of the Infinite." I will confess that the form of this answer which contemplates the existence of these eternal relationships in the Divine nature as most clearly and positively personal, is more conclusive to my mind than any other. But if other men think otherwise on this point, we are not therefore divided from each other, nor from the Christian faith. The question is one of metaphysics. It is not a question of religion. All modes of defining the Trinity as a doctrine must be kept subordinate to the purpose for which it exists. All attempts to express it are valuable only in so far as they help us to keep in view the unveiling of the Divine nature which centres in him who was manifested in the flesh, justified in the Spirit, seen of angels, preached among the nations, believed on in the world, received up in glory.[1]

V

Now wherein is a message like this, the gospel of a personal unveiling of God in the person of Christ, adapted to the needs of the present age?

1. It seems to me first of all that the course of modern thought has prepared the way for it by destroying the *a priori* objections to the Incarnation. Shallow agnosticism makes two assumptions which are contradictory. It assumes that man is unable to attain to the knowledge of God; and that it is impossible for God to reveal himself to man. But if we cannot know him, how can we know that he cannot reveal himself? This would be in effect the most intimate kind of knowledge. To take it for granted that an Incarnation of God is impossible or incredible is to profess a most perfect and exclusive understanding of the

[1] 1 Tim. 3 : 16.

Divine nature. "At one time," says Mr. Romanes, "it seemed to me impossible that any proposition, verbally intelligible as such, could be more violently absurd than that of the Incarnation. Now I see that this standpoint is wholly irrational. . . . 'But the Incarnation is opposed to common sense.' No doubt: utterly so; but so it ought to be if true. Common sense is merely a rough register of common experience. But the Incarnation, if it ever took place, whatever else it may have been, was not a common event. 'But it is derogatory to God to become man.' How do you know? Besides, Christ was not an ordinary man. Both negative criticism and the positive effects of his life prove this; while if we for a moment adopt the Christian point of view for the sake of argument, the whole *raison d'être* of mankind is bound up in him. Lastly, there are considerations *per contra*, rendering an Incarnation antecedently probable."[1]

2. Now these considerations to which Romanes alludes are not foreign to the intellectual atmosphere of our age; they are native to it; they are in fact the offspring of the times, born of the spirit which now leads the best thoughts of men.

[1] *Thoughts on Religion*, p. 186.

THE UNVEILING OF THE FATHER

The whole doctrine of development, as it is conceived by the deepest and clearest minds, looks forward to the discovery of an Incarnation which shall be at once the crown and the completion of the process of evolution. If nature is an orderly and progressive manifestation of an Unseen Power; if each successive step in this manifestation realizes and exhibits something higher and more perfect, to which all that has gone before has pointed, and in which the potentialities of all previous developments are not only summed up, but raised to a new power; if the mechanical structure of inorganic substances contains a prophecy (only to be interpreted after the event) of organic life, and organic life is a basis for instinct and the elementary processes of intellect, and the rude forms of thought and feeling in the lower animals foreshadow the unfolding of reflective reason and moral consciousness in man, —then surely this reflective reason and this moral consciousness, in themselves confessedly imperfect, must be only the foundation for a fuller and more perfect manifestation of that Unseen Power out of whose depths all preceding manifestations have come forth. And if the universal verdict of human science and philosophy is correct in assuming that the lower must precede the higher, and that organic life is above inorganic life, and that reason is above instinct, and that virtue is above automatic action, then it is to be expected that the complete manifestation of that Unseen Power which makes for Reason and Righteousness will neither be omitted nor intruded before its time. It cannot come too soon, without violating the order of evolution. It cannot fail to come, without destroying the significance of evolution.

But in what form can it come except one which at once sums up all that has gone before it, and advances to a new level? If the universe contains an unveiling of the might, and wisdom, and reasonableness, and righteousness, of its Primal Cause, then certainly it must contain at last an unveiling of his personality. This is the only thing that remains to be added. This is the only thing that embraces all the rest and raises it to a new power. The highest category known to our minds is that of self-conscious life. Without the conception of a personal God, man's view of the universe must remain forever incomplete, incoherent, and unreasonable. Without the revelation of a personal God, the process of evolution as the unfolding of the real secret of the universe must remain unfinished and futile. Philosophy as well as religion pushes us forward to this conclusion. Personality is the ultimate reality. Personality must be the final revelation. But a person can be unveiled only in a personal form. Therefore all the presumptions of reason are in favour of an Incarnation of the Deity, not outside of nature, but in nature, to consummate and crown that visible evolution whereby the invisible things of him from the creation of the world are clearly seen. And all the processes of intelligence are satisfied, and rest and repose in the conviction that the Word, which was in the beginning with God and which was God and by whom all things were made, finally became flesh and dwelt among us, revealing his glory, the glory as of the only-begotten of the Father, full of grace and truth.

3. Moreover, this view of Christ is adapted to the present age because it is historically consistent. We have seen that it underlies the very existence and growth of the Christian Church. The testimony of eighteen centuries to the impossibility of explaining the personality of Christ on humanitarian grounds is in itself an evidence of his divinity.

Lincoln was right when he said: "You can fool some of the people all of the time, and all

of the people some of the time, but you cannot fool all of the people all of the time." A
thousand attempts to account for the life of
Christ without admitting his divinity have
been made. Not one of them has succeeded
in winning the assent and approbation of any
great mass of men for any great length of time.
They have hardly survived the lives of those
who have invented them. Each new naturalistic theory of Christ has discredited and de-
molished its predecessors. And if any one of
them is alive and finds credence to-day, it is
only because it is the latest, and it is but waiting
for its successor (as the theory of Socinus waited
for the theory of Strauss, and the theory of
Strauss for the theory of Renan) to be its judge
and destroyer.

Meantime historic Christianity, which beholds God incarnate in Christ, stands as a rock
around which the tides of opinion ebb and flow.
The Church has changed in some things, but
not in this. It has modified, enlarged, dimin-
ished, or abandoned some articles of faith, but
not this. If it be an error, it is such an error
as the world has never seen anywhere else; for
it has not only stood firm through the fiercest
and most persistent storm of criticism that has
ever been directed against any human opinion,

but it has also been the foundation of the strongest and saintliest lives that humanity has ever known. If it be a truth, it must be for every Christian preacher the central truth. For it is certain that this age of ours, with its ruthless critical spirit, with its keen historical sense, will never respect the intelligence, though it may acknowledge the good intentions, of a man who professes to speak in the name of Christianity without proclaiming, as the core of his message, the Divine Christ.

4. And this gospel meets the need of our times because it is the satisfaction of humanity. More urgent and painful even than the questions of the intellect in regard to the being and nature of God, are the misgivings of the heart in regard to his relations to us. If he is that remote and inaccessible Sovereign

> *"Who sees with equal eyes, as Lord of all,*
> *A hero perish or a sparrow fall,"*

what possible answer can we find in him to the longings and desires of our souls for a Divine love? what possible support can we find in him for our struggles against outward temptation and indwelling evil? what possible sympathy can we find in him for our hopes and aspirations and upward strivings, out of the quicksands of heredity and environment, towards liberty and light? The religion of the Incarnation is the only one that brings us near to God, assures us of our kinship with him, and of his infinite, practical, helpful love for us. This faith alone bridges the chasm that divides the eternal self-existent Spirit from our finite, despondent, earthbound souls. This faith alone gives us any knowledge of the things that we most need to know about him. Deism is like a message written in an inscrutable hieroglyph which conveys no clear meaning to the mind. Theism is like a message which is intelligible to the intellect, but unsatisfactory to the heart, because it has no personal address and no signature. Christianity is a personal message, signed by the hand of a Father, and conveyed to us by the hand of the Son.

The comparison is imperfect. It falls far short of the truth. In Christianity the messenger is the message. The love which sent and the love which delivered it are the same. Christ is Immanuel, God with us. The gospel of the Incarnation does not profess to remove all intellectual perplexities in regard to the existence of God and our own souls. It professes simply to establish such a conscious relation between our souls and God that our ethical needs shall be satisfied at once; and thus it shall be infinitely easier, either to dissolve, or to endure, our intellectual perplexities. This relation is possible only in Christ. And it is possible in him only when we receive him as the unveiling of the Father. This requires an act of faith. But it is a faith which is simpler in its form, more natural in its method, and more profound in its spiritual results than any other. For in the last analysis it is just an act of personal confidence in a person. And this does not demand perfect knowledge, but absolute trust.

To imagine that we can adapt our preaching to this age of doubt by weakening, concealing, or abandoning the truth of the Deity of Christ is to mistake the great need of our times. It is to seek to commend our gospel by taking away from it the chief thing that men really want,—an assurance of sympathy and kinship with God. "One of the great marks of the youth of to-day," says Ernest Lavisse,—"I speak of thinking youth,—is a longing for the Divine." This longing is to be met not by slighting, but by emphasising, not by clouding, but by clarifying, not by withdrawing, but by advancing, the true Deity of our Lord Jesus Christ. Let us take up the words of the ancient

106

THE UNVEILING OF THE FATHER

creed: *"We believe in one Lord Jesus Christ, the Son of God, only-begotten of the Father, that is of the substance of the Father, God of God, Light of Light, very God of God, begotten, not made, being of one substance with the Father: by Whom all things were made which are in heaven and earth: Who, for us men and for our salvation, came down, and was incarnate, and was made man, and suffered, and rose the third day, and ascended into the heavens, and shall come to judge the quick and the dead."*

IV

THE HUMAN LIFE OF GOD

NEARLY fifty years ago, Horace Bushnell, the most mystical of logicians, or the most logical of mystics, delivered before Yale University a magnificent discourse upon *The Divinity of Christ*. In that fine work of genius, wrought out of darkness and light, like an intricate carving of ebony and ivory, I find these words: "Christ is in such a sense God, or God manifested, that the unknown term of his nature, that which we are most in doubt of, and about which we are least capable of any positive affirmation, is the human."

This sentence, it seems to me, is not of light, but of darkness. It does not represent that illuminating and harmonious kind of truth which comes directly from the divine revelation of Christ. It belongs rather to that obscured and discordant manner of presenting truth which is the consequence of studying it too much at second-hand and too little at first-hand, too much in the speculations and reasonings of men and too little in the facts of life wherein it was first manifested. Whatever may be said of this sentence as a statement of the result of dogmatic theology,—and in this sense I do not question its accuracy,—when we consider its plain meaning as an expression of Christian experience and faith, one thing is clear: It is utterly out of touch with the experience and faith of the first disciples. It is in sharp and striking discord with the consciousness of the primitive Church. For if there is anything in regard to which the New Testament makes positive and undoubting affirmation, it is the complete, genuine, and veritable humanity of Christ. If there is any fact which stands out luminous and distinct in the experience of the early Christians, it is that they saw in Christ, not merely a mysterious manifestation of the Divine, but something utterly different. They saw the mystery reduced to terms of simplicity, the revelation levelled to the direct apprehension of man, the unveiling of the Father under conditions which were so familiar that they dissolved doubts and difficulties They saw in Christ *the human life of God.*

THE HUMAN LIFE OF GOD

I

Definition is dangerous. And this is the nature of the danger: the definition has an inherent tendency to substitute itself for the thing defined. The terms in which a fact is expressed creep into the place of the fact itself. The reality is removed insensibly to a remote distance behind the verbal symbols which represent it. The way of access to it is blocked, and its influence is restricted by the forms of expression invented to define it.

I do not know where we can find a more vivid illustration of this process than that which is given, in many ways, in the history of art. The first pictures of Christ, traced in colour upon the walls of the Catacombs, or carved in stone upon the sarcophagi of the Christian dead, do not give us indeed the very earliest conception of him; for the Christian art of the first two centuries, if it ever existed, has perished. But that which remains, dating from the third and fourth centuries, bears witness to an idea of the Christ which was simple and natural and humane. He appears as a figure of youthful beauty and graciousness; the good Shepherd bearing a lamb upon his shoulders; the true Orpheus drawing all creatures and souls by the charm of his amiable music. These are only symbolic representations, yet they evidence a conception of him which was still in touch with the facts. A little later we find an effort to conceive and depict him with more realism. His face appears in pictures which resemble the description given in the spurious Epistle of Lentulus: "A man of dignified presence, with dark hair parted in the middle and flowing down, after the custom of the Nazarenes, over both shoulders; his brow clear and pure; his unfurrowed face of pleasant aspect and medium complexion; his mouth and nose faultless; his short, light beard parted in the middle; his eyes bright and lustrous."

But when we pass on to the creations of so-called Byzantine art, we find ourselves face to face with an utterly different view of the Christ. His countenance now stares out in glittering mosaic from the walls of great churches, huge, dark, threatening, a dreadful and forbidding face. The fixed and formal lines are repeated and deepened by artist after artist. Every feature of naturalness is obliterated; every feature that seemed to express awfulness is exaggerated and emphasised. The wide-set eyes, the long narrow countenance, the stern, inflexible mouth, —in this ocular definition the man Christ Jesus

111

has vanished, and we see only the immense, immutable, and terrible Pantokrator, who cannot be touched with the feeling of our infirmities.

When we turn to the intellectual life of the Church out of which this type of art grew, we see there the process explained. The early Greek Fathers, like Irenæus, went directly to the Holy Scriptures for their view of the person of Christ, and frankly accepted all the features of the living portrait there disclosed. They recognized without reserve the reality of Christ's human growth in wisdom and stature and in favour with God and men; the actual limitations of Christ's human knowledge as expressed in the questions that he asked and in his profession of ignorance in regard to the time of his second advent; the intimacy of his sympathy with us in temptation, suffering, and death. But with the development of theological definition this direct view of Christ was modified, obscured, and at last totally eclipsed. Instead of looking at God through his revelation in Christ, the Fathers began to look at Christ through a more and more abstract, precise, and inflexible statement of the metaphysical idea of God. It became necessary to harmonize the Scripture record of the life of Jesus with the theories of the divine nature set forth in the decrees of councils and defined with amazing particularity in the writings of theologians. In the effort to accomplish this, two main lines of thought were followed. One line abandoned the belief in Christ's real and complete humanity, and reduced his human life to a tenuous and filmy apparition. The other line distinguished between his humanity and his Divinity in such a way as to divide him into two halves, either of which appears virtually complete without the other, and both of which are united, not in a single and sincere personality, but in an outward manifestation and a concealed life, covering in some mysterious way a double centre of existence. It is only fair to say that the extreme results of these two lines of thought were condemned by the Church in the heresies of Doketism and Apollinarianism, Eutychianism and Nestorianism. But it is equally fair to say that the influence of these theories was by no means checked nor extirpated. They continued to make themselves felt powerfully and perniciously; now in the direction of dissolving the humanity of Christ into a mere cloud enveloping his Deity; and again in the direction of dividing and destroying the unity of his person in the definitions of his dual nature.

113

THE HUMAN LIFE OF GOD

It is not necessary, nor would it be possible, for us to trace this process in detail through all its complexities and self-contradictions. It will be enough to give two or three specimens of the kind of work to which it led in dealing with two essential features of the picture of Christ which is given to us in the Gospels: his human limitation of knowledge, and his human growth in wisdom, stature, and grace. Both limitation and growth are unexempt conditions of manhood. Both are unquestionably attributed to Christ in the New Testament. Both are explicitly denied by theologians. Ephrem Syrus, commenting upon the *Diatessaron* of Tatian, says: "Christ, though he knew the moment of his advent, yet that they might not ask him any more about it, said, *I know it not.*" Chrysostom, in his explanation of St. Matthew 24 : 36, paraphrases Christ's words in this extraordinary fashion: "For if thou seek after the day and the hour thou shalt not hear them of me, saith he; but if of times and preludes, I will tell thee all exactly. *For that indeed I am not ignorant of it*, I have shown by many things.—I lead thee to the very vestibule; and if I do not open unto thee the doors, this also I do for your good." John of Damascus, defending the orthodox faith, declares that,

114

THE HUMAN LIFE OF GOD

"Christ is said to advance in wisdom and stature and grace, because he grows in fact in stature, and through his growth in stature brings out into exhibition the wisdom which already existed in him. . . . But those who say that he really grew in wisdom and grace as receiving increase in these, deny that the flesh was united to the word from the first moment of its existence." Peter Lombard does not explicitly adopt, but quotes with evident approval, the opinion that the person of the eternal Word put on a human body and soul as a robe, in order that he might appear suitably to the eyes of mortals, yet in himself he was not changed by this incarnation, but remained one and the same, immutable.

A very full and clear exhibition of the darkness and unreality in which the patristic and mediæval theologians involved the person of Christ may be found in Professor A. B. Bruce's great book on *The Humiliation of Christ,* and in Canon Charles Gore's two admirable volumes on *The Incarnation,* from which I have taken some illustrations after verifying them. Professor Bruce sums up the matter by saying: "The effect, though not the design, of theories of Christ's person has been to a large extent to obscure some of these elementary truths,—the unity of the person, or the reality of the humanity, or the divinity dwelling within the man, or the voluntariness and ethical value of the state of the humiliation. That is, certainties have been sacrificed for uncertainties, facts for hypotheses, faith for speculation."

Canon Gore, in his Bampton Lectures, adroitly uses the Jesuit theologian De Lugo as a man of straw through whom he may safely and vigorously attack the false conceptions of Christ's person which are still current, and to a considerable degree dominant, in dogmatic theology. He says that De Lugo depicts a Christ "who, if he was, as far as his body is concerned, in a condition of growth, was, as regards his soul and intellect, from the first moment and throughout his life in full enjoyment of the beatific vision. Externally a wayfarer, a *viator*, inwardly he was throughout a *comprehensor*, he had already attained. . . . It is denied that he can be strictly called 'the servant of God' even as man, in spite of the direct use of that expression in the Acts of the Apostles. He is spoken of at the institution of the Eucharist as offering sacrifice to his own Godhead."

Canon Gore condemns this picture by De Lugo as in striking contradiction to that which the New Testament presents. But the point which I wish to make clear and distinct, is that, in spite of this contradiction, the picture has not been discarded in Christian theology. It still exercises an obscuring influence upon the vision of Christ. It still produces representations of him in which definitions dominate facts, and formulas hide realities. We do not need to go back to the seventeenth century, nor abroad to the Jesuits, for our examples. We may turn to Archdeacon Wilberforce's book on *The Incarnation*, and find him representing the body of Christ as miraculous in its freedom from sickness, its power over animals, its exemption from the necessity of death, and its inherent power of communicating life to others. In regard to the mind of Christ, he says that "since it would be impious to suppose that our Lord had pretended an ignorance which he did not experience, we are led to the conclusion [astonishing conclusion!] that what he partook, as man, was not actual ignorance, but such deficiency in the means of arriving at truth as belongs to mankind." We may turn to the *Dogmatic Theology* of Dr. W. G. T. Shedd and read: "Jesus Christ as a theanthropic person was constituted of a divine nature and a human nature. The divine nature had its own

117

form of experience, like the mind in an ordinary human person; and the human nature had its own form of experience, like the body in a common man. The experiences of the divine nature were as diverse from those of the human nature as those of the human mind are from those of the human body. Yet there was but one person who was the subject-ego of both of these experiences. At the very time when Christ was conscious of weariness and thirst by the well of Samaria, he also was conscious that he was the eternal and only-begotten Son of God, the second person in the Trinity. This is proved by his words to the Samaritan woman: 'Whosoever drinketh of the water that I shall give him shall never thirst; but the water that I shall give him shall be in him a well of water springing up into everlasting life. I that speak unto thee am the Messiah.' The first-mentioned consciousness of fatigue and thirst came through the human nature in his person; the second-mentioned consciousness of omnipotence and supremacy came through the divine nature in his person. If he had not had a human nature, he could not have had the former consciousness; and if he had not had a divine nature, he could not have had the latter. Because he had both natures in one person, he

could have both." We may turn to Canon
Liddon's magnificent work on *The Divinity of
our Lord* and find him writing: "Christ's Manhood is not of itself an individual being; it is
not a seat and centre of personality; it has no
conceivable existence apart from the act whereby the Eternal Word in becoming Incarnate
called it into being and made it his own. It
is a vesture which he has folded around his
person; it is an instrument through which he
places himself in contact with men and whereby he acts upon humanity."

If we accept this picture of Christ, the manhood of Jesus fades, retreats, grows dim and
shadowy. It wavers like a veil. It dissolves
like mist. It descends again mysterious and
impenetrable, illusory and impersonal, to en-
velop him whom we love and adore in its strange
and unfamiliar folds. We grope after him, but
we can touch nothing but the hem of his mystic
robe. We long for him, but he approaches us,
and comes into contact with us, only through
an instrument. He is not what he seems. The
Son of God behind that veil is beyond our reach.
The Son of man, whom human eyes beheld and
human hands touched, is not the real, living,
veritable Saviour, but only the form, the garment, of an inscrutable life. And if, in our dire

confusion, our reasoning faith still succeeds in holding fast to the Eternal Logos, our confiding faith is maimed and robbed by the loss of that true, near, personal, loving, sympathizing Jesus, who was born of a woman, suffered under Pontius Pilate, was crucified, dead, and buried. He is gone from us, as certainly as if the Pharisees had spoken truth when they said that his disciples came by night and stole him away. The thing of which we are most in doubt, and about which we are least capable of any positive affirmation, as Dr. Bushnell said, is the humanity of Christ. We are left with a perfectly orthodox doctrine of two natures, but we no longer have a clear and simple gospel of One Person to preach to doubting men.

II

But the heart of Christendom has never rested content with this distant, vague, uncertain view of the real manhood of our Lord. There has always been a protest against it. There has always been an effort to escape from it.

We can see a strange and indirect but indubitable evidence of this deep inward dissatisfaction, in the rise and growth of an impassioned devotion to the human mother of Jesus. The worship of the Virgin Mary was a reprizal for the obscuration of the humanity of her Son. In the thought of her true womanly tenderness and affection, her real and unquestionable sorrows, her simple and familiar joys, her intimate, genuine, unfailing sympathy with all that makes our mortal life a bitter, blessed reality to us, the souls of the lowly and the lonely found that peace and consolation which they could no longer find in the contemplation of the distant Second Person of the Trinity through the telescope of theology. That which Jesus himself was to John and Peter, to the household of Bethany, to the penitent publican, and to the woman which was a sinner, Mary became to the baffled and confused faith of a later age,—an approachable mediator of the divine mercy, a helper who could really understand and feel the need of those who cried for help, a warm and living image of the Eternal Sympathy in flesh and blood. In the light of mediæval dogmatics Mariolatry appears not without its justification. And for my part, I should not wish to be bound to the Christology of Peter Lombard and Thomas Aquinas, without finding the compensation which their followers found in personal devotion and confidential trust, flowing instinctively and irresistibly towards the blessed Virgin.

But, after all, this was only a substitute. It gave to faith the image of a lovely and adorable humanity in closest union with God; but it did not give back the old vision of *the human life of God*. And so through all the ages we see men turning, now in solitary thought, now in great companies, to seek that vision. The renaissance of Christian art, with its beautiful pictures of the infancy of Jesus, with its piercing and pathetic representations of the sufferings of Jesus, bears witness to the eagerness of that search. The revivals of Christian life, seen in such diverse yet cognate forms as the rise of the "Poor Men of Lyons" and the foundation of the "Brotherhood of St. Francis" are evidences of the same movement back to Christ. Peter Waldo outside of the Church, and Francis of Assisi within the Church, were awakened by the same vision of Jesus, "a man of sorrows and acquainted with grief," and were inspired by the same desire to make his real human life the pattern of all piety and the example of all goodness. The Reformation, which was at once and equally an intellectual and a spiritual protest against the arrogance of current theology and the coldness of religious life, supplies no better watchword to express its great motive than the saying of Erasmus:

THE HUMAN LIFE OF GOD

"I could wish that those frigid subtleties either were completely cut off, or were not the only things that the theologians held as certain, and that *the Christ pure and simple might be implanted deep within the minds of men.*" Modern Biblical scholarship, with its splendid apparatus of linguistic and historical learning, proceeding in part, at first, from a sceptical impulse, has developed in our generation, either through the conversion of sceptics in the process of research, or through the awakening of believers to the necessities of their faith, into a reverent and eager quest for the historic Christ, the Jesus of the Gospels, the Lord of the primitive Church, that we may see him as the first Christians saw him, in the integrity of his person and the sincerity of his life, and receive from him what they received,—a faith that dissolved doubts and an inspiration that conquered difficulties. Back to the New Testament of our Lord and Saviour Jesus Christ,—back to the facts that lie behind the definitions, back to the Person who embodies the truth, back to the record and reflection of that which the apostles "heard, and saw with their eyes, and looked upon, and their hands handled of the word of life,"—this, and this only, is the way that leads us within sight of

THE HUMAN LIFE OF GOD

*"the heaven-drawn picture
Of Christ, the living Word."*

Now it is a marvellous thing, and one for which we can never be grateful enough, that when we come to the New Testament in this spirit, we find in it exactly what we need; not an abstract formula, not a collection of definitions, but the graphic reflection of a Person seen from a fourfold point of view, and the simple record of manifold human experience under the direct and dominant influence of that Person. And the one fact that emerges clear and triumphant from the reflection and the record, is that the writers of the New Testament never were in doubt of the human nature of Christ and never hesitated to make the most positive affirmations in regard to it.

The Christ of the Gospels is bone of our bone, flesh of our flesh, mind of our mind, heart of our heart. He is in subjection to his parents as a child. He grows to manhood. His character is unfolded and perfected by discipline. He labours for daily bread, and prays for Divine grace. He hungers, and thirsts, and sleeps, and rejoices, and weeps. He is anointed with the Spirit for his ministry. He is tempted. He is lonely and disappointed. He asks for information. He confesses ignorance. He in-

124

THE HUMAN LIFE OF GOD

terprets the facts of nature and life with a
prophetic insight. But he makes no new disclosure of the secrets of omniscience. There is
no hint nor indication that he is leading a double
life, reigning consciously as God while suffering
apparently as man. His personality is simple
and indivisible. The glory of what he is and
does, lies not only in its perfection, but in the
hard conditions of its accomplishment. Superhuman in his origin, as the only-begotten Son
of God; superhuman in his office and work,
as the revealer of the Father and the redeemer
of mankind; in his earthly existence the Christ
of the Gospels enters without reserve and without deception into all the conditions and limitations which are necessary to give to the world,
once and forever, *the human life of God*.

When we turn to the Epistles to see how this
view of Christ was affected by the recognition
of his divine glory and power as one who had
been raised to the right hand of God and made
head over all things to the Church, two things
strike us with tremendous force. First, the
identity of his person was not lost, nor the con-
tinuity of his being broken: the exalted Christ
is none other than "this same Jesus."[1] Second,
the reality and absoluteness of his humiliation

[1] Acts 1 : 11.

are emphasised as the ground and cause of his exaltation.

How vividly these two things come out, for example, in the writings of St. Paul. It has been well said that "the Christ whom Paul had seen was the risen Christ, and the conception of him in his glorified character is the one which rules his thoughts and forms the starting-point of his teaching." Corresponding to this present glory, Paul assumes an eternally pre-existent glory of Christ as the image of the invisible God, the medium and end of creation.[1] Now it is of this Person, divinely glorious in the past as the One who is before all things and in whom all things consist,[2] divinely glorious in the present as the One who is far above every name that is named, not only in this world but in that which is to come,[3]—it is of this Person that Paul writes, in words so strong that they touch the very border of the impossible: "For our sakes, *he beggared himself* that we through his beggary might be enriched."[4] And again: "He, existing in the form of God, did not consider an equal state with God a thing to be selfishly grasped and held, but *emptied himself*, and took the form

---

[1] Col. 1 : 16.   [2] Col. 1 : 17.   [3] Eph. 1 : 21.
[4] 2 Cor. 8 : 9.

of a slave, being made in the likeness of man."[1]

These powerful expressions, "self-beggary," "self-emptying," seem to be directly designed to break up the conventional moulds in which dogmatic theology has attempted to cast the truth and let it harden. They bring back a vital warmth and motion into the facts of the Incarnation. Once more it glows and flows. Once more we see that it is not a mere exhibition of being but a process of becoming. The idea of self-beggary mightily overflows the mere statement that a human nature was added and united to the divine nature; for that would have been no impoverishment but an enrichment. The idea of self-emptying shatters the narrow dogma that the Son of God suffered no change in himself when he became man. It was a change so absolute, so immense, that it can only be compared with the vicissitude from fulness to emptiness. He laid aside the existence-form of God, in order that he might take the existence-form of man. Whatever right he had to an equal state of glory with God, that right he did not cling to, but surrendered, in order that he might become a servant. And upon this real self-emptying there followed a

[1] Phil. 2 : 6, 7.

127

real self-humiliation, wherein, being found in
fashion as a man, he became obedient unto
death, even the death of the cross.[1] It was on
account of this,—and by "this" we must understand the entire actual operation of the self-
denying, self-humbling, self-sacrificing mind of
Christ,—it was for this reason, St. Paul declares, that "God highly exalted him, and gave
unto him the name which is above every
name."[2] And I know not how to interpret
such language with any reality of intelligence,
unless it means that the present glory of the
Son of God is in some true sense the result of
his having become man and so fulfilled the
will of God.

This view, which St. Paul condenses into a
single pregnant "wherefore," is expanded in
the Epistle to the Hebrews. The object of
this Epistle is to show the superiority of the
priesthood and sacrifice of Christ, which are
substantial and enduring, to the priesthood and
sacrifice of the old dispensation, which were
shadowy and transient. But the method which
the writer follows is not to deny, but to assert
the verity of Christ's humanity. Without this
he could not be the true priest nor offer the
true sacrifice. "In all things it behoved him

[1] Phil. 2 : 8.　　　　　　　　[2] Phil. 2 : 9.

to be made like unto his brethren."[1] "For we have not an high priest which cannot be touched with the feeling of our infirmities: but was in all points tempted like as we are, yet without sin."[2] "Though he were a Son, yet learned he obedience by the things which he suffered, and being made perfect, he became the author of eternal salvation unto all them that obey him."[3] This complete incarnation, this thorough trial under human conditions, this perfect discipline of obedience through suffering, was a humiliation. But it was in no sense a degradation. On the contrary, it was a crowning of Christ with glory and honour in order that he might taste death for every man. "For it became him, for whom are all things, and by whom are all things, in bringing many sons to glory, to make the captain of their salvation perfect through suffering."[4] If the Epistle to the Hebrews teaches anything, it certainly teaches this. The humanity of Jesus was not the veiling but the unveiling of the divine glory. The limitations, temptations, and sufferings of manhood were the conditions under which alone Christ could accomplish the greatest work of the Deity,—the redemption of a sinful race.

[1] Heb. 2 : 17. [2] Heb. 4 : 15.
[3] Heb. 5 : 8, 9. [4] Heb. 2 : 9, 10.

THE HUMAN LIFE OF GOD

The centre of the divine revelation and of the divine atonement was and is the human life of God.

III

Here, then, we may pause for a moment and try to sum up the conclusions to which the New Testament leads us in regard to the person of Christ.

I am sincerely anxious not to be misunderstood. On the one hand, I would not conceal for a moment my conviction that current theology has failed, very often and very largely, to do justice to the meaning of the Incarnation on the human side, and that we *must* go back to the image of Jesus Christ as it is reflected in the Gospels to purify, and refresh, and simplify our faith. We should not suffer any reverence for ancient definitions of doctrine, however well founded, nor any fear of incurring reproach and mistrust as innovators, to deter us from that necessary and loyal return to the reality of the Person in whom our creed centres and on whom it rests. To find Jesus anew, to see him again, as if for the first time, in the wondrous glory of his humility, is the secret of the revival of Christianity in every age. This is not innovation; it is renovation.

On the other hand, we have no right and we ought to have no inclination to insist exclusively upon any particular theory as the only possible explanation of the facts of the Incarnation. Every earnest and thoughtful man must feel that these facts are so profound and mysterious that the plummet of human reason cannot sound their ultimate depths. With all our thinking upon this subject, there must ever mingle a consciousness of insufficiency and a confession of ignorance. But with this confession of ignorance there must go also a clear recognition of those portions of the truth which are unquestionably revealed in the New Testament. Three things are there made plain to faith.

1. God is so closely related to man, and the likeness of God in man is so real, that the Divine Logos is able to descend by a free act of self-determining love into the lower estate of human existence, and humble himself to the conditions of manhood without losing his personal identity.

2. The essence of the Gospel is its declaration of the fact that this act of condescension, of self-humiliation, actually has been performed, and that Jesus Christ is the eternal Son of God who has taken upon him the existence-form of a servant, and lived a truly human life, and

131

been obedient even unto death, in order to reveal to the world the saving love of God.

3. The distinctive attributes of personality (self-consciousness and self-determination) are not dual in Christ, as of two persons, the one divine and the other human, co-existing side by side in a double life. They are individual, and manifested as the life of one person. That person is the Son of God, who laid aside the glory which he had with the Father, and emptied himself, and so became the Son of man; and on account of this humiliation God hath highly exalted him and crowned him with glory and honour as the God-man forever.

These are the points which are vital to the reality of the Gospel of the Incarnation. All theories which make these points clear, safeguard the truth in its integrity and in its reconciling power. The question of the method of the divine humiliation and the human exaltation of Christ, lies beyond these points. It is not necessary to insist upon any particular form of its solution. Indeed, it may well be that the profundity of the question, the inherent mystery of the facts of life and personality with which it deals, and the limitations of human thought and language, preclude the possibility of a complete and final answer at present.

THE HUMAN LIFE OF GOD

It must be frankly acknowledged that none of the solutions which have been propounded hitherto are free from serious perplexities. But it must be recognized with equal frankness that the theories which have been put forward in modern times, with new earnestness and power, by men of unquestionable loyalty to the Christianity of the New Testament, who have sought to find a clear and positive meaning for the great word *Kenosis*, which St. Paul uses to describe the self-emptying of Christ in the Incarnation,—theories which have been stigmatized as *kenotic*, as if the name were enough to mark them as unorthodox,—are so far from being heretical that they have the rare merit of conserving and emphasizing a truth of surpassing value, undoubtedly taught in the Bible, and too much neglected, if not practically denied, during many centuries of theological speculation.

It may be that the distinctive attributes of personality are, abstractly considered, identical in God and man, so that, by the divine self-limitation in the Incarnation, they are actually unified, like two circles which have a common centre. It may be that the Son of God, being the eternal representative of the filial relationship within the Godhead, the symbol of the created within the uncreated, needed but to

surrender the form and status of the uncreated
Son in order to assume, by the same act, the
form and status which man as the created Son
was intended to realize. It may be that the
Incarnation was by deprivation, and that the
Eternal Word renounced his divine mode of
being, and entered into life, without omniscience, omnipresence, or omnipotence, as an
unconscious babe. It matters little in what
form of words we try to express the transcendent truth. But it matters much, it is supremely important for the integrity of our
Gospel and for its influence upon the heart of
this doubting age, that we should hold fast to
the fact that the life of Jesus of Nazareth is
simply and sincerely *the human life of God*.

The time is at hand when this simple and
profound view of Christ, which beholds in him
the God-man in whom Deity is self-limited and
humbled in order that humanity may be divinely exalted and perfected, must break
through the clouds which have obscured it,
and become the leading light of religion and
theology. The life of Christ needs to be re-
studied and rewritten under this luminous
guidance, in absolute and unhesitating loyalty
to the facts as they lie before our eyes in the
Gospels. The doctrine of Christ's person needs

to be restated in this light. It must include not only the truth of a sameness of nature and experience with God; but also the equal truth of a sameness with man, which the future is to unfold as the universality of Christ's manhood is exhibited through his progressive triumphs among all the races of men and all the modes of human life. The humanity of the incarnate Christ must stand out as clear, as positive, as indubitable, as his Deity. Nay, more, it must stand where the New Testament puts it, in the foreground of faith. For it is only in this humanity that we can truly find the Son of God who loved us and gave himself for us.

Life is now the regnant idea; personality its utmost expression. It is in the facts of life, its secret potencies, its mysterious limitations in germ and seed, its magnificent unfoldings in the process of development that we must seek our comparisons for the Incarnation. And the very search will bring us face to face with the conviction that life in all its manifestations transcends analysis without ceasing to be the object of knowledge.

We know many facts and forms of life whose modes of becoming we cannot imagine. It is just as impossible for us to conceive how the life of the oak, root and trunk and branch and leaf, form and colour and massive strength, is all folded in the tiny, colourless, unshaped seed, as it is to conceive how the life of God is embodied in the man Christ Jesus. But the difficulty of conceiving the manner of this infolding, this embodiment, does not destroy for us the reality of the life. Indeed, if we could explain it entirely, if we could trace it perfectly as in a diagram, if we could observe it completely, as in one of those beautiful models of flowers which a skilful artist has recently made to illustrate his lectures on botany, we should know that it was not life, but only a picture of it. The picture is useful, but it is not vital. The metaphor has its value, but it falls far short of the truth. *Self-beggary* and *self-emptying* are but "words thrown out towards" an unimaginable but not unreasonable manifestation of the Divine Love as life. The reality to which they point us is the Son of God descending to live under all the conditions and limitations of energy and consciousness which are proper to the Son of man: the Word made flesh and dwelling among us, like unto his brethren in all things.

THE HUMAN LIFE OF GOD

IV

It is impossible to overestimate the significance of this view for the present age, and the importance of setting it forth as a living truth in the language of to-day. It is the only view which gives us any ground of reality for our faith in the kinship of man with God. If the Son of God, who is the image of the Father, by laying aside the outward prerogatives of his divine mode of existence, actually becomes human, then, and only then, the divine image in which man was created is no mere figure of speech, but a substantial likeness of spiritual being. There is a true fellowship between our souls and our Father in heaven. Virtue is not a vain dream, but a definite striving towards his perfection. Revelation is not a deception, but a message from him who knows all to those who know only a part. Prayer is not an empty form, but a real communion.

"Speak to Him, thou, for He hears, and Spirit with Spirit can meet:
Closer is He than breathing, and nearer than hands and feet."

This view of the spiritual relation of man to God cannot possibly have any foundation in fact, deep enough and strong enough to withstand the sweeping floods of scepticism, unless it builds upon the rock of a veritable Incarnation. The discoveries of modern science, enlarging enormously our conceptions of the physical universe, have not only put man (as we said in the first lecture) in a position to receive a larger and loftier vision of the glory of God, but they have made such a vision indispensable. And they have emphasised, with overwhelming force, the form in which that vision must come in order to meet our needs and strengthen faith for its immense task. If we are not to be utterly belittled and crushed by the contemplation of the vast mass of matter and the tremendous play of force by which we are surrounded; if we are still to hold that the vital is greater than the mechanical, the moral than the material, the spiritual than the physical; if we are to maintain the old position of all noble and self-revering thought, that "man is greater than the universe,"—there is nothing that can so profoundly confirm and establish us in that faith, there is nothing that can so surely protect and save us from "the distorting influences of our own discoveries," as the revelation of the Supreme Being in an unmistakably vital, moral, spiritual, and human form.

Such a revelation at once rectifies, purifies,

138

and elevates our view of God himself. For if the Son of God can surrender omnipresence, omniscience, and omnipotence without destroying his personal identity, then the central essence of the Deity is neither infinite wisdom nor infinite power, but perfect holiness and perfect goodness. And so from the very lowest valley of humiliation we catch clear sight of the very loftiest summit of theology, the shining truth that God is Love.

In the light of this truth we behold also the highest perfection of man and the path which leads to it. Love is the fulfilling of the law, and the supreme pattern of love is the example of Christ. And whether we look at it from the divine side as the supreme self-sacrifice of God, or from the human side as the complete obedience of man, everything depends upon the genuineness and sincerity of this example. Unless the Son of God truly became man, the Incarnation cannot be "a revelation of human duties." What strength could we draw from his victory over temptation if he was not exposed as we are to the assaults of evil? What consolation could we draw from his patience if he was not a man of sorrows and acquainted with grief? "Jesus Christ," says one of the greatest of French theologians, "is not the

Son of God hidden in the Son of man retaining all the attributes of Divinity in a latent state. This would be to admit an irreducible duality which would withdraw him from the normal conditions of human life. His obedience would become illusory, and his example would be without application to our race. No, when the Word became flesh, he humbled himself, he put off his glory, being rich he made himself poor, and became as one of us, only without sin, that he might pass through the moral conflict with all the risks of freedom." When we see him thus, we know what it means to follow him and to be like him.

Finally, the whole value of the Atonement, in its reconciling influence on the heart of man, in its exhibition of the heart of God, depends upon the actuality of the Incarnation. If he who died on Calvary was a mere theophany, like the angel of Jehovah who appeared to Abraham, then his death was merely a dramatic spectacle. The body of Jesus was broken, but God was not touched. But if the Father truly spared not his own Son, but delivered him up for us all, then the Father also suffered by sympathy, making an invisible sacrifice, an infinite surrender of love for our sakes. Then the Son also suffered, making a visible sacrifice, and pouring out his soul unto death to redeem us from the fear of death and the power of sin. And this becomes real to our faith and potent upon our souls only when we see *the human life of God*, agonizing in the garden, tortured in the judgment-hall, and expiring upon the cross. Then we can say

> "*Oh Love Divine! that stooped to share*
> *Our sharpest pang, our bitterest tear.*"

Then we can look up to a God who is not impassible, as the speculations of men have falsely represented him, but passible, and therefore full of infinite capacities of pure sorrow and saving sympathy. Then the dumb and sullen resentment which rises in noble minds at the thought of a Universe in which there is so much helpless pain and hopeless grief, created by an immovable Being who has never felt and can never feel either pain or grief,—that sense of moral repulsion from the idea of an unsuffering and unsympathetic Creator which is, and always has been, the deepest, darkest spring of doubt, fades away, and we behold a God who became human in order that he might bear, though pure and sinless, all our pains and all our griefs.

Thus men who believe in *the human life of*

THE HUMAN LIFE OF GOD

God can speak to the doubting age, as David
sings to the disillusioned, downcast, despondent
Hebrew king, in Robert Browning's splendid
poem of "Saul." The word, sought in vain
among the glories of nature, among the joys of
human intercourse, the word of faith and hope
and love and life, comes to us, leaps upon us,
flashes through us.

"*See the King—I would help him, but cannot, the wishes
fall through.*
*Could I wrestle to raise him from sorrow, grow poor to
enrich,*
*To fill up his life, starve my own out, I would—knowing
which,*
*I know that my service is perfect. Oh, speak through me
now!*
*Would I suffer for him that I love? So wouldst Thou—
so wilt Thou!*
*So shall crown Thee the topmost, ineffablest, uttermost
crown—*
*And Thy love fill infinitude wholly, nor leave up nor
down*
One spot for the creature to stand in! It is by no breath,
*Turn of eye, wave of hand, that salvation joins issue with
death!*
*As Thy Love is discovered almighty, almighty be proved
Thy power, that exists with and for it, of being beloved!*
*He who did most, shall bear most; the strongest shall stand
the most weak.*
*'Tis the weakness in strength, that I cry for! my flesh,
that I seek*

142

THE HUMAN LIFE OF GOD

In the Godhead! I seek and I find it. O Saul, it shall
*   be*
A Face like my face that receives thee; a Man like to me,
Thou shalt love and be loved by, forever; a Hand like this
*   hand*
Shall throw open the gates of new life to thee! See the
*   Christ stand!"*

V

THE SOURCE OF AUTHORITY IN
THE KINGDOM OF HEAVEN

PREACH CHRIST, is the apostolic watchword that rings to-day, with all the force
and charm of a new commandment, through
the heart of a Church, which has felt, more
deeply than it has yet confessed, the age-per-
vading chill of a winter of doubt and discontent.
The very entrance of that reviving word has
already brought a glow of enthusiasm into the
Christian life, and caused new blossoms of hope
and love, manifold and beautiful activities of
help and healing, to appear in the earth. It
seems as if some fresh and secret tide of vitality were flowing through the veins of Christendom, and breaking everywhere towards the
light in deeds of charity and enterprises of
mercy. Hospitals, asylums, red cross societies,
rescue missions, salvation armies, spring into
existence as if by magic. Never has there been
a time when Christian men have tried to do
so much for their fellow-men in the name and
for the sake of Christ. Never has there been

a time when they have recognized so clearly and fully that there was so much yet to be done. It is an age of secular doubt, as many other ages have been. But it is also an age of Christian beneficence, as hardly any other age has been. And this beneficence is not self-satisfied and complacent. It is self-reproachful, and, in its best expressions, nobly discontented with all that has been accomplished hitherto. It seeks, not always wisely, but with splendid eagerness, for plans which shall lead beyond the relief, to the prevention of human suffering. It aims to bring about not only the immediate mitigation, but also the ultimate abolition, of war. It demands that charity shall be translated into the terms of national, as well as of individual life. It will not be satisfied until in some real and palpable sense the kingdom of this world is become the kingdom of our Lord and of his Christ.[1]

Now this splendid expansion of Christian activities, evident by many signs to all thoughtful observers, depends for its power and permanence upon the setting forth of Christ, vividly, personally, practically, as the pattern of all virtue and the Prince of Peace among men. The sense of absolute confidence in him

[1] Rev. 11 : 15.

as the perfect example of goodness, and of thorough loyalty to him as the Master of noble life, is the hidden reservoir of moral force. The organized charities of Christendom are the distributing system.

But in all this renewal and expansion of what is well called practical Christianity, there is, if I mistake not, a danger, or at least a serious possibility, of loss. The life of man is not only practical, it is also intellectual. His relations to his fellow-men are important, but his relation to truth is no less important. He cannot help acting; neither can he help thinking. When his thinking is divorced from his acting, when he has one standard for truth and a different standard for conduct, he is like a house divided against itself. If the Christianity of to-day, by dwelling exclusively or too much on the ethical side of the Gospel as a beautiful and beneficent rule of conduct illustrated by a perfect Example, tends to ignore the intellectual necessities of man and fails to realize that it has a message to deliver in the realm of truth as well as in the realm of righteousness, it cannot meet the deepest wants of the present age. Indeed, it may even aggravate those wants and make them more painful. It may seem to give assent, by silence, to the desperate assumption

146

of scepticism that the unseen world is unknown and unknowable, even to the most perfect of men. It may foster the sad feeling that the reality of religion is beyond our reach and that we must content ourselves with the convenient dreams of virtue. It may preach, in effect, a Christ whose character and conduct are to be accepted as infallible, but whose thoughts and convictions in regard to God and the soul and the future life are mere fallacies and illusions.

Preach Christ, if it is to be a true watchword for our ministry to the present age, must be cleared and vivified in our consciousness. We must know what we mean by it, and we must try to know what we ought to mean. We must ask ourselves again and again whether the thing that we do mean is always quite, or even approximately, the thing that we ought to mean when we use this precious and powerful phrase. It was commonly employed, say fifty years ago, to describe by way of distinction a presentation of Jesus which dwelt chiefly or entirely upon his death as the vicarious sacrifice for sin. It is frequently employed now as if it meant little or nothing more than the graphic description of Christ's life and actions as the supreme type of virtue and love. But surely to preach Christ exclusively in either of these ways is to divide him. It is not enough to have a Christocentric theology. It is not enough to have a Christocentric morality. We must not only put him at the centre; but we must also draw the circumference so that it shall embrace the whole of human life.

If Christ is the Lamb of God that taketh away the sin of the world,[1] he is also the true Light which lighteth every man that cometh into the world.[2] If he is the fulfilment of all dim prophecies of good, he is also the head and source of a new unfolding of spiritual vision. If he is the way and the life, he is also the truth.[3] If he is immortal love, regenerating the affections, he is also immortal wisdom reorganizing the thoughts, and immortal power strengthening the wills, of men. If his heart is to be the norm of our feeling, his mind is to be the norm of our thinking. If he is the herald and founder of a new and celestial dominion upon earth, he is also the source of authority in the kingdom of heaven.

I

The idea of the kingdom of heaven, as an actual reign of God over living men, in which all ancient anticipations of good are accom-

[1] St. John 1 : 29.   [2] St. John 1 : 9.   [3] St. John 14 : 6.

148

plished and a new state of virtue and blessedness is established on earth, was foremost and dominant in the teaching of Jesus.[1] It was the keynote of his ministry. Everything that he said, everything that he did, was in harmony with this master thought.

It is passing strange to see how often and how utterly this keynote has been changed in the variations which men have woven about the original theme of Christianity; and how far we are, even yet, from hearing it clearly, and sounding it with dominant fulness in the music of religion. At times the kingdom of heaven has been identified with the visible church as an outward embodiment of power in the world. And surely this interpretation is far enough away from the thought of Christ, who taught expressly that the kingdom was invisible and inward. At other times men have removed their conception from the present to the future, and looked for its realization in the life of the redeemed after death, or in the second coming of Christ to reign in millennial glory. And surely this interpretation is equally remote

[1] The word "kingdom" is used in the Gospels more than a hundred times to express the new condition of human life which Christ came to announce and establish. In St. Matthew's Gospel the favourite phrase is "the kingdom of heaven." St. Mark and St. Luke use "the kingdom of God."

149

from Christ's teaching, at the very outset of
his ministry and all through its course, that
the kingdom of heaven was at hand, that it
had already come near to men, and was lying
all around them, close to them, pressing upon
them from every side so that many were already entering into it and dwelling within it.

The unreality and incompleteness of these
two opposite interpretations of the kingdom
produced their natural results. The idea fell
out of its true place in Christian thought. It
became obscure, subordinate, and was finally
almost obliterated.

But in recent times there has been an intense revival of interest in this idea and an immense amount of good work done in the study
and explication of it. Such books as those which
Dr. James S. Candlish and Professor A. B.
Bruce have written upon "The Kingdom of
God," are valuable gifts to Christian literature.
Yet I will frankly confess that these books, and
others like them, seem to me rather to point
the way than to reach the goal. The fulness of
the conception of the kingdom of heaven is
not yet restored in current theology. There is
still a great deal of work to be done in this direction by the Christian thinker. The vision
of the kingdom is obscured, the proclamation

of the kingdom is weakened, because it is still presented too exclusively as a kingdom of grace, and not with equal emphasis as a kingdom of truth: it is set up too partially as a standard for the character and conduct of men, and not with equal clearness as a standard for their thoughts and convictions.

One reason of this one-sidedness, it seems to me, lies in the fact that we have hitherto been looking almost entirely to the first three Gospels as the source of our knowledge of the true meaning of the kingdom of heaven. But the Fourth Gospel, if indeed it be, as the best modern scholars say it is, "the most faithful image and memorial of Jesus that any man could produce," must be no less important, no less significant in the light which it throws upon this controlling idea of his mind. And when we turn to study it with this aim in view, we find at once that it gives us what we need. It completes and rounds out the record of the three other Gospels. It answers the questions which they suggest. And it is only when we take the fourfold narrative in its entirety that we begin to catch sight of the satisfying and convincing fulness of the idea of the kingdom of heaven.

This idea underlies the whole Gospel according to St. John. It is no less fundamental, no less necessary here than it is in the Synoptic Gospels. It is presented in different forms, because the type of the writer's mind and the purpose of his book are different. But it is the same idea. And this presentation of it is essential to its completeness.

In the Synoptics we have the conditions of entrance into the kingdom, a child-like spirit,[1] faith,[2] repentance,[3] and obedience.[4] In St. John we have the spiritual birth by which alone those requisites are made possible.[5] In the Synoptics we have the laws of the kingdom.[6] In St. John we have the new life in which alone those laws can be fulfilled.[7] In the Synoptics we have the parables and pictures of the kingdom.[8] In St. John we have the inmost sense of those parables, spoken directly to the soul, in words of which Christ himself says "they are spirit, and they are life." [9] In the Synoptics we have the new order of human society in the imitation by the disciples of Christ's obedience to the will of God.[10] In St. John we have the organizing principle of that new order in Christ's

---

[1] St. Matt. 18 : 3.
[2] St. Matt. 9 : 22; St. Mark 10 : 52.
[3] St. Luke 13 : 3.
[4] St. Matt. 5 : 20.
[5] St. John 3 : 5.
[6] The Sermon on the Mount.
[7] St. John 6 : 22–65.
[8] St. Matt. 13, 21, 25; St. Luke 13, 17, 19, etc.
[9] St. John 6 : 63; 8 : 12–51.
[10] St. Matt. 12 : 50.

revelation of himself to the disciples as the way, the truth, and the life.[1] In the Synoptics we have the supremacy of Christ's example over men's hearts. In St. John we have the supremacy of Christ's teachings over men's minds.

Of course, I do not mean to say that either of these aspects of the kingdom is confined exclusively to the source in which it is most fully and clearly exhibited. But this is what I mean. The Synoptics give us the first and simplest description of the nature of the kingdom. St. John gives us the fullest and clearest revelation of the mind of the King. We cannot understand the former without the latter. We cannot enter into the full meaning of the initial proclamation of Jesus, when he walked beside the Sea of Galilee crying "The kingdom of heaven has come near," [2] unless we go on with him to the judgment-hall and hear him give his final answer to Pilate: "Thou sayest that I am a King; to this end have I been born, and to this end am I come into the world, that I should bear witness unto the truth; every one that is of the truth heareth my voice." [3]

When we stand at this point, when we accept this declaration as the key to unlock and open the inmost meaning of the manifestation

[1] St. John 14 : 6.　　　[2] St. Matt. 4 : 17.　　　[3] St. John 18 : 37.

of the Father in the human life of the Son, we begin to apprehend the inexhaustible scope and significance of our call to preach Christ to an age of doubt. It is a gospel not only for the affections, but also for the intellect. It takes up his words as well as his works and makes them vital in the lives of men. It conceives and proclaims the kingdom of heaven as something more than "the reign of divine love exercised by God in his grace over human hearts believing in his love and constrained thereby to yield him grateful affection and devoted service." It is also the reign of divine truth exercised through a faithful witness over the minds of men who submit to his guidance and are led by him into inward peace and unity of thought. And the source of authority in this kingdom of heaven, which is equally a realm of truth and a realm of grace, is Jesus the Christ, whose doctrine, as well as his example, is ultimate and supreme.

II

Let us observe in passing that we have precisely the same basis to rest upon in our preaching of the doctrine of Jesus as in our preaching of his character and life. If historical criticism gives us good reason to believe, as all candid inquirers now admit, that the four Gospels contain a veritable picture of an actual personage who once lived on earth, there is equally good reason to believe that they have preserved for us a trustworthy account of his teaching in its substance and spirit. If we can justly claim that his character is so perfect and transcendent that no man of that age, however gifted or learned, and least of all such men as the writers of the New Testament, could possibly have invented it; we can make the same claim, with equal justice, for the body of doctrine which is attributed to Christ. In its coherence, its clarity, its sublimity, and its universality it altogether surpasses the mental abilities and the religious insight of the writers of the four Gospels. Indeed, it is frankly confessed that the disciples of Jesus were so far from being able to invent his doctrine, that they actually misunderstood and misinterpreted many of its truths when they first heard them. It was contrary to their prejudices and expectations. They did not put it into his mouth. He revealed it to their minds. Their faith in it rested upon his personal authority. And it was only as they kept company with him and followed him, receiving his word into their souls and translating it into their lives, that it became to them luminous and satisfying and convincing.

We are entitled, or rather we are compelled, to regard the teaching of Jesus as an objective fact just as much as his life and character. The record of it bears on its face the overwhelming evidence of verity. All the results of literary criticism are squarely against the supposition that such a doctrine as that which is presented to us under his name in the four Gospels, could ever have been pieced together out of the thoughts and imaginations of widely separated and divergent minds, and attributed to an unknown and perhaps mythical Master. It is not a mosaic; it is a living unity. It is not a creation of faith; it is the creator of faith. The hypothesis that four men agreed, or happened, to gather together, out of the Hebrew prophets, and the heathen philosophers, and the mysterious and inexplicable inner consciousness of the new-born Christian churches, certain beautiful ideas in regard to God and the soul and the future life, and ascribe them to Jesus, utterly breaks down at the touch of reality. The central, unifying, formative quality of the teaching of Christ is the one thing that is most evident in the record. It is emphasised by all the phenomena of growth, of vital development,

156

of deepening power, which may be traced from the sermon in the synagogue at Nazareth to the discourse in the upper room at Jerusalem. It shines out unmistakably through all the living variety of impressions which it made upon various minds, and through all the consequent many-sidedness of the report which is given of it. Not more certainly did the character of Christ inspire and unite the lives of his followers than his doctrine illuminated and controlled their beliefs. The only view which meets the facts is that Jesus really lived, and really taught thus and so, as he is presented to us in the Gospels.

This brings us at once to the most important feature in the record of his teaching. It is not given to us in the form of an abstract system, a treatise on theology, or a summary of doctrine, written down by the hand of Jesus. He himself made no record of his words. Only once do we see him writing,—in the beautiful episode which a later tradition has added to the eighth chapter of St. John's Gospel. Historical or not, the incident is profoundly suggestive. For Jesus wrote not with a pen upon enduring parchment, nor with a stylus upon imperishable brass

"*He stooped*
And wrote upon the unrecording ground."

He would not leave even a single line of manuscript where his followers could preserve it with literal reverence and worship it as a sacred relic. He chose to inscribe his teaching upon no other leaves than those which are folded within the human soul. He chose to trust his words to the faithful keeping of memory and love; and he said of them, with sublime confidence, that they should never pass away.[1] He chose that the truth which he declared and the life which he lived should never be divided, but that they should go down together through the ages.

And this is precisely what has come to pass. The Church in past ages has often been inclined to abstract the doctrines of Christianity concerning the person and work of Christ from their union with his human life, and to condense them into a purely formal system of dogma for the intellect. The Church in the present age shows at least a tendency to separate the image of Jesus from the truths which he taught, and hold him up to men merely as an ideal of holiness and goodness. But the one barrier that stands firm against both these false tendencies is the marvellous narrative of the Gospels, in which the life and the doctrine of Christ are

[1] St. Mark 13 : 31.

158

woven together, one and inseparable, like a robe without seam.

How can we understand his grace, unless we accept his truth? How can we appreciate his truth, unless we receive his grace? At every step, his action is interpreted and explained by his words. He trusts in Providence, and he commands his disciples to trust, not merely because submissive confidence is a beautiful and happy thing, but because he knows and declares that God is really a Father, worthy to be trusted.[1] He prays, secretly and openly; secretly because he is sure that God hears him always, and openly because he would fain give this assurance to others.[2] He seeks the sinful and the lost, not merely because such a ministry is lovely and gracious, but because he knows and declares that it is the will of God, and that there is more joy in heaven over one sinner that repenteth than over ninety-and-nine just men that need no repentance.[3] He cares for the bodies of men and he relieves their wants, but he cares infinitely more for their souls and he teaches them to care more, because he knows that the soul is capable of immortality and more precious than all that this world can give.[4] He

---

[1] St. Matt. 6 : 25–30. [2] St. John 11 : 41, 42.
[3] St. Luke 15 : 7. [4] St. John 6 : 27; St. Mark 8 : 36, 37.

moves willingly and obediently to the cross, not because it is inevitable, not because resignation is the crown of virtue, but because he knows and declares that this is the sacrifice appointed for him as the Christ, the laying down of his life as a ransom for many, the lifting up by which he is to draw all men unto himself.[1] He goes down into death with unshaken courage, not because it is a fine thing to be brave, but because he knows and declares that he is returning to the Father and that he will bring those who love him to be with him where he is forever.[2]

Now these are declarations of great truths. If we deny them, if we make them uncertain, the life which was built upon them has no meaning, no substance, no power in it. It becomes a splendid illusion, a heroic mistake. But if we accept them, then, and only then, that life becomes the rock of our confidence, the substance of things hoped for and the evidence of things not seen. For it was on the knowledge of these things that Jesus actually founded his own character and his conduct. It was by believing thus and so, and by living up to his belief, that he was made perfect. And it was

[1] St. Mark 9 : 12; St. Matt. 20 : 28; St. John 12 : 32.
[2] St. John 14 : 1–3.

by teaching his disciples to believe thus and
so that he would bind them to follow his example and inspire them to share his life. "Whosoever heareth these sayings of mine and doeth
them, I will liken him unto a wise man which
built his house upon a rock."[1] "Now ye are
clean through the word which I have spoken
unto you." "If ye abide in me, and my words
abide in you, ye shall ask what ye will and it
shall be done unto you."[2]

III

The importance which Christ ascribed to
his words as the authoritative revelation of
unseen verities to the confused and darkened
minds of men, cannot be denied or overlooked
by any one who reads the Gospels candidly and
intelligently. It is true, indeed, that he expressly disclaimed the idea that his doctrine
was created, or invented, or even discovered
by himself. He said, "My doctrine is not mine
but his that sent me,"[3] "All things that I have
heard of my Father I have made known unto
you."[4] But it is equally true that he claimed
an absolute infallibility for the message which

[1] St. Matt. 7 : 24.
[2] St. John 15 : 3, 7.
[3] St. John 7 : 16.
[4] St. John 15 : 15.

was revealed in him, committed unto him, and
delivered by him. This claim is made with
equal force in the Synoptics and in St. John.
"No one knoweth who the Son is, save the
Father; and who the Father is, save the Son,
and he to whomsoever the Son willeth to reveal him."[1] "We speak that we do know, and
bear witness of that we have seen."[2] This is
not the language that an honest and conscien-
tious teacher would use to describe his religious
opinions or his spiritual hopes. The wisest and
the best of men have always hesitated to assume this tone of certainty in regard to their
deepest reflections upon the mysteries of being.
But from first to last this tone marks the teaching of Jesus. "They were astonished at His
teaching; for he taught them as having authority, and not as the scribes."[3]

It is evident that he intended to speak thus.
For nothing is more striking in the manner of
his teaching than the absence of all reliance
upon corroborative testimony or traditional
support. He did not seek to defend his posi-
tions with a formidable array of great names.
He did not make a long catena of quotations
from learned sources. He gave out his doctrine from the depth of his own consciousness,

[1] St. Luke 10 : 22.　　[2] St. John 3 : 11.　　[3] St. Mark 1 : 22.

as a flower breathes its odour, fresh, pure, original, and convincing. He certainly felt a Divine inspiration in the ancient Hebrew Scriptures. The law and the prophets conveyed to him the word of God. He used them on certain occasions to repel the assaults of evil, as in the temptation in the wilderness. He used them on other occasions to convince and convict the Scribes and Pharisees out of their own Scriptures. But he never rested upon them as the sole and sufficient basis of his doctrine. He was not a commentator on truths already revealed. He was a revealer of new truth. His teaching was not the exposition; it was the text. And this higher revelation not only fulfilled, but also surpassed, the old; replacing the temporal by the eternal, the figurative by the factual, the literal by the spiritual, the imperfect by the perfect. How often Jesus quoted from the Old Testament in order to show that it was already old and insufficient; that its forms of speech and rules of conduct were like the husk of the seed which must be shattered by the emergence of the living germ! His doctrine was in fact a moral and intellectual daybreak for the world. He did far more than supply a novel system of conduction for an ancient light. He sent forth from himself a new illumination, transcending

163

all that had gone before, as the sunrise over-floods the pale glimmering of the morning star set like a beacon of promise upon the coast of dawn.

He did not rely upon reasoning for the proof of his doctrine. He put no trust in the compulsion of logic, in the keenness of dialectics. We look in vain among his words for an exhibition of the "evidences of Christianity." He did not endeavour to demonstrate the existence of God or the immortality of the soul. What he said was meant to be its own evidence. His method was not apologetic; it was declaratory.

"He argued not, but preached, and conscience did the rest."

The result of this is marvellous and magnificent. His teaching is cleared and disentangled from all that is temporary and transient in human thought. If he had reasoned with men, it must have been done upon the premises and in the forms of philosophy current in that age. Otherwise he could not have reached their intelligence, his reasoning would have been of none effect. But because he passed by all these processes and left them on one side while his doctrine moved simply, directly, and majestically to the heart of the truth, it comes to us to-day free, and unencumbered by any of those theories of physical science, of psychology, of political economy, which the growth of knowledge has changed, discredited, or discarded. His teaching is neither ancient nor modern, neither deductive nor inductive, neither Jewish nor Greek. It is universal, enduring, valid for all minds and for all times. There are no more difficulties in the way of accepting it now than there were when it was first delivered. It fits the spiritual needs of the present as closely as it fitted the spiritual needs of the first century. It carries the same attractions, the same credentials in the Western Hemisphere as it carried in the Eastern. It stands out as clearly from all the later, as it did from all the earlier, philosophies. It finds the soul as inevitably to-day as it did at first. And the men of this age who hear Christ can only say, as his disciples said long ago, "Lord, to whom shall we go? Thou hast the words of eternal life."[1]

And yet how few are those words, compared with the utterances of other teachers. How small in compass is the doctrine of Jesus as it has come down to us. Eighty pages of a duodecimo book will hold all of his recorded discourses and the story of his life. Other words he must have spoken while he was on earth,

[1] St. John 6 : 68.

but I doubt not that they moved within the same circle. For even in the present record we find the same truths recurring again and again, expressed in different language, arranged in different sequence, as the evangelists retrace, each from his own point of view, the memory of the things which Jesus taught to the multitudes and to his disciples. The literature of the world holds no other doctrine so limited in bulk, so limitless in meaning.

The teaching of Christ differs from that of all other masters in its *fontal quality*. It is comprised in a little space, but it has an infinite fulness. Its utterance is closely bounded, but its significance is inexhaustible. The sacred books of other religions, the commentaries and expositions on the Christian religion, spread before us a vast and intricate expanse, like lakes of truth mixed with error, stretching away into the distance, arm after arm, bay after bay, until we despair of being able even to explore their coasts and trace their windings. When we come back to Christ, we find, not an inland sea of doctrine, but a clear fountain of living water, springing up into everlasting life.

Calm, pure, unfathomable, it is never clouded and it never fails. The inspiration of other teachers rises and falls like an intermittent

166

spring. To-day it is brimming full; to-morrow it is empty and dry. But the truth that flows from Jesus is constant and unvarying. The Spirit always rests upon him. The Father is always with him. Out of the deep serenity of his soul, as from some secret vale of peace high among the eternal hills, the spring of truth wells up forever, and forever the crystal stream runs down to refresh and revive the souls of men.

New meanings come out of the teaching of Jesus in every land and in every age. New stars are mirrored in its depths. New flowers blossom on its banks. New fields of love are fertilized by its waters. It is not that each succeeding century and race adds something of its own to the doctrine of Christ. It is that each finds in that source something which was meant to become its own, and so to satisfy its deepest needs. The old questions are repeated in new words, and the new answer comes in the old words. The truth as it is in Jesus does not have to be changed and adapted to fit it for a world-wide missionary enterprise. It needs only to be purified from the things that men have mingled with it, restored to the simplicity that is in Christ, and it proves itself as fresh, as satisfying, as life-bestowing to the thirsty soul in America or in the islands of the sea, as it did in Galilee or on the hillsides of Judea.

When we ask ourselves why it is that the doctrine of the Master has this enduring, self-renewing, *fontal* character, I think we must find the answer in the fact that it simply bears witness, with a directness and inevitableness altogether unparalleled, to the actual existence of a spiritual world corresponding to the spiritual faculties and aspirations of men. It does not turn aside to discuss metaphysical problems or theological subtleties. The distinction between the natural and the supernatural does not even appear in the teaching of Jesus. There may, or there may not, be such a distinction. If there is, he at least does not think it important enough to speak of it. The one thing of which he wishes to make men sure is that the same God who sends his sunshine and his rain upon the evil and upon the good, the same God whose bounty feeds the birds of the air and clothes the lilies of the field with beauty, hears in secret the prayers of the penitent and believing and rewards them openly. The question of the how and the where of the life after death is not even touched in the teaching of Jesus. It matters little. The one thing that he declares with unfaltering certainty is the reality of that life. The one thing that he presses home upon the minds of men with calm intensity is the danger of losing it through sin and unbelief. The one thing that he tenderly and urgently pleads with them to do, is to make sure of its immortal blessedness through faith and love and obedience to him. And so, at every point, he passes by the non-essential to touch the essential, he disregards the passing curiosity to satisfy the real anxiety, he neglects the shadows to reveal the substance of the unseen world.

Teaching like this is the only kind of teaching that will always renew itself, always have something more to bestow upon us. It cannot grow obsolete. It cannot be drained of its significance. It is like life. Nay, it is life, and it gives life.

IV

Let us understand, then, that if our Christianity is to satisfy our whole nature, if it is to have its real and full meaning, and power to bring in the kingdom of heaven, it must include this element. We must be as loyal to the teaching of Jesus as we are to his example. We must count no pains too great to spend

169

upon the study of that teaching as it lies in the records, and no effort too severe to make in order that it may be restored in its integrity and entirety, rounded and harmonized, within the very centre of our minds. And then we must preach it, simply, sincerely, certainly, as the only doctrine which can lead men out of the intellectual anarchy of doubt into the peaceful realm of truth.

This is what the age is looking and longing for. It can find no joy in the kingdom of heaven unless it finds there a source of authority for the mind as well as for the heart. Authority is what the sociologist demands, in order that he may have a sure basis for the precepts of altruism. Authority is what the philosopher seeks, in order that he may have a fixed point of departure and certain limits of speculation. Authority is what the poet craves, as he clings to

> "*The truths that never can be* proved,
> *Until we close with all we loved*
> *And all we flow from, soul in soul.*"

Men are crying lo here! and lo there! We must find the source of authority in an inerrant Book, or in an enlightened reason, or in an infallible Church, or perhaps in all three; as if there could be three sources of one authority, or as if a channel could ever be rightly called a source! Let us not hesitate to pass through this confusion of tongues and of ideas, serene and untroubled, with the message of a more excellent way.

Christ is the Light of all Scripture. Christ is the Master of holy reason. Christ is the sole Lord and Life of the true Church. By his word we test all doctrines, conclusions, and commands. On his word we build all faith. This is *the* source of authority in the kingdom of heaven. Let us neither forget nor hesitate to appeal to it always with untrembling certainty and positive conviction. If Christ did not know and preach the truth, then there is no truth that can be known or preached. Unless we are sure of this, we would better go out of business entirely. It is inconceivable that the loftiest character in history should be the most mistaken man who ever thought about the real basis and meaning of life. It is incredible that the noblest life in the world should be founded upon a faith that was vain. It is impossible that a supreme devotion and a real likeness to Christ should have been produced and perpetuated in the world without a veritable apprehension of that which he knew and taught concerning God and man.

To have this apprehension clearly formed

within us must be our ardent and joyful intellectual endeavour. We are not to rest content with the study of single words and separate phrases. The limitations of language, the conditions of transmission, will always expose us to error if we follow that course. The truth as it is in Jesus does not lie in fragments, but in the rounded whole. We must get back to the unity and integrity of the thoughts of Jesus, the creed of Christ. The broad outline of his vision of things human and divine, the central verities which appear firm and unchangeable in all the reports of his teaching, the point of view from which he discerned and interpreted the mystery of life,—that is what we must seek. And when we find it, we must take our stand there as men who feel the solid ground beneath their feet. Illustrations and confirmations we may gather from science and history and philosophy. But the rock of certainty is the mind of Jesus, expressed in his living words and in his speaking life. Beyond this we need not and we cannot go. Here is the ultimatum. This is the truth, we say to men, because Jesus knew it, and said it, and lived it.

But one thing we may not, we dare not, forget. The condition of apprehending, and how much more of preaching, the truth revealed by

Christ is that we abide in him. The word of Jesus in the mind of one who does not do the will of Jesus, lies like seed-corn in a mummy's hand. It is only by dwelling with him and receiving his character, his personality, so profoundly, so vitally that it shall be with us as if, in his own words, we had partaken of his flesh and his blood, as if his sacred humanity had been interwoven with the very fibres of our heart and pulsed with secret power in all our veins,—it is thus only that we can be enabled to see his teaching ьs it is, and set it forth with luminous conviction to the souls of men.

And if ever we ourselves become afraid of our own task, and shrink from it; if the scepticism of our age appalls us and chills us to the marrow; if we question whether a gospel so simple, so absolute, as that which is committed to us can find acceptance in such a world, at such a time as this,—be sure it is because we have gotten out of fellowship with him who is our Peace and our Hope, our Light and our Strength. A Christless man can never preach Christ. We have been anxious and troubled about many things, and have forgotten the one thing needful. Peace we must have before we can have power. Let us straightway return, in prayer, in meditation, in trust, in faithful simple-hearted obedience, to him who is the only centre of Peace because he is the only source of authority.

> "*I have a life in Christ to live,*
>   *But ere I live it must I wait*
> *Till learning can clear answer give*
>   *Of this and that book's date?*
> *I have a life in Christ to live,*
>   *I have a death in Christ to die;—*
> *And must I wait till science give*
>   *All doubts a full reply?*
>
> *Nay, rather, while the sea of doubt*
> *Is raging wildly round about,*
> *Questioning of life and death and sin,*
> *Let me but creep within*
> *Thy fold, O Christ, and at Thy feet*
> *Take but the lowest seat,*
> *And hear Thine awful voice repeat*
> *In gentlest accents, heavenly sweet,*
> *Come unto Me and rest;*
> *Believe Me, and be blest.*"

VI

LIBERTY

THERE are three points at which the teaching of Jesus comes into closest contact with the needs of the present age. Three problems of profound difficulty are pressing to-day upon all thoughtful men: the psychological problem of the freedom of the will; the theological problem of the actual relation of God to the universe; and the moral problem of man's duty to his fellow-men in a world of inequality. Most of the intellectual perplexities and practical perils of our times come directly from these questions, to which modern scepticism gives an answer of despair, or at best only a dubious and uncertain reply.

But the gospel of Christ, rightly apprehended and interpreted, offers us a solution of these problems which is full of light and hope. Three truths emerge in his doctrine, and stand out clear and sharp as mountain peaks against the blue: the truth of human liberty, the truth of Divine sovereignty, and the truth of universal service. Of these three truths we must never lose sight, if our thinking is to be in accordance with the mind of Jesus. To these three truths we must bear witness, unhesitatingly, faithfully, and joyfully, if our preaching is to be a gospel for this age of doubt.

I

No one who has looked steadily upon the face of modern life as it is reflected in popular literature can deny that it is "sicklied o'er" with the shadow of fatalism. It is evident in the writings of the learned and in the scribblings of the ignorant. Everywhere there is a tendency to explain the whole life of man as the product of heredity and environment. The student of physiology, tracing the subtle correspondence between the processes of consciousness and the changes and movements of the nervous system, makes the enormous assumption that the correspondence amounts to identity. He takes for granted that the hopes, affections, and aspirations, which glorify this mortal life, are in their last analysis the result of certain puckerings of the gray matter of the nerves. The actions which flow from them are as necessary as the fall of an apple when the stem is broken. The caress which a mother gives to her child, and the blow with which a murderer strikes his victim dead, are equally automatic and inevitable. They are the motions of delicately constructed puppets, and the triumph of modern investigation is the discovery of the string which moves them and the forces which pull it.

It is true that many of the teachers who steer us, more or less openly, towards this conclusion are careful to disavow the idea that they are teaching materialism. The name is highly unpopular at present, and there is hardly one of the men of science of to-day who has not protested with indignation that no one should dare to call him a materialist. They have devised subtle theories of something called "mind-stuff" which they hold, with W. K. Clifford, "is the reality which we perceive as matter." They distinguish, with Huxley, between matter and force, and a third thing which they call consciousness and which they admit cannot conceivably be a modification of either of the first two things; but they go on to say that "what we call the operations of the mind are functions of the brain, and the materials of consciousness are products of cerebral activity." In short, they give a materialistic explanation of the origin and processes of thought, and then protect themselves against the imputation of being materialists, by solemnly averring that they have not the slightest idea of what matter really is, nor the slightest intention of suggesting that it has any resemblance to the so-called mental operations which are probably produced by one of its own forms of activity.

A scheme like this certainly has no room for free-will or personal responsibility. It makes a man's character and action entirely dependent upon the amount and quality of nervous energy that has been transmitted to him by his ancestors and developed by the circumstances of his life. He lives, as Tyndall says, in a realm of "physical and moral necessity,"—though why he should be at pains to say "moral," I can hardly conceive. One adjective would serve as well as two, when they both mean the same thing. It requires but a little exercise of this nervous energy on our part, in the form of imagination, to trace it back to its previous form of heat stored up in certain hundredweights of food and appropriated by digestion. From this point our cerebral activity skips lightly and altogether without volition along the various lines of animal and vegetable life, of chemical and physical transformations of energy, until we arrive at the idea of the sun. From this idea a certain uncontrollable change in the gray

substance of our brain produces the further notion that the arrangement of certain quantities
of matter and force which took place in some
inexplicable way long before the birth of the
solar system was really the thing that settled
the question whether you and I should prefer
telling the truth to lying,—if we do. Indeed,
there never has been any question at all about
it; it was fixed from the beginning. We have
no more responsibility for it than we have for
the colour of our eyes or the shape of our noses.

I have found a brief and explicit statement
of the position to which this method of thinking forces those who follow it, in an article ironically entitled "Thoughts of a Human Automaton" in a recent English periodical.

"I am an automaton—a puppet dangling on
my distinctive wire, which Fate holds with an
unrelaxing grip. I am not different, nor do I
feel differently, from my fellow-men, but my
eyes refuse to blink away the truth, which is,
that I am an automatic machine, a piece of
clockwork wound up to go for an allotted time,
smoothly or otherwise, as the efficiency of the
machinery may determine. Free-will is a myth
invented by man to satisfy his emotions, not
his reason. I feel as if I were free, as if I were
responsible for my thoughts and actions, just

as a person under the influence of hypnotism believes he is free to do as he pleases. But he is not; nor am I. If it were once possible for a rational being to question this fact, the discoveries of Darwin must have set his doubts at rest. . . .

"What is crime? A crime is an action threatened by the law with punishment, says Kant; and freedom of action or free-will is a legally necessary condition of crime. But the law of heredity conclusively demonstrates that free-will and freedom of action stand in the category of lively imaginings. Therefore crime, as the law understands it, is non-existent, since no imputability can be recognized when a man is not responsible for his actions. Therefore the law is not justified in inflicting punishment. . . .

"Briefly to conclude. Religion can no more mix with science than oil with water. Science acknowledges no necessity for the existence of religion, and finally severs the bonds between morality and religion. Morality, altogether independent of religion, is entirely based upon self-interest. The supposed connection between religion and morality is an illusion most pernicious to the general welfare and advance of mankind. Religion, as a superfluity, should

180

be excluded from all educational institutions. Its place will be supplied by the creed of scientific philosophy—Determinism. The primary principle of Determinism, namely, that a human being is an automaton, and therefore not responsible for his thoughts or his acts, taken together with its corollaries, more than suffices for every intellectual need hitherto provided for by religion. For the two great factors in the value of religion are its ethics and its sedative properties, and in both these uses Determinism displays overwhelming intellectual superiority. Its ethics are more universal and its consolation more assured; for they both rest on irrefragable scientific truth. The Determinist is consequently never harassed by doubts—the Rock of Ages is fragile compared with the adamantine foundation of his creed."

This curious claim of an automaton to have a "creed" would be humorous, if it were not so sad and so dangerous. For though, as a matter of fact, there are few men who will make, even under an assumed name, such a candid confession of faith in their own moral non-entity as that which we have just read, there are many men who are, consciously or unconsciously, preaching the same black creed of Necessity in the subtle forms of literary art, and multitudes who are silently accepting it as gospel truth. Fatalism broods over modern fiction and the modern drama like a huge, shapeless spectre; and its influence is felt in all the judgments and conceptions and unspoken but clearly revealed sentiments of a society which finds its chief intellectual pabulum in novels and plays.

Here is the famous French realist, Zola, of whose books it is said that enough have been sold to build a pile as high as the Eiffel tower. He writes a novel called *La Bête Humaine*, in which he shows how unswervingly the lines of evil run through the plan of life. He describes seven inevitable murders, occurring within eighteen months in close connection with a certain fated house, and closes his book with the description of a railway train, crowded with soldiers, dragged by an engine whose driver has been killed, dashing at headlong speed into the midnight. The train is the world; we are the freight; fate is the track; death is the darkness; God is the engineer,—who is dead.

Here is the leader of the Dutch sensitivists, Louis Couperus, who writes a romance called *Noodlot*, "*Destiny*," in which four human lives are tangled together in an inextricable and horrible coil. One of his characters pauses for an instant in the shameful career to which he is impelled. "He threw himself back in his chair, still feebly wringing his hands, and the tears trickled again and again down his cheeks. He saw his own cowardice take shape before him. He stared into its frightened eyes, and he did not condemn it. For he was as fate had made him. He was a craven, and he could not help it. Men called such an one as he a coward; it was but a word. Why coward, or simple and brave, or good and noble? It was all a matter of convention, of accepted meaning; the whole world was mere convention, a concept, an illusion of the brain. There was nothing real at all—nothing!"

Here is the Norse dramatist, Ibsen. He writes a drama of life which he calls *Ghosts*, and shows how every player is haunted by dead ancestors who look through his eyes, speak in his words, and act in his deeds. Echoes of spent passion, shreds and patches of worn-out sin, rags and tatters of the past,—that is the stuff of which life is fabricated, like a piece of shoddy cloth, in the great mill of circumstance which stands on the banks of the river of time and turns out the shabby lives of men and women.

Nor is this view of life confined to the great foreign masters of realism. It pervades almost all the minor schools of fiction; it diffuses itself

183

insensibly through the work of the feeble and
fatuous imitators. A keen and wholesome
critic of our own literature, Mr. Charles Dud-
ley Warner, put his finger upon the fact when
he wrote: "It has come about that the novels
and stories which are to fill our leisure hours
and cheer us in this vale of tears have become
what we call tragic. It is not easy to define
what tragedy is, but the term is applied in modern fiction to scenes and characters that come
to ruin from no particular fault of their own,—
not even when the characters break most of
the ten commandments,—but by an unap-
peasable fate that dogs and thwarts them. This
is the romance of fatality, and if it is tragedy,
it is the tragedy of fatalism."

It is not possible that such a theory of existence should prevail without bringing sadness
and heaviness into the hearts of men. The
modern melancholy of which we spoke in the
first lecture is largely the result of this general
sense of a godless predestination. It is Calvinism with the bottom knocked out. It robs life
of all interest, of all joy, of all enthusiasm. Pessimism exudes from fatalism like sepia from
the cuttlefish. What could be more dispiriting
than to doubt the reality of all effort, to deny
the possibility of self-conquest and triumph

184

over circumstances, to find heroism an illusion and virtue a dream? What could break the spring of life more completely than to feel that our feet are tangled in a net whose meshes were woven for us by our ancestors, and for them by tailless apes, and for them by gilled amphibians, and for them by gliding worms, and for them by ciliated larvæ, and for them by amœbæ, and for them by God does not know what? To baptize fatalism with a Christian name does not change its nature. To hold fast to the metaphysical conception of God while accepting Heredity and Environment as his only and infallible prophets is simply to add a new ethical horror to the dismal delusion of life, and to fall back into the pessimism of Omar Khayyám.

"We are no other than a moving row
Of Magic Shadow-shapes, that come and go
Round with this Sun-illumined Lantern, held
In Midnight by the Master of the Show;

Impotent Pieces of the Game He plays
Upon this Checker-board of Nights and Days;
Hither and thither moves, and checks, and slays,
And one by one back in the Closet lays.

The Moving Finger writes; and, having writ,
Moves on; nor all your Piety nor wit

LIBERTY

Shall lure it back to cancel half a Line,
Nor all your tears wash out a Word of it.

And that inverted Bowl they call the Sky,
Whereunder crawling coop'd we live and die,
Lift not your hands to It for help—for it
As impotently rolls as you or I."

II

This is the solution which modern positivism,
christened or unchristened, offers for the problem of the freedom of the will. Before we turn
to consider the very different answer which
Christ gives to the same question, let us stay
for a moment to ask whether this current and
popular solution is of the nature of a demonstration, or of the nature of a doubt. Is it so
clearly proven that science forces us to accept
determinism? Or is it an unverifiable assumption, which is made under the influence of a
general scepticism in regard to spiritual realities, and which leaves out of view quite as many
and quite as important facts as those which it
professes to explain? Are we compelled to admit it; or is it only one of two alternatives,
neither of which is scientifically demonstrable,
so that the choice between them must rest upon
other considerations?

I do not hesitate to say that the whole weight

of sober and sane criticism inclines to the latter conclusion. Determinism has not yet been established either by physiological, psychological, or metaphysical argument.

The common assumption that the abstract reasoning of Jonathan Edwards against the liberty of the will has never been and cannot be refuted, is based upon ignorance of the facts. An American philosopher, Mr. Rowland Hazard, has answered it with great clearness and force. Professor George P. Fisher says: "The fundamental point of Mr. Hazard's criticism of Edwards is fully established. It must be allowed that his confutation of that conception of the will which underlies the reasoning of the great theologian is sound and conclusive."

The support which modern science is supposed to give to the theory of determinism turns out, upon closer examination, to be altogether illusory. The soundest and most careful investigators utterly decline to commit themselves to that metaphysical dogma, or to bind science as a maid-of-all-work in the service of fatalistic theology.

Lord Kelvin recently said: "The influence of animal or vegetable life on matter is infinitely beyond the range of any scientific inquiry hitherto entered on. Its power of directing the motions of moving particles, *in the demonstrated daily miracle of our human free-will*, and in the growth of generation after generation of plants from a single seed, are infinitely different from any possible result of the fortuitous concourse of atoms. The real phenomena of life infinitely transcend human science."

The theory that consciousness is a function of the brain breaks down completely when it attempts to explain the phenomena of sleep. Why should all the other functions of the body be carried on without fatigue and without interruption while consciousness alone demands rest and admits of intervals of cessation? If it is a function of nerve-matter, sleep abolishes it. How does it come back again without losing the sense of personal identity? Is it conceivable that the highest character, the loftiest genius, is purely an intermittent secretion of certain nerve-cells, and that during the hours of sleep, embracing one-third of its entire history, it is absolutely non-existent? "Function," says an eminent neurologist, "is a physiological term, and it is, I submit, improper to speak of states of consciousness as being functions of the brain. . . . It is not the mind, but the physical basis of mind, which is a product of physical evolution. It is the organ of mind, not the mind of itself, which being an evolution out of the rest of the body is representative of it."

The fact that the brain is a double organ,—that there are really two brains, only one of which is used,—cannot be explained on the theory that consciousness is merely the result of the vibration of nerve filaments, as the music of the Æolian harp is the result of the passage of the wind over its strings. A distinguished physiologist has cleverly shown that if this were the case a double brain would mean a double amount of thought, just as twice the number of strings would mean twice the quantity of music. But the fact that this is not so, points clearly to the hypothesis that the brain is not an Æolian harp helplessly vibrating under external impulses, but a double organ with two sets of keys, and the mind is like the player who can use either one of them to make the music. And this corresponds closely with our own sense of the process. For we are conscious not only of passive thoughts and feelings, evoked within us by external causes, but also of thoughts and feelings voluntarily directed and combined, woven together in creative harmonies, and moving under the guidance of chosen ideals towards a symphonic completeness. Even the sense of discord and conflict which often rises within us is an evidence that there is a player as well as an instrument. For it is inconceivable that an Æolian harp, ill-strung, should dislike its own bad music, and endeavour, or think that it could endeavour, to make a better, sweeter sound.

Heredity is undoubtedly a real and powerful force. It supplies the outfit of life. But does it determine the use which we shall make of it? The very extension of the doctrine by the investigations of science dissolves this narrow and absolute conclusion. We inherit from thousands, from hundreds of thousands, of ancestors. The blood of many families and tribes and races is mingled in our veins. What is it that decides which of these many lines we shall follow? It must be either blind chance or free choice. All the phenomena of society, all the facts of consciousness, are in favour of the latter supposition. We see men whose heritage is of the lowest and the worst, working their way up, by sheer strength of moral choice and effort, to a higher plane. We see men whose heritage is of the loftiest and the best, declining

> "*thro' acted crime,*
> *Or seeming-genial venial fault,*
> *Recurring and suggesting still,*"

190

to the very depths of infamy. It is true that a man cannot bring out of himself anything that is not already there. But it is true also, by virtue of heredity, that there are many potential men in every man, and which of them is to emerge, he chooses for himself by a thousand silent moral preferences; by yielding or by resisting; by the cowardice and corruption, or by the courage and purification of his own free-will.

Even those who write of human life from a professedly naturalistic standpoint cannot get rid of this conviction. Take Zola, for example. If he were consistent, he would speak with equal and impassive coldness of all his characters, tangled together in the inextricable toils of heredity. But he cannot help letting his hatred and contempt for the selfish, the luxurious, the vicious, express itself in the very accent with which he describes them. He cannot help showing his admiration and affection for those who, like *Denise* and *Doctor Pascal*, and *Clotilde*, rise out of the infamy which envelops the family *Rougon-Macquart*. Virtue and vice may be scientifically treated as if they were merely natural products like sugar and vitriol; but when we come to talk of them from a human standpoint, there is something within us which

demands that we shall recognize a merit in being
virtuous, and a shame in being vicious,—qualities which can never belong to mere secretions,
whether of plants or of nerves,—qualities which
have no possible meaning unless there is a free
will in man, capable of choosing between the
evil and the good.

That a free will is possible, modern psychology assures us, as the result of its latest
researches. It does not attempt to demonstrate
the existence of such a power by physiological
investigation. It confesses that this demonstration is impossible with our present knowledge.
But it declares with equal candour that the
contrary attempt to show that the sense of
freedom is a delusion, is inconclusive. "The
last word of psychology here," says Professor
William James, "is ignorance, for the forces
engaged are too delicate and numerous to be
followed in detail." He points out the ex-
tremely reckless and inconsequent nature of
the reasoning by which the determinists seek
to make mere analogies drawn from the course
of rivers, and reflex actions, and other material
phenomena, serve as proofs that the will is a
mechanical effect. He exposes the bold assumption by which they ignore the testimony

of consciousness in the presence of feeling and effort. He shows that the utmost which any argument for determinism can do is to present a possible hypothesis, which a man who has already determined to hold fast to the idea that the whole universe is one chain of inevitable causation may accept if he likes. But meanwhile the other alternative stands equally open. The moral arguments all point in that direction. The only course, in such a situation, is voluntary choice. "For scepticism itself, if systematic, is also voluntary choice. If, meanwhile, the will be indetermined, it would seem only fitting that the belief in its indetermination should be voluntarily chosen from amongst other possible beliefs. Freedom's first deed should be to affirm itself. . . . Thus not only our morality but our religion, so far as the latter is deliberate, depends on the effort which we can make. *'Will you or won't you have it so?'* is the most probing question we are ever asked: we are asked it every hour of the day, and about the largest as well as the smallest, the most theoretical as well as the most practical, things. We answer *by consents or non-consents*, and not by words. What wonder if these dumb responses should seem our deepest organs of communication with the nature of things! What wonder if the effort demanded by them should be the measure of our worth as men! What wonder if the amount which we accord of it be the one strictly underived and original contribution which we make to the world!"

III

Here, then, modern science, careful, exact, reverent, as distinguished from modern scepticism, leaves us before the two doors. And here Christ comes to us, calling us to enter through the door of liberty into the pathway of eternal life. "Ask, and it shall be given you; seek and ye shall find; knock and it shall be opened unto you."[1] "If any man willeth to do his will, he shall know of the teaching."[2]

The whole life and ministry of Jesus is a revelation of moral freedom. His entrance into the world was voluntary. His continuance in human life was voluntary. His death was voluntary. At the first crisis of his life he chose to go about his Father's business. In the temptation he chose to resist the allurements of the Evil One. On the way to the cross he chose not to call on God for the deliverance which he knew would come in answer to his call. He was, indeed, fulfilling an appointed task, tread-

[1] St. Matt. 7 : 7.   [2] St. John 7 : 17.

ing the path which had been marked out for the feet of the Christ; but he was fulfilling the task freely; he was walking in liberty because he loved to do the will of God. The triumph of his virtue lay in the freedom of his choice.

There was a singular propriety in the text of his first public discourse. It was a declaration of liberty, as well as of grace. It was an emancipation proclamation as well as a gospel of comfort and help. "The spirit of the Lord is upon me, because he anointed me to preach good tidings to the poor; he hath sent me to proclaim release to the captives, and recovering of sight to the blind, to set at liberty them that are crushed, to proclaim the acceptable year of the Lord."[1] And what was the oppressive bondage from which he proclaimed release? Was it not the tyranny of a false doctrine of necessity over the minds of men, as well as the enslaving influence of sin over their inert and hopeless wills?

Here were the scribes and Pharisees teaching that the whole world was divided into two classes,—the chosen and the not-chosen, the righteous for whom salvation was secure whatever they might do, and the sinners for whom salvation was impossible whatever they might

[1] St. Luke 4 : 18.

do. Here were the outcast, the lost, the neglected, shut out, by no choice of their own, but
by their birth, by the occupations in which
they were engaged, by their ignorance, by the
very conditions of their life, from all part in
the kingdom of heaven as the scribes and Pharisees conceived it; not only the harlots and the
publicans, but also *Am Haarez*, "the people of
the land," with whom it was not fitting that a
righteous person should have any dealings;
miserable souls, bound by inheritance to a desperate and unhallowed fate. Here came Jesus,
taking his way directly to these lost ones, these
outsiders, and telling them that all this doctrine of inevitable doom was a chain of lies,
breaking the imaginary fetters from their souls
and assuring them by his first word that they
were free, even though they were ignorant of
it. "Repent," he cried, "for the kingdom of
heaven has approached unto you."[1] "Except
ye be converted and become as little children,
ye shall not enter into the kingdom of heaven."[2]
And what is the significance of these words,
"repentance" and "conversion,"—their real
significance, I mean, not that which has been
read into them by centuries of false and formal
theology? They are not passive and involun-

[1] St. Matt. 4 : 17.   [2] St. Matt. 18 : 3.

tary words; they do not rest upon the idea of qualifications which may or may not be in the possession of those to whom Christ speaks. They are active words,—words of inward movement and exertion. "Repent" means change your mind; make that simple effort of the soul for internal change which is the ultimate act of the free will; put forth that power of fixed attention to the new motive which is the central essence of liberty and the creative force of the soul. "Be converted," as Christ spoke the word, is not passive; it expresses an action exercised by the soul within itself; it means simply "turn around"; set yourself in a new relation to God, to truth, to virtue. The name of this relation is faith. "Believe" is Christ's great word. It is the *"open sesame"* of the kingdom. "Believe in God, believe also in me."[1] "He that believeth hath everlasting life."[2] "All things are possible to him that believeth."[3] But it is never spoken of as a mere intellectual opinion, or emotional experience, an irresistible conviction wrought by external evidence in the mind, or bestowed without effort upon the soul. The Bible never says that faith is a gift. There is a voluntary element in it. It is something to be done by the

[1] St. John 14 : 1.　　[2] St. John 6 : 47.　　[3] St. Mark 9 : 23.

197

exercise of an inward power. It is a coming of the soul to Christ; it is a following of the soul after him; it is the first step in a long course of spiritual activity. It is a deed. The disciples said unto Christ, "What must we do that we may work the works of God?" Jesus answered, "This is the work of God, that ye believe on him whom he hath sent." [1]

Now there is not a hint in all the teaching of Jesus that this first act of freedom is impossible for any soul to whom he speaks. He has no idea of an eternal predestination binding some to belief and others to unbelief, a secret decree including certain men in the kingdom and excluding others from all possibility of entering into it. It is true that he says, "No man can come unto Me except the Father draw him"; [2] but what he means by this drawing he tells us in the parable of the Lost Son, where it is the simple knowledge of the Father's abundant love that draws the prodigal back from the far country of sin; [3] and in the parable of the Publican in the Temple,[4] where it is the sense of the Divine mercy and forgiveness that makes the outcast man cry, "God, be merciful to me a sinner." There is prevenient grace in

[1] St. John 6 : 28, 29.   [2] St. John 6 : 44.
[3] St. Luke 15.   [4] St. Luke 18 : 10-14.

the doctrine of Jesus. But the grace is there. It has already come. All that man has to do is to meet it, to put himself into the upward swing of it, that it may lift and help him heavenward.

A calling and a choosing by God are necessary before any man can be saved. But Jesus does not speak of this choosing and calling as eternal. Christ himself is the call, and all who answer it are chosen. "If any man thirst, let him come unto me and drink."[1] "Him that cometh unto me I will in no wise cast out."[2] The heavenly invitation is set forth in all its generosity and sincerity in the story of the Marriage Feast.[3] The bidding went out into the highways and hedges, to the bad and to the good; and all who heard and accepted it were welcome. And if a single guest was turned away, it was only because his own conduct showed that he had not really taken the invitation honestly and accepted willingly all that was provided for him.

There is not a single word in all that Jesus said to suggest any other reason than this for the exclusion of a single person from the blessings of the kingdom. "*Ye will not* come unto

[1] St. John 7 : 37. [2] St. John 6 : 37.
[3] St. Matt. 22 : 1-14.

me that ye might have life."[1] "How often would I have gathered thy children together even as a hen gathereth her chickens under her wings, *and ye would not.*"[2] There is not one statement that anything else but mercy and grace has been eternally prepared by God for any human soul. In that awful parable of judgment which discloses the convincing picture of the final separation of the evil from the good, Christ says distinctly that the joy of the blessed has been prepared for them from the foundation of the world, but of the punishment of the cursed, he says with equal distinctness that it was not prepared for them, but for the devil and his angels.[3] No one is ever lost because he cannot do good, but only because he will not do what he can.

Christ recognizes the undoubted truth which lies in the doctrine of heredity; but he exposes, and almost ridicules, the false and fatal extremes to which men think it out. To the Jews, who claimed that because they were Abraham's seed they must be free, he showed that they were in bondage to their own sins. They had chosen to break away from the heredity of faith and righteousness, and were no longer the true

---

[1] St. John 5 : 40. [2] St. Matt. 23 : 37.
[3] St. Matt. 25 : 34–41.

children of Abraham. They had become the
children of the devil, because they had "willed
to do his works." [1] He said to his disciples who
took up the cant of the day about hereditary
sin and punishment, asked whether the blind
man or his parents had sinned that he was born
blind, "Neither hath this man sinned, nor his
parents, but that the works of God should be
made manifest in him." [2] The true inheritance,
the deepest inheritance which Jesus recognizes
in the human race, is an inheritance from God;
a nature made in the Divine image, spiritual,
free, responsible, and capable, though so sadly
marred, though so far astray, of returning to
communion with the Heavenly Father.

Undoubtedly Christ perceived and taught
the immense difficulty of being good; the infirmity which long centuries of sin has wrought
into the very fibres of the soul; the awful and
almost inaccessible height of true holiness; the
enormous obstacles which lie in the way of at-
taining it. The gate is strait, and we must
agonize to enter in by it. The road is steep,
and we must toil to climb it. "How hardly
shall they that have riches enter into the kingdom of God." [3] And yet "the kingdom of
heaven suffereth violence, and men of violence

[1] St. John 8 : 33–47.   [2] St. John 9 : 3.   [3] St. Mark 10 : 23.

take it by force." [1]   There is an effort which
succeeds even in this greatest of all endeavours,
not in its own strength, but because it is sure
of a Divine assistance.   "With man it is impossible, but not with God." [2]   To the human
will, enfeebled and corrupted, so that it is like
a sick man, barely able to turn himself upon
his couch, and look and long and cry for help,
three great sources of strength are always open
and accessible.

The first is prayer.   "Men ought always to
pray, and not to faint." [3]   How sweet and serene
is the voice that rings through the vain dis-
putations and doubtful wranglings of the scribes
and Pharisees, and calls every sinful soul to
pray!   Pray! you may not be able to realize
your own ideal, but you can ask God to help
you hold fast to it and struggle towards it.
Pray!

> *"More things are wrought by prayer*
> *Than this world dreams of."*

Pray!   For God is not deaf, nor sleeping, nor
gone upon a journey; he has not bound you
to an inexorable fate and bound himself not to
interfere with it.   Pray!   The liberty of your
own soul, and the liberty of God himself, dwells

[1] St. Matt. 11 : 12.   [2] St. Mark 10 : 27.   [3] St. Luke 18 : 1.

in that word; for when you stretch your feeble hand to him, a Divine hand will meet it, and break your fetters, and lift you out of darkness and death into life and light.

The second source of strength is the Holy Spirit. It is inconceivable, morally impossible, that there should be such a Spirit, and yet that his influence should be withheld from those who need and implore it. "If ye then, being evil, know how to give good gifts unto your children, how much more shall your heavenly Father give the Holy Spirit unto them that ask him." [1]

The third source of strength is Christ himself. Does the sense of past guilt stand in the way of future effort? He says, "I have power on earth to forgive sins." [2] Does the soul feel dead and hopeless under the burden of evil habits? He says, "I came that they may have life, and may have it abundantly." [3] Do the works of a true and vital righteousness seem far beyond our power? He says, "Without me ye can do nothing"; [4] but, "Lo, I am with you alway, even unto the end of the world." [5] "He that believeth on me, the works that I do shall he do also, and greater works than these shall

---

[1] St. Luke 11 : 13.　　[2] St. Mark 2 : 10.　　[3] St. John 10 : 10.
[4] St. John 15 : 5.　　[5] St. Matt. 28 : 20.

he do, because I go unto the Father." ¹ The
whole life of Christ is summed up in the words,
"But as many as received him, to them *gave
he power* to become the sons of God." ²

But this receiving, we need to remember and
assert again and again, is not a passive thing.
It is an action of the soul, the opening of a door
within the heart, the welcoming of a heavenly
master. God does not save men as a watch-
maker who repairs and sets a watch, but as a
King who recalls his servants to their duty, as
a Father who makes new revelations of his love
to draw his lost children back to himself. The
dogmas of the schools in regard to the working
out of what they call the scheme of redemption
sound like the creak and rattle of some vast
machine. The doctrine of Christ is like the
soft breath of spring, evoking the songs of birds
and the unfolding of new life. No fiery chariot
of grace swoops down to snatch men to glory.
But a living Messenger comes forth from God
to ask men to turn and walk back with him to
their soul's home. The invitation itself is a
guarantee of the power to accept it. With authority Christ commanded the winds and the
sea and they obeyed him. But with gracious
pleading he invited the hearts of men, and those

¹ St. John 14 : 12.   ² St. John 1 : 12.

204

who were willing gladly heard and followed him.

"If any man *wills* to come after Me," [1]—that is the prelude of his message. He offers a leadership to men who can follow, a mastership to men who can obey. Out of this first movement he promises to guide and direct the whole development of the new life,—not a passive life of retirement, of ascetic meditation, of reflection upon secret truth,—but an active life of service, of warfare against evil in the world, a life which translates truth into conduct.

Contrast the religion of Jesus in this respect with the Oriental religions, and with those forms of Christianity which have borrowed the garments of Buddha or speak with the accent of Mahomet. They despise and slight personality. Christ respects and emphasises it. They aim to reduce and evaporate responsibility. Christ aims to deepen and increase it. They point forward to a blank Nirvana in which the individual is lost and absorbed, or a Paradise in which he is forever lapped in sensual ease and pleasure. Christ speaks of the perfecting of the individual through the Divine communion and service on earth, and his entrance in heaven upon a new stage of the same communion, the

[1] St. Matt. 16 : 24.

same service,—"not in a blessed idleness, but in an exalted kingly work and activity." And the entrance into this kingdom on earth, the continuance in its realm of liberty, the attainment of its final glory, are all through an act of the will. The freedom which originated in God is only to be preserved by returning to God and abiding in him.

> *"Our wills are ours, we know not how;*
> *Our wills are ours, to make them Thine."*

That is the teaching of Jesus. That is the truth which, when it comes to men, makes them and keeps them free.

IV

It is impossible that we should be faithful preachers of Christ to the present age, unless we preach this truth. There may have been ages in which it was important to dwell upon other sides and aspects of the manifold reality of the spiritual world. But to-day this is the important side; this is the aspect which demands a clear recognition and an unfaltering proclamation by those who mean to be true to Christ and loyal to the needs of humanity. I do not believe that there is a single passage in the Old Testament which contradicts Christ's doctrine of the real liberty of the soul. But if there were such a passage, I would leave it forever alone, as belonging to that knowledge which was in part, and which was done away when that which was perfect had come. I do not believe that there is a single word in the writings of St. Paul which stands against this doctrine of the real liberty of the soul. I cut loose from the false interpretations which men have read into his words. I take the light of Christ's teaching in my hand, and I go back to interpret by that light the teachings of the great Epistle to the Romans with its glorious revelation of "the mystery which hath been kept in silence through times eternal, but now is manifested, and by the Scriptures of the prophets, according to the commandment of the eternal God, is made known unto all the nations *unto obedience of faith*." [1] I hear again the cry of the struggling, labouring, conquering apostle: "*To will is present with me*, but to do that which is good is not. . . . O wretched man that I am, who shall deliver me out of the body of this death? I thank God *through Christ Jesus our Lord*"; [2] and I know that St. Paul also was a believer in the freedom of the will, and that he received this gospel and the

[1] Rom. 16 : 26.　　　　[2] Rom. 7 : 18, 24, 25.

power to fulfil it, through the proclamation of
liberty in Jesus Christ.

"This matter of free-will," wrote one of the
most orthodox of theologians, but a few years
before his death, "underlies everything. If
you bring it to question, it is infinitely more
than Calvinism. . . . I believe in Calvinism,
and I say that free-will stands before Calvinism. Everything is gone if free-will is gone;
the moral system is gone, if free-will is gone;
you cannot escape except by Materialism on
the one hand or by Pantheism on the other.
Hold hard therefore to the doctrine of free-
will."

Yes, and we may say more than this. Not
only is the moral system gone, but the great
attraction of Christ is gone, the power of his
gospel to liberate men is gone, if free-will is
gone.

The age has hypnotized itself. It is drifting
steadily towards fatalism. It denies freedom,
and therefore it is not free. It is in bondage
to its own doubt. It is enslaved by its own
denial. If there is such a thing as liberty, it
can only be developed, as everything else has
been developed, by action, by exercise. Life is
self-change to meet environment. Liberty is
self-exertion to unfold the soul. The law of

natural selection is that those who use a faculty
shall expand it, but those who use it not shall
lose it. Religion is life, and it must grow under
the laws of life. Faith is simply the assertion
of spiritual freedom; it is the first adventure
of the soul. Make that adventure towards
God, make that adventure towards Christ,
and the soul will know that it is alive. So it
enters upon that upward course which leads
through the liberty of the sons of God to the
height of heaven,

> *"Where love is an unerring light*
> *And joy its own security."*

This is the truth with which we are to go
out a-gospelling in this age of doubt. We are
to tell men that though much has been determined for them by causes beyond their control,
—their circumstances, their talents, their faculties,—one thing has not been determined, and
that is what they will do with them. Much has
been ordained before their birth,—their nationality, their family, their station in life,—but
one thing has not been ordained, and that is
whether they are to move from this starting-
point towards life or towards death. They
may be like men sunken in a nightmare dream
of helplessness, muttering in their sleep, "If I

am to be saved, I shall be saved; if I am to be lost, I shall be lost,"—but we must cry to them with the voice of the Spirit: "Awake, thou that sleepest, and arise from the dead, and Christ shall give thee light."

VII

SOVEREIGNTY

THE questions about the world which science considers and answers, all have to do with secondary causes. Beyond that sphere she does not need to go, and within that sphere her wisdom is sufficient. We come to her like curious children. We "want to see the wheels go round." We want to know what the wheels are made of. She tells us, and there she stops. All that we have a right to ask of her is that she shall be true to facts, and that she shall confine herself to them. When the astronomer Laplace was reproached for not mentioning God in his treatise on the dynamics of the solar system, he answered, "I had no need of that hypothesis." And this reply was just, as Mr. John Fiske has pointed out, because "in order to give a specific explanation of any single group of phenomena, it would not do to appeal to divine action, which is equally the source of all phenomena."

But the moment we take this reasonable

and modest position, we perceive that curiosity in regard to single groups of phenomena by no means satisfies or exhausts the activity of the questioning spirit in man. There is a deeper curiosity in regard to the relation of these single groups of phenomena to each other, and to ourselves, and to the possibility of a meaning, a purpose, an end, underlying all things and all their workings. Out of this deeper curiosity rise the questions which are most urgent and vital,—questions which, when we consider them abstractly, are philosophical, and condition the unity of our intellectual life; but when we consider them personally, they are religious, and upon their answer our spiritual peace and moral action absolutely depend. How are we to think about the things that we know? What are we to believe in regard to the things that science tells us we cannot know, but which we still feel are necessary conditions of all intelligent and right conduct? Is there an invisible unity beneath all the visible diversity of phenomena? What is the nature of that unity, personal or impersonal, conscious or unconscious? Is there anything behind the mechanical working of the world which corresponds to what there is in us when we make and use a machine or an instrument, when we plant and cultivate a garden, or when we select and train a noble breed of animals? Is there a final cause towards which things work together, and a supreme power which guides them to that end?

This is the question of sovereignty. We can no more help asking it than we can help thinking.

We are in the world like voyagers on a ship. We inquire what the ship is made of; and science tells us,—iron and wood. And what makes it float? The buoyancy of the air which it contains. And what makes it go? Steam. And what makes the steam? The heat of the furnace. Then, if we are sufficiently interested, science takes us down into the engine-room, and shows us all the condensers and pistons and cranks and wheels, more fully than they have ever been shown before; and we are amazed and profoundly grateful. We come up again into the light of day. We look into the overarching heaven, the home of sunshine and storm, the deep mother of light and darkness. We look out upon the great and wide sea, full of mystery and terror. New questionings spring to our lips. Where is the ship going? Is there a captain on board? Does he know, does he care, what is to become of it? Is he wise, is he a good captain? Can he direct the vessel through tempests and dangers? Can he tell us how to work with him? Can we be sure of him, can we trust him?

Now to this questioning, scepticism gives a reply of desperate uncertainty; and positivism answers with a stern No! The world is a derelict vessel, and we are masterless and lost mariners. This answer has been expressed by a French poet in powerful and pathetic verse.

"*Jouet de l'ouragan, qui l'emporte et le mène,*
Encombré de tresors et d'agrès submergés,
Ce navire perdu, mais c'est le nef humaine,
Et nous sommes les naufragés.

L'equipage affolé manœuvre en vain dans l'ombre;
L'Épouvante est à bord, le Désespoir, le Deuil;
Assise au gouvernail, la Fatalité sombre
Le dirige vers un écueil."

But Christ gives a very different answer. It seems as if his very words were chosen to contradict this view of life as a helpless, hopeless voyage, and humanity as a shipwrecked race. For what is it that he says to his disciples as they look out upon the mystery of existence?

"Seek not what ye shall eat, and what ye shall drink, *neither be ye as a ship that is tossed on the waves of a tempestuous sea* (μὴ μετεωρί-

214

SOVEREIGNTY

ζεσθε), for your Father knoweth that ye have
need of these things." [1]

The vessel is not driving masterless over the
ocean. The Captain is on board. He is God.
He is also our Father. For all who trust and
serve him, it is a sure voyage, a certain port,
a safe harbour.

I

The doctrine of the presence and sovereignty
of God in his world, in one form or another, is
essential to the validity of any reasoning which
attempts to go beyond the mere appearance of
things. Without it we find ourselves, as one
has well said, "put to permanent intellectual
confusion." Without it the world lies before
us, as Pope wrote in the first draft of his *Essay
on Man*,—

> "*A mighty maze, but not without a plan.*"

And if we follow the poet in that cold philosophical deism which led him to revise his famous line so that it now reads

> "*A mighty maze, and all without a plan,*"

we are still in the dark, still confused and hopeless, unless we go further and learn enough of

---

[1] St. Luke 12 : 29.

215

him who made the plan, to trust him even when we cannot perfectly understand his working, and to confide absolutely in "His most holy, wise, and powerful preserving and governing all his creatures and all their actions."

This is what Christ gives us: a view of God in his world which requires faith to accept it, but which when it is accepted, satisfies the reason and the heart better than any other view, clears away many of the intellectual and moral difficulties which beset us, and becomes the inward source not of doubt and distress, but of certainty and peace.

This is not true, we must admit, of some of the forms in which the doctrine of divine sovereignty has been preached in Christ's name. They have often disregarded the facts of nature. They have often outraged the moral instincts of humanity. They have created new obstacles to faith. They have driven men back in dumb resentment to believe in the positivist's "sombre Fatality," rather than in an absentee God who has foreordained, by one and the same decree, all the evil and all the good, all the sorrow and shame and suffering that are in the world.

Not so with Christ's teaching. It is sane and sweet. It gives a reconciling, harmonizing, atoning view of God's sovereignty. And if we can see it clearly and preach it faithfully, it will be to-day, as it was in his day, one of the great attractions of the gospel for an age of doubt.

II

Christ's doctrine of the divine sovereignty was both old and new. It was old because it recognised the truth, uttered so magnificently by prophets and psalmists, of God's right and power to rule the universe which he has made. "Thy throne, O God, is for ever and ever." [1] "The Lord hath prepared his throne in the heavens and his kingdom ruleth over all." [2] "He doeth according to his will in the army of heaven, and among the inhabitants of the earth: and none can stay his hand, or say unto him, What doest Thou?" [3]

But Christ's doctrine was new because it revealed the presence of the sovereign God in the physical universe more simply, more naturally, more intimately, than it had ever been revealed before. How gentle, how plain is the language in which Jesus expresses this truth, compared with the flashing, rolling speech of the prophets!

[1] Psalm 45 : 6.   [2] Psalm 103 : 19.   [3] Daniel 4 : 35.

SOVEREIGNTY

The manifestations of divine power in the Old Testament appear chiefly as mighty works, exceptional forthputtings of supernal force. It seems sometimes as if they came from a distance; as if God had withdrawn from the world and had been called back to it by the peril and the cry of his people. But Christ would teach us to feel that he has never gone away for an instant. He is always here. Nothing that happens is hidden from him. Nor does he hide himself from any who would behold him. We may see him every day, in the feeding of the birds, in the blossoming of the flowers,

"And every wayside bush aflame with God."

This view of the relation of God to the material world is not external and mechanical. It is inward and vital. God has not made the world and wound it up and left it to run by itself. He is in it, as really as a man is in the house that he inhabits, and all the potencies that move and animate it flow directly from him. The Jews thought that God had fabricated the universe in six days and sat down to rest on the seventh, laying aside his work as a clock-maker would put down a finished clock. But Christ said, "My Father worketh until now, and I work." [1] Creation is not ended, it

[1] St. John 5 : 17.

is going on all the time. Yesterday was a creative day; and so is to-day; and so to-morrow will be. The divine thought is still weaving its beautiful garment on the roaring loom of Time.

But God's activity in the world is not capricious or disorderly. No one was more sensitive than Jesus to "the rhythmic element in nature,—the flow of rivers, the procession of stars, the antiphony of day and night, the silent but inviolate order of the seasons." It was he who expressed the law of growth: "first the blade, then the ear, and after that the full corn in the ear." [1] It was he who suggested the analogy of natural law in the spiritual world, applying the figure of germination to his own death and resurrection: "Except a corn of wheat fall into the ground and die, it abideth alone; but if it die, it bringeth forth much fruit." [2] The parables which he used to describe the kingdom of heaven were drawn from nature and based on law. It was like "leaven which a woman took and hid in three measures of meal until the whole was leavened," or "like a grain of mustard seed, which a man took and sowed in his field; which indeed is the least of all seeds, but when it is grown it is the greatest among

[1] St. Mark 4 : 28.　　　　[2] St. John 12 : 24.

herbs." [1] He taught his disciples to look upon the regular and steadfast ordinances of nature as the proof that their Heavenly Father was mindful of them and would take care of them. You will not find any such superfluous phrase as "special Providence" in the teaching of Jesus. His thought was of a general and universal Providence, wide enough and deep enough to embrace the wants of all creatures and provide for them. God's children were not to trust in miracles for their daily bread; they were not to be always looking and calling for manna from the sky, water from the riven rock. They were to rest rather upon the course of nature in quiet confidence, and work with it in cheerful joy, knowing that he who clothes the grass of the field will much more clothe them,[2]—and by the same power working in the same way.

Yet Jesus did not think of God as having exhausted all possible modes of his activity in those which are familiar to us. His presence in the world is of such a kind that it necessarily brings with it the power of direct, personal, infinitely varied action. Out of this power spring those strange signs and wondrous works which we call miracles. Jesus never said that they were against nature. He never even said

[1] St. Matt. 13 : 32, 33.   [2] St. Matt. 6 : 30.

that they were supernatural. He claimed only that they were proofs of a divine mission, because they were such works as could only come from God. They were signs, just as all uncommon and extraordinary acts are signs. But signs of what? Of personality, of that power of choice in modes of action which is the essential attribute of a free spirit. They were wrought in order that men might believe, not in order that they might be astonished; and just as truly in order that they might believe in the order of nature as in the Person who upholds it by his presence.

"An energy," says Ruskin, "may be natural without being normal, and divine without being constant." Jesus did not teach the reign of law. He taught the reign of God through law. And in order that men might be sure that the law did not bind God like a chain, but freely expressed his sovereign will, it was given unto Jesus to show men those rare works, unique and transcendent, like strokes of genius, which reveal, as if by flashes of light, the true relation between the sovereign God and the universe which he is making and ruling.

It is always to this personal God that Jesus would direct the thoughts and confident affections of men. How is it possible for any one to miss his meaning, and translate it into something entirely different, as Matthew Arnold does in his misinterpretation of what he calls "the secret of Jesus"? It is not merely the joy and peace of *self-renunciation* that Jesus sets forth to his disciples. It is the inward quietude and rest of *self-surrender* to a loving Father who is also the Mighty God. And it is not from the sense of his resistless power, but from the consciousness of his love, of his Fatherhood, that peace comes. "Yea, Father, for so it was well-pleasing in thy sight." [1] "Father, all things are possible unto thee; remove this cup from me: howbeit not what I will, but what thou wilt." [2] "Father, into thy hands I commit my spirit." [3] This is the secret of Jesus. He does not teach bare sovereignty to which we must yield because it is irresistible. He teaches sovereignty of a certain kind,—the sovereignty of a Father, who is better and more powerful than all earthly parents or rulers, and who will never forsake his world, nor suffer his children to slip from his mighty hand.

III

But sovereignty of this kind necessarily implies distinctions in the manner of its exercise.

[1] St. Matt. 11 : 26.   [2] St. Mark 14 : 36.   [3] St. Luke 23 : 46.

SOVEREIGNTY

It cannot possibly be conceived of in terms of any single force or confined to any one mode of operation. It must be flexible and discriminating. It must include within itself as many forms of rule as there are forms of being under its dominion. What, for example, should we say of a king who had but one way of dealing with all his subjects, young and old, wise and ignorant, loyal and disloyal, and who treated his servants under precisely the same conditions as his horses and his chariots? Or what should we say of a father who attempted to regulate and rule his children without reference to their character, and who made no distinction between them and the furniture of his house? Yet this, in effect, is the theory of the divine sovereignty which has frequently been set forth by theologians as if it were the only one which did justice to the glory of God.

"The will of God," according to this theory, "is the irresistible force. It is the source of all things, all persons, all events. From it they all proceed, under it they all act, by an invariable necessity. This will has already determined from all eternity everything that comes to pass. Every character in the world, like every rock and every plant, is just what God willed it to be. Everything that happens, happens because he willed it and precisely as he willed it. The life of mankind is far from being in any sense a voyage, an adventure, a probation. It is simply the process of printing a history which has already been written and set in type down to the last letter. The great press is in motion. Our souls are the blank pages. On one is printed a foreordained prayer. On another a foreordained blasphemy. Death is the folding knife. Judgment is the act of binding, in which the fair pages will be preserved and the foul pages rejected and burned. The sovereignty of God is exercised in seeing that the book goes through the press exactly as it was written, without the addition or subtraction of a single syllable of the foreordained text."

But surely, even if this theory were true and could be proved, it is not of a nature to give aid and comfort to those who are zealous for the glory of God. It does not really exalt and magnify the divine sovereignty, but narrows and degrades it. It does not call for the perfect wisdom and unlimited resources of a potent Ruler able to meet emergencies, to overcome oppositions, to guide and direct intelligent and free subjects like himself, and to conduct a high enterprise, through all the difficulties that

SOVEREIGNTY

may arise, to a successful end. It calls for qualities of a lower kind and a strictly limited scope; the exact knowledge and the applied strength of a skilful machinist; not the broad intelligence, the swift genius, the inexhaustible patience, and the triumphant personal influence of a great Captain, a Master and Lord of men.

It is conceivable, of course, that God might have chosen to create a universe in which his sovereignty should be exercised in this one unvarying line of foreordained necessity. Being supreme, he has both the right and the power to make such a sphere, or spheres, for the revelation of his attributes as may please him. But it is not humanly conceivable that he should have made this particular choice which is ascribed to him for his own glory. If he had chosen this kind of a universe, so far as we can see, it must have lowered and hidden his glory. It must have left him with a field in which the highest qualities of personality could not possibly be exercised. It must have made all subsequent choice, and all approval or disapproval, and all truly moral government impossible. The existence of rewards and punishments, the sense of merit or demerit among the creatures of such a world, would be inexplicable. To claim that this sense of responsibility, like all other parts of the system, may be a necessity, a legal fiction which is essential to the working of a scheme far above our comprehension and therefore above our judgment, makes it more awful, but not more admirable. If there is any validity whatever in our moral instincts, we need not hesitate to say, that from our present point of view, (which is for us the only one attainable,) this theory of the absolute and unconditional sovereignty of God, exercised by one law of necessity over all creatures, is so far from being for God's glory that it is apparently for his shame and dishonour.

As a matter of fact, it has been, and still is, the most fertile mother of doubts. "A universe in which all the power was on the side of the creator, and all the morality on the side of creation, would be one compared with which the universe of naturalism would shine out as a paradise indeed." The idea of an irresponsible God ruling by an eternal and inflexible *fiat* over responsible men, is a moral nightmare, under which humanity groans, and from which it struggles to awake, even though it should have to open its eyes upon the blank darkness of an unsearchable night. Between the unknowable God of agnosticism and the unlov-

able God of absolutism, there is indeed little
to choose. But the choice, such as it is, lies
on the side of agnosticism. It is unspeakably
better to doubt God's personality, his supremacy, his very being, than it is to doubt his
eternal goodness and his moral integrity.

But the teaching of Jesus is designed and
fitted to deliver us, if we will accept it, from
both of these doubts. He reveals a God who
is not only Lord of all, but who exercises his
sovereignty in discretion, in justice, and in
love. He does not look upon all his creatures
with the same eyes. He discriminates, he dis-
tinguishes, he has regard to their differences
of nature and character. The human soul is
of more value to him than many sparrows.[1]
How much is a man better than a sheep?[2] By
so much as he is more like God, spiritual, free,
responsible, immortal. These qualities, which
God himself has created, God himself respects.
Every word of Jesus takes it for granted that
God is not an infinite Autocrat, a hard master,
reaping where he has not sown, and gathering
where he has not strewed, but a fair and equi-
table Lord, who takes into consideration all the
conditions of his subjects and renders unto all
their dues. The forces of nature obey his will

---

[1] St. Matt. 10 : 31. [2] St. Matt. 12 : 12.

227

inevitably, and for them there is neither praise nor blame. The souls of men are invited to love him, and commanded to serve him, but they are left free to choose whether they will obey or disobey, and upon their choice the approval and blessing of God depend.

Who can question for a moment that this is the view of the divine sovereignty which underlies all the parables of Christ? The omnipotence which he teaches is not sheer, absolute, unconditioned. It is a self-restrained power. It is able to limit itself, to act in such a way and under such conditions as God chooses to create. If he could not do this, he would not be truly omnipotent. If there were but one method in which he could manifest his will, and that the method of necessity, he would be forever shut out from personal relations, which can only exist where there are different wills, capable of agreement or disagreement, of cooperation or conflict, of harmony or discord.

Jesus taught that God has actually chosen to limit the autocratic exercise of his sovereignty by creating beings who have the power of yielding to his will or of resisting it.

From this resistance flow all the evil, sorrow, misery of the world. God does not ordain sin. God does not even permit sin, in the sense that he allows it to exist without condemnation on his part. It may be a necessary feature of a world of free choice and moral probation. Jesus seems to imply as much when he says "It must needs be that offences come." But he adds at once, "Woe unto that man by whom the offence cometh."[1] That man is not doing the will of God. He is a rebel, a traitor, an apostate. When the tares appear in the field, Christ does not leave us to suppose for a moment that they were planted by the same hand that sowed the good seed. He says, "An enemy hath done this."[2] Satan, who is the embodiment of evil and the leader of all who are opposed to God, is the great enemy, the adversary not only of souls, but also of the Divine will.

Turn for a moment to the narrative of the temptation of Christ.[3] He was led up by the Spirit into the wilderness to be tempted of the devil. But did the same Spirit lead the devil? Was Satan acting under the divine sovereignty in the same sense, in the same way, that Jesus was? Set aside, if you will, the question of the personality of the evil one. There was a suggestion of evil before the mind of Jesus. Did that suggestion come from the same source as the holy strength that resisted it,—the all-

[1] St. Matt. 18 : 7.   [2] St. Matt. 13 : 28.   [3] St. Matt. 4 : 1–11.

229

creating, all-controlling will of God? Can the same fountain send forth sweet and bitter water? Why then should the one be called cursed and the other blessed? Such a view simply obliterates all moral distinctions. It completely undermines and ruins the significance of Christ's life as a free obedience to the will of God, and it utterly paralyses his gospel as a divine call to men to enter freely into the same obedience.

Jesus teaches very distinctly that there are two spheres in which the sovereignty of God is exercised,—in heaven and on earth. These two spheres are not conceived locally but spiritually. They are realms in which the power of God is working under different conditions. In heaven the Divine will is unopposed, and therefore the empire of heaven is peace and holiness and unbroken love. On earth the Divine will is opposed and resisted, and therefore earth is a scene of conflict and sin and discord. For this reason the kingdom of heaven must *come* to earth, it must win its way, it must strive with the kingdom of darkness and overcome it. God's sovereignty in heaven is triumphant. God's sovereignty on earth is militant, in order that it may triumph,—and triumph not in universal destruction, but in the salvation of all who will submit to it and embrace it and work with it,—triumph not by bare force, as gravitation triumphs over stones, but by holy love, as fatherly wisdom and affection triumph over the reluctance and rebellion of wayward children.

It must be admitted frankly that this view of Divine sovereignty does not seem to be consistent with the theory of absolute divine foreknowledge of all volitions and all events. This has been urged as a fatal objection against it. But the objection cannot be pressed because it lies in a region where our ignorance is so great that dogmatism is, to say the least, unbecoming. There may be some way of reconciling the self-limitation of God's omnipotence with the certainty of his foreknowledge, which is beyond the reach of our logic. But whether there be any such reconciliation or not, one thing is clear: we have not the right to make a logical statement of our ignorance of one divine attribute a reason for refusing to accept, frankly and sincerely, Christ's revelation of the mode in which another divine attribute is exercised.

God knows everything. But when we say that, we mean simply that he knows everything which can be the object of knowledge.

He knows all things as they are. He does not know them as they are not. The very perfection of his knowledge consists in its exact correspondence with the nature of its object. If an event is certain and foreordained, then God knows it as certain and foreordained. If it is contingent upon the free, self-determining action of a human will, then God knows it *as contingent*, for he himself has foreordained that it should be so.

God waits to hear whether his children will call upon him in their distress; and if they call, he hears and helps them. If Jesus teaches anything, he teaches that prayer really influences the purpose and action of God.

God waits to see whether his husbandmen will return to him the fruits of his vineyard; whether they will receive and honour the messengers whom he sends unto them; and if they are rejected, he sends other messengers; and last of all he sends his son, saying, "It may be they will reverence him." [1] But when this last *maybe* does not come to pass, then judgment falls upon the wicked husbandmen, not because they have fulfilled the secret will of the King, but because they have rebelled against him.

This conception of God in his world, not as

---

[1] St. Luke 20 : 13.

the mere spectator of the fulfilment of his own immutable decrees, but as the Lord of Hosts, presiding over the great scene of conflict between good and evil in the souls of men who can only attain to real holiness through real liberty, and warring mightily on the side of good in order that it may win the victory, infinitely exalts and glorifies him. We see him in the teaching of Jesus, as the High Captain of the armies of love, working salvation in the midst of the earth, pleading with men to accept his mercy, warning them to escape from his judgments, sustaining the good in their goodness, overthrowing the wicked in their wickedness, bringing light out of darkness and triumph out of defeat, amid all strifes and storms maintaining his kingdom of righteousness and peace and joy in the Holy Ghost. His sovereignty embraces human liberty as the ocean surrounds an island. His sovereignty upholds human liberty as the air upholds a flying bird. His sovereignty defends human liberty as the authority of a true king defends the liberty of his subjects,—nay, rather, as the authority of a father tenderly and patiently respects and protects the spiritual freedom of his children in order that they may learn to love and obey him gladly and of their own accord. For this is the end of God's sovereignty: that his kingdom may come; that his will may be done on earth,—not as it is done in the circling of the stars or in the blossoming of flowers,—but as it is done in heaven, where created spirits freely strike the notes that blend in perfect harmony with the music of the Divine Spirit.

IV

But does not the acknowledgment that God has thus limited the operation of his sovereignty on earth by conditioning his actions upon the character and conduct of other beings than himself, throw us back into confusion and uncertainty? Does it not make the course of the world insecure and the end of all things doubtful?

It would do so if it were not for the other truth which Jesus reveals with equal clearness, that God is in the world guiding, ruling, and directing it, and that he has kept the supremacy in his own hands. He is the master of the ship; his hand is on the helm; and whether the sailors obey or mutiny, he will guide the vessel to her appointed haven.

The power of evil is a finite, transient, self-destroying power. It disintegrates, it dies, it passes away with the enfeeblement and destruction of the soul that yields to it. But the power of goodness is eternal and incorruptible, because it is of God. Satan is the prince of this world, but his might is limited to the perverted and enslaved wills that submit to him. He is not the ruler of nature. God is the master of winds and waves and earth and stars. The great battalions are on his side and under his control. If for one instant the cause of Christ were in real danger, he could summon celestial hosts without number to his assistance.[1] But because he knew this, he knew also that his cause was never in danger. He knew that his kingdom was an everlasting kingdom. He knew that he had already overcome the world.

How serene and splendid are the words with which he reassures his disciples, again and again! *"Fear not! Care not! Be not anxious! O thou of little faith, wherefore didst thou doubt? Have faith in God! Upon this rock will I build my church and the gates of hell shall not prevail against it! Fear not, little flock, for it is your Father's good pleasure to give you the kingdom!"* How glorious is the vision of that kingdom which Jesus unfolds as he looks forward to the new birth of earth and heaven in the perfect

[1] St. Matt. 26 : 53.

fulfilment of the purpose of God! How absolute is the confidence with which he rests upon
God's power to work out all that may be needed
to bring about that blessed consummation.

Communicated by his divine influence to the
hearts of his disciples, this faith has been a force
of incalculable potency and inspiration in the
lives of men. The noblest deeds of heroism
and self-sacrifice and liberation have been
wrought in the strength of it. The greatest
conquests over self and sin, the supreme vic-
tories of righteousness and love and peace in
human hearts, have been won through this
faith. *Deus vult*—God wills it!—is the war-
cry that rouses the human will to its highest
endeavour.

Here is a man struggling against evil, longing and striving to rise to high and holy life.
And if he is alone in the struggle, what assurance has he, what promise or hope of success?
He may fail, he may perish. But when the
great truth flashes into his heart that God is
with him in the fight, that God is "not willing that any should perish but that all should
come to repentance," [1] that God is the captain
of his salvation and the leader of his soul,—
then he is emancipated, then he triumphs, then

---

[1] 2 Pet. 3:9.

he is joined to the Invincible. He cries with Paul, "If God is for us, who is against us?" [1]

Here is a good man called to endure sharp and heavy trials, to drink the waters of affliction, to pass through the fires of pain, to go down into the dark valley of the shadow. Alone, it would be impossible; human patience could not endure it, human courage could not face it, human wisdom could not solve the mystery of goodness called to suffer. But with God, believing that he is sovereign, and that he is love,—how different it is! Now you shall see the wondrous spectacle of a frail, gentle, mortal soul, strengthened by simple submission to God's will, persecuted but not forsaken, cast down but not destroyed, trembling but victorious. Such a soul cries: "The will of God be done. It cannot be his will that I should lose my faith. It cannot be his will that I should deny him. It cannot be his will that I should be lost, for he is good, he is my King, my Father, he will save me. It may be his will that I should suffer trial for the purifying of my faith, for a more perfect fellowship with Christ, for a better reward in heaven. Even so, Father, for so it seemeth good in Thy sight."

[1] Rom. 8 : 31.

SOVEREIGNTY

"I welcome all Thy sovereign will,
For all that will is love;
And when I know not what Thou dost,
I wait the light above."

How radiant and magnificent is that truth
as it appears in the history of the Church! The
people of God have often been persecuted and
oppressed, yet God has been on their side, and
no weapon that has been formed against them
has prospered. How often has God proved his
sovereignty by preserving and rescuing and
delivering his people from overwhelming perils!
Even when it has seemed to be otherwise, even
when the Church has appeared forsaken and
helpless, when the billows of persecution have
rolled fathom-deep above her head, when ava-
lanches of falsehood have buried the truth out
of sight, it has only been for a time, and the
end has been the victory of the defeated. The
blood of the martyrs has been the seed of the
Church. The boastful shouts of error have been
the advertisement of the silent truth. Error
has had kings and generals, philosophers and
orators, empires and armies; truth has had
God. Error has had swords and spears, ships
and cannons, fortresses and dungeons, racks
and fires; truth has had God. God and one
make a majority. Unless the Church doubts,

she cannot fear. Unless the Church denies, she cannot despair. In the darkest days, when the confusion seems greatest, the conflict most unequal, she can look out on the great battle-field and cry

"History's pages but record
One death-grapple in the darkness 'twixt old systems and
the Word;
Truth forever on the scaffold, Wrong forever on the throne,—
Yet that scaffold sways the future, and behind the dim un-
known
Standeth God within the shadow, keeping watch above his
own."

But is it for the Church alone, is it not for the whole world that this truth of God's sovereignty shines? To our eyes the conflict of life and death, of good and evil, seems to be undecided, and we think it may be perpetual. The dust blinds us; the uproar bewilders us; as far as our sight can pierce we see nothing but the rolling strife,—sin always in arms against holiness, the created will always resist-ing and defying the creator. But Christ sees that the conflict is decided, though it is still in progress. Christ sees that the victory is won, though it is not yet manifest. On the hill of the cross the captain of salvation met the captain of sin and conquered him. Calvary is victory. Through death Christ hath overcome him that had the power of death, that is the devil.[1] Satan has received his mortal wound; and if he still fights more fiercely, it is because he knoweth that he hath but a short time.[2] The day is coming when he must perish; the day is coming when sin and strife shall be no more; the day is coming when Christ shall put all enemies under his feet[3] and shout above the grave of death, "O thou enemy, destructions are come to a perpetual end"; the day is coming when the great ship of the world, guided by the hand of the Son of God, shall float out of the clouds and storms, out of the shadows and conflicts, into the perfect light of love, and God shall be all in all. The tide that bears the world to that glorious end is the sovereignty of God.

> "*O mighty river, strong, eternal Will,*
> *In which the streams of human good and ill*
> *Are onward swept, conflicting, to the sea,—*
> *The world is safe because it floats in Thee.*"

[1] Heb. 2 : 14.   [2] Rev. 12 : 12.   [3] 1 Cor. 15 : 25-28.

VIII

SERVICE

THAT strange and searching genius, Nathaniel Hawthorne, in one of his spiritual phantasies has imagined a new Adam and Eve coming to the earth after a Day of Doom has swept away the whole of mankind, leaving their works and abodes and inventions,—all that bears witness to the present condition of humanity,—untouched and silently eloquent. The representatives of a new race enter with wonder and dismay the forsaken heritage of the old. They pass through the streets of a depopulated city. The sharp contrast between the splendour of one habitation and the squalor of another fills them with distressed astonishment. They are painfully amazed at the unmistakable signs of inequality in the conditions of men. They are troubled and overwhelmed by the evidence of the great and miserable fact that one portion of earth's lost inhabitants was rich and comfortable and full of ease, while the multitude was poor and weary and heavy-laden with toil.

SERVICE

This feeling of sorrowful perplexity over the unevenness and apparent injustice of human life, which the prose poet puts into the heart of his new Adam and Eve, is really but a reflection from the tender and pitiful depths of his own. Who is there that has not sometimes felt it rising within his own breast,—this profound sentiment of inward trouble and grief, this feeling of spiritual discord and wondering repugnance at the sight of a world in which the good things of life are so unequally distributed, in which at the very outset of existence, before the factor of personal merit or demerit, the element of work and wages, enters into the problem at all, so much is given to one man and so little to another man that they seem to be forever separated and set at enmity with each other by the unfairness with which they are treated?

This sentiment has been strangely deepened and intensified in the nineteenth century by innumerable causes, until it has become one of the most marked characteristics of the present age. Never before have men felt the sorrows and hardships of their fellow-men so widely, so keenly, so constantly as to-day. In one sense this is the honour and glory of our age.

But in another sense it is the greatest peril
of our age. For it has been seized by the spirit
of scepticism and transformed into an ally of
doubt. It has been used as an argument against
the possibility of discovering a moral order in
such a "hungry, ill-conditioned world" as this.
Man's inhumanity to man has been employed
to prove God's indifference or injustice to man.
The feeling of sorrow and perplexity has been
aggravated by wild and whirling words into
a passion of resentment against the present
conditions of life. Rash and sweeping schemes
for their total destruction have been proclaimed
as a new gospel. Christianity has been first
claimed as a supporter of these schemes, and
then denounced and repudiated as the chief
obstacle to their success. The cry goes up that
the whole world is out of joint. "Everything
is wrong and crooked and unfair: the race of
man has been deceived and maltreated and
oppressed by the creation of such an order of
life as the present. If God created it, so much
the worse for God. But it is almost certain
that he did not create it, almost certain that
there is no God. The world of inequality is
man's mistake. There is but one thing to do,
and that is to break it all up, at once and utterly, and begin anew. Create a new world

if possible. If not, then let the old wreck sink and be blotted out, for it is worse, infinitely worse, than the blank desolation of an unconscious chaos."

This cry of anger and despair rings to-day in the ears of all earnest and thoughtful men and women. We are filled with perturbation and distress and deep anxiety to know the right and to do it, to understand the meaning of this exceeding great and bitter cry, and the duty to which it calls us. Is it indeed the utterance of true equity and wisdom? Is it the voice of a new Adam, appearing after so many ages of delusion, with open eyes to condemn the old world, and with ruthless hand to break it in pieces? Must we welcome him and hearken to him and believe in him, as the true judge and regenerator and leader of mankind?

The very form of the question points the way to the only Master who can answer it. Hawthorne's picture of the second Adam was a poetic dream. But the Apostle Paul uses the same figure to reveal a historic truth. "The first man Adam became a living soul. The last Adam became a life-giving spirit. Howbeit that is not first which is spiritual, but that which is natural; then that which is spiritual. The first man is of the earth, earthy; the

244

second man is of heaven." [1] The new Adam
has already come upon the earth, eighteen centuries ago. He was called Jesus. With pure
and perfect heart he entered into the world,
not desolate and depopulate, but thronged
with the myriads of toiling, suffering men.
With clear eyes he looked upon their different
conditions, their manifold inequalities, their
outward and inward joys and sorrows. With
steadfast heart he set himself to the divine
task of beginning a new humanity and inaugurating the kingdom of heaven on earth.

He did not strive nor cry, neither was his
voice heard in the streets.[2] He did not protest
against the moral government of the universe,
because one man was rich and another poor,
one strong and another weak, one happy and
another wretched, one good and another evil.
He did not say that God must be unjust because he has given, in things spiritual as well
as in things temporal, much to one and little
to another. He did not teach his followers
that the only way to help the world was to rebel
against this order, and refuse to submit to it,
and denounce it, and fight against it. He did
not even proclaim a social and political revolution. He was one of the most peaceful, orderly,

[1] 1 Cor. 15 : 45-47.   [2] St. Matt. 12 : 19.

245

obedient, loyal citizens of all that subject land
of Palestine; rendering unto Cæsar the things
that were Cæsar's, discharging every duty of
his lowly lot with cheerful fidelity, and labouring patiently for his daily bread.

He was not blind, nor dull of heart to feel
the troubles of life. The problem of inequality lay wide open before him. But it did not
agitate nor distract him. He neither raved nor
despaired. He was serene and sane.

"He saw life clearly and he saw it whole."

He looked through the problem to its true solution. He knew the secret which justifies the
ways of God to man. He knew the secret by
which an eternal harmony is to be brought
into the apparent discords of life. He knew
the secret by which men living in an unequal
world, and accepting its inequality as the condition of their present existence, can still become partakers of a perfect, peaceful equity,
and citizens of an invisible, imperishable city
of God. That secret was none other than the
highest, holiest teaching of Jesus, the divine
truth of election to service.

SERVICE

I

Before we set our hearts to take in the meaning of this truth, let us try to get them in tune for it by listening to some of the other teachings of Jesus which are meant to quiet and steady us in the contemplation of the unevenness of human existence.

And first of all he reminds us that our real happiness in this world does not depend upon our outward condition, but upon our inward state. "The life is more than meat and the body than raiment." [1] "A man's life consisteth not in the abundance of the things which he possesseth." [2] The land of wealth is not the empire of peace. Joy is not bounded on the north by poverty, on the east by obscurity, on the west by simplicity, and on the south by servitude. It runs far over these borders on every side. The lowliest, plainest, narrowest life may be the sweetest. Most of the disciples of Jesus were peasants, but they were as happy, as contented, even in this world, as if they had been princes. There was more gladness and singleness of heart in that frugal breakfast of broiled fish and bread beside the boats on the shore of the sea of Tiberias,[3] than in the splen-

[1] St. Matt. 6 : 25.   [2] St. Luke 12 : 15.   [3] St. John 21 : 1-13.

247

did feast in the house of Simon the Pharisee. Life has its compensations and its comforts for all estates. Work means health. Obscurity means freedom. The best pleasures are those that are most widely diffused.

I do not mean to say that Jesus overlooked the bitter hardships of toil under bad masters, under false and cruel and oppressive laws. I do not mean to say that he would not have been full of pity and indignation at the sight of the crushed and crippled state of great multitudes of human beings in our modern cities. But I am sure that he teaches us to believe that the real source of human misery is not in poverty, but in a bad heart; that envy is not a virtue, but a vice; that life is a great gift to all who will receive it cheerfully and contentedly, even in a world where its material things are unevenly distributed; and that the true beatitudes are not monopolies reserved for the few, but blessings within the reach of all, and gloriously independent of all outward contrasts in the lives of men. Indeed it seems as if he would go even beyond this, and remind us that some of these blessings could not be ours except in a world of contrast and temporal inequality. Of the eight beatitudes which Jesus pronounced, four at least,—the blessing of the

248

mourners, and of the meek, and of the merciful, and of the peace-makers,—imply the existence of differences and degrees among men; and one—the blessing of those who are persecuted for righteousness' sake—is only possible in a world where evil is sometimes actually more powerful and prosperous than good.

I have not been able to find a single word of Christ that looks forward to a time in which there shall be no more inequalities on earth, no more rich and poor, no more masters and servants, no more wise men, and no more babes. But there are many words of his that pierce with mild and gracious light through all these outward distinctions to reveal the truth that this kind of inequality is superficial and illusory, that the babes rejoice in beholding those mysteries which are hidden from the wise and prudent, that servants are often nobler and more free than their masters, that the poor may have treasures laid up in heaven which are beyond all earthly reckoning, and that this is the true wealth which brings contentment and peace.

It is a great mistake to suppose that Jesus preached a gospel which was melancholy and depressing for those who received it in this world. It is a great mistake to suppose that he taught men that they must resign themselves to earthly misery and make the journey of life as a weary and mournful pilgrimage. He came to cheer and brighten the hearts of all who would accept his guidance and tread the path of virtue with courage and fidelity and hope. He came to give us rest in the midst of toil, and that refreshment which only comes from weariness in a good cause. He came to tell us not to despair of happiness, but to remember that the only way to reach it on earth is to seek first usefulness, first the kingdom of God, and then the other things shall be added. He that loseth his life for Christ's sake shall not lose it but find it,[1]—find it in deep inward contentment,

> "*And vital feelings of delight,*"

which make up the true and incomparable joy of living.

Jesus does not differ from other masters in that he teaches us to scorn earthly felicity. The divine difference is that he teaches us how to attain earthly felicity, under all circumstances, in prosperity and in adversity, in sickness and in health, in solitude and in society, by taking his yoke upon us, and doing the will of God, and so finding rest unto our souls. That

[1] St. Matt. 10 : 39.

is the debt which every child of God owes
not only to God, but also to his own soul,—
to find the real joy of living.

> *"'Joy is a duty,'—so with golden lore*
> *The Hebrew rabbis taught in days of yore.*
> *And happy human hearts heard in their speech*
> *Almost the highest wisdom man can reach.*
>
> *But one bright peak still rises far above,*
> *And there the Master stands whose name is Love,*
> *Saying to those whom heavy tasks employ*
> *'Life is divine when duty is a joy.'"*

The second point in the teaching of Jesus
which is meant to rectify our views of the unevenness of the world, is his doctrine of a future
life,—not a different life, but the same life moving on under new conditions and to new issues.
This world is not all. There is another world,
a better age, a more perfect state of being, in
which the sorrows and losses of those who now
suffer unjustly will be compensated, and in
which—let us not hesitate to say it as calmly
and as firmly as Jesus said it—those who have
unjustly and selfishly enjoyed their good things
in this world will suffer in their turn. It is the
fashion nowadays to sneer at such teaching
as this; to call it "other-worldliness"; to declare that it has no real power to strengthen
or uplift the hearts of men. Jesus did not think

so. Jesus made much of it. Jesus pressed home upon the hearts of men the consolations and warnings of immortality. He showed the miserable failure of the man who filled his barns and lost his empty soul.[1] He bade his disciples, when they suffered and were persecuted for righteousness' sake, "rejoice and be exceeding glad, for great is your reward in heaven." [2]

Let us not impoverish our gospel by flinging away, in our fancied superiority, this precious truth. It is impossible to justify the present fragmentary existence of man if we look at it and speak of it as the whole of his life. Earth has mysteries which naught but heaven can explain. Earth has sorrows which naught but heaven can heal. Yes, and earth has evils, black and secret offences of man against man, false and foul treasons against the love of God, crimes which take a base advantage of his patience and long-suffering and hide themselves like poisonous serpents in the shelter of the very laws which he has made for the good of the world, sins all entangled with the present structure of society and beyond the reach of human law, undiscoverable iniquities, unpardonable and unpunishable cruelties,—which naught but hell can disclose and consume. The

[1] St. Luke 12 : 16–21.   [2] St. Matt. 5 : 12.

errors of time call for the balance of eternity. Patient labour, patient endurance, patient resignation in this present life shall be greatly rewarded in the life to come. Now is the day of toil and trial; but the pay-day will surely dawn. Much of the best that is done in this world receives no earthly wages. Those to whom it is done,—the poor, the maimed, the lame, the blind,—"they cannot recompense thee; but thou shalt be recompensed at the resurrection of the just." [1]

Thus Jesus teaches; and he shows us that the present order of inequality, so far from being an obstacle to this result, is the very means by which it is to be accomplished. The discipline of this uneven life is the education by which alone we can be prepared for the heavenly life. Jesus does not present himself as a rectifier of life's unequal conditions of outward fortune. He distinctly refuses this office. "Man, who made me a judge or a divider over you?" [2] Jesus does not preach an equality which is synonymous with life on a dead level. He does not preach equality at all. He preaches fraternity. And fraternity implies differences, —older and younger, stronger and weaker, higher and lower. The elder brother is the

[1] St. Luke 14 : 14.   [2] St. Luke 12 : 14.

heir; all that the father has is his; but his sin lies in holding fast to his inheritance selfishly, in shutting out his younger brother, in forgetting and denying that he is a brother at all.[1] The distinctions of life are not meant to obscure, but to reveal and to beautify its best virtues. Out of dependence spring the sweet blossoms of gratitude and loyalty. Out of mastership flow the refreshing streams of forbearance and justice and mercy. The apostle tells us that the love of money is a root of all kinds of evil.[2] But Christ shows us the deeper truth that the right use of money is a means of all kinds of good. "It is more blessed to give than to receive." [3] Every gift of Providence to us is an opportunity and therefore a responsibility, and the blessing does not come with the gift until we recognize the responsibility, and use the opportunity. The mammon of unrighteousness can only be destroyed by a process of transformation which transmutes it into the pure gold of the celestial treasury.[4] The name of that process is charity. And the translation of that name is wise and holy love.

It is said nowadays that Christianity means communism, and that it is the duty of all Christians to give away everything that they possess. It is strange that Christ never proclaimed this duty except to one man, and that man was not a Christian.[1] Of course it must be admitted at once that this would be the duty of all Christians if it could be shown that it would be for the real good of their fellow-men. But this never has been shown. On the contrary, communism has always turned out badly. It was tried in Jerusalem, in a limited way, when the early Christians sold all that they had and made a common purse; but it led, in less than ten years, to confusion and strife, and sank the Jerusalem church into a condition of pauperism and dependence upon the other churches, which had avoided the well-meant but dangerous experiment. It was tried in France, under atheistic auspices, and its fruit was wide-spread misery and injustice. It was tried to some degree in England, under a system of poor laws which were based upon the idea that every man had a right to eat whether he would work or not, and it resulted in such disorder and demoralization that it had to be discarded as a menace to society.

There is nothing in the teachings of Christ which would make us blind to these plain les-

[1] St. Mark 10 : 21.

255

sons of history. On the contrary, he desires and commands us to discover and do that which will really bless and help our fellow-men. "Thou shalt love thy neighbour as thyself," [1]— the same kind of love, the same inward regard for the higher ends and aims of life, which is the saving grace of the individual soul, is to be the saving grace of society. And what kind of love is that? It is a wise and holy love, a love which puts character first and comfort second, a love which seeks to purify and bless and uplift the whole man. Such a love may be shown by withholding as truly as by bestowing. False charity pampers self and pauperizes others. True charity educates self by helping others. The so-called Christian who never gives is a false Christian. The Christian who gives carelessly, blindly, indiscriminately, however generously, is a very imperfect Christian. The Christian who gives thoughtfully, seriously, fraternally, bending his best powers to the accomplishment of a real benefaction of his fellow-men, bestowing himself with his gift, is in the true and only way of the following of Jesus.

Preach this truth. Preach it home to the hearts of men, without fear or favour for rich

[1] St. Matt. 22 : 39.

or poor. Preach it home to your own heart
so close that it shall save you from the minister's besetting sins of spiritual selfishness and
cant. Tell the Lady Bountiful that she is not
called to discard her ladyhood, but to give herself with all her refinements, with all her ac-
complishments, with all that has been given to
her of sweetness and light, to the ennobling
service of humanity. Tell the Merchant-Prince
that he is not called to abandon his place of
influence and power, but to fill it in a princely
spirit, to be a true friend and father to all who
are dependent upon him, to make his prosperity a fountain of blessing to his fellow-men, to
be a faithful steward of Almighty God. And
then let us tell ourselves, as members of the
so-called "educated classes," to whom God has
given even greater gifts than those of rank and
riches,—privileges of knowledge, opportunities
of culture, free access to the stored-up wisdom
of the ages,—let us tell ourselves with unflinching fidelity that God will hold us to a strict
account for all these things. If our salt loses
its savour it shall be trodden under foot of men.
If our culture separates us from humanity we
shall be cast into the outer darkness. Our light
must shine or be shamefully extinguished.
Every faculty and every gift we possess must

be honestly and entirely consecrated to the service of man, in Christ's name and for Christ's sake. This is the gospel for the present age, and for every age. This is the way in which the kingdom of heaven is to be established on earth. This is the way in which the inequality of this mortal life is to be transfigured and ir-radiated with a divine equity. "What we look for, work for, pray for, as believers, is a nation where class shall be bound to class by the fullest participation in the treasure of the one life; where the members of each group of workers shall find in their work the development of their character and the consecration of their powers: where the highest ambition of men shall be to be leaders of their own class, so using their special powers without waste and follow-ing the common traditions to noble issues: where each citizen shall know, and be strength-ened by the knowledge, that he labours not for himself only, nor for his family, nor for his coun-try, but for GOD."

II

Thus far the teaching of Christ leads us with clear serenity in our understanding of the dif-ferences among men in the distribution of the goods of this present world. But the deeper problem still remains untouched. There is an apparent inequality in the bestowal of spiritual blessings. In the life of the soul also, it seems that much is given to one and little to another. Some men are born very close to the kingdom of heaven and powerfully drawn by unseen hands to enter its happy precincts. Other men are born far away from the gates of light, and it looks to us as if all the influences of their life were hindrances rather than helps to holiness. There is an undeniable contrast in the religious world which can only be interpreted as a divine foreordination,—that is to say, an act by which some men are set before others, given the precedence, offered an earlier and apparently an easier opportunity of spiritual life. If God is sovereign, this act, by which the means of grace are unevenly dispensed, must be the result of a divine choice.

The formal recognition of this choice is the doctrine of election. It is an inevitable doctrine. It is founded upon facts which admit of no denial. And it brings every thoughtful and earnest soul face to face with the question of questions, upon the answer to which the nature and reality of religion depend.

Is God arbitrary, is God partial, is God unjust? Does he bless some of his children and leave the rest under an irremediable curse without a single reason which can be exhibited to human faith and justified in perfect love? In the last and highest realm of life, the realm of the spirit, does he make it more blessed to receive than to give, and exercise his sovereignty in favouritism, and establish heaven as a kingdom of infinite and eternal and inexplicable inequality?

It is an idle thing to answer this question by an appeal to God's absolute right to dispose of all his creatures as he will. For the very essence of true religion is the faith that he is such a God that he wills to dispose of all his creatures wisely and fairly and in perfect love. And the very essence of a true revelation, as the message which calls religion into being, is that it makes God's wisdom and fairness and love manifest, and so helps us to understand and adore and trust him, not only for ourselves but for the whole world.

It is an idle thing to answer this question by saying that God is under no obligation to be good to everybody, and therefore that he may be good to whomsoever he pleases. The idea of an irresponsible God is a moral mockery. Poisonous doubt exhales from it as malaria from a swamp. To teach that all men are God's

debtors, and that therefore it is right for him
to remit the debt of one man, and to exact the
penalty from another to the last farthing, is to
teach what is logically true and morally false.
Our hearts recoil from such a doctrine. If God
has made us, and made us spiritual paupers,
utterly incapable of anything good, we are not
his debtors. Jesus teaches us that God asks of
us only to give as freely as we have received.[1]
He demands only that which he himself has
made us able to pay. And he forgives like the
good master in the parable, with a free pardon
which needs but the confession of helplessness
and poverty to call it forth.[2]

It is an idle thing to answer this question by
an appeal to ignorance, and to say that God
elects some men to be saved and leaves the rest
of mankind to be lost simply for his own unsearchable and inexplicable glory! For God's
glory, as revealed by religion, is identical with
his goodness. Faith, true and joyful and uplifting faith, answers only to a gospel which
makes that identity more clear and luminous,
and shows that the divine election in the realm
of grace is perfectly consistent with that wide
and deep love wherewith God so loved the whole
world that he sent his only begotten Son that

---

[1] St. Matt. 10 : 8.   [2] St. Matt. 18 : 27.

whosoever believeth in him should not perish but have everlasting life.

Now it is because men have forgotten this that they have found no answer, or a false and misleading answer, to the problem of inequality in the spiritual world. It is because they have torn the doctrine of election from its roots in the divine love, and petrified it with unholy logic, that it has lost its beauty, its perfume, its power of fruitfulness to everlasting life. We must go back from the dead skeleton as it is preserved in the museum of theology to the living plant as it blossoms in the field of the Bible. We must go back of Jonathan Edwards, and back of John Calvin, and back of Augustine, to St. Paul, and see how, under his hand, all the mysterious facts of election as they are unfolded in human history, break into flower at last in the splendid faith that "God hath shut up all unto disobedience that he might have mercy upon all." [1] We must go still farther back, to Christ, and learn from him that election is simply the way in which God uses his chosen ones to serve the world,—the divine process by which the good seed is sown and scattered far and wide and the heavenly harvest multiplied a thousand-fold. "I elected

[1] Romans 11 : 32.

262

you," he says to his disciples and to us, "I elected you, and appointed you, that ye should go and bear fruit, and that your fruit should abide."[1]

Christ's doctrine of election is a living, fragrant, fruitful doctrine. It is one of the most beautiful things in Christianity. It is the very core and substance of the gospel, translated from the heart of God into the life of man. It is the divine law of service in spiritual things. It is the supreme truth in the revelation of an all-glorious love; the truth that God chooses men not to be saved alone, but to be saved by saving others, and that the greatest in the kingdom of heaven is he who is most truly the servant of all.

Is not this true of Christ himself? He is the great example of what it means to be elect. He is the beloved Son in whom the Father is well pleased. And he says "Behold, I am in the midst of you as he that serveth."[2] Service was the joy and crown of his life. Service was the refreshment and the strength of his soul, the angel's food, the "meat to eat" of which his disciples did not know.[3]

Was not this the lesson that he was always teaching them by practice and by precept, that

[1] St. John 15 : 16.   [2] St. Luke 22 : 27.   [3] St. John 4 : 32.

they must be like him if they would belong
to him, that they must share his service if they
would share his election! "I have appeared
unto thee for this purpose," he said to Saul,
"to make thee a servant (ὑπηρέτην, *a rower in
the ship*), and a witness both of those things
which thou hast seen and of the things in the
which I will appear unto thee." [1] The vision
of Christ is the call to service. And if Paul
had not been obedient to the heavenly vision
could Saul have made his calling and election
sure? But he answered it with a noble faith.
"It pleased God to reveal his son in me *in order
that I might preach him among the nations*." [2]
Henceforward, wherever he might be, among
his friends in Cilicia, in the dungeon at Philippi,
on the doomed vessel drifting across the storm-
tossed sea, in the loneliness of his Roman prison,
this was the one object of his life, to be a faithful servant of Christ, and therefore, as Christ
was, a faithful servant of mankind. [3]

How can we interpret Christ's parables, without this truth? The parables of the Pounds
and the Talents are both pictures of *election
to service*. They both exhibit the sovereignty
of God in distributing his gifts; they both turn
upon the idea of man's accountability for re-

[1] Acts 26 : 16.   [2] Gal. 1 : 16.   [3] 2 Cor. 4 : 5.

ceiving and using them; and they both declare that the reward will be proportioned to fidelity in serving. The nature and meaning of this is explained by Christ in his great description of the judgment, which immediately follows the parable of the Talents in St. Matthew's Gospel.[1] Many of those who have known him will be rejected at last because they have not served their fellow-men. Many of those who have not known him will be accepted because they have ministered lovingly, though ignorantly, to the wants and sorrows of the world.

Service is the key-note of the heavenly kingdom, and he who will not strike that note shall have no part in the music. The King in the parable of the Wedding Feast[2] chose and called his servants, not to sit down at ease in the palace, but to go out into the highways and bid every one that they met to come to the marriage. And if one of those servants had refused or betrayed his mission, if he had neglected his Master's business, and sat down on the steps of the palace or walked pleasantly in the garden until the supper was ready, do you suppose that he would have found a place or a welcome at the feast? His soul would have stood naked and ashamed without the wedding-

[1] St. Matt. 25 : 31–46.   [2] St. Matt. 22 : 1–13.

garment of love. For this is the nature of God's kingdom: a selfish religion absolutely unfits a man from entering or enjoying it. Its gate is so strait that a man cannot pass through it if he desires and tries to come alone; but if he will bring others with him, it is wide enough and to spare.

> *" Who seeks for heaven alone to save his soul,*
> *May keep the path, but will not reach the goal;*
> *While he who walks in love may wander far,*
> *Yet God will bring him where the blessed are."*

How wonderfully all this comes out in the intercessory prayer of Christ at the last supper.[1] That prayer is the last and highest utterance of the love wherewith Christ, having loved his own which were in the world, loved them unto the end. He prays for his chosen ones: "I pray for them: I pray not for the world but for those whom thou hast given me." "Holy Father, keep them in thy name which thou hast given me, that they may be one even as we are. For their sakes I consecrate myself, that they themselves also may be consecrated in truth. Neither for these only do I pray, but for them also that believe on me through their word; that they may all be one, even as thou, Father, art in me, and I in thee, that

[1] St. John 17.

they also may be in us; that the world may believe that thou didst send me." How the prayer rises, like some celestial music, through all the interwoven notes of different fellowships, the fellowship of the Father with the Son, the fellowship of the Master with the disciples, the fellowship of the disciples with each other, until at last it strikes the grand chord of universal love. Not for the world Christ prays, but for the disciples in the world, in order that they may pray for the world, and serve the world, and draw the world to faith in him. And so, in truth, while he prays thus for his disciples, he does pray for the whole world. Circle beyond circle, orb beyond orb, like waves upon water, like light from the sun, the prayer, the faith, the consecrating power spread from that upper room until they embrace all mankind in the sweep of the divine intercession. The special, personal, elective love of Christ for his own is not exclusive; it is magnificently and illimitably inclusive. He loved his disciples into loving their fellow-men. He lifted them into union with God; but he did not lift them out of union with the world; and every tie that bound them to humanity, every friendship, every fellowship, every link of human intercourse, was to be a channel for the grace of

God that bringeth salvation, that it might appear to all men.[1]

This is Christ's ideal: a radiating gospel: a kingdom of overflowing, conquering love; a church that is elected to be a means of blessing to the human race. This ideal is the very nerve of Christian missions, at home and abroad, the effort to preach the gospel to every creature, not merely because the world needs to receive it, but because the Church will be rejected and lost unless she gives it. 'Tis not so much a question for us whether any of our fellow-men can be saved without Christianity. The question is whether we can be saved if we are willing to keep our Christianity to ourselves. And the answer is, No! The only religion that can really do anything for me is the religion that makes me want to do something for you. The missionary enterprise is not the Church's afterthought. It is Christ's forethought. It is not secondary and optional. It is primary and vital. Christ has put it into the very heart of his gospel. We cannot really see him, or know him, or love him, unless we see and know and love his ideal for us, the ideal which is embodied in the law of election to service.

For this reason the spirit of missions has

[1] Titus 2 : 11.

always been the saving and purifying power of the Christian brotherhood. Whenever and wherever this ideal has shone clear and strong, it has revealed the figure of the Christ more simply and more brightly to his disciples, and guided their feet more closely in the way of peace and joy and love.

In the first century it was the spirit of foreign missions that saved the Church from the bondage of Jewish formalism. Paul and his companions could not live without telling the world that Christ Jesus came to seek and save the lost—lost nations as well as lost souls. The heat of that desire burned up the fetters of bigotry like ropes of straw. The gospel could not be preached to all men as a form of Judaism. But the gospel must be preached to all men. Therefore it could not be a form of Judaism. The argument was irresistible. It was the missionary spirit that made the Emancipation Proclamation of Christianity.

In the dark ages the heart of religion was kept beating by the missionary zeal and efforts of such men as St. Patrick, and St. Augustine, and Columba and Aiden, and Boniface, and Anskar, who brought the gospel to our own fierce ancestors in the northern parts of Europe and wild islands of the sea. In the middle ages

it was the men who founded the great missionary orders, St. Francis and St. Dominic, who
did most to revive the faith and purify the life
of the Church. And when the Reformation
had lost its first high impulse, and sunken into
the slough of dogmatism; when the Protestant
churches had become entangled in political
rivalries and theological controversies, while
the hosts of philosophic infidelity and practical
godlessness were sweeping in apparent triumph
over Europe and America, it was the spirit of
foreign missions that sounded the *réveille* to the
Christian world, and lit the signal fire of a new
era—an era of simpler creed, more militant
hope, and broader love—an era of the Christianity of Christ. The desire of preaching the
gospel to every creature has drawn the Church
back from her bewilderments and sophistica-
tions closer to the simplicity that is in Christ,
and so closer to that divine ideal of Christian
unity in which all believers shall be one in him.
You cannot preach a complicated gospel, an
abstract gospel, to every creature. You cannot
preach a gospel that is cast in an inflexible
mould of thought, like Calvinism, or Arminian-
ism, or Lutheranism, to every creature. It will
not fit. But *the* gospel, the only gospel which
is divine, *must* be preached to every creature.

Therefore, these moulds and forms cannot be an essential part of it. And so we work our way back out of the tangle of human speculations towards that pure, clear, living message which Paul carried over from Asia to Europe, the good news that God is in Christ, reconciling the world to himself.

This is the gospel for an age of doubt, and for all ages wherein men sin and suffer, question and despair, thirst after righteousness and long for heaven. There are a thousand ways of preaching it, with lips and lives, in words and deeds; and all of them are good, provided only the preacher sets his whole manhood earnestly and loyally to his great task of bringing home the truth as it is in Jesus to the needs of his brother-men. The forms of Christian preaching are manifold. The spirit is one and the same. New illustrations and arguments and applications must be found for every age and every race. But the truth to be illuminated and applied is as changeless as Jesus Christ himself, in whose words it is uttered and in whose life it is incarnate, once and forever. The types of pulpit eloquence are as different as the characters and languages of men. But all of them are vain and worthless as sounding brass and tinkling cymbals, unless they

speak directly and personally and joyfully of
that divine love which is revealed in Christ in
order that all who will believe in it may be saved
from doubt and sin and selfishness in the everlasting kingdom of the loving God.

This is the gospel which began to shine
through the shadows of this earth at Bethlehem,
where the Son of God became the child of
Mary, and was manifested in perfect splendour
on Calvary, where the Good Shepherd laid
down his life for the sheep. For eighteen centuries this simple, personal, consistent gospel
has been the light of the best desires and hopes
and efforts of humanity. It is the bright star
that shines, serene and steady, through the
confusion of our perplexed, struggling, doubting age. He who sees that star, sees God. He
who follows that star, shall never perish.

If I have failed to make this view of religion
clear, if an imperfect utterance has beclouded
and obscured the message, at least let this last
word be plain, at least let nothing hide from
your soul or from mine, this supreme saving
truth of *election to service.*

The vision of God in Christ is the greatest
gift in the world. It binds those who receive
it to the highest and most consecrated life. To
behold that vision is to be one of God's elect.

But the result of that election depends upon the giving of ourselves to serve the world for Jesus' sake. *Noblesse oblige.*

Let us not miss the meaning of Christianity as it comes to us and claims us. We are chosen, we are called, not to die and be saved, but to live and save others.

BOOK II

THE GOSPEL FOR A WORLD
OF SIN

I

THE MIST AND THE GULF

DOUBT is the mist that rises between man's spiritual vision and the eternal truth. Sin is the gulf that separates man's moral character from the divine ideal. The mists gather, and thicken, and melt, and disperse. The gulf is always there. Ages of doubt come and go, in a world of sin. The pain of doubt is an evidence that man was made for faith. The shame of sin is an evidence that man was created for goodness.

A gospel for humanity must be good news both for doubters and for sinners. The depth of its sympathy will always be the measure of its power. It must not condemn doubt as if it were a sin: neither must it deny sin as if it were merely an illusion of doubt. To doubting men and to sinful men it must speak the message of a divine love,—a revealing love that pierces the mist with rays of light and brings clearness and joy to the confused and darkened spirit,—a redeeming love that bridges the gulf of separation and leads the guilty conscience back into peace and harmony with God.

An age of doubt is a transient phase of a sinful world. Through such an age I think we have been passing, in the latter half of the nineteenth century. Of the intellectual causes which have led to this increase of doubt; of the qualities which characterize it,—qualities for the most part sympathetic and hopeful,—its reverence for the questioned faith, its deep unrest and sorrow, its loyalty to ethical ideals; and of the gospel which it needs, the gospel of the personal Christ clearly revealing the reality and fatherhood of God, the liberty and responsibility of man, and the immortality of the soul, —of these things I have written in the first part of this volume.

But such a presentation of the gospel, from the point of view of a particular age, and with the purpose of meeting certain intellectual needs, certain urgent questionings of the human spirit, could not be (and indeed it was not intended to be) complete and sufficient. Man has other needs than those of the intellect. After the question of the reality of God is answered, then remains the question of our personal relation to him.

THE MIST AND THE GULF

The age of doubt is already passing, and we are entering, if the signs of the times fail not, upon a new era of faith.

There is a renaissance of religion. Spiritual instincts and cravings assert themselves and demand their rights. The loftier aspirations, the larger hopes of mankind, are leading the new generation forward into the twentieth century as men who advance to a noble conflict and a glorious triumph, under the captaincy of the Christ that was and is to be. The educated youth of to-day are turning with a mighty, world-wide movement towards the banner of a militant, expectant Christianity. The discoveries of science, once deemed hostile and threatening to religion, are in process of swift transformation into the materials of a new defence of the faith. The achievements of commerce and social organization have made new and broad highways around the world for the onward march of the believing host. Already we can discern the brightness of another great age of faith.

But an age of faith, when the mist of doubt is dissolved and driven away, is always the time when the gulf of sin is most clearly visible.

The souls that are most sure of the reality of God and the future life are always those

279

that feel most deeply their separation from him and their guilt in his sight. The evil that is in their own hearts presses upon them more heavily, the more vividly they realize the actual existence of the spiritual realm and its eternal significance. The evil that is in the world does not disappear nor change through all the coming and going, the darkening and dissolving of human doubts in regard to its origin, nature, and meaning. It remains an unalterable fact in human experience. The interpretation which religious faith gives to it intensifies the necessity of a divine salvation from it.

Those who have accepted the gospel for an age of doubt are those who feel most keenly the need of the gospel for a world of sin.

There cannot be two gospels. I do not believe that there is any essential difference or contradiction between the message which Christianity has for one age and that which it has for another. It is always the good tidings of the personal Christ, the revealer of God and the Saviour of men. To those who are doubtful and confused, to those who have lost the sense of spiritual things, the divine voice says, "This is my beloved Son; hear him." [1]

[1] St. Luke 9 : 35.

THE MIST AND THE GULF

To those who are sinful and sorrowful, upon whom the sense of evil rests like an intolerable burden, the voice says, "Behold the Lamb of God, which taketh away the sin of the world." [1]

These two elements of the gospel are interwoven and inseparable. Christ could not take away the sin of the world unless he were the Son of God. Christ would not be the divine Saviour unless he took away the sin of the world.

In trying to set forth the personal Christ as God's answer to the doubts and questionings of this age, I could not help speaking of him as the deliverer from sin. Nor will it be possible to present his sacrifice on the cross as the world's redemption without confessing a constant faith in him as God manifest in the flesh.

Indeed, this second book is written chiefly because I feel the need of a fuller utterance to complete the message of the former book. I would have the two books stand together and interpret each other. They are but windows looking towards Christ from two different points of view.

The message of the first book was this: Christ saves us from doubt, because he is the incarnation of God.

[1] St. John 1 : 29.

THE MIST AND THE GULF

The message of the second book is this: Christ is the revelation of God, because he saves us from sin.

The gospel for a world of sin cannot be preached by any except those who need it for themselves. An angel could not deliver it aright. Its language is always in the first person plural, drawing the speaker and the hearers into a brotherhood of penitence and forgiveness.

"God commendeth his love towards *us*, in that, while *we* were yet sinners, Christ died for *us*." [1]

Christ himself did not come to preach this gospel.

He came to live it.

It was when the Apostles Peter and Paul and John had seen him delivered for their offences and raised again for their justification that they began to understand and preach this gospel for a world of sin. Ever since it has had but one message.

"*Through his name whosoever believeth in him shall receive remission of sins.*" [2]

"*God was in Christ reconciling the world unto himself.*" [3]

[1] Romans 5 : 8.   [2] Acts 10 : 43.   [3] 2 Cor. 2 : 19.

282

THE MIST AND THE GULF

"If any man sin, we have an advocate with the Father, Jesus Christ the righteous: and he is the propitiation for our sins, and not for ours only, but also for the sins of the whole world." [1]

[1] 1 John 2 : 1, 2.

II

THE SIN OF THE WORLD

THE sins of the world are many. The sin of the world is one.

It is like the grass of the field. Below the separate shoots and blades, which stand up individual and distinct, as if each one grew by itself, there is a network of branching roots and fibres, knotted together, interwoven, tenacious, spreading far, and propagating itself more swiftly the more it is cut and divided. The separation is on the surface. The unity is underground.

But before we can have any idea of what sin means, either separately in the individual or collectively in the race, we must give some thought to the problem of evil, starting not from the point of view of philosophy, but from the point of view of experience.

I

THE PRESENCE OF EVIL

Beneath all the particular forms of evil that exist in the world, men have always recognized a common ground of evil in human nature. Something has happened to the race, something has entered into it and taken possession of its vital powers, which makes it bring forth bad fruit. This is not a theory. It is a fact.

The experience of mankind, thus far, is a mass of cumulative evidence that there is a radical twist in humanity which runs through it from top to bottom, and produces crooked results in every sphere of human life. So far as we can judge by our own experience, and by observation of others, every child of man who comes to moral consciousness, comes not only with a freedom of will which makes the choice of evil possible, but also with a propensity which makes such a choice easy. This probability is so strong that we always reckon with it, in dealing with ourselves or with others.

No man gets fairly started in the journey of life without knowing that he has a tendency to go wrong. It is the folly of the fool that he forgets it. The wise man remembers, fears, and tries to guard against it.

Human society is organized around two facts: the desire of good and the recognition of evil. Every institution in the world which is of any value has in it a defensive, corrective, punitory side, which is an unconscious confession that mankind is prone to do wrong. Men take this for granted in all the relations of life. Whether they are making systems of education or of government, whether they are devising enterprises to increase their property, or laws to protect it, or wills to distribute it, they always take into account the fact that there is a strain of evil running through all humanity.

The advance of modern science and philosophy has not reduced or weakened the evidence of this common ground of evil in the world. On the contrary, it has done much to deepen and intensify the conviction that there is a radical twist in human nature. The easy-going and superficial optimism of the eighteenth century is thoroughly discredited and obsolete. Men have turned away from Rousseau's skin-deep philosophy of the "original goodness and unlimited perfectibility" of human nature, to the profounder view of the Hebrew prophets, the Greek dramatists, Dante's *Divine Comedy*, Shakespeare's *Hamlet*, Tennyson's *Idylls of the King*, the great poetry of all lands and ages, —the clearer, deeper, sadder view, which sees the mysterious shadow resting on the life of man, and traces the lines of conflict, disaster, and death that run through human history, back to their origin in the separation of man's moral character from the divine ideal.

Science, with its new theory of evolution, puts a stern emphasis upon the strength of the ties which bind man to the brute. It lays bare the workings of the selfish, sensual, egotistical impulses in the career of the race. It lengthens the cords and strengthens the stakes of the fatal net of heredity which holds all men together in an entanglement of defects of nature and taints of blood.

"I know of no study," wrote Professor Huxley, "which is so unutterably saddening as that of the evolution of humanity as set forth in the annals of history. Out of the darkness of prehistoric ages man emerges with the marks of his lowly origin strong upon him. He is a brute, only more intelligent than the other brutes; a blind prey to impulses which as often as not lead him to destruction; a victim to endless illusions which make his mental existence a terror and a burden, and fill his physical life with barren toil and battle. He attains a certain degree of comfort, and develops a more or less workable theory of life in such favourable situations as the plains of Mesopotamia or of Egypt, and then for thousands and thousands of years struggles with various fortunes, attended by infinite wickedness, bloodshed, and misery, to maintain himself at this point against the greed and ambition of his fellow-men. He makes a point of killing and otherwise persecuting all those who first try to get him to move on; and when he has moved a step farther he foolishly confers post-mortem deification on his victims. He exactly repeats the process with all who want to move a step yet farther."

This was written by a teacher of science, for a periodical called *The Nineteenth Century.* If it had been uttered by a Hebrew prophet, in the sixth century before Christ, it could not give a darker picture of human nature.

Modern philosophy is permeated with the flavour of pessimism,—the bitter tincture drawn from the twisted, tangled roots of sorrowful perversity which underlie the life of man.

Modern literature is haunted by the persistent spectre of evil, which "will not down." A novel by Zola, or Turgenieff, or Thomas Hardy, is little more than a commentary on Jeremiah's text, "The heart is deceitful above all things, and desperately wicked." [1]

Gloomy as such a view of life is, unmitigated by any real explanation of its mysterious ailment, unillumined by any hope of its cure,

---

[1] Jer. 17 : 9.

there is still something wholesome and medicinal in it. It is better to know the saddest truth than to be blinded by the merriest lie. The sober, stern-browed pessimism which looks the darkness in the face is sounder and more heroic than the frivolous, fat-witted optimism which turns its back, and shuts its eyes, and laughs.

Man, indeed, is framed to live and rise by hope. But a hope which begins by denying the facts is a false hope whose path leads upward—a few steps—to the edge of a precipice of deeper despair.

The Bridge-Builders in Rudyard Kipling's story would have been fools if they had tried to accomplish their work by ignoring the steady downward thrust of gravitation, or shutting their eyes to the destructive rage of the Ganges-flood.

No less foolish is the man who tries to build a life, or a theory of life, in forgetfulness of the steady downward thrust of human nature, or in denial of the reality and universality of the evil that is in the world.

Hidden, dormant it may be; unrealized it may be in the fulness of its possibilities and powers. The river sleeps in the smoothness of its flow. The force that draws all foreheads downward to the dust is checked and countervailed by other forces. But evil is always there,

a potency of disaster and destruction. All the
ills that have been wrought in the world come
from that secret source. In form they are manifold. In origin and essence they are one.

II

THE UNANSWERABLE QUESTION

How came evil into being?

This is the question which man has always
asked, and to which he has never found a perfect answer.

He cannot help asking it, because curiosity,
in the nobler sense of the word, is the main-
spring of his mind. He cannot find the perfect
answer, because his reason is limited and conditioned, and because his intellectual power itself has developed under the shadow, and within the sphere, of the very malign presence which
he seeks to account for.

A spirit whose life was beyond the influence
of evil might be able to understand and solve
the problem of its origin. But even so, it would
hardly be possible for such a spirit to com-
municate this knowledge to other spirits who
were born and lived within the domain of evil.

And yet, that man should ask this question,
and continue to ask it after thousands of years

of baffled thought and disappointed search, is in itself a hopeful and illuminating fact. It is a question which implies a faith not to be eradicated, a courage not to be conquered. It speaks of a conviction that evil is not eternal, but temporal; not sovereign, but subordinate; not native to the universe, but a foreigner and an intruder. It testifies to man's knowledge that evil is not the whole, but a part; not the straight line, but the deflection; not a necessary element in the perfect harmony of being, but a false note which breaks the chord.

If man should ask, "How came good into being?" he would be in the region of despair. While he continues to ask, "How came evil into being?" he is in the region of hope.

All the answers to this question which have been attempted, may be classified under three forms. The first amounts to a denial of the existence of evil. The second destroys the reality of the distinction between evil and good. The third confesses that the primal origin of evil is a mystery, and bids us seek a knowledge of its reality and its mode of manifestation in the world.

All theories which are based upon the idea of the essential *nothingness* of evil, amount to a practical denial of its existence. Traces of such theories may be found even in Christian writers. A theologian as orthodox as Thomas Aquinas has said, "God created everything that exists; but sin is *nothing;* so God was not the author of it." In Robert Browning's poem of "Abt Vogler," the idea is put into a single verse.

" The evil is naught, is null, is silence implying sound."

Darkness is but the absence of light. Evil is but the negation of good.

The rock upon which all these negative theories go to pieces is the practical conviction that evil is just as real to us in our experience, just as solid, just as operative, as good is. The desire which seeks a wrong pleasure is no less vivid than that which seeks a right pleasure. The will which determines a wicked action is just as strong as that which determines a righteous action. The end sought is no more negative in one case than it is in the other. If evil is a nothing, it is a strangely active, positive, and potent nothing, with all the qualities of a something. The theories which attempt to account for its origin by tracing it to a mere negation or absence of good, raise a harder question than that which they attempt to answer. Instead of asking how evil came into being, we must ask, How did evil, if it is a mere nothing, come to have the reality, the life, and the power of a something?

All theories which are based upon the idea of the *necessity* of evil lead to a practical denial of the distinction between evil and good. For if the necessity be purely natural, that is to say materialistic, then there is no possible ground for making such a distinction. The inexplicable constitution of the original atoms of the universe has produced mother's love and murderer's hate in precisely the same way, and the one is as good as the other. But if the necessity be ordained by any kind of a Divine Being, then all its results must be according to his will and must serve his purpose. Any essential difference between the evil and the good becomes unimaginable. All that is left is a formal difference, in which evil is good in disguise, a necessary but unrecognized element in the development of the world. We must accept the statement of Pope's *Essay on Man:*

> "*All nature is but art, unknown to thee;*
> *All chance, direction which thou canst not see;*
> *All discord, harmony not understood;*
> *All partial evil, universal good;*
> *And spite of pride, in erring reason's spite,*
> *One truth is clear, Whatever is, is right.*"

THE SIN OF THE WORLD

The rock upon which these theories of the necessity of evil go to pieces is the practical knowledge of the nature of evil, which comes to us through the same moral sense which makes us aware of its existence. There is absolutely no variation in the testimony of human consciousness on this point. Evil is recognized not merely as something which is, but also as something which "ought not to be." This is the mark by which we know it. If from this mark we set out to trace its origin to a divine necessity which has ordained it and called it into being to serve a good purpose, then we must admit that our original mark of evil is an illusion, a false label. It is not "that which ought not to be." It is "that which had to be." The whole problem of the origin of evil dissolves into an absurdity. We are left to face a still harder question. How did our moral consciousness, with such an error at the very heart of it, come into being? Is it a mistake? Or is it a lie? Or is it perhaps a divinely imposed delusion?

But if our common sense turns away from these theories of evil as originating in nothingness, or in necessity, in what direction shall we look for an answer to the question of how it came into being? There is only one line left open; and that is the line of the facts as they lie before us in the world of experience.

What, then, are the facts of evil recognized by the moral sense of mankind? First of all, that it is "that which ought not to be." Then, that it actually is. Then, that it manifests itself in our own experience in connection with voluntary acts,—acts of choice, or acts of compliance,—contrary to "that which ought to be." But "that which ought to be," must be the will of God. Therefore "that which ought not to be," can only make itself known in the world through the will of a creature capable of going contrary to God. The possibility of evil depends upon the liberty of the created will. Liberty, then, which means the power of contrary choice, must be the door through which evil entered the world.

But what lies behind that door? From what secret region does the evil that passes through it draw its birth and its power? Why does it enter in? Why does God permit it? Here we stand face to face with the mystery.

Certainly God as creator must have bestowed the gift of liberty with a good purpose. He must have intended man to choose the good in order to attain real and permanent freedom; that is, the power of self-realization in harmony with the ideal of his nature. But when evil comes in through liberty, the purpose of liberty is violated, the very end of its being is frustrated. The will, choosing evil, comes into subjection to it, and cannot realize itself in a lasting freedom of concord with good.

Evil, then, as it manifests itself in the world, is a purposeless, aimless thing. It is an abuse of the power of choice. It is caprice. It is violence to reason. We can give no rational explanation of its origin, because its origin appears irrational. It is incomprehensible. There is a madness about it which confuses the mind. The Greeks took refuge from it in their myth of Atë, "the eldest daughter of Zeus, the power of bane, who blindeth all." But this was only a shift of desperate ignorance to get rid of the difficulty by transferring it from the human to the divine.

A wiser, humbler, more reverent thought holds fast to the conviction that wherever the madness of evil comes from, it does not come from God. Its origin is beyond our ken. "Evil is the inscrutable mystery of the world; it ever remains, in its inmost depths, impenetrable darkness." It is not to be comprehended in its cause. It is to be known in its effects, which are symptoms of its nature.

THE SIN OF THE WORLD

This is the point to which our line leads us, and here it leaves us. To go farther is to abandon fact for fancy. Christianity itself does not profess to give us light beyond this point. It presents no doctrine of the origin of evil. It tells us only how it came into the world, and what it means in the life of man. Where it came from is unrevealed.

There are two places in the Bible where the entrance of evil and the fall of man are described—and they both teach the same lesson. Christ's parable of the Prodigal Son[1] is just as true, just as significant, as the poem of Adam's lost Paradise.[2] In both stories the birthplace of the evil is hidden. The serpent that tempted Eve, and the far country that allured the Prodigal, are symbols of a mystery. In both stories the entrance of the evil is through self-will— blind, perverse, ruinous, but free, and therefore responsible. In both stories the nature of the evil is rebellion, self-injury, separation from God. In both stories the result of the evil in man's heart is the sense of sin.

Adam's story stops there; but the Prodigal's story goes on to salvation.

[1] St. Luke 15.　　　　　　　　[2] Gen. 3.

THE SIN OF THE WORLD

III

The sense of sin is deeper than the consciousness of evil. Evil is a broad, vague word. It covers all that ought not to be, but it does not make clear the nature of the "ought not." It is a general description of that which prevents perfection, destroys happiness, produces discord and misery.

Sin is a precise, sharp word. It translates the idea of evil from the language of philosophy into the language of religion. It defines the nature of the "ought not" as opposed to a divine law. It recognizes the presence and the guilt of a contrary will in disobedience to that law.

The consciousness of evil is universal. There is a feeling of conflict, of disorder, of moral perturbation and unrest, diffused through humanity. This is the great mark of division between the life of man and the life of nature. Emerson has described it in his poem of "The Sphinx." Nature is harmonious, joyful, unconscious of strife between the real and the ideal.

> *"But man crouches and blushes,*
> *Absconds and conceals;*
> *He creepeth and peepeth,*

THE SIN OF THE WORLD

He palters and steals;
Infirm, melancholy,
Jealous glancing around,
An oaf, an accomplice,
He poisons the ground.

Out spoke the great mother,
Beholding his fear;—
At the sound of her accents
Cold shuddered the sphere;
'Who has drugged my boy's cup?
Who has mixed my boy's bread?
Who, with sadness and madness,
Has turned my child's head?' "

This mysterious unrest, this vague trouble,
is an utterance of man's consciousness that he
belongs to another world from that which is
ruled by mere necessity. It is an instinctive
confession that beyond the power of control,
to which all physical life is subject, he feels a
power of command, to which his spiritual life
ought to be subject. This power of command
makes itself known to him through conscience,
which is the power of perceiving the difference
between the "ought to be" and the "ought
not to be."

"Whom do you count the worst man upon
earth?" says Robert Browning in "Christmas
Eve."

THE SIN OF THE WORLD

"Be sure that he knows, in his conscience, more
Of what right is, than arises at birth
In the best man's acts that we bow before:
This last knows better—true, but my fact is,
'Tis one thing to know, and another to practise."

This contrast between knowledge and practice is the root of the consciousness of evil, whose symptoms are unrest, shame, and fear.

"Thus conscience doth make cowards of us all."

It is a feeling of resistance to a moral pressure, of disobedience to a commanding power, of discord with a dim ideal. But it is also a sense of compliance with an inward impulse, of obedience to a native desire, of agreement with a secret passion.

It is not altogether dark. It could not exist in a world where there was nothing but evil. In a universe wholly material there could be no materialism. In a race utterly and totally evil there could be no consciousness of evil.

Neither could it exist in a world where separate evils stood alone and had no common ground in human nature. Each misdeed would then be a miracle. It would be a rootless, unrecognizable, nameless thing. Conscience perceives evil not only in its individuality, but also in its solidarity. When a man does wrong

300

he feels that he is a partner in a great conspiracy, a sharer, by choice or by compliance, in a widespread rebellion.

"There is in man," wrote Frederic Amiel in his diary, "an instinct of revolt, an enemy of all law, a rebel which will stoop to no yoke, not even that of reason, duty, and wisdom. This element in us is the root of all sin—*das radicale Böse* of Kant."

But this feeling of radical evil and of its presence and potency in every misdeed, needs more light to make its meaning clear. Evil is known as sin only when good is known as the will and command and ideal of a personal and holy God.

This is what St. Paul teaches. Revelation is given to make clear the nature of the gulf between man as he is and man as he ought to be. Evil is not a step in a progress towards the ideal. It is a chasm which cuts us off from the ideal. The reason why it cuts us off is because it is contrary to God's will, through which alone the ideal can be realized. The moral law reveals that will to us as positive, personal, righteous, and immutable. The law enters that the offence may abound, for "by the law is the knowledge of sin." [1]

The sense of sin, therefore, is a step beyond

[1] Rom. 3 : 20; 5 : 20.

301

the consciousness of evil. And it is a step towards light.

It is the interpretation of evil as an offence against God, a disobedience to God, a separation from God. It comes into being only with Theism, the faith in a holy, wise, and righteous Spirit as creator of the world. It is not until this light breaks upon the soul that Amiel's words become true: "All men long to recover a lost harmony with the great order of things, and to feel themselves approved and blessed by the author of the Universe. All know what suffering is, and long for happiness. All know what sin is, and feel the need of pardon."

Religion must begin, then,—even if we hold that its ultimate aim is the deliverance of men from evil,—religion must begin not with a doctrine of evil, but with a doctrine of God.

Its keynote must be the first article of the creed, "I believe in God, the Father Almighty, maker of heaven and earth." When he is hidden, forgotten, denied, the gospel for an age of doubt must prepare the way for the gospel for a world of sin. Over the vague unrest, the inarticulate shame, the uncomprehended fear, of an evil world, the light of God's love and God's law must be poured. Thus only can the evil doer find his way to that place of penitence, where he cries, "Against thee, thee only, have I sinned, and done this evil in thy sight." [1]

The sense of sin, therefore, is not by any means a hopeless thing. It is an evidence of life, in its very pain; of enlightenment, in its very shame; of nearness to God, in its very humiliation before him.

There is a passage in Margaret Deland's *Old Chester Tales* that puts the truth very simply and beautifully. A woman that was a sinner has come to a minister of Christ to confess her sin. The old man speaks to her as she kneels at his feet, weeping.

"You have sinned, and suffered for your sin. You have asked your Heavenly Father to forgive you, and he has forgiven you. But still you suffer. Woman, be thankful that you can suffer. The worst trouble in the world is the trouble that does not know God, and so does not suffer. Without such knowledge there is no suffering. The sense of sin in the soul is the apprehension of Almighty God."

IV

THE HOPEFUL FEAR

Sin is not a thing to be defined. It is a thing to be felt. Every attempt at a definition comes

[1] Psalm 51 : 4.

short of the reality. If it is insisted upon as the full truth, it becomes a guide to error. Every genuine feeling of sin throws some light upon the reality and helps us to perceive that which we can never explain.

One of the inexplicable elements of sin is the connection between its root in the race and its fruits in the individual. We cannot explain how it is that each man should feel himself free enough to be fully responsible for his own evil thoughts and feelings and actions, and yet conscious at the same time that they are joined to a common ground of evil in human nature. Stranger still is the fact that this propensity to evil is felt to be not an excuse but an aggravation. The man who injures his brother in a fit of passion, takes no comfort in the remembrance of his anger. The anger itself is part of his condemnation. Who ever excused a foul deed, to his own conscience, with the saying that he had a foul nature? Sin is not only an act: it is a condition, a state; and separate sins are not better, they are worse, because they spring from a common root. "It is of sin," says Boetius, "that we do not love that which is best."

Christ taught the truth of original sin. He did not explain it, but he declared it when he said, "Out of the heart proceed evil thoughts, murders, adulteries, fornications, thefts, false witness, blasphemies." [1] Side by side with this truth he proclaimed the guilt of actual sin when he said, "Whosoever looketh on a woman to lust after her hath committed adultery with her already in his heart." [2] He taught also that all men need to be delivered from both original and actual sin when he said, "Ye must be born again," [3] and "Except ye repent ye shall all likewise perish." [4] But when his disciples pressed him to explain this mystery of the connection between the root and the fruit of evil, with their question, "Lord, who did sin, this man or his parents, that he was born blind?" Christ refused to answer them. He said, "Neither did this man sin nor his parents" (that is, in relation to the point of their question), "but that the works of God might be made manifest in him." [5]

Original sin makes originality in sins impossible. There is a fatal resemblance and relationship in all the evils that are done under the sun, from the days before the flood even until now.

And yet every sin originates in the heart that

---

[1] St. Matt. 15 : 19.   [2] St. Matt. 5 : 28.   [3] St. John 3 : 7.
[4] St. Luke 13 : 3.   [5] St. John 9 : 2, 3.

commits it. Each individual will that consents to evil chooses for itself. The ground of this choice is hidden in darkness. It may lie in a region beyond the sphere of time and space, an antenatal state. But the operation of this choice is manifest in the light. Every sin is a fall of man.

To be really conscious of a single sin is to feel its secret connections and infinite possibilities. It is to catch sight of the bottomless gulf and have a sense of the immeasurable peril of walking beside it with unguarded feet.

In Goethe's *Confessions of a Beautiful Soul* there is a singular and searching passage which goes very deep into human experience.

"For more than a year,"—so runs the confession,—"I was forced to feel that if an unseen Hand had not protected me, I might have become a Girard, a Cartouche, a Damiens, or almost any moral monster that one can name. I felt the predisposition to it in my heart. God, what a discovery!"

John Bunyan's exclamation, when he looked from his window at a condemned malefactor going to execution,—"There goes John Bunyan, but for the grace of God,"—has found an echo in many a heart. But this echo is not a defence; it is a confession.

THE SIN OF THE WORLD

The sense of sin covers character as well as deeds. It clings not only to what we have done, but also to what we are prone to do. It was in this region below the surface that Jesus touched and exposed it, with his searching tenderness, his holy insight, his relentless love. Not only his word, piercing like an arrow of light to the roots of evil in pride and selfishness and lust and greed and hypocrisy, but also his life in its stainless purity and flawless truth, was an infallible detective of the furtive evil seeking to hide itself, like Adam and Eve in the poem of Eden, among the trees of the garden. It was for this reason that the scribes and Pharisees hated him, because he made them hate themselves. It was for this reason that Peter feared to be with him, and cried, "Depart from me, for I am a sinful man, O Lord." [1] It was for this reason that the woman of the city streets drew close to him, and bathed his feet with her tears, because she knew that he knew that she was a sinner.[2]

There are four elements in a true sense of sin: shame, pain, fear, and hope.

The shame comes from its ugliness, its defilement, its marring and mocking of those elements in us which we feel belong to the divine

[1] St. Luke 5 : 8.   [2] St. Luke 7 : 38.

307

image and our better nature. No man is born without an ideal.

> *"Take all in a word: the truth in God's breast,*
> *Lies trace for trace upon ours impressed:*
> *Though he is so bright, and we so dim,*
> *We are made in his image to witness him."*

The failure to be true to this ideal, the befouling and breaking of this image, is the shame of sin.

The pain comes from its enslaving and imprisoning power. Man was made for liberty. But sin is bondage to evil. "Whoso committeth sin is the servant of sin." [1] The conflict within our members, the law of the flesh warring against the law of the spirit, the weight of the chains of evil habit, the tyranny of sensual lusts and passions,—these make the misery of human life. Stevenson's parable of *Dr. Jekyll and Mr. Hyde* is a commentary on the seventh chapter of the Epistle to the Romans.

> *"The gods are just, and of our pleasant vices*
> *Make instruments to plague us."*

"Crime and punishment," says Emerson, "grow out of one stem. Punishment is a fruit that, unsuspected, ripens within the flower that concealed it."

[1] St. John 8 : 34.

THE SIN OF THE WORLD

The fear comes from the sense of disobedience to a high, mysterious, inexorable command. It is not possible to feel sin without fear, except by denying the existence of all moral law. As a matter of fact, the consciousness of evil has always carried with it in all human experience a feeling of secret apprehension, a troubled expectation and dread of punishment. Fear is related to guilt as personality is related to law. The reality of the one relation carries with it the reality of the other. Here we come face to face with a crucial question in religion.

Is there anything objective and actual which corresponds to this human element of fear in the sense of sin? Is there anything for sinful man to be afraid of?

Certainly there must be, unless the whole testimony of our moral nature is an illusion. The condemnation of sin rests not merely upon the feeling that sin is self-injury, self-mutilation, but upon the deeper sense that it is an offence against a law outside of us, and above us, and justly sovereign over us. Such a law must have within itself the right, the power, the inexorable necessity of punishment. Resting upon the will, and expressing the character of a righteous God, the ruler of the universe,

it implies in him a holy indignation against all
that breaks and dishonours it.

"For consider," says one of the greatest
preachers whose voice has been heard in the
nineteenth century, "sin violates and defies
the Moral Law of God. And what is God's
Moral Law? Is it a law which, like the laws
of nature, as we call them, might conceivably
have been other than it is? Certainly not.
We can conceive much in nature being very
different from what it is—suns and stars moving in smaller cycles; men and animals in different shapes; the chemistry, the geology, the
governing rules of the material universe, quite
unlike what they actually are. God's liberty
in creating physical beings was in no way limited
by his own laws, whether of force or of matter.
But can we, if we believe in a Moral God, conceive him saying, 'Thou mayest lie,' 'Thou
mayest do murder'? . . . The Moral Law is
not a code which he might have made other
than it is; it is his own Moral Nature, thrown
into a shape which makes it intelligible and
applicable to us his creatures; and therefore
in violating it we are opposing, not something
which he has made, but might have made otherwise, like the laws of nature,—but himself.
Sin, if it could, would destroy God."

THE SIN OF THE WORLD

The penalty of sin under moral law is not less certain, but more certain, than the penalty of disobedience to natural law. The wholesome fear which makes a burnt child dread the fire is trustworthy in the same way as the salutary fear which makes a sinful man dread the divine indignation. Both are premonitions of an actual peril, safeguards against a real danger. But the latter, if Christ knew the truth, is far more needful, far more terrible. For he said: "Be not afraid of them that kill the body, and after that have no more that they can do. But I will forewarn you whom ye shall fear: Fear him, which after he hath killed, hath power to cast into hell; yea, I say unto you, fear him." [1] And this he said, not unto his enemies to terrify them, but unto his friends to warn and save them.

The fear that lurks in sin is not an illusion. It is an admonition. It corresponds to something real outside of us. And that something is the reality which religion calls "the wrath of God."

It is inconceivable that this holy wrath should be perfectly comprehended or explained by us. It is equally inconceivable that it should be doubted or denied. A righteous judge incapa-

[1] St. Luke 12 : 5.

ble of indignation against crime would be unfit
to sit in the seat of justice. A holy God incapable of wrath against sin would be disquali-
fied to rule the world.

There must be a moral necessity in God which
calls for the condemnation of evil as sin. This
necessity comes from every side of his nature,
—from his justice first, but also from his purity,
his wisdom, his goodness, his love. And the
condemnation expresses every side of his relation to the world. As Creator, he disapproves
the marring of the ideal. As Judge, he condemns the transgression of the law. As Lord,
he resents and reproves treason and rebellion
against his government. As Father, he is
wounded and offended by ingratitude against
his love and separation from his fellowship.
All these holy perfections are included and implied in that mysterious reality of which the
Scripture speaks as "the wrath of God, coming
upon the children of disobedience." [1]

But there is a form in which this truth of
the divine wrath has been presented which
makes it utterly hateful, and, indeed, incredible. It is the form which forgets and denies
those perfections of God out of which his indignation proceeds. It is the form which in-

[1] Eph. 5 : 6.

troduces sin itself into the very heart of God's feeling against sin. It is the form which makes him fierce, vindictive, implacable, and cruel.

To defame and dishonour the divine wrath is worse than to doubt or deny it. To separate God's indignation against sin from his love towards man is to blaspheme his name.

This is the fault of which, alas, human theology has too often been guilty,—a fault which has brought its own deep punishment in the revolt of human nature against the hideous misrepresentation of religion. Take two examples of this black caricature of God's feeling towards sin, from the writings of Robert South, one of the eloquent preachers of the seventeenth century.

"The same relation of a Creator that endears God to the innocent, fires him against a sinner. God looks upon the soul as Amnon did upon Tamar: while it was a virgin he loved it; but now it is deflowered he hates it."

"A physician has a servant; while this servant lives honestly with him he is fit to be used and to be employed in his occasions; but if this servant should commit a felony and for that be condemned, he can then be actively serviceable to him no longer; he is fit only for him to dissect, and make an object upon which to show the experiments of his skill. So while man was yet innocent he was fit to be used by God in a way of active obedience; but now having sinned, and being sentenced by the law to death as a malefactor, he is a fit matter only for God to torment and show the wonders of his vindictive justice."

The world is to be congratulated that such teaching as this has become obsolete and incredible. Whatever system of theology it may have belonged to is now as dead as Dagon. A God who had any resemblance in his character to that despicable sinner, Amnon, a God who could use his children, even after they had disobeyed him, as "fit matter to torment and show the wonders of his vindictive justice," would be a nightmare horror of moral monstrosity, infinitely worse than no God at all. To worship such a God would be to worship an omnipotent devil.

God cannot be angry, even against sin, as sinful men are angry, because in him there is no sin. Whatever his holy wrath against evil may mean, it certainly must be eternally consistent with his purity, his goodness, his compassion, and his love.

Therefore, the true fear which is an element
314

in the sense of sin,—the fear which is simply seeing what evil is, what judgment is, what law is, and what punishment is,—the fear which is not spiritual cowardice, but an incitement to courage, not abject superstition, but a reasonable awe,—the fear which comes upon every sinful soul as an influence of quickening intelligence, a powerful movement of imperilled life, in the presence of the just and holy God, —this fear carries in its heart a secret and imperishable hope.

The hope that dwells in the sense of sin! Strange mystery of the deepest of all sorrows, —seed of light hidden in the womb of darkness, —indomitable testimony of the lost soul to its faith that some one is seeking for it in the wilderness!

Sin is the separation of man from God.

The sense of sin is God's unbroken hold upon the heart of man.

The sacrifices on myriad altars bear witness to it. The prayers of penitence rising from all dark corners of the earth bear witness to it. The tremulous homeward-turnings of innumerable souls from far countries of misery and loneliness bear witness to it.

THE SIN OF THE WORLD

"Father, I have sinned against heaven and in thy sight, and am no more worthy to be called thy son!"

But mark,—he still says, *Father!*

III

THE BIBLE WITHOUT CHRIST

THE Bible, if indeed it be the true text-book of religion, must contain the answer to man's cry as a sinner to God as a Saviour. It must disclose to man a remedy for the pain, a consolation for the shame, a rescue from the fear, and a confirmation of the secret hope, that he dimly and confusedly feels in the sense of sin. A Bible with no message of deliverance from sin would be a useless luxury in a sinful world. It would lack that quality of perfect fitness to human need which is one of the most luminous evidences of a divine word. The presence of a clear message of salvation is an essential element in the proof of inspiration.

That there is such a message of salvation in the Bible, no intelligent reader can deny. That it centres in Christ, is what this chapter is intended to show.

Jesus himself took this view of the Scriptures. To the unbelieving Jews, who trusted in their sacred books but felt no need of him, he said, "Search the Scriptures; for in these ye think ye have eternal life: and these are they which testify of me." [1]

Suppose for a moment that this were a mistake. Suppose that there were no testimonies to Christ in the Old Testament, no promises of his coming, no foreshadowings of his saving mission and power,—only law and ritual, poetry and history, philosophy and prophecy.

Suppose also that the New Testament contained nothing but the record of the moral teachings of Jesus and his followers, without reference to his life and death as a visible revelation of divine justice and mercy in personality and action. Suppose that it had not a word to say about his work in relation to men as sinners. Suppose, in short, that it gave the words of Jesus about the reality and nature and guilt of sin, about the pain and shame and fear of humanity, but no revelation of him, no recognition of what he did and suffered, no view of his crucifixion and resurrection, in their bearing upon the sin of the world.

Suppose the Bible without Christ. What hope of salvation would it contain? What would it be worth to us? What would be left of it as the divine answer to the need of a sinful world?

[1] St. John 5 : 39.

318

THE BIBLE WITHOUT CHRIST

In the Old Testament, with its partial and imperfect vision of the nature of evil, an unbroken shadow.

In the New Testament, with its poignant disclosure of the secret of sin, an intolerable light.

We can never realize the true meaning and value of this book of the world's hope until we try the experiment of reading it without the message which makes it hopeful. How the Bible centres in Christ can be learned best by trying to take Christ out of the Bible.

I

THE UNBROKEN SHADOW

The Old Testament does not begin with a theory of the nature of God and the origin of evil. It begins with a picture of creation, followed immediately by a picture of the entrance of evil into the world, and from this point it unrolls a graphic panorama of human life.

Some people interpret this panorama of Genesis as a series of scientific diagrams. Others interpret it as a series of poetic illustrations. It makes little difference in regard to their value for purposes of spiritual instruction. Upon the whole, the vital truths by which

319

the souls of men live, have been conveyed in poetic illustrations rather more frequently and fully than in scientific diagrams. Dante's *Divine Comedy* has taught more than Euclid's *Geometry*.

One thing is clear in the book of Genesis. By whatever method we translate its records, their meaning is the same. They show a vision of human sin, conflict, and suffering, against a divine background of offended love, righteous indignation, and just retribution. This view of human life corresponds very closely with what we know of it from other sources.

Unruly appetite, lustful passion, envy and discord, violence and terror and guilt, are written as clearly in the story of the beginnings of all tribes and nations and families, as in the story of Adam and Eve, Cain and Abel, Noah, Abraham, and Jacob.

It is difficult to conceive how a pure and righteous God could look upon such a race, made in his own image, with dominion over the creatures, and with capacities of infinite development in wisdom and virtue and power, yet descending to lower depths of animalism than the very beasts of the field, developing passions more cruel and treacherous and base than those of the brute creation,—upon such a race it is impossible that God should look without holy wrath. Not wrath as we know it, always tainted with selfishness, but wrath as only God can know it, absolutely unselfish and springing out of frustrated benevolence. The more he loves men and women, the more he must hate the evil which mars his image in their characters and defeats his design in their lives.

Now take away out of these pictures which are given in Genesis, that one ray of light which flashes in the Messianic promise that the seed of the woman shall bruise the serpent's head,[1] that one thread of gold which runs from this promise through the lives of those who believe in God, keeping them in touch with him, making them his faithful seed, because from them there is to come a star, a sceptre, a Shiloh unto whom the nation shall be gathered,[2]—take away that ray of light, that thread of gold, and what remains? Sin and shame and struggle below; baffled love, frustrated benevolence, inevitable condemnation above. The expulsion from Eden—the thorn-cursed soil—the brand on the brow of Cain—the shattered Babel—the whelming flood—the fiery tempest on Sodom and Gomorrah—wars and disasters, tumults

[1] Gen. 3 : 15.   [2] Gen. 49 : 10.

and captivities—man a rebellious, wretched, wandering creature—God justly offended at the violation of his law—a sin-twisted, suffering, fearful world below—a stainless, silent heaven above,—and no bridge across the gulf.

Now turn to the law given through Moses. His part in history was twofold. He was the leader of the Exodus; and that means emancipation from human tyranny. He was the explorer of Sinai; and that means subjugation to divine justice.

Moses talked with God face to face. But there was a frown upon the divine countenance, and the voice which spoke to him was as stern as fate. The people heard it only as the voice of a trumpet, mysterious and inarticulate, whereat they did exceedingly fear and quake, and entreated that it should not be spoken unto them any more. But Moses heard the words, and knew that they were inevitable and eternal.

Ten commandments he brought down from the mount, written out clearly so that all men should understand them, and on stone so that they should endure to all generations. One of the commandments was positive. Nine of them were negative.

But the point that pierces us, in this revelation through Moses, is that every "Thou shalt not" is a disclosure of what men have done, and are prone to do, and would like to do again if they dared. The commandments sound like a shouting from the mountain-top of the secrets of many hearts. After each divine word which says, "Thou shalt not," follows a human murmur which says, "But I will."

A Bible was once published in which, by a typographical error, the *not* was omitted from the seventh commandment. It was called "the wicked Bible." The history of Israel, starting from Sinai, reads like a commentary on a wicked Bible with the printer's error multiplied by ten. Carry the commandments through the books of the Judges and the Kings, and you must acknowledge that they compel the conclusion that man is what he ought not to be, and ought not to be what he is.

The one bright spot in the law given by Moses is the commandment to make a mercy-seat in the Tabernacle, where the sins of the people may be confessed before Almighty God,[1] and where the blood of sacrifice, sprinkled upon the Ark, may symbolize an atonement between man and God. The one good hope which cheered Moses in his ministry to a disobedient

[1] Ex. 25; Lev. 16.

and gainsaying folk, was the promise that God would raise up a prophet from among his brethren unto whom the people should hearken.[1] Blot out that prediction of Christ, and Moses stands as an embodiment of failure,—a leader who emancipated the nation and condemned the race,—the messenger of a divine law which was broken even while he was carrying it down from the burning mount.

Turn from history and law to poetry and experience. In the Psalms the thunders of Sinai are set to music and translated into song. But what is that song? It is the song of the unattainable. It is the lyric utterance of desire and disappointment, shame and penitence. Those broken-hearted Psalms! How they ring the changes on human frailty and suffering and remorse! How sad and searching the light with which they are illuminated in the story of David's life! He could sing divinely, but he could not live as he sang.

Sin is the shadow on genius.

Literature full of beauty and harmony: life full of ugliness and discord. A book written with simplicity and purity and noble sentiment: a writer touched with vanity and self-

[1] Deut. 18 : 15.

324

ishness, impurity and vengeful passion. How often has that strange contrast been discovered!

David knew his own infirmity and guilt. He knew the corruption and disgrace of his house. He laid hold on the promise of divine mercy in the Christ. He looked and longed for the coming of that King who should reign in righteousness forever. He did not understand the full meaning of that hope. He held fast to it as a drowning man clings to a rope in the night. He does not see it. He feels it.

Take away that rescuing hope of divine help laid upon one who is mighty to save,[1] and what is left in the Psalms? A passion of longing for inaccessible holiness.

The poetry of the Bible without Christ is a musical confession of the impossibility of getting out of God's sight, and of the hopelessness of being pure enough in heart to have sight of God.

Does the philosophy of the Bible bring us any different message, apart from Christ?

Solomon stands in the Old Testament as the representative of wisdom. In the books that bear his name the divine commandments are cut and polished into the jewels of an ethical

[1] Psalm 89 : 19.

325

system. They become brilliant, symmetrical, memorable; compact treasures of morality, fit to keep—in a storehouse. A hundred epigrams flash from the divine law, in the hands of Solomon, like rays of light. Its wisdom, reasonableness, and beauty are exhibited from every side. We see how prudent, how profitable, how admirable it is to be perfectly good,—and how impossible! The king who made these diamond proverbs was the man who showed us how easily they may be burned to coal in the flame of passion.

The eleventh chapter of the First Book of Kings is the record of an experiment in the reduction of philosophy to ashes. The lover of wisdom chooses folly for his bed-fellow. The sage whose shining words rise like an airy ladder towards the skies, finds, like other men, that the downward path is the easiest. The wisest of mankind, in theory, becomes the meanest, in practice,—an idolater despising idols, a sensualist praising virtue, a tyrant extolling justice, an unchained prisoner of his own despair.

The book of Ecclesiastes, whoever wrote it, contains the epitaph of Solomon. "Vanity of vanities, all is vanity." It is the hand-book of pessimists; the tragic monodrama of man's

self-betrayal; the epic of the suicide of hope.
Close the book, and write upon it this sentence,
"The world by wisdom knew not God." [1]

Beyond philosophy rises prophecy,—the
mount of vision, whose top touches the stars
and whose horizon spreads beyond the encircling ocean-stream of time.

The human name that is graven highest on
this mountain is the name of Isaiah. Whether
that name represents the prophetic elevation of
only one among the sons of men, or of more
than one, matters little to us in our present
study. The Isaiah-spirit is the same, whether
the mount was climbed but once, or more than
once. The loftiest point reached in the Old
Testament is that at which we see, in lonely
grandeur, a human figure called Isaiah. There
he stands, above the confusions and perturba-
tions, the wrecked hopes, and the onrushing
calamities, the shames and fears, the desola-
tions and disasters of his people. He looks
around him, with unsealed eyes, and what is it
that he beholds? He sees "one that cometh
from Edom, with dyed garments from Bozrah,
glorious in his apparel, travelling in the greatness of his strength, speaking in righteousness,

[1] 1 Cor. 1 : 21.

mighty to save." [1] But this vision, if there is
no Christ in the Old Testament, is a delusion,
a mirage, a Brocken-spectre. It vanishes. And
what is left?

An unbroken shadow of disgrace, despair,
and gloom, resting like night upon the world.
"Ah sinful nation, a people laden with iniquity,
a seed of evil doers, children that are corrupters:
they have forsaken the Lord, they have pro-
voked the Holy One of Israel unto anger, they
are gone away backward." [2] Burden after
burden, in the prophet's song,—the burden of
Babylon, the burden of Moab, the burden of
Damascus, the burden of Egypt. Doom after
doom, around the prophet's horizon,—the doom
of Israel, the doom of Judah. "The whole
head is sick, and the whole heart faint. From
the sole of the foot even unto the head there
is no soundness in it; but wounds, and bruises,
and putrefying sores." [3]

Never man lived on earth who felt so deeply
the world's want of a Saviour from sin as Isaiah
felt it. Never man saw so clearly that humanity is helpless and hopeless under the power
of evil unless God comes to the rescue. The
law's maker must be its keeper. He who cursed
sin must come and take it away. A redeeming

[1] Is. 63 : 1.   [2] Is. 1 : 4.   [3] Is. 1 : 5, 6.

God, holy and therefore obedient, loving and therefore suffering, faithful and therefore triumphant,—this is the Immanuel who is needed in a world of sin. Isaiah's soul was driven by that need upward and upward on the mount of vision, higher and higher in the divine solitude of inspiration. From that lofty height his voice floated down in songs of glorious cheer to his fellow-men. "Comfort ye, comfort ye, my people." [1] "Rejoice ye with Jerusalem, and be glad with her, all ye that love her: rejoice for joy with her, all ye that mourn for her." [2]

But what was it that he saw to kindle that singing hope in his soul? Nothing. He dreamed, but there was really nothing for him to see.

There was no roseate dawn on the far edge of night, no radiance of a virgin-born Prince of Peace, no prophetic gleam of the glory of a Kinsman Redeemer who should bear our griefs and carry our sorrows, who should be wounded for our transgressions, and by whose stripes we should be healed. When Isaiah thought that he saw the upward-streaming rays of such a brightness, it was but an illusion of sleep. There was no Christ. There was to be no

[1] Is. 40 : 1.   [2] Is. 66 : 10.

Christ. God never intended it. Man only imagined it. The high and holy One who inhabiteth eternity looked upon the inhabitants of earth, "and he saw that there was no man, and wondered that there was no intercessor." [1] But his arm did not bring salvation unto him, neither did his righteousness sustain him. The Redeemer never meant to come to Zion. He was too great, too infinite to enter into human life, and be numbered with the transgressors, and bear the sin of many, and make intercession for the transgressors. The very thought of such an advent was folly and presumption.

Isaiah awakes from his dream. Every trace of the Christ disappears from his vision, blotted out in the encircling night. What is his message now? What song is left on his lips?

A cry of woe and desolation. "They shall look unto the earth; and behold trouble and darkness, dimness of anguish; and they shall be driven to darkness." [2] "Your iniquities have separated between you and your God, and your sins have hid his face from you, that he will not hear." [3]

There is no explanation of the mystery of evil. There is no light upon the future. There is only a shadow resting over all the earth, a

[1] Is. 59 : 16.   [2] Is. 8 : 22.   [3] Is. 59 : 2.

shadow hiding the very face of God,—an unbroken shadow falling from the Old Testament without Christ.

II

THE INTOLERABLE LIGHT

It may seem as if it were impossible to take Christ out of the New Testament without destroying it altogether. So entirely does the personality of Jesus pervade the book, that if he were withdrawn it would fall to pieces, like a tower from which the mortar had been all removed.

But it is not of Jesus as an example of noble manhood, a teacher of moral truth, a worker of social reform, that I speak. It is of Jesus as the Christ, the divinely anointed redeemer of men, the bringer of salvation from sin. These two aspects of Jesus were, indeed, vitally united in fact. Yet it is possible to separate them in thought. It is conceivable that the New Testament might have reported Jesus to us as a prophet without making any revelation of him as the Saviour.

Such a conception has already been entertained among men. It has been presented by some teachers, whose literary and historical sense is very imperfect, as an interpretation of what the New Testament actually is. It has been put forward by others, whose scholarship is better, as a theory of what the New Testament ought to be, and probably would have been, if it had been written in an age free from superstition.

"That which is really valuable in the book," we are told, "is its picture of a beautiful character, its rules for good conduct, its spirit of piety and virtue, the clear light which it throws upon God and human life and immortality. If it contained only the Sermon on the Mount, it would still be complete and sufficient. The substance of it all could be put into an ethical creed. The essential Jesus is only the teacher and illustrator of a perfect morality. He is the central figure of Christianity not because he did more than man can do, but simply because he did what every man ought to do. All that goes beyond this in the New Testament,—all that refers to him as the sacrifice for sin, the mediator between God and man, the only begotten Son who came forth from the bosom of the Father, was born and lived, was crucified and died, was buried and rose again, in order to redeem and reconcile the world to God,— is partly imaginary, and partly superstitious, and wholly unnecessary. A New Testament without Christ in this sense, would be not only possible, but very desirable."

The experiment may be tried. The testimony of Jesus and the Apostles in regard to his work as the Saviour may be obliterated, as the censor "blacks out" the passages of a book which he deems dangerous. The cross as the central scene of the great reconciliation between man and God may be hidden. Christ as the deliverer from sin and death may be annulled in our thought. We shall then be able to estimate the meaning and value of the New Testament without him.

There are two things in the book which must strike every fair-minded reader. In two points it is distinguished among all the books of the world. It gives a new and intensely searching view of the problem of moral evil. It is written from beginning to end in sight of death as the door which leads into eternity.

On these two points the New Testament pours an unrivalled light. Does it give us any comfort or hope in regard to them, without Christ?

It was Jesus of Nazareth who illuminated the moral evil in the world most deeply and clearly. He showed its spring, its secret workings, and the power which lies behind it. Calmly, steadily, with a sublime indifference to theory, with an inexorable sense of the facts of human life, he pressed his serene and faithful analysis of sin home to its centre in the inner life of man.

A falsehood on the lips means a lie in the heart. Violence in conduct means a cruel streak in character. Uncleanness in the life means impurity in the soul. "Those things which proceed out of the mouth come forth from the heart; and they defile the man." [1]

Jesus does not say that everything in human nature is evil. He does not say that all men are entirely depraved. He recognizes the good things that a good man bringeth forth out of his good treasure.[2] But he says also that all men, even the best, have need to be converted and become as little children;[3] all men owe a vast debt which they are unable to pay;[4] all men are unprofitable servants;[5] all men have something to repent of, in the presence of God.[6]

And this something which demands repentance is not outward and accidental; it is inward and personal. It is the angry passion; it is the impure imagination; it is the secret

[1] St. Matt. 15 : 18. [2] St. Matt. 12 : 35. [3] St. Matt. 18 : 3.
[4] St. Matt. 18 : 23. [5] St. Luke 17 : 10. [6] St. Luke 13 : 3.

unbelief which blinds the soul. All the excuses with which men cover and hide their sin grow thin and transparent in the light of this searching analysis. Jesus reveals the underlying facts. The sins of men are not the result of circumstances, the fruit of outward temptations, things which belong to the world and the age in which we live. They are things which belong to us and come from us. The fashions and forms of sin change with the centuries and differ in different lands. But the essence of it is always the same. It comes from within. The man in whose heart the root is hidden is responsible for the fruit. This is what Jesus says about the source of sin.

No less clear and penetrating is his teaching in regard to its secret workings and its fatal results. He reveals the truth that goodness does not consist in obedience to the letter of the law, but in harmony with its spirit. A man may keep all the commandments, as the young ruler did, and yet because he is selfish he is outside of the kingdom of God.[1] A man may observe all the Mosaic precepts and perform all the ritual of religion, as the Pharisee did, and yet be a greater sinner than the Publican

[1] St. Matt. 19.

335

who stands afar off and beats upon his breast.[1] Men are strangers to their own sins; they do not recognize them when they meet them in the street. They are blind leaders of the blind, whose feet stumble in the gulf. The angry impulse is the "blot in the 'scutcheon." The real stain of blood is on the inside of the heart. The idle, irreverent word is blasphemy. There are no human lips that have not taken God's name in vain. The scorn of brethren is the little spark that kindles unquenchable flames. They in whose breast this spark smoulders are "in danger of hell-fire." [2] But they do not know it. They carry their lighted candles through the powder-magazine with their eyes shut.

The Sermon on the Mount contains the most thorough diagnosis of sin that has ever been made. It proceeds by contrast with the symptoms of spiritual health and soundness. The Beatitudes are not only blessings to be desired; they are also tests to be applied to the heart. It was not without significance that this discourse was delivered from a lofty place. "Be ye perfect even as your Father which is in heaven is perfect." [3] That summit is inacces-

---

[1] St. Luke 18.　　　　　　　　[2] St. Matt. 5 : 22.
[3] St. Matt. 5 : 48.

sible if there is no divine Christ to lead us thither.

But there is another element in the doctrine of Jesus in regard to sin which we must not forget. He discloses a secret power behind it, which clothes it with strange terror and might. He teaches that there is a force, an influence, a spirit in the world, which is altogether evil, and which is continually desiring, seeking, and working sin. It is the unclean spirit rejoicing in the defilement of the house which it inhabits.[1] It is the father of lies ready to beget falsehood in every listening mind.[2] It is the enemy of souls sowing tares in the field by night.[3] It is Satan longing to get possession of the soul that he may sift it as wheat.[4]

Whether we take this teaching of Jesus literally or not, whether we believe that evil is embodied in demonic personality or not, one thing is unquestionable. Jesus regarded evil as a positive, organic, ever active, malignant power, a Prince of this world, whose domain lies all around us, whose influence touches us on every side, the friend of sin and the foe of the soul. There is a conflict going on in the world.

[1] St. Matt. 12 : 43 ff. [2] St. John 8 : 44.
[3] St. Matt. 13 : 39. [4] St. Luke 22 : 31.

THE BIBLE WITHOUT CHRIST

It is not a mere game. It is an elemental warfare between right and wrong. We are cast into the midst of this conflict. An unseen, mighty, skilful, relentless adversary is against us. And in every heart there is a traitor ready to betray the citadel into his hands.

The additional fear which this mysterious teaching of Jesus lends to the sense of sin made itself felt in human experience for many centuries. Doubtless it was over-emphasised and exaggerated, by a false interpretation of his words, into an immense and shapeless terror. A grotesque and impossible devil tyrannized over ages of superstition. Men believed in a Satan who was practically the rival of God, equal in power if not in glory, and as immortal in evil as God is in good. There is no trace of such a doctrine in the words of Jesus. It was natural, it was inevitable, that men should react from the exaggeration, and cast off almost entirely, as they have done to-day, the thought of an actual power of evil, outside of the human soul and inexorably hostile to it.

But when we return to the teachings of Jesus, and study them with candour and calmness, we see that thought in his mind clearly and unmistakably. He teaches us that our conflict is not merely with ourselves. There is an enemy against us who is mightier than man. We need a defender, a deliverer, a divine friend to fight with us and for us.

Where, then, shall we look for such a powerful friend? If Jesus was not the Christ who came to save us from our sins, then there is no captain of salvation, no conqueror of Satan, no liberator of captive souls. We must fight the battle alone against unknown and heavy odds. The triumph of Jesus over evil was for himself only. It gives no assurance that we also shall overcome the world. On the contrary, it makes our victory seem the more doubtful, when we remember his perfect courage and inflexible strength, in contrast with our waverings and the many defeats that we have already suffered. We have begun to lose the battle already. Who shall turn the tide for our discouraged forces?

The sinlessness of Jesus comforts us little unless it has some remedial bearing upon our sins. If it is but an example of what every man ought to be, its very perfection daunts and disheartens us. Something less absolute and flawless would be better suited to our need.

In fact, men have never dared or cared to make the stainless Jesus the real pattern of their lives, until they have learned to believe in him as the redeeming sacrifice for their sins. They have chosen other ideals, other heroes, other examples,—less exacting, less disheartening, less depressing by contrast with themselves.

It is the ransoming faith that "Christ suffered for us," that gives his disciples courage to say that he also left us "an example that we should follow in his steps." [1] The idea of "The Imitation of Christ" is hopeful and inspiring only to the heart that has first felt the liberating touch of his pierced hand. Sinners do not venture to go after the sinless Jesus unless they hear him say "The Son of man hath power on earth to forgive sins." [2]

But in a Christless gospel this word would have no place, no meaning. There would be no such unique power in the hands of Jesus. All the consoling, reassuring, inspiriting utterances of Jesus, which are connected with his sublime confidence in his divine mission and authority to seek and save the lost,—utterances which strangely enough are closely and inseparably connected with the prevision of his death, his laying down his life for the sheep,[3] his lifting up upon the cross,[4]—all these words of saving hope would be "blacked out."

[1] 1 Peter 2 : 21.   [2] St. Matt. 9 : 6.
[3] St. John 10 : 11.   [4] St. John 3 : 14.

They lose their significance, if the Redeemer is lost. There was no ransom wrought upon the cross. There was only the payment of the debt of nature. The good Shepherd laid down his life. But it was not for the sheep. It was only to show the cruelty of the robbers. There was no victory on Calvary. It was a defeat, in which the one sinless being on earth was crushed and killed *by* the sin of the world,— but not *for* it.

Let us turn from the Gospels to the Epistles, and consider what they have to say to us about sin, when we have taken out of them the idea of a work wrought by Jesus Christ for the salvation of the world. It is evident that the Apostles have received the teaching of their Master in regard to the source, the workings, the guilt, and the danger of sin, and that it has made a profound impression upon them.

No doubt there was some difference between St. John and St. Paul in regard to the philosophic forms in which they expressed their thought upon this subject. St. Paul was trained in the rabbinical theology of Jerusalem. St. John was influenced by the Platonic philosophy of Alexandria. St. Paul lays emphasis upon the connection of sin with "the flesh," with man's lower, physical nature.[1] St. John brings out "the darkness" of sin as contrasted with the light of God.[2] St. Paul traces the entrance of sin into the world to Adam's disobedience.[3] St. John speaks of "the world" as an order of existence estranged from God, which must not be loved because it is opposed to the love of God,[4] and declares that "the whole world lieth in the Evil One."[5] But both agree in teaching that sin is transgression of the divine law;[6] and that its fruit is death.[7] It is their sense of the reality and guilt of the transgression, their overwhelming sense of the greatness of the disaster which threatens all men on account of it, that separates them as writers from the easy-going, reckless pagan world. "If we say we have not sinned," says St. John, "we deceive ourselves and the truth is not in us."[8] "When I would do good," cries St. Paul, "evil is present with me. O wretched man that I am, who shall deliver me from the body of this death?"[9]

But if this is all that they have to say to us, if they bring us no message of a divine Christ

---

[1] Rom. 7 : 5; 8 : 4, 6; 2 Cor. 10 : 2; Gal. 5 : 17; Eph. 2 : 3.
[2] 1 John 1 : 6; 2 : 9, 11; Rev. 16 : 10.
[3] Rom. 5 : 12–21.   [4] 1 John 2 : 15.   [5] 1 John 5 : 19.
[6] 1 John 3 : 4; Rom. 7 : 13.
[7] Rom. 6 : 23; 8 : 6; 1 John 3 : 14; 5 : 16; 2 Cor. 15 : 56.
[8] 1 John 1 : 8.   [9] Rom. 7 : 21, 24.

who hath appeared to put away sin, how lame and impotent is their conclusion! Read St. Paul's answer to his own question, who is to deliver him, with Christ left out: 'I thank God, *through nobody.*' Read St. John's consolation to those who have sinned, without the gospel of atonement. 'If any man sin, we have no advocate with the Father, neither is there any propitiation for our sins, nor for the sins of the whole world.' 'Herein is love, not that we loved God, but that he did not love us, neither did he send his Son to be the justification for our sins.'

Go on a little further with this Christless New Testament. Listen to St. Paul again: 'For as through one man sin entered into the world, and death through sin, and so death passed unto all men, for that all sinned,—even so there was no grace of God, and the gift of grace by the one man, Jesus Christ, did not abound unto many.' 'Sin reigned unto death, but grace did not reign through righteousness unto eternal life through Jesus Christ our Lord.' 'God commendeth his love towards us in that while we were yet sinners nobody died for us.' 'Wherefore remember that ye were aliens from the commonwealth of Israel and strangers to the covenants of promise; and now ye that were far off are not made nigh by the blood of Christ.' 'God is not in Christ reconciling the world unto himself.' 'There is no mediator between God and man.' 'The life that I now live in the flesh I live by faith in myself, for the Son of God did not love me, nor give himself for me.'

Listen to the author of the Epistle to the Hebrews: 'Having then no high priest who hath passed into the heavens, let us not draw near with boldness unto the throne of grace, for we have no promise of mercy, nor grace to help in time of need.' 'For we are not come unto Jesus the mediator of the new covenant, and to the blood of sprinkling which speaketh better things than that of Abel, but unto Mt. Sinai that burns with fire.'

Listen to St. Peter: 'We know that we were not redeemed, neither with corruptible things as silver and gold, nor with the precious blood of Christ as of a lamb without blemish and without spot.' 'Wherefore, not having seen him, we love him not, neither do we rejoice in him, since we receive not the end of our faith, nor the salvation of our souls.'

This is what the New Testament would say to a world of sin, without Christ. It is surely not consoling.

But the significance of this teaching is very much intensified and deepened by the view which the New Testament gives of death as the gateway of another life.

The heathen world in the first century was for the most part inclined to cover up the fact of death as much as possible, to hide it in flowers, to put it out of sight. But the Christians, perhaps because they were persecuted and afflicted and continually in danger of death, perhaps because they had a truer and a braver philosophy of life, followed another course. They faced death steadily, looked it in the eyes, prepared to meet it, and conquered all its terrors by their faith in Christ as the Saviour.

There is no other book in the world which can compare with the New Testament in its serene, unflinching recognition of death's inevitableness. There is no other book in the world which has so clear and courageous an insight into its eternal issues. From beginning to end it is pervaded with the conviction that "It is appointed unto all men once to die, and after death the judgment."

Now the burden of death is twofold. There is a burden of present sorrow and anguish, in the sufferings of the flesh which precede and accompany it, and in the pains of the spirit which are associated with the breaking of human ties and the bereavement of love. There is also a burden of fear and anxiety for the future, a sense of apprehension in regard to the perils and mysteries of the unknown world.

Both of these burdens, in the New Testament, are lifted by trust in Christ. It is the sense of fellowship with him in their sufferings that sustains the Christians in the valley of the shadow of death. It is the confidence that he has risen from the dead and that he will plead for them at the judgment, that enables them to face the future with composure. But if Christ is taken away, both burdens fall back with new and crushing weight upon the heart. "If Christ be not risen, then is our preaching vain, and your faith is also vain." "If in this life only we have hope in Christ, we are of all men most miserable." [1]

What practical assurance, what tangible proof, is there of a divine sympathy in our sufferings, without the vision of the Son of God who has borne our griefs and carried our sorrows? The God of nature, the God who made the heavens bright and beautiful with stars, and ordained the immutable glories of the revolving year,—what can he understand of the

[1] 1 Cor. 15 : 14, 19.

pains that rack our human hearts, what part
has he in the broken and tragical drama of mortal life? A sublime spectator,

> *"He sees with equal eyes, as God of all,*
> *A hero perish or a sparrow fall."*

I think a man or woman with a breaking
heart, pierced with the spear of pain, smitten
with the anguish of inexorable separation, might
go out into this splendid world in the spring,
when the glory of earth's face is renewed with
joy and the time for the singing of birds is come,
—such a lonely, desolate, perishing man or
woman might walk among the unconscious
flowers, and look up to the silent-shining sky,
and the unfriended heart would break again
with the thought that there is after all no clear
word of divine sympathy with it,—no human
life of God, no Christ who wept at the grave
of Lazarus, and agonized in the garden, and
died on the cross, in order that he might know,
with us, the mortal sorrows of a world of sin
and death.

What comfort, what peace, is there in the
New Testament view of death, unless we can
see beyond it what St. Paul saw when he said,
"I know whom I have believed, and am per-
suaded that he is able to keep that which I

have committed unto him against that day." [1]
—"O death, where is thy sting? O grave, where
is thy victory? The sting of death is sin; and
the strength of sin is the law. But thanks be
to God, which giveth us the victory through
our Lord Jesus Christ." [2] Annul that gospel
of victory over death by One who has taken
away the sting of sin, and what remains? A
certain fearful looking-for of judgment; a vision
of futurity with no reasonable hope of escape
from evil and its consequences; a prospect of
dying without getting rid of the disease which
kills us.

Read again the words of the Apostles after
you have blotted out their gospel of the conquest of death by Christ. 'Through death
he was destroyed by him that had the power
of death, that is, the devil, and brought no
deliverance to them who through fear of death
were all their lifetime subject to bondage.'
'God hath not raised him up, neither were the
pains of death loosed, because it was not possible that he should escape from it.' 'The
enemy that shall never be destroyed is death.'
'This same Jesus shall never come again.'
'He liveth not to make intercession for his people.' 'Even as he never was offered to bear

[1] 2 Tim. 1 : 12.   [2] 1 Cor. 15 : 55–57.

the sin of many, so shall he never again appear without sin unto salvation to them that wait for him.' 'If we believe not that Jesus died and rose again, even so them also which sleep with Jesus will God never bring with him.'

> *"Christ is not risen!*
> *Eat, drink, and die, for we are souls bereaved;*
> *Of all the creatures under heaven's high cope,*
> *We are most hopeless, who once had most hope,*
> *And most beliefless, that had most believed.*
> *Ashes to ashes, dust to dust,*
> *As of the unjust, also of the just;*
> *Yea, of that Just One too,*
> *It is the one sad Gospel that is true,—*
> *Christ is not risen!"*

To take Christ out of the Bible is to make it worse than useless to a sinful world. It is to make it crushing, disheartening, terrifying,— the saddest book that was ever written. The Old Testament casts upon us an unbroken shadow of gloomy fate. The New Testament pierces it with an intolerable light of conscious guilt and coming judgment.

But restore Christ to his place in the Bible, and it becomes the book of hope and joy. The unbroken shadow is changed into the adumbration of the coming Redeemer. The intoler-

349

able light is transformed into a healing radiance: the light of the knowledge of the glory of God in the face of Jesus Christ, the Saviour of the world.

IV

CHRIST'S MISSION TO THE INNER LIFE

THE ultimate mission of Christ was to the inner life of man. His ministry there was not in words alone, but in character and action; in what he was and what he did for men; the heart of his message was himself, his life, his death. The central gospel of this message is the reality and completeness of peace with God through the forgiveness of sins. The forgiveness of sins brings with it the freedom and power of a new inner life of divine righteousness.

These four statements may serve to mark out, in a broad way, the line of thought that I wish to follow in this chapter.

I

THE KINGDOM IS WITHIN YOU

Christ came into the world to proclaim and establish the kingdom of God among men. The sway of that kingdom extends over every region of our life. But its seat must be within us.

It must reach and reconcile and rule that interior region of the heart which lies behind audible utterance and visible action, below social ties and bonds of human fellowship, underneath conscious reasonings and formulated theories,—that undiscovered country where the moral sentiments, the religious feeling, the sense of dependence, and the joy or grief of living, have their home.

It is there that the real forces of human life are generated. Man could not "live by bread alone," even if he would. Every phase of his existence betrays the presence of an energy, whether for good or for evil, which is drawn from some secret source deep within him.

Vitality, in man, is a spiritual force conditioned, but not created, by a material embodiment. A *vitometer* will never be invented, because there is no instrument delicate enough to take the temperature of the inner life. Even in dealing with bodily disease, the wise physician, while he may make his diagnosis absolute, always recognizes an element of uncertainty in his prognosis. "While there is life there is hope," he says. He might add, "While there is hope there is life." Hope has healed more diseases than any medicine.

The life of man is a demonstrated daily miracle. It shows that the physical laws which we know and the physical forces which we can measure, are traversed by spiritual laws which we do not know and spiritual forces which we cannot measure. It proves the reality and potency of that which is invisible and imponderable.

The various kinds of energy which are developed from heat are not more real, nor more powerful, than the actual working force which is developed in the world from love in the inner life of man. Gravitation itself does no more to insure the stability of the material order, than inward peace of soul does to maintain the stability of the social order. The wind that bloweth where it listeth, is no more efficient in purifying and vitalizing the atmosphere, than are the secret spiritual currents of penitence and faith and aspiration which breathe through the hearts of men, in cleansing and renewing the inner air which keeps the soul alive.

This is the reason why sin is a power of disorder and death. It is not because it affects the outer life, not because it sows the seeds of physical corruption and decay, not because it brings forth crimes of violence and destruction. It is because it pervades the inner life, because it poisons the streams of human existence at the fountain-head, because it paralyzes the vital energies of humanity.

Sin is a separating, secluding, imprisoning power which shuts the soul off from the purifying breath of the divine Spirit and leaves it in a dungeon, to breathe the same air over and over again until it is smothered. Sin is a rebellious, turbulent, tormenting power which destroys the inward peace of the soul, agitates it with restless passion, tortures it with haunting fear. Sin is a selfish, envious, hateful power which takes the very life out of love and makes it impotent for good.

The supreme simplicity of Jesus as the bringer of a new kingdom into the world, came from the clearness with which he saw that the world's chief trouble and man's deepest need lie in the inner life. He wasted no strength in polishing the outside of the cups and platters on which man's exterior wants are served. He spent no time in whitening sepulchres. He knew that the seat of real goodness and permanent happiness must be in the inner life. The incomparable service to mankind which was to give him the chieftaincy in the spiritual life, was a service to the soul.

There can be no real empire of peace unless

this deepest region is reached. There must be no nook or corner or crevice of man's life left unexplored, unsubdued, unreconciled; no lurking-place of rebellion; no fountain of discord; no

> "*little rift within the lute,*
> *That slowly widening makes the music mute.*"

The kingdom must go in to the centre and down to the bottom of personality, and work from within outward,—from below upward. This was the programme of Christ; and to carry it out he directed his journey to the inner life of man.

On the way thither, like a prince in progress, he conferred inestimable gifts and blessings in the outer circles of human existence. The doctrine of Jesus has widened the thoughts of men. The example of Jesus has crystallized the moral aspirations of men into a supreme ideal. The precept of Jesus has struck the keynote for a new harmony of human fellowship. The influence of Jesus has given inspiration and guidance to philosophy and literature and the fine arts.

But as we follow him through these regions we are aware that he is pressing inward to a goal beyond. He seeks the thinker, we say, behind the thought; the person, behind the social order. He aims to elevate man by uplifting men. His mission is not to masses, nor to classes; it is to the individual. But when he finds the individual, as a thinker, as a social unit, what then? Still Christ seems to press inward, to seek a yet deeper point.

His mission to society is through the individual. But when we have said that, we have not yet said all. His mission to the individual is through the inner life. He has not arrived at the goal of his journey, he has not spoken the last word of his message until he has said to the paralytic, "Son, be of good cheer, thy sins are forgiven thee"; and to the woman of Syro-Phœnicia, "Go in peace"; and to the disciples, "Let not your heart be troubled"; and to all the weary and heavy-laden, "Come unto me, and ye shall find rest unto your souls."

The kingdom of God which Jesus proclaims and establishes is a kingdom of the soul. Its deepest meaning is a personal experience. Its essence is righteousness and peace and joy in the Holy Ghost. Its dwelling-place and seat of power is in the inner life.

TO THE INNER LIFE

II

THE PICTURE OF JESUS IN THE SOUL

If this be true, it is perfectly natural, and altogether reasonable, that the earliest and clearest and most enduring manifestation of Christ should be in this region of man's inmost being. The traces of his presence in the world should be most distinct and most indelible in the records of spiritual experience. The evidences of his healing, harmonizing power should be found first and most abundantly in those underlying relations, those mysterious sentiments and propensities,—

"those obstinate questionings
Of sense and outward things,
Fallings from us, vanishings;
Blank misgivings of a creature
Moving about in worlds not realized,
High instincts before which our mortal Nature
Doth tremble like a guilty thing surprized:
Those first affections,
Those shadowy recollections,
Which, be they what they may,
Are yet the fountain light of all our day."

And so in fact we find it to be. The image of Jesus comes to light, first of all, in the spiritual experience of man. The earliest and the most wonderful picture of him is simply a living reflection of him in man's inner life.

Before we can discern any influence of his teaching, as a great reformer, upon the institutions of society; before we can perceive any effect of those large, simple truths which he brought to light, upon the orderly thinking of the world; before we can trace the rudest beginnings of Christian art, the most ancient formulas of Christian worship, the earliest foundations of Christian temples; yes, even before we can find any narrative of the life of Jesus, any collection of his sayings, any record of his deeds,—first of all, and most vivid of all, we see the person of Jesus printed upon the hearts and revealed in the letters of certain men who loved and trusted and adored him as their Saviour from sin.

In time, the Epistles come before the Gospels. I do not say they are more authentic, more precious, than the Gospels. I do not say they are ever to be read or interpreted apart from the Gospels. But I say they are sacred to all Christian hearts, because they are the place where we first catch sight of Jesus Christ in this world. And their personal testimony, their peculiar significance, their religious meaning, must never be forgotten or denied, if we want to know what Christ came to do, and what Christ really did, for the life of man.

For what are these Epistles? They are not formal treatises of theology, of ethics, of church government. They are simply transcripts of the spiritual experience of real men,—St. Peter and St. Paul and St. John, and perhaps some others whose names we do not know.

No one can doubt that the centre of these letters is Jesus Christ. He is their theme and their inspiration, their impulse and their aim. They are written in his name. They bear witness to his power, they glow with his praise. They are, first of all, and most of all, evidences of the place which Jesus held in the inner life of these men, testimonies to the change which he wrought in their souls,—a change so great, so deep, so joyful, that it was like a new birth, a veritable passing from death unto life. Listen to a description of this change, in words as fresh and glowing as if they had been written but yesterday:—

"Therefore if any man be in Christ, he is a new creature: old things are passed away; behold, all things are become new. And all things are of God, who hath reconciled us to himself by Jesus Christ, and hath given to us the ministry of reconciliation; to wit, that

God was in Christ, reconciling the world unto himself, not imputing their trespasses unto them; and hath committed unto us the word of reconciliation. Now then we are ambassadors for Christ, as though God did beseech you by us: we pray you in Christ's stead, be ye reconciled to God. For he hath made him to be sin for us, who knew no sin; that we might be made the righteousness of God in him."

This is an authentic description of the mission of Christ to the inner life of man. This is a reflection of what he really effected in the secret place of the human heart. This is the voice of that new tide of peace which silently rose through man's experience,—

> "*One common wave of thought and joy*
> *Lifting mankind again.*"

This is the original gospel, which began to win the world eighteen hundred years ago, and has never ceased to spread from heart to heart, from land to land, like music mixed with light.

And it is the faithful and persistent witness to this experience, more than anything else, that has made Christianity a world-religion. A changed heart, uttering its new-found felicity in sweet and searching tones,—this is the miracle that has drawn the attention of men, century after century, to the teachings of Christianity.

Its apostles won their way chiefly by the evidence which they gave that something had happened to transform their life at the fountain-head. The sense of *newness* in their souls was the source of their power. Whenever this sense of newness has faded and grown dim, the self-propagating force of Christianity has waned. Whenever this sense of newness has been deep and vivid, Christianity has advanced swiftly and found a wide welcome. Its most potent argument has been this simple and direct testimony to the pacification and renewal of the inner life by the acceptance of Jesus Christ as the Saviour.

I am not concerned at present to justify it, to defend it, to argue for its truth or its morality, to find a place for it in a system of theology or philosophy. What I want to do is to tell what it was; to show what it meant to the men who received it; to look at it, not as a theory, not as a doctrine, but as a spiritual experience; to let the inner life speak for itself about what Christ has done for the souls of those who have believed on him.

III

PEACE WITH GOD THROUGH CHRIST

That Christ's mission was one of joy and peace needs no proof. The New Testament is a book that throbs and glows with gladness. It is the one bright spot in the literature of the first century. The Christians were the happiest people in the world. Poor, they were rich; persecuted, they were exultant; martyred, they were victorious. The secret of Jesus, as they knew it,. was a blessed secret. It filled them with the joy of living. Their watchword was, "Rejoice and be exceeding glad."

But what were the elements of that joy? What was it that had entered into their inner life thus to transform and illuminate it?

To answer this question fully would be to give a summary of the primitive records of Christianity. All the manifold aspects of human existence were affected, unmistakably and immediately, by faith in Jesus Christ as the Son of God and the Saviour of men. Those who received him thus into their hearts felt that they were saved. And if one had asked them from what they were saved, doubtless they would have wondered at the question, and would have answered, "From everything

362

that brings trouble and fear and anguish and death into our souls."

The world looked to them like a new place, and they felt like new men. Sorrow was changed. Instead of a hopeless burden of affliction, it had become the means of working out for them a far more exceeding and eternal weight of glory. Death was changed. Instead of a gloomy shadow enveloping the end of all things, it had become the gateway into a world of light. Duty was changed. Instead of an impossible compliance with an inexorable law, it had become a new obedience with divine help to accomplish it. They felt that they had received power in the inner life to become the sons of God. And the chief element in this power, according to their own testimony, was the sense of deliverance from the weight, the curse, the condemnation of sin, through the work of the Lord Jesus Christ.

It is of this strange and wonderful feeling of salvation from sin that I wish to speak more particularly, not as a doctrine, not as a theory, but as an actual fact brought by Christ into the inner life of man.

1. The normal Christian experience, as it is expressed by those who stand nearest to Christ, utters itself, first of all, as a great sense

of peace with God through something which Christ has done to sweep away the barrier of sin between the human and the divine.

Nowhere else in the world do we find such a deep and keen sense of sin, and of its three deadly facts, as Henry Drummond calls them, —its power, its stain, and its guilt; nowhere else in the world do we find these facts so clearly recognized, so profoundly felt, as in the New Testament.

In many of our modern religious writers this sense of sin seems to be a vanishing quantity. Mr. Gladstone says: "They appear to have a very low estimate both of the quantity and the quality of sin; of its amount, spread like a deluge over the world, and of the subtlety, intensity, and virulence of its nature." It is chiefly in the secular writers, the dramatists like Ibsen, the novelists like Hardy, that we find a full and clear recognition of the facts of moral evil to-day. And they offer no remedy, give no hope.

But when we turn back to the New Testament we come into touch with men who faced the facts, and, at the same time, felt that they had found the cure.

Nothing that Jesus said or did, led his disciples to minimize or disregard sin, to cover it up with flowers, to transform it into a mere defect or mistake, to deny its reality and explain it away, to say

"The evil is naught, is null, is silence implying sound."

The whole effect of his mission, whatever form it may have taken, whatever its teaching may have been,—its undeniable effect was to intensify and deepen the consciousness of sin as a fatal thing from which men must needs be saved.

"This is the condemnation," says St. John, "that light is come into the world, and men loved darkness rather than light, because their deeds were evil." [1] "All have sinned and come short of the glory of God," says St. Paul; "death passed upon all men, for that all have sinned." [2] "For whosoever shall keep the whole law," says St. James, "and yet offend in one point, he is guilty of all." [3] "If we say we have not sinned," says St. John, "we make God a liar and his truth is not in us." [4]

But with this overwhelming sense of sin which Christ brought into the inner life, he brought also an equally great and deep sense of deliverance from it.

[1] St. John 3 : 19.
[3] St. James 2 : 10.
[2] Rom. 5 : 12.
[4] 1 John 1 : 10.

"There is therefore now no condemnation to them that are in Christ Jesus, who walk not after the flesh but after the Spirit." [1] "And you, being dead in your sins, hath he quickened together with him, having forgiven you all trespasses." [2] If any man "have committed sins, they shall be forgiven unto him." [3] "I write unto you, little children, because your sins are forgiven you for his name's sake." [4]

Now it is an extraordinary thing that men should speak thus, in one breath condemning themselves and in the next breath declaring their freedom from condemnation. And when we come to look into this strange utterance of the inner life, we find that it flows from a twofold experience.

2. First of all, there is a profound, unalterable conviction that the life and death of Jesus Christ are an expression of the forgiving love of God towards man. The old idea of God as a stern, angry, revengeful being, demanding and delighting in the death of the sinner, has vanished from the inner life of the true Christian. Somehow Christ has blotted it out. Somehow the Christian knows that God is love. And if we ask how he knows it, the answer is,

[1] Rom. 8 : 1.   [2] Col. 2 : 13.
[3] St. James 5 : 15.   [4] 1 John 2 : 12.

366

that the only begotten Son came forth from the bosom of the Father to reveal him. "Herein is love, not that we loved God, but that he loved us, and sent his Son to be the propitiation for our sins." [1] "God commendeth his love towards us, in that while we were yet sinners, Christ died for us." [2] All the meaning of Christ's life and death, with us and for us, hangs upon his being the true Son of God, the word of God, the brightness of the Father's glory and the express image of his person. It is this that makes us sure that God is not a fierce, vindictive, relentless God. He is more than a ruler, a judge of all the earth, an almighty king. He is our friend, the lover of our souls. He is willing to live among us, to suffer with us, to die for us.

The entire significance of Christ as a revelation of divine Love depends upon his real oneness with the Father, and the essential voluntariness of his sacrifice. It is not a punishment inflicted from without, by the inexorable law of God. It is a revelation made from within, by the immeasurable love of God, showing mercy at the heart of righteousness.

The faith in Christ's divinity underlies the faith in his sacrifice as an expression of the kind-

[1] 1 John 4 : 10.   [2] Rom. 5 : 8.

ness of God's heart. It could not speak to us of the love of God unless the love of God were in it. Love is the light within the lantern. There would be no colour in the glass, the figure of the crucifix would be black and indistinguishable, if it were not transfigured by that inner radiance.

The love of God goes before the gift of Christ. "God so loved the world that he gave his only begotten Son." He did not give his only begotten Son in order that he might learn to love the world.

The love was expressed not only in the life, it was summed up and crowned in the death, of Christ. "Greater love hath no man than this, that a man lay down his life for his friends."

Love's consummation is the cross. It is not intended to produce a change in the mind of God. It is intended to show what is already in the mind of God. It is not designed to make him feel differently towards men. It is designed to reveal what he has always felt.

Men say that repentance is the condition of forgiveness. Only let a man repent of his sin, only let him be sorry for it, and hate it, and turn to God, crying for pardon, and he shall be forgiven. This is an inspiring view of the readiness of divine mercy.

But the picture of Jesus in the soul, as it is drawn in the New Testament, goes far beyond the glory of this thought. It shows us that in Christ forgiveness is the creator of repentance. God is ready to forgive long before man is ready to repent. God gives his Son to die for us while we are yet sinners. At the heart of the gift lies the desire to make us sorry for our sins. "The goodness of God leadeth thee to repentance." [1] To forgive is divine; that comes first. To repent is human; that follows afterward.

In all the New Testament I can find no trace of the idea that Christ did anything, or needed to do anything, to make God love the world.

There is a noble passage in the works of St. Augustine, which sets forth the true image of Christ as the expression of God's readiness to forgive sins. "What is meant," he asks, "by 'being reconciled by the death of his Son'? Was it, indeed, so that when God the Father was angry with us he saw the death of his Son, and was appeased? Was, then, the Son already so appeased towards us that he was willing to die for us; while the Father was so angry that unless the Son had died he would not have been appeased? What does it mean,

[1] Rom. 2 : 4.

then, when the same teacher of the Gentiles
says, in another place, 'What shall we say to
these things? If God be for us, who can be
against us? He that spared not his own Son
but freely delivered him up for us all, how has
he not with him also freely given us all things?'
Unless the Father had been already appeased
would he have delivered up his own Son, not
sparing him for us? Is there not a contradiction between these two views? In the former
the Son dies for us, and the Father is reconciled
by his death. In the latter the Father, as if
out of love for us, does not spare the Son, but
himself, for our sake, delivers him up to death.
But I see that the Father loved us beforehand,
—not only before the Son died, but also before
the world was created, according to the testimony of the Apostle who says, 'He hath chosen
us in him before the foundation of the world.'
Nor was the Son unwillingly offered, for it is
said of him, 'Who loved me, and gave himself
for me.' Therefore together, both the Father
and the Son, and the Spirit of both, work all
things at the same time equally and harmo-
niously; yet we are justified in the blood of
Christ, and we are reconciled to God by the
death of his Son."

So stands the picture of Christ the mediator,

the reconciler, as it is reflected in the soul of those who first trusted in him.

His atonement does not reconcile God to the world. No need of that. God has loved the world forever. It does reconcile the world to God. Great need of that. For it breaks down the barrier of fear and mistrust; it rends the veil of dreadful dreams that sin has woven before the divine face, and discloses the countenance of a pitying, forgiving Father; it moves men to repentance by the mightiest force of mercy; it binds men to holy living by the enduring bonds of gratitude and love.

3. But could the sacrifice of Christ have meant this much to the inner life of man unless it had also meant something more? Suppose for a moment that the disciples had thought that it was not really a necessary sacrifice; that there was no reason why he should suffer, except perhaps that his sufferings might move their hearts; that his death was nothing more than the accidental consequence of his being entangled in a world like this; that God could have forgiven sin and would have forgiven sin in just the same way if there had been no crucifixion on Calvary. What then? Would Christ still have had the same atoning power to draw their hearts to God?

371

It is love that reconciles. And it is self-sacrifice that reveals love. But does an unnecessary sacrifice, a useless sacrifice, reveal love in a way that moves and compels our hearts? No, the moment we perceive that an offered proof of love has no relation to our real needs, and is not intended to do us any real good, it loses its power upon us, becomes unreal and futile.

Suppose, for example, that you are rowing a boat on a river, in no danger of any kind. A friend comes down to the shore and hails you; he tells you that he is about to show his devotion to you in a way that you cannot possibly doubt. He intends to give his life for you. So he throws himself into the water and is drowned. Are you impressed with gratitude and love? Is the proof of devotion so manifest and indubitable that you cannot resist it? Does it not seem more like a vain show of heroism, a display made not so much for your sake as for the sake of him who made it?

But if your boat had been sinking? Ah, then it would have been another matter. The man who gives up his life to rescue you from an actual peril, commands your love because he is your saviour. The crown of love is service. The glory of sacrifice is usefulness. The love of Christ, the sacrifice of Christ, draw their deepest power upon the inner life of man from the conviction they really have accomplished a deliverance for sinners from the guilt and curse and doom of sin.

The first message that the disciples received from the risen Jesus, while their minds were still overwhelmed by the apparent tragedy of the crucifixion, was the truth that it was not a useless loss, but a fruitful gain. The subject of his conversation with the two sad-hearted disciples on the road to Emmaus,—sad because they could not see why it was necessary for Christ to die,—the theme of his talk with them was the need of his death. "Ought not Christ to have suffered these things and to have entered into his glory?"

How much the first Apostles, who had been with Jesus from the beginning, who had loved him and trusted that he was the promised Redeemer of Israel,—how much these men needed this gospel of a real victory in his death, we who have always heard it, even though we may not have believed it, can hardly realize. Think what it must have meant to see the holy and loving Master die upon the cross. What a crushing catastrophe, what an inexplicable tragedy, what an irreparable loss for the world! How was it possible to have any trust in the wisdom and goodness of a God who would permit such a cruel disaster? How was it possible to have any hope for a humanity which had no other use for the perfect life than to blot it out in anguish and disgrace? Faith itself must have died with Christ, unless it had been able to discover a meaning, a purpose, a necessity, a triumph in his death great enough to make it the accomplishment of all that he had lived for. A bitter waste, or an unspeakable gain: those were the alternatives in the cross.

One would think that the words of Jesus while he was with the disciples had been clear enough to show them which was the true explanation. He had spoken of his death as inevitable; he had moved forward to it as the fulfilment of his mission; he had interpreted it as an infinite benefit to his disciples. "The Son of man came to give his life a ransom for many." "The bread that I will give is my flesh, which I will give for the life of the world." "Except a corn of wheat fall into the ground and die, it abideth alone; but if it die, it bringeth forth much fruit." "I, if I be lifted up, will draw all men unto me." "This cup is the New Covenant in my blood which is shed for many for the remission of sins."

But the meaning of these words was withheld from their eyes. They did not dare, they

374

were not willing to look the fact of Christ's coming death in the face, as he did. So its significance escaped them. It needed the lifting up of the cross, it needed the vision of the Master's death, to make them realize the true alternative.

On Calvary all was lost,—unless, on Calvary all was won! The disciples stood between utter despair and immeasurable hope. The risen Lord came back to tell them that all was won by the needful sacrifice of the cross. That is the testimony of the first Apostles.

Paul's testimony comes out of a different experience but leads to the same result. He had been an unbeliever in Jesus, a hater and a persecutor of the Nazarene. To him the man of Nazareth had appeared as a false prophet, a blasphemer. He found no fault with the death of Jesus from that point of view. It was not only necessary; it was desirable. Paul would have willingly consented to it, if he had been in the palace of Caiaphas, and in the judgment-hall of Pilate, and on the hill called Golgotha.

But when Paul was overwhelmingly convinced that he was wrong in his judgment of the Nazarene, his old point of view was utterly destroyed.

From the moment on the Damascus road

when Paul saw that the crucified Jesus whom
he had been persecuting was not a heretic Jew,
justly slain for his blasphemies, but the true
and living Christ of God,—from that moment
it became absolutely necessary for him to find
a new interpretation of the cross. He never
dreamed that it could be regarded as a mere
incident, a needless sacrifice, a disastrous close
of a beautiful life. It must be an essential element, an indispensable factor in the mission
of the Messiah. It must complete the revelation of God which was made in him. It must
be the corner-stone of that divine kingdom
which he came to establish.

This was the starting-point of Paul's theology. While he thought that Jesus was not
the Christ, he saw in the death on the cross
nothing but the punishment of the folly and
falsehood of the Nazarene. As soon as he was
convinced that Jesus really was the Christ,
the death on the cross was transformed into
the revelation of the righteousness and love of
God. There was no other alternative. The
sinless one, the glorious one, did not die for
sins of his own. He could not have died in
vain. Therefore he must have died for us.
God was manifest in him reconciling the world
unto himself.

This was certainly the interpretation which the Christians put upon the death of their Lord and Master on the cross. This was the effect that it actually wrought in their inner life. They did not deem it an accident, nor a catastrophe. It was not the defeat, nor merely the termination, of his work. It was the crown and consummation of his work. It gave Christ to them more than it took him from them. They did not think that he died for naught. His death for sinners was the greatest service that love could perform. It accomplished and declared God's righteousness in the remission of sins that are past. It made it possible for God to be just and the justifier of him who believeth in Jesus.

The Apostles did not teach that forgiveness could not have taken place without the crucifixion of Christ. They kept within the horizon of experience. They testified of what they knew, and bore witness of what they had seen.

They simply taught that, without the death of Christ, forgiveness would not have been what it is. They taught it because they felt it. They did not dream that the tragedy of the cross made any change in God. But they were sure that it made a change in the relation of the sinful world to God. It took away the curse of the law. It blotted out the handwriting of ordinances. It redeemed us. It brought us near to God. It put away sin. It cleansed us from sin in the blood of Christ. It is the one offering by which Christ hath perfected them that are sanctified.

Now, what were the secret laws and what were the mysterious relations of the world to God which made this offering of the sinless life of Jesus necessary for the rescue of mankind from sin, no man knoweth, nor can any man explain them and set them in order. But their existence does not depend upon our knowledge of them. Nor is the satisfaction of them rendered unreal by our ignorance of the way in which they are satisfied. If God is such a being as the moral ruler of the universe must be, it is not to be expected that we should be able to fathom the necessities which are present to his mind. There must be a world of eternal laws and wants and needs lying about us of which we can form no adequate conception. Into this world Christ entered by his death. Whatever was needed there for the forgiveness and blotting out of man's sin he provided. Whatever the law required for its righteous vindication he performed. It was the Father's will that he should die to redeem men; and so he died, and men were redeemed.

Thus the atonement appears in the New Testament. Not only from the side of man, but also from the side of God, it is the supremely necessary, and the supremely successful, peace-making sacrifice. "Therefore, being justified by faith, we have peace with God through our Lord Jesus Christ."

IV

NEWNESS OF LIFE

What forgiveness would have been without Christ (if it were possible), no man knows.

What forgiveness is in Christ, what it means to "have redemption through his blood, even the forgiveness of sins,"—this is the gospel that rings like music through the whole New Testament. It is inward peace, and secret joy, and newness of life. ·

An experience like this cannot possibly be expressed in any language that is fixed and formal. It must utter itself in vital speech because it is a vital experience. The attempt to transform any of the glowing words which the Apostles use to describe it into an abstract, scientific definition inevitably results in a mis-

379

representation. The attempt to interpret any
of the terms which are associated with the experience of atonement as if they described legal
transactions or artificial adjustments destroys
their real significance as utterances of conscious
life.

Take, for example, Paul's famous phrase,
"justified by faith." Suppose we attempt to
define that by making it mean that the guilt
of the sinner has been legally transferred to
Christ, and the merits of Christ have been
legally transferred to the sinner; so that Christ
on the cross is declared guilty and is punished
for sin, while the sinner, believing, is pronounced
righteous and escapes from punishment. What
effect would such an idea of the atonement
have upon the inner life? Apart from the
frightful confusion which it must introduce
into the moral sense to think of God as the
author of such an arrangement, what conceivable influence of a real and permanent nature
could such a thought have upon the soul? Does
it bring inward happiness to a man's heart to
be pronounced righteous when he knows that
he is still unrighteous? Does it give a man
inward peace to be set free from punishment
when he is conscious that the evils which de-
served it are still within him? Does it reconcile

a man's inner life with God to have the righteousness of another person attributed to him
by a legal fiction, while his own soul is still out
of harmony with God?

Merely to put these questions is to answer
them. No; if Christ's mission is to the inner
life, then his work in the inner life must be real
and vital. In this region there is no room for
anything that is merely formal and artificial.
There is no room for what Phillips Brooks calls
"the fantastic conception of the imputation to
Christ of a sinfulness which was not his, of
God's counting him guilty of wickedness which
he had never done." There is no legal fiction
in the real atonement. God is not a maker of
fiction, nor can the inner life of man be satisfied with formalities. The human heart revolts
at the idea of the punishment of the innocent
in the place of the guilty. Those instincts which
lie deeper than all reasoning, are insulted and
wounded by the thought of the arbitrary transfer of the merits of one person to the credit of
another person. The moral sense could never
find peace in the contemplation of such a purely
forensic transaction.

But the testimony of the Apostles is that
their moral sense, their conscience, actually
did find peace through the atonement as they

believed in it. "Justification by faith," as they use the words, must therefore mean something very different from the definition which has sometimes been given to it. It must mean that righteousness is not merely imputed, but actually imparted through faith. It must mean that sinners are not merely declared just, but actually made just, by Christ's work as the Saviour. It is not justification of law, it is "justification of life." [1]

There is not a single passage in the New Testament where the merits of one person are transferred, or reckoned, or counted to another. But there are a hundred passages where the righteousness and obedience of Christ are spoken of as the source of a new righteousness, a new obedience in us. "How much more shall the blood of Christ purge your conscience from dead works to serve the living God." [2] "Elect according to the foreknowledge of God the Father, through sanctification of the Spirit, unto obedience and sprinkling of the blood of Christ." [3] "Our Saviour Jesus Christ, who gave himself for us that he might redeem us from all iniquity and purify unto himself a peculiar people, zealous of good works." [4] "If

[1] Rom. 5 : 18.   [2] Heb. 9 : 14.
[3] 1 Pet. 1 : 2.   [4] Titus 2 : 14.

we walk in the light as he is in the light, we have fellowship one with another, and the blood of Jesus Christ his Son cleanseth us from all sin." [1]

What, then, does Paul mean when he says that "faith is counted for righteousness"? [2] He means not that faith is taken in the place of righteousness, as if it were enough for a man to believe that Christ was holy without making any effort to attain to holiness himself. He means that faith is regarded as an actual beginning of righteousness, a seed of divine promise and power in the soul of man, to be unfolded, by the grace of God, into a holy life. He means that there is infinitely more hope and potency of goodness in the man who trusts in God's mercy to save him, and in God's holiness to purify him, and in God's grace to make him righteous, than there is in the man who tries to work out salvation in his own strength according to the law. This is Paul's personal consciousness of the atonement. It is not the peace of death: it is the peace of new life joined to God. It involves a spiritual crucifixion with Christ unto sin. It involves also a real resurrection with Christ unto righteousness. "Therefore we are buried with him by baptism into

[1] 1 John 1 : 7.   [2] Rom. 4 : 5.

death, that like as Christ was raised up from the dead by the glory of the Father, even so we should walk in newness of life." [1]

Newness of life,—new hopes, new powers, new inspiration, new courage,—that is the practical side of regeneration. And that, according to the New Testament, is the result of the atonement which Christ brings into the inner life of man.

Paul was certainly the one writer among the Apostles who took the most legal point of view in considering the work of Christ. His temperament, his training, inclined him to this method of thought and expression. He was the lawyer of the gospel. But Paul never for a moment dreamed that his forensic figures of speech exhausted or limited the meaning of the gospel.

Nothing could be more absurd, more false to the facts, than to make the message of Paul a mere gospel of escape from the law by belief in the vicarious sacrifice of Christ. Such a view of his gospel would make it and keep it a purely legal gospel. Satisfaction of the law would be still its main theme and motive. It would differ from the religion of the Pharisees only in the way in which it proposed to satisfy

[1] Rom. 6 : 4.

the law. It would present a view of justification based upon a different ground indeed, but which in its results, if they did not go beyond escape from the law, would be just as incomplete, just as formal, just as dead, as justification by works.

Paul's message was certainly a gospel of escape from the law; but it was that because it was something infinitely more. It was *the gospel of escape into life.*

This was the new birth that came to him when he saw Christ. In the old life his chief concern had been to fulfil the demands of the law; and that was not really a life at all; it was a kind of death, not only because it was a hopeless struggle, but also because it was a subordination of the inward to the outward, of the vital to the formal, of the spirit to the letter. In the new life Paul felt that he was set free from the task of fulfilling the law, not merely because Christ had satisfied all its conceivable demands, but also because Christ had brought him into an utterly different relation to God; not outward, but inward; not formal, but vital; not artificial, but spiritual.

Paul's message was more than a doctrine of law satisfied in Christ. It was a proclamation of life begun in Christ. There was as much righteousness in this new life as there was in the old law. But it was a new kind of right-eousness. Certainly it was not a fictitious kind of righteousness, a mere legal justification, a formal transfer of the merits of Christ, by some mysterious decree of a supreme court, to the credit of the believer. It was a real righteous-ness, living and working itself out in the life of man. But it differed from the old righteous-ness in two things. First, in its origin: it was not human, but divine; and therefore it must be received by faith. Second, in its operation: it was not conformity to a rule, but guidance by the Spirit; and therefore it must be per-fected by love.

Paul's teaching amounts to this. We are not saved through law; we are saved through life. Life does not mean outward obedience. That is only the shell of life. Real life means faith and hope and love. The only source of this life is in God. Christ alone brings this life near to us, makes it accessible, sweeps away all hindrances, and invites us to enter into it by giving ourselves entirely to him. To live, according to Paul, means to believe in Christ, to hope in Christ, and to love Christ, because he is the human life of God, "delivered for our offences and raised again for our justification." [1]

[1] Rom. 4 : 25.

TO THE INNER LIFE

Mark well the words. Why *"raised again for our justification"*? If the taking away of our sins means only the release from their punishment because he has borne them upon the cross, then his resurrection makes no difference in the result. If our justification means only the imputation of the merit of his obedience and the value of his sacrifice to our account, then his rising again from the dead has nothing to do with it. Everything would be secure, whether he rose, or whether he did not rise.

Why *"raised again for our justification"*? Because the taking away of our sins means an actual separation from sin by union with the crucified Christ. Because our justification means a living entrance into his righteousness in the risen life. The mission of Christ to the inner life was just this: to make such an atonement that sin should no more divide the soul from God: to make such an atonement that the broken law should no more keep the soul at enmity with God: to make such an atonement that the inner life of all who truly live, should be "not unto themselves, but unto him who died for them and rose again."

V

THE FULNESS OF ATONEMENT

ATONEMENT is the word that seems best fitted to express the meaning of the gospel of Christ in relation to a world of sin. I have used it thus far without defining it, for three reasons.

First, because a final definition is impossible. The work of Christ for the saving of sinners can never be confined within the phrases which men invent to describe what they can see of it. It overflows the boundaries. Its fulness makes it indefinable.

Second, because the very attempt to define it has so often led to misconception and strife between men who believed in it with equal sincerity. I have read many books on the atonement. If the titles and references were given here, they would fill several pages. In almost all of these books I have found truth; in none of them the whole truth. The writers have helped me most when they have expressed their own experience of the saving power of

Christ. They have helped me least when they have been making definitions to shut out and condemn the views of other writers. Yet even in this they have not been altogether unprofitable. An attack upon a book has often led me to read it sympathetically, and so to discover in it a new source of illumination, a new testimony of experience.

The third reason why I have not tried to give a definition of the atonement is because it is not needed. The word is clear enough and plain enough already. It denotes a certain mystery,—the entire work of Christ in reuniting man to God,—the perfect result of that work in the establishment of peace between man and God,—the redeeming relation of that work to human sin,—the satisfying relation of that work to divine righteousness,—it denotes a mystery, but it denotes it in language which brings it into analogy with things that we know, and throws upon it light enough to enable us to see at least some of its essential elements.

What is this word, *atonement*, and where does it come from? It comes directly out of human life and experience. It is derived from an older word, "*onement*," which means unity or concord. To set two persons or things "at onement" means to bring them together in harmony after discord. Atonement is simply the process, or the result of reuniting and reconciling those who have been separated. Thus, in Shakespeare's *Richard III*, Buckingham says to the Queen:

> "*Ay, madame; he desires to make atonement*
> *Between the Duke of Gloster and your brothers.*"

From this original and broadest meaning, the word is sometimes narrowed a little to denote some particular action or offering by which the reconciliation is effected. It may come either from one of the separated parties, or from a third person who offers himself as a reconciler. But in any case three elements must always enter into the idea of an atonement.

First, the motive of it must be love. It cannot possibly spring from any other cause. Justice, or righteousness, or authority,—and least of all anger or hate,—would never account for the desire of making a reconciliation. It can only come from a sincere love for the persons to be reconciled, and an earnest wish that they shall love each other.

Second, the condition under which this love works is the sense of a present separation, arising out of a fault, an offence, which has created

390

a real obstacle between the persons who are separated.

Third, the purpose which this love has in view is a real state of harmony, in which the persons who are to be brought together shall be vitally at one.

These, then, are the three marks of all atonement. Its creative cause is the power of love. Its occasional cause is the recognition of an offence. Its final cause is the restoration of vital union.

Atonements have been going on in the world from the beginning; between man and man, and between man and God. Those who have been conscious of injury and offence against their fellow-men have been trying to make some reparation, to show some contrition for the wrong, and to reëstablish peace. Those who have been grieved at the prevalence of enmity and strife among their friends have been trying to bring about reconciliation, by mediating between the offended and the offender.

This mediation involves suffering and sacrifice on the part of the peacemaker. It is hardly possible to obtain forgiveness and love for a guilty person without bearing something of his pain and punishment. Many a father has suffered for the sake of making peace among his children who were at strife. Many a mother has borne not only grief, but also actual trouble and loss, for the sake of reconciling a rebellious boy to an offended father. Many a brother has shared the disgrace and paid the debts of a brother for the sake of bringing him back into the harmony of the social order. And in such sufferings of love for the cause of atonement there is always something which propitiates the heart and inclines it to show favour. The father's compassion towards an erring son is always quickened by the thought of the mother's love as expressed in sacrifice. The sentiment of society, which after all is the final earthly court of appeal in all questions of conduct, is certainly affected favourably towards an offender by the fact that an innocent friend is willing to stand beside him and share in some degree the consequences of his fault. All this is of the nature of atonement, and there is no corner of the world where the letters of this word may not be spelled out, like a dim and broken inscription, on the fragments of human life.

The same word runs through the history of religion from the beginning until now. Sacrifice is another way of spelling it; and sacrifice is primitive and universal.

THE FULNESS OF ATONEMENT

"Both for themselves and those who call them friend" men have not only prayed, but also presented gifts and offerings to God, in the desire to take away the obstacle of sin and reconcile the human heart to him.

Atonement is spoken of in the Old Testament in many places. It is said that an atonement was made when Moses interceded for the people at Sinai,[1] when Aaron burned incense in the midst of the congregation,[2] when Phinehas executed judgment on Zimri,[3] and when Nehemiah established ordinances in the restored city of Jerusalem.[4] The Hebrew word which is used in these passages, and in many others where some form of the verb "to atone" occurs in our English version, is from a root which means "to cover." It carries with it the idea of guilt which needs to be expiated. But the object of the expiation is the renewal of fellowship between man and God. Sacrifice has this twofold meaning. The slaying of the victim is the confession that sin deserves punishment. The offering of the blood, which is the sign of the life, is the utterance of the worshipper's desire to return into union with God.

Now all these kinds of atonement, which men

[1] Ex. 32 : 30.   [2] Num. 16 : 46.
[3] Num. 25 : 13.   [4] Neh. 10 : 33.

have been making through the centuries, and are making still, are but shadows and reflections of the great work which Christ came to do for a sinful world. Its purpose and design, its nature and conditions, the depth of its motive and the breadth of its scope, cannot be expressed by any lesser, narrower, more precise word.

It takes up into itself the significance of all sincere and pure sacrifices which have been offered on human altars, visible and invisible. Christ is the eternal embodiment of the sacrificial spirit.[1]

It utters the great peace-making desire of all those blessed human mediators who have laboured and suffered to bring together divided hearts and to restore harmony between discordant lives.[2] In this light it reveals Christ as standing between God and man, and touching both the human and the divine.

It is the perfect consummation of all those imperfect offerings which have been made in behalf of those who are guilty, to propitiate One who has a right to be offended with them. In this sense Christ appears as the High Priest of sinful and repentant humanity.[3]

It is the divine interpretation and consecra-

[1] Heb. 9 : 26.   [2] Eph. 2 : 14–18.   [3] Heb. 10 : 10–14.

tion of all those royal acts of compassion and mercy in which men and women who have been sinned against have expressed their forgiveness and sought to win their enemies back to peace. In this aspect Christ is revealed as the incarnate love of God, coming forth from the bosom of the Father, to seek and to save his lost children.[1]

No word which fails to cover all these meanings, no word which sharply emphasises one side of the truth at the expense of the other sides, no word which leaves out of its significance the sweetness of any of those things most "pure and lovely and of good report" which have been done in the spirit of reconciliation, is broad enough to describe the work of Christ in closing the gulf which sin had made between man and God. Sacrifice is not broad enough. Mediation is not broad enough. Propitiation is not broad enough. Redemption is not broad enough. Substitution is not broad enough. Satisfaction is not broad enough. Embracing all these things, Christ's work goes beyond them all. It is simply *the fulness of atonement*.

The word occurs but once in the English version of the New Testament, in a passage

[1] 1 John 3 : 16.

395

where St. Paul declares that "we joy in God through our Lord Jesus Christ, by whom we have now received the atonement."[1] But the same Greek noun which is here rendered "atonement," occurs again in a later verse, where he speaks of "the reconciling of the world,"[2] and in a still more important passage of another epistle, where he describes the gospel as "the word of the reconciliation," and the preacher's work as "the ministry of the reconciliation."[3] The translation should be made uniform in all three places. Then we should have "the atonement of the world," "the word of the atonement," and "the ministry of the atonement."

This would prepare us to appreciate the full force of another passage in which we find, not the noun, but the verb from which it is derived, in an intensive form which gives it new value, and in a connection which seems to pour fresh light upon it from all sides of human experience. The classic passage on the atonement is in the first chapter of the Epistle to the Colossians, and the central idea of it is in the twentieth verse, in which St. Paul declares that it pleased the Father, by Christ, "to atone all things with himself; by him, I say, whether they be things in earth, or things in heaven."

[1] Rom. 5 : 11.   [2] Rom. 11 : 15.   [3] 2 Cor. 5 : 18, 19.

THE FULNESS OF ATONEMENT

Go backward and forward from this point, and see how many meanings converge in St. Paul's idea of the great atonement. Deliverance from the power of darkness;[1] redemption through Christ's blood, even the forgiveness of sins;[2] a new birth from the dead;[3] peace-making by the cross;[4] the winning back of enemies;[5] the taking away of blame and reproof;[6] the interpretation of human sufferings in fellowship with the afflictions of Christ;[7] and finally the making known of the riches of the glory of a mystery, "which is Christ in you, the hope of glory."[8] This, indeed, is atonement made perfect.

The perfection of it lies in the fulness and clearness with which it embodies and expresses the three essential elements of all lesser atonements. Its purpose is a true, deep, eternal harmony of spirit between man and God, a peace which the world can neither give nor take away. Its condition of operative power is a full acknowledgment of the immense obstacle which sin has put between man and God. Its motive is pure and perfect love,—the love which meets all needs as man feels them in his repentant heart,—the love which passeth

[1] vs. 13. [2] vs. 14. [3] vs. 18. [4] vs. 20.
[5] vs. 21. [6] vs. 22. [7] vs. 24. [8] vs. 27.

397

knowledge in its power to cover the whole mystery of sin as it is known to God alone.

I

THE LOVE THAT MEETS ALL NEEDS

There is no truly Christian view of the atonement which does not begin with the love of God. This love involves the primal purpose of self-revelation, of union with man, of a divine incarnation. There is a gospel, a promise of God's communication of himself to man, in the very act of creation. "The faith of the atonement presupposes the faith of the incarnation."

If this be true, it follows that we may believe that the Son of God would have come into the world whether man had sinned or not. God has chosen and loved mankind in his Son before the foundation of the world. There is a profound truth in the saying of Robertson of Brighton, "God's idea of humanity is, *and ever was*, humanity as it is in Jesus Christ."

Atonement, therefore, is the form which is given to the incarnation by the presence of sin in the world. Christ would have come to us as the revealer of the divine love, even though the world had never been separated from God. But because the separation had actually taken place, because man had offended against God, and departed from his ideal, and fallen into enmity with him, Christ must reveal the divine love as a suffering love, a sacrificial love, a reconciling love, in order to bring man back to God.

This atoning form of incarnation appears to us more glorious, more wonderful, than any other form, because it costs more: It is love put to the test. It is love overcoming obstacles. It is love militant and victorious. And its perfection is manifest in the freedom and fulness with which it meets all the needs imposed by the fact of sin.

Our consciousness of these needs is the measure of our power to understand the atonement. But beyond this consciousness there is another region wherein the results of evil, the disorders which it has introduced into the world, surpass our comprehension. In that region we cannot fully understand the atonement. We can only accept it, and rest upon it, as a great fact through which the concord of an untuned universe is restored, and infinite mercy is harmonized with infinite justice in the redemptive government of the world.

In music there are notes too high and too low for us to hear. But the chord which fills

the range of our hearing with harmony must
be harmonious also in the undertones and over-
tones. Our faith in the unmeasured values of
the atonement in the spheres beyond our ken
is inseparably connected with an experience of
its active power to meet our conscious wants
as sinful men.

What are these wants? They spring from
the four elements which are present in the sense
of sin,—the shame of impurity, the pain of
bondage, the apprehension of guilt, and the
hope of mercy. To these four elements, and
to the needs which arise out of them, there are
four things in the atonement which correspond,
—a power to cleanse the soul, a power to liberate the life, a power to satisfy the law, and a
power to reveal forgiveness. And these four
things are spoken of in the New Testament
under four principal expressions,—a sin-offer-
ing;[1] a ransom;[2] a satisfaction, the payment
of a debt;[3] and a reconciliation.[4]

There is a famous passage in Coleridge's
Aids to Reflection in which he explains that
these expressions are figures of speech, which
do not describe the real nature of the atone-

[1] Heb. 9 : 19–28; 1 John 1 : 7; Rev. 1 : 5.
[2] 1 Tim. 2 : 6; Gal. 4 : 5; Eph. 1 : 7; Col. 1 : 14.
[3] Gal. 5 : 3; 2 Cor. 5 : 21; 1 Pet. 3 : 18.
[4] Eph. 2 : 14, 16; 2 Tim. 2 : 5.

ment, but only illustrate "the nature and extent of the consequences and effects of the atonement, and excite in the receivers a due sense of the magnitude and manifold operation of the boon, and of the love and gratitude due to the Redeemer."

I should accept the positive part of Coleridge's explanation, but I should reject the negative part of it.

Undoubtedly these metaphors are intended to express the great benefits which sinners receive from the atoning work of Christ. They describe the results which it produces in the consciousness of man,—a sense of cleansing from defilement, a sense of deliverance from slavery, a sense of being right with the law, and a sense of God's willingness to pardon. These are subjective effects. They are within us. But do they not belong to the real nature and intention of the atonement? Are they not clear indications of its purpose and meaning? Is not this complete reconciliation with God, in spite of sin, precisely what it was intended to accomplish? Are not these consequences in man's spiritual consciousness just as real, just as veritable, as any other consequences that we can imagine?

The atonement, as has been said, "is the

meeting-point of the objective and subjective elements of Christianity." It covers all the ground that lies between God and man, so far as sin has touched it. It has a reference to every element of the divine nature which condemns sin, and to every element of human nature which is affected by sin. It acts directly upon the divine will and upon the human will. There is no possible metaphor, drawn from any real relation of man to God, which is without its value in illustrating the real nature of the atonement.

So far, then, from denying the verity of these four figures of speech, we should accept them as expressions of substantial truth. We should seek to make them as real and living as possible in our own experience. And we should go back to the New Testament to see if there are not other metaphors of the atonement which fit in with our consciousness of need as sinners.

There are four other figures of speech, less familiar, and less frequently used, which throw new light upon the subject. They are used by Christ himself to describe the effects of his sacrifice. It would be well if they were taken more deeply into our conception of the atonement.

The first figure is the metaphor of germination. "Except a corn of wheat fall into the ground and die, it abideth alone: but if it die, it bringeth forth much fruit." [1] This means that Christ's death is the means of communicating new life—pure, holy, immortal—to the souls of men. It answers to the need which springs out of the shame of sin as the conscious deadening of the higher life.

The second figure is the metaphor of vicarious suffering. "I am the good shepherd: the good shepherd giveth his life for the sheep." [2] This means that because Christ loves us, and has identified himself with us, he is willing to die for us in order to rescue us from sin, the robber of our souls. It is another aspect of redemption, the ransom of a life willingly laid down for others in the conflict with evil. It answers to the painful sense of helplessness in our struggles to escape from sin. It is the voice of the victor who stands by the vanquished and promises deliverance.

The third figure is the metaphor of consecration. "For their sakes I sanctify myself, that they also might be sanctified through the truth." [3] This means that Christ's death is the completion of his holy obedience to God. It is more than the payment of a debt exacted

[1] St. John. 12 : 24.   [2] St. John 10 : 11.   [3] St. John 17 : 19.

403

by the law. It is the fulfilment of a service prompted by love. "Lo, I come to do thy will, O God." [1] And so it becomes in us the spirit of a new obedience.

The fourth figure is the metaphor of a new covenant of pardon. "This is my blood of the new covenant, which is shed for many for the remission of sins." [2] This means that Christ's death is the seal of God's entering into a new engagement with us, not of works, but of grace, in which he will deal with us as a father, forgiving our sins for his name's sake. An ancient covenant was always sealed with blood. But it was not made on account of the blood. That was simply the sign of the solemnity and binding force of the engagement. The covenant itself rested upon the willingness of both parties to enter into it and to keep it. Christ's death does not make God willing to forgive. It reveals his forgiveness as ready and waiting for us to claim it.

Now take these four latter metaphors of the effects of the atonement in its relation to us, and lay them beside the four others which are more familiarly employed. See how they mutually illuminate one another, and how the light which comes from each reminds us that

[1] Heb. 10 : 9.   [2] St. Matt. 26 : 28.

THE FULNESS OF ATONEMENT

no one of them can be interpreted alone as the
secret of "the true doctrine of atonement."

There is a sacrificial element in it, assuredly.
It is an offering for sin. But it is not in any
sense an offering which is separate from us. It
is implanted in us, in our human nature, as a
seed is planted in the earth, to germinate and
bear fruit.

There was a substitution on Calvary. But
it was not the substitution of a sinless Christ
for a sinful race. It was the substitution of
humanity with Christ, for humanity without
Christ. He bore our sins, not apart from us,
but with us. He expressed, in his willing submission to the death of the cross, the ideal and
representative repentance of mankind for sin.
And this sacrifice is the sufficient atonement
for the original sin of the whole race. He is
joined by his cross to every sinful soul that
repents of actual sin, and thus there is no further need of sacrifice, since the offering of Christ
abides forever and germinates in each heart
that believes in him. To be crucified with
Christ is to feel the guilt of sin in like manner
(though never in like degree) as he felt it. It
is to acknowledge the righteousness of the law
which condemns sin, even as he acknowledged

it by suffering with the race which lay under condemnation. It is to present to God, by faith, our lesser sacrifices of a broken and a contrite spirit, not now standing alone in their imperfection, but purified and made precious by union with that perfect sacrifice in which Jesus Christ poured out his soul unto death.

There is also a redemptive element in the atonement, undoubtedly. It is a ransom which emancipates us from the tyranny of evil. But it is not, as the patristic writers imagined, a ransom paid to the devil. There is no trace of such an idea in the New Testament. It is, as Christ himself teaches us, a victory over the evil one. It is our ransom, just as the death of a heroic leader who conquers in a good cause and in conquering dies, is the ransom of his people from defeat and slavery. The liberating power of Christ's death for us is never to be separated from his spiritual victory over evil, nor from the courage which it inspires in our hearts to know that we have such a mighty, faithful, triumphant Shepherd.

There is also an element of satisfaction to the righteous law in the atonement, undoubtedly. Christ fulfilled all that the law of God required. He paid the debt of righteousness to the full. But the emphasis in this satisfaction is not to be laid exclusively, nor chiefly, upon his sufferings, but upon his holiness, upon his willing and complete obedience to the Father in all things. As St. Bernard said, *Non mors, sed voluntas placuit sponte morientis.*

The value and meaning of Christ's atonement as a satisfaction depend upon the connection of his sufferings and death with his perfect life. It was "the mind that was in Christ Jesus" that made him "obedient unto death, even the death of the cross." [1] That mind of obedience was the priceless jewel worth more than enough to pay the whole debt of righteousness.

The truth of this view is self-evident. How can we think of it in any other way? Suppose for a moment that Christ had died in infancy. Suppose that instead of escaping into Egypt with the Virgin Mary and St. Joseph, the babe Jesus had been slain with the other children of Bethlehem. His death would still have been the sacrifice of an innocent victim. It would still have shown the hatefulness and cruelty of human sin. It might still be regarded, in imagination, as the substitution of the guiltless for

[1] Phil. 2: 5-8.

407

the guilty. It might still be defined, by a legal fiction, as the transference of a penalty to one who had not transgressed. It might still be presented, by a purely forensic theory, as an exhibition of a supposed vindictive element in the law, which could only be satisfied by the shedding of innocent blood. All this might still be attributed to the death of Christ if it had befallen him in helpless infancy. But would it then have been, in any satisfactory sense, an atoning sacrifice? Would it have had any power to really reconcile our hearts with the law which requires righteousness?

No, a thousand times no! That which gives the obedience of the cross its reconciling power is the fact that it was voluntary suffering, holy suffering, suffering which made Christ perfect,[1] the crown and consummation of his patient, faithful, self-denying, stainless life.

It is only when we look at it in this way that the holiness of Christ becomes, not the substitute for our holiness (which would contradict the spirit of the law), but the source of our holiness,—the consecration of our Kinsman High-Priest, in which and by which the consecration of his brethren is secured.[2] "Christ is the end of the law for righteousness to every one

[1] Heb. 2 : 10.   [2] Heb. 2 : 11-18.

that believeth." [1] Thus, and thus only, the law is satisfied in him.

Once more, there is a reconciling element in the atonement, undoubtedly. It does remove a real obstacle between man and God. It does bring God nearer to man, in order that man may come close to God. But this obstacle is never to be thought of as an unwillingness on God's part to pardon and restore the guilty. This reconciliation is always to be interpreted in the light of Christ's word of "the new covenant," freely and gladly made by the divine mercy, and sealed with the most holy seal in the universe,—"the precious blood of Christ, as of a lamb without blemish and without spot." [2]

The atonement, then, is never to be regarded as the cause of God's grace. It is the result and the seal of his grace. It is the channel made by grace, through which all the blessed effects of the divine love may flow, across the bitter waste that sin has made, to all who hunger and thirst after righteousness, in order that they may be filled.

If any one should ask, therefore, "What has the atonement done for you?" our answer

[1] Rom. 10 : 4.   [2] 1 Pet. 1 : 19.

should be broad enough to cover all our needs. With Christ God has freely given us all things: an assurance of mercy, divinely sealed; a satisfaction of the law, divinely perfected; a ransom from evil, divinely accomplished; a sacrifice for sin, divinely offered; a covenant of peace; a spirit of consecration; a good Shepherd of our souls; a seed of everlasting life,—and if there be any other thing that sinners need for their salvation, doubtless this also is in the atonement.

The only false view is that which questions the reality of any of these blessings. The only dangerous view is that which interprets any one of them in such a way as to make it merely formal and artificial, and to deny the necessity of the others. All views are true which recognize, through experience, the love of God in Christ meeting any of our needs as sinful men, and which preserve a grateful openness of heart to welcome every new ray of light that comes from the cross through the experience of other men.

After all is said, out of the fulness of each ransomed heart, there still remains a secret reason for gratitude, unuttered because not yet perfectly realized. "Thanks be unto God for his *unspeakable* gift." [1]

[1] 2 Cor. 9 : 15.

THE FULNESS OF ATONEMENT

II

If there is a mystery in sin, there must also be a mystery in the atonement.

We can know the love of God in Christ which meets all our conscious needs as sinners. But that love, as it makes provision for all the unsearchable necessities of God's moral government of the universe, must be a love that passeth knowledge.

There are some theologians who object strenuously to this acknowledgment of a mystery in the atonement. It seems to them that it leaves "in the very focus of revelation a spot of pure impenetrable black." I would rather say that it leaves a centre of "light inaccessible and full of glory."

The humility of partial knowledge is not the same as the despair of total ignorance. "We know in part, and we prophesy in part."[1] This was the last text from which President James McCosh spoke in the chapel of Princeton University. "We know in part," said he; "*but we know!*"

We know sin, for example, in its qualities and results, since they are manifested in human

[1] 1 Cor. 13:9.

life and in our own souls. But we do not perfectly know it; for its origin, and the secret forces which keep it alive and operative, though it be in itself a kind of death, and the strange subterranean relations which give it a unity amid all its diversity, and the mysterious power by which it destroys freedom of will while seeming to express it,—these things are hidden from us. They are inscrutable. Sin is a bottomless gulf. To account for it rationally would be to justify its existence. "Sin explained," said Dr. Edward G. Robinson, "would be sin defended." It is in fact a kind of reversed miracle. It is the action of the creature without the creator. It takes place in a sphere below the reach of our thought. It transcends reason,—*downward*.

It is fitting, therefore, it is altogether to be expected, that the atonement which is to take away sin should also transcend reason,—but *upward*. It ought to be, as it is, an inexplicable and unsearchable mystery of redeeming love, just as sin is an inexplicable and unsearchable mystery of enslaving hate. It ought to cover, as it does, all those secret relations in which the unity of righteousness consists, just as sin entangles the soul in that network of subtle bondage wherein the unity of evil consists.

THE FULNESS OF ATONEMENT

The atonement, in its divine essence, must go as far above our knowledge, as sin, in its mortal perversity, goes below it.

Consider the subject from another point of view. The atonement is undoubtedly the manifestation of God's mercy in harmony with his justice. But what are mercy and justice, in our knowledge of them, but fragments of a great circle which sweeps far beyond our vision? So far as logic goes, the forgiveness of sins appears like an absolutely impossible thing. An offence once committed must stand on the books forever as a thing to be condemned and punished. So far as logic goes, the execution of absolute justice seems to be equally impossible. We have never seen it. We cannot conceive nor explain it. "Justice is a fragment, mercy is a fragment, mediation is a fragment; justice, mercy, mediation as a reason of mercy —all three; what indeed are they but great vistas and openings into an invisible world in which is the point of view which brings them all together."

And yet in this mysterious region into which the divine side of the atonement reaches, there are two things which we ought to believe, even though we cannot fully comprehend them.

THE FULNESS OF ATONEMENT

First, it is necessary to the reality of faith to believe that the atonement has a practical relation to God, an actual and direct effect upon the divine will as well as upon our will. "Christ's work can be regarded as efficacious in the justification and reconciliation of men only in so far as we, at the same time, recognize a reference of that work to God. Nay, rather, his saving operations upon men cannot be understood except it be presupposed that his doing and suffering for that end had also a value for God, whether that be expressed in the motives of satisfaction, merit, propitiation, or somehow otherwise."

Second, it is essential to the moral integrity of faith that we should believe that the divine justice and mercy, which are harmonized in the atonement, are not different in kind, but only in degree, from mercy and justice as they are revealed in our fragmentary knowledge. There can be no satisfaction of divine justice which does not justify itself in the moral sense. There can be no propitiation of mercy which introduces a conflict, or an appearance of conflict, among the attributes of God. Mercy must be merciful; and justice, just.

This shuts out at once the possibility of interpreting the mystery of atonement by analogy with ideas and figures drawn from imperfect and cruel systems of human government, or from corrupt and superstitious systems of religion. The notion of a God whose vindictive anger demands a precise equivalent of suffering as the condition of release from penalty does not belong to Christianity. It belongs to the moral ill-temper of a civilization which, like that of the middle ages or of the sixteenth and seventeenth centuries, was essentially harsh and cruel. It belongs to a conception of life in which law was relentless and vindictive,—in which men were hung for petty larceny and burned alive for heresy; in which war was simply a colossal public revenge, and a captured city was certain to be sacked. It belongs, in its religious kinship, to paganism, to fetichism, to the cruel, sensual religions of Mexico and Africa.

Shadows of their darkness have fallen upon the outer form of Christianity. Strange and uncouth words have found their way into the dogmatic books which vainly seek to reduce life to logic. Wild and wandering phrases of bewildered theologians have represented Christ as exposed to the divine wrath in our place, or as "wiping away the red anger-spot from the brow of God." Dismal echoes from the chants of blood-stained heathen temples have crept into the hymns of the church,—echoes which say that

"On Christ Almighty vengeance fell
Which must have sunk a world to hell,"

or that

"One rosy drop from Jesus' heart
Was worlds of seas to quench God's ire."

These echoes, these phrases, these words, have undoubtedly penetrated, in a wavering and uncertain way, into the ritual, the dogma, the outer circle, of Christianity. It seems as if, to use the expression of that great German theologian, Rothe, "in his work for man it were the constant fate of God to be misunderstood." But these misunderstandings cannot enter, and they have not entered, into the inner life where Christ is truly manifested as the living sacrifice and Saviour.

There is not a word in all the New Testament which implies that Christ offered a sacrifice to the anger of God. It is morally inconceivable that the Redeemer coming from the bosom of the Father to do his work should ever have been, in any sense, an object of the divine wrath. For that wrath, as we have already seen, is not a vindictive anger against sinners; it is a pure and holy indignation against sin. How, then, could it have rested for a single moment upon Christ?

Nor is there anything in the Bible to imply that Christ has taken that wrath against sin away. It still exists. It still hates and condemns sin as much as ever.

Christ delivers us from the fear of it, not by subjecting himself to it, but by separating us from the sin against which it is directed.

How, then, shall we interpret Christ's sufferings?

There was no infliction of punishment upon the innocent instead of the guilty. There was no transference of the demerits of the sinful to the sinless. Christ remained guiltless; man remained guilty. But Christ entered into humanity, freely, willingly, taking on himself all its limitations, burdens, pains, and sorrows. Christ lived and died with man and for man. He was not merely a substitute: he was a representative. He was not thrust into our place: he shared our lot; and if that sharing involved a sacrificial death upon the cross, if there was no other way in which he could be one with sinners, and make them one with himself, and lift them out of guilt and doom, save by dying for their sins, what then?

Does the recognition of this, as a mysterious

fact revealed in the crucifixion, cast any stain upon the justice of God? Not so thought Christ, who shrank from the cross, yet said, "Father, not my will, but thine be done." Not so thought the Apostles, who saw in Christ crucified the perfect revelation of the righteousness and love of God. Not so thought such a Christian as Phillips Brooks. The inner life of Christendom finds a true expression in his sermon on *The Conqueror from Edom*.

"My friends," he says, "far be it from me to read all the deep mystery that is in this picture. Only this I know is the burden and soul of it all, this truth, that sin is a horrible, strong, positive thing, and that not even Divinity grapples with him and subdues him except in strife and pain. What pain may mean to the Infinite and Divine, what difficulty may mean to Omnipotence, I cannot tell. Only I know that all that they could mean, they mean here. This symbol of the blood bears this great truth, which has been the power of salvation to millions of hearts, and which must make this conqueror the Saviour of your hearts, too, the truth that only in self-sacrifice and suffering could even God conquer sin. Sin is never so dreadful as when we see the Saviour with that blood upon his garments. And the Saviour himself

418

is never so dear, never wins so utter and so tender a love, as when we see what it has cost him to save us. Out of that love, born of his holy suffering, comes the new impulse after a holy life; and so, when we stand at last purified by the power of grateful obedience, binding our holiness and escape from our sin close to our Lord's struggle with sin for us, it shall be said of us that we have 'washed our robes and made them white in the blood of the Lamb.' "

That the divine mercy is satisfied in this conception of the atonement, no one can doubt. But how is the satisfaction of the divine justice manifested in this view? What glimpse does it give us of a holy law vindicated, an eternal righteousness maintained?

It seems to me that it certainly shows us one thing, however much it leaves still hidden from our knowledge in the unsearchable counsels of God. It shows us that God so honours and upholds the moral law by which he governs the world, that not even Christ could come into union with humanity, not even Christ could become man, without sharing the consequences of man's sin. Christ was not punished for sins that he had never done. Christ was not punished for our sins. Christ was not punished at all. But because our sins deserve punishment,

THE FULNESS OF ATONEMENT

Christ, having become one with us, endured the shame and the cross, poured out his soul unto death and was numbered with the transgressors, suffered and died as *the human life of God*, because suffering and death have justly come upon the world of sin.

This is indeed the noblest vindication of the law that we can possibly conceive. It elevates and illuminates the atonement, so that it shines far above us, as a mountain-peak of righteousness. It makes it a part of an eternal moral order, resting upon the very nature of God, and his relation to the world as its moral governor. It is a doctrine of majesty and power.

Forgiveness without atonement, if we could conceive of such a thing, would leave us far more in the dark, would present a far greater mystery. But forgiveness with atonement assures us that God is in eternal harmony with his own law. He has not permitted suffering and death to come into the world merely to execute a personal vengeance on sin as an insult offered to his majesty. They are the expression of an eternal and righteous mode of government. Their presence is necessary, and just, and consistent with God's goodness and love as well as with his wisdom and holiness. The Son of God, entering the world to redeem

420

it, not from without but from within, must submit to these conditions.

He could not be punished. That was impossible. But he could suffer and die. And so he did, confessing and glorifying the integrity and solidarity of God's attributes in the moral law of the universe.[1]

Wherein that solidarity consists, what is the eternal fitness and propriety of atonement by sacrifice and suffering, we can neither fully understand nor perfectly explain. "The nature of the redemptive act in itself is not to be compassed nor uttered by the language of human understanding." When we look upon it "we are in the presence of forces which issue from infinity, and pass out of our sight even while we are contemplating their effects."

This confession of something beyond our comprehension in the atonement runs through all the literature of the Christian religion. Some theologians, indeed, scoff at it and reject it. But the heart of the church has always felt it profoundly, and acknowledged it with adoration. On Calvary we behold the "love of Christ which passeth knowledge." [2]

If the meaning of the cross were perfectly plain to us it would be less precious. We know

[1] Rom. 3 : 25.　　　　　[2] Eph. 3 : 19.

that we need more than we can know. The cross is most dear to our hearts because it is the sign of an unsearchable mystery of saving love.

VI

THE MESSAGE OF THE CROSS

I

THE cross speaks silently but surely of God's great love for sinners. For this reason it has become the sign under which Christianity has won its way in a world of sin. This is not a dogma of theology. It is a fact of history. Wherever the religion of Christ has advanced, its song of victory has been the burden of the ancient Latin hymn:

> *"Forward the royal banners fly,*
> *The sacred cross shines out on high,*
> *Where man's Creator stooped to die*
> *In human flesh, to draw man nigh."*

The same burden is repeated in the music of the modern church:

> *"Onward, Christian soldiers,*
> *Marching as to war,*
> *With the cross of Jesus*
> *Going on before."*

Nothing could appear more strange, if we leave out of view that interpretation of the death of Jesus which comes from the faith of the atonement, than that the cross, the emblem of the world's shame and reproach, should become the symbol of Christian faith, the treasure of Christian hope, the banner of Christian victory. How came it to be thus transformed? What miracle has exalted the instrument of death to the place of glory?

When Christianity came to China under this banner, the Chinese wondered at it, mocked at it, issued an edict against it. This edict said: "Why should the worshippers of Jesus reverence the instrument of his punishment, and consider it so to represent him as not to venture to tread upon it? Would it be common sense, if the father or ancestor of a house had been killed by a shot from a gun, or by a wound from a sword, that his sons or grandsons should reverence the gun or the sword as their father or ancestor?" It is a searching question; and the only answer to it is in the inner life, where the cross of Jesus has been planted as the tree of peace and blessing, the sign of divine forgiveness and redeeming love; so that the first cry of faith is

" *Simply to Thy cross I cling*,"

and the last breath of prayer is

"*Hold Thou Thy cross before my closing eyes*."

THE MESSAGE OF THE CROSS

There is a passage in Goethe's *Confessions of a Beautiful Soul* which tells the story of human experience before the cross.

" 'Now, Almighty God, grant me the gift of faith!' This was the prayer that came out of the deepest need of my heart. I leaned upon the little table beside me, and hid my tear-stained face in my hands. At last I was in the state in which we must be, if God is to hear our prayers, but in which we so seldom are.

"Yes, but who could ever express, even in the dimmest way, the experience that came to me then? A secret influence drew my soul away to the cross, where Jesus once expired. It was an inward leading, I cannot give it any other name, like that which draws the heart to its beloved one in absence, a spiritual approach doubtless far truer and more real than a dream. So my soul drew near to him who became man and died upon the cross, and in that moment I knew what faith was.

" 'This is faith!' I cried, and sprang up as if half frightened. I tried to make sure of my experience, to verify my vision, and soon I was convinced that my spirit had received a wholly new power to uplift itself.

"In these feelings words forsake us. I could distinguish clearly between my experience and all fantasy. It was entirely free from fantasy. It was not a dream-picture. And yet it gave me the sense of reality in the object which it brought before me, just as imagination does when it recalls the features of a dear friend far away."

Many are the souls that have passed through that indescribable experience. Millions of men who have been unmoved by philosophy and unconvinced by argument, have yielded to the mystic attractions of the cross of Jesus. The story of this divine charm runs like a thread of gold through all the many-coloured literature of Christianity.

If I were asked to name the three books outside of the New Testament which lie closest to the Christian heart, and are entitled to be called the classics of Christian faith, I should choose *The Imitation of Christ* and *The Pilgrim's Progress* and *The Christian Year*. There is no difference among them in their testimony to the power of the cross of Jesus to draw men to him.

"Take up, therefore, thy cross," says Thomas à Kempis, "and follow Jesus, and thou shalt go into life everlasting. He went before bearing his cross, and died for thee on the cross, that thou mightest also bear thy cross and die on the cross with him."

426

THE MESSAGE OF THE CROSS

"So I saw in my dream," says John Bunyan, "that just as Christian came up with the Cross, his burden loosed from off his shoulders and fell from off his back, and began to tumble, and so continued to do, till it came to the mouth of the sepulchre, where it fell in, and I saw it no more. Then was Christian glad and lightsome, and said with a merry heart, he hath given me rest by his sorrow, and life by his death."

"Is it not strange," says John Keble in his poem on the Crucifixion,—

"Is it not strange, the darkest hour
  That ever dawned on sinful earth,
Should touch the heart with softer power
  For comfort than an angel's mirth?
That to the cross the mourner's eye should turn,
Sooner than where the stars of Christmas burn?
  .   .   .   .

Lord of my heart, by Thy last cry,
  Let not Thy blood on earth be spent:
Lo, at Thy feet I fainting lie,
  Mine eyes upon Thy wounds are bent;
Upon Thy streaming wounds my weary eyes
Wait, like the parched earth on April skies.

Wash me, and dry these bitter tears;
  Oh, let my heart no farther roam,—
'Tis Thine by vows and hopes and fears,
  Long since.   Oh, call Thy wanderer home,—
To that dear home, safe in Thy wounded side,
Where only broken hearts their sin and shame may hide."

THE MESSAGE OF THE CROSS

II

The healing, purifying, pacifying power of the cross comes from its silent proclamation of the holy and self-sacrificing love of God. It reveals him to us as he really is,—eternally willing to forgive sin, and entirely ready to suffer for the sake of making its forgiveness perfect and pure and altogether beyond question. It carries in itself the marks of an immeasurable mercy; a tender resolution to meet, for our sake, requirements that are beyond our ken; a tranquil assurance that God's pardon is a holy pardon, a righteous pardon, a pardon through which "there is no condemnation to those who are in Christ Jesus." [1]

But we do not say that this message of the cross is the only ministry of peace and blessing and enrichment that Christ has brought to the life of man. Nor do we say that those who have failed to hear in this message the very same words which it brings to us, or to interpret these words as they have been interpreted in our experience, have not been blessed in any way by Christ.

Some have followed him, as Peter did at first, unwilling to think of his cross. Some

[1] Rom. 8 : 1.

have trusted his forgiving power, as Mary Magdalen did, without apprehending what his forgiveness would cost. Some have called upon him for salvation, as the penitent thief did, without understanding the great significance of his sacrifice. And there are some to-day who belong to Christ in their hearts and lives, but who have not yet read clearly the writing above the cross.

Pure and patient souls, companions of the merciful labours of Jesus, lovers of his gracious doctrine, worshippers of his divine perfection, illustrators of his meek and lowly spirit, whose lives are fragrant with the sweetness of the Master's name, of whose presence the world is glad, in whose lowly service the heart of the Lord rejoiceth,—surely of them we may say, *If any man have the spirit of Christ, he is one of his.*

The saving shadow of the cross falls upon these gentle lives, though they know it not. Christ did not die only for those who call him "Lord." He died also for those who minister to him without knowing it.

But the message which is proclaimed to the world by these serene and untroubled lives,— it is certainly a gospel; but is it, indeed, *the* Gospel for which the great mass of men, sin-

ful, struggling, weary, despondent, are longing?
No; it is imperfect. It does not go down to
the bottom of human experience. It does not
meet the full need of those who labour and are
heavy-laden under the weight of sin, of those
who are tormented with remorse, of those who
would give all that they have if they could blot
out the fatal past and cast away the burden
of their conscious guilt. Poor strugglers under
the curse of evil, the vast majority of mankind
long passionately for the blessedness of the man
whose sins are forgiven, whose transgressions
are covered. To such men the gospel of the
Son of God, who bore our sins in his own body
on the tree, is the real gospel, the veritable
"good tidings of great joy."

III

There is no final formula of the cross. Perhaps if it could have been put into a series of
logical propositions, the divine sacrifice would
not have been necessary. But God has seen fit
to save men, not by a system of definitions, but
by an experience of grace.

This experience takes into itself all the permanent elements of the soul's life. It includes
and interprets also all those elements which are
progressive, the factors of man's moral being

which are in process of development through the discipline of the individual and the race.

It has been well said that "one of the objects of the atonement is to form the conscience to which it makes its appeal."

It would be strange, indeed, if, with the education of man's ethical nature, there were not also a real progress in the interpretation of the message of the cross. It does not change; it unfolds.

We can see how it grew in the epistles of St. Paul. It was the same gospel from the beginning to the end of his life. But it found new expressions and took larger forms. It meant one thing in Thessalonica, and more of the same thing in Galatia, and more of the same thing in Corinth, and more of the same thing in Rome, until, finally, it rose to its height in the epistles of the imprisonment, where it appears as the good news of the reconciliation of all things, "whether they be things in earth or things in heaven." [1]

There are three great ideas in which the human race has made an immense ethical advance. And it seems to me that all of these advancing ideas must have an influence upon

[1] Col. 1 : 20.

our interpretation of the message of the cross, and must open new vistas of wondrous glory in the circle of its universal significance.

The first of these ideas is the unity and solidarity of mankind. It is characteristic of modern thought that, in its view,

" The individual withers, and the world is more and more."

Vast sociological tables are compiled, covering the physical peculiarities and social customs, the arts and industries, the family ties and ethical conceptions, the forms of government and modes of worship of all sorts and conditions of men, in all quarters of the globe. The causes of the rise or decline of certain tribes are investigated; the secret bonds which unite the generations on an upward or downward scale are traced; the average intelligence of communities is measured; the average welfare of the world is estimated; the collective view of mankind predominates in the thoughtful mind of to-day.

It would be singular and unfortunate if this new view of life did not bring new and larger meanings into the message of the cross. It must be the meeting-point of races, as well as the landmark of centuries. It must reconcile man with men, as well as men with God. It must be an opener of closed doors, a conciliator of estranged peoples.

The universal charter of the cross,—"Go ye therefore and disciple all nations," [1]—forgotten and obscured in ages of particularism, revives in ages of human brotherhood. A gospel of limited atonement becomes a manifest absurdity of selfishness. Sacrifice for others—one man for another, one race for another, and Christ for all—is seen to be built into the very structure of Christianity.

If the modern world is to hear the message of the cross, the church must speak the language of to-day—the language of universal atonement and foreign missions.

Another idea in which there has been a great advance is the notion of law. In the first stage of human progress, the concept of law is chiefly vindictive; it simply destroys the offender. In the next stage, it takes on a nobler aspect and becomes a system which inflicts retribution on the law-breaker in order that its majesty may be upheld and the peace of society secured by the wholesome restraints of fear. Under this conception, law punishes the offender in order that other men may be afraid to offend. In

[1] St. Matt. 28 : 19.

the third and highest stage, the reformative principle of law comes into clear view and takes the leadership. The regulative idea does not vanish. The idea of a positive guilt in crime is not lost. But both become subordinate to the higher idea of a moral purpose in law,— the rescue and reformation of the offender. Rectoral justice still remains a necessity of government, but reformative justice appears as the supreme necessity in a moral order of society.

No man can study the history of laws, no man can read the story of prison reform and compare the penal statutes of three centuries ago with those of to-day, without perceiving that there has been a wonderful progress in this direction. And side by side with it, not always with equal steps, but always in the same direction, we see a progress in the interpretation of atonement.

The old idea, that Christ died because God was insulted and must punish somebody, fades out. The conception of the death of Jesus as a mere exhibition of governmental severity for the sake of keeping order in the universe, becomes too narrow. The measuring of the precise amount of Christ's suffering, as a *quid pro quo* for an equal amount of penalty incurred by human sin, no longer satisfies the moral sense. The cross itself, with its simplicity, its generosity of sacrifice, its evident reforming and regenerating power upon the heart,—the cross itself leads the race upward and onward in the interpretation of its message.

Whatever else the sufferings of Jesus may mean, whatever unsearchable necessities of the divine government they may meet, they must meet this great requirement, this ultimate ideal of all moral law. Their end must be righteousness, their purpose must be "to make us good."

So the cross comes with a deeper message than mere vindication of law, or mere exemption from penalty. It says to every man: "Christ was crucified with thee, that thou mightest be crucified with him. He died for thee, that thou shouldest not henceforth live unto thyself, but unto him who died for thee and rose again. Rise with him into the new life. Never despair. Never surrender to remorse or fear or death. Come up with Christ, come on with Christ, into the ransomed life."

There is one more idea in which there has been a real advance; and that is, the idea of sin. Here I do not think it is possible for us to trace the progress through the centuries, as we can trace the ideas of human solidarity and of law. But certainly there is in the deepest and best modern thought a more profound and vital conception of the nature of sin, than there was in the ages when it was imagined that a murderer or an adultress could "square the record" by building a church or endowing a monastery. I think we feel now, if we admit that there is such a thing as sin at all, that it cannot be in any sense a mere external. "The laws of God are written in the human soul, and the sin of man is a sin against the law of his own nature."

There is an unnaturalness in sin which is the worst kind of unworthiness. It cannot possibly be taken away by any outward pardon, by any formal justification at the bar of a law which is external to us. Not only must the law which is above us be fulfilled, but also the law which is within us must be restored. This can only be done by the renewal of a vital communion with God, who is the author of both laws. He must be our deliverer outwardly and inwardly,—

> "*Be of sin the double cure*
> *Save me from its guilt and power.*"

The cross speaks to us not only of the death of Christ for us, but of the life of the Spirit in us. This was the interpretation which Jesus himself put upon it. He said, "It is expedient for you that I go away: for if I go not away the Comforter will not come unto you."[1] Certainly we have not entered into the full meaning of Christ's death until we have learned to see in it the condition and the means of the dispensation of the Spirit.

We may not know the significance of this on the divine side. Why the Comforter would not come unless Christ went away, we cannot tell. But on the human side the truth is not difficult to apprehend. The vision of Christ's suffering and death makes it infinitely easier for us to receive the Comforter. It breaks the bonds of that rigid and pedantic notion of God which exhibits him as remote, inflexible, impassible. It shows us that he is great enough and good enough to suffer with us in order to deliver us from sin. It diffuses through the soul the fragrance of a new kind of forgiveness, —the only real forgiveness,—a forgiveness which not only blots out guilt, but opens the heart's door to the Spirit and restores divine fellowship.

Thus it seems to me that the message of the cross, because it is a living message, must be

[1] St. John 16 : 7.

437

ever growing and drawing new words into its service, and charging them with richer meaning.

The theory of the atonement will never be completed until the discipline and education of humanity are completed.

You come to a man with your theory of the atonement, and he says, "Yes, perhaps it means that to you, but it means something else, something far more precious, to me." You come to another man, and he says: "No doubt there is truth in your view, but it is not all the truth. Christ crucified means more than that to me." And so it ought to be, so it must be, if the atonement has a real place in the inner life. We ought not to expect, we ought not to wish, that it should ever be defined or explained in a formula valid for all men and for all time. Whatever it may be in itself, whatever it may be in its objective relations to God's government of the world, for us it must be a progressive, growing, expanding element of spiritual peace and power.

IV

This expanding message of the cross, then, is what I believe to be the true gospel for a world of sin. The heart of it never changes. "Herein is love, not that we loved God, but that he loved us, and sent his Son to be the propitiation for our sins."

Is such a gospel as this unsuited to the present age? Is such a gospel as this a low gospel, a narrow gospel, an immoral gospel, an obsolete gospel, a gospel to be ashamed of in the presence of learning and refinement and moral earnestness? Let the men whose hearts have been cleansed and ennobled by it—the men like Paul, and Augustine, and Francis of Assisi, and Martin Luther, and John Wesley—make answer.

Is such an experience as this an unreal experience, a fantastic thing, a thing of no great consequence, of no large influence in

> "*The very world which is the world*
> *Of all of us,—the place where in the end*
> *We find our happiness, or not at all*"?

Let the answer come from the triumph in the midst of sorrow, the courage in the face of death, and the steadfast devotion to every noble cause, of those who have learned to say, "The life that I now live in the flesh I live by the faith of the Son of God, who loved me and gave himself for me."

Is such a message as this to the inner life of

man no longer needed, in these latter days?
Let the unchanged, struggling, sinful heart of
man make answer.

Burdened with the weight of responsibilities
to which we have never lived up, disenchanted
by the sad advance of a knowledge with which
our vital wisdom has not kept pace, stained
and dishonoured by sins of selfishness and pride
and impurity and unbrotherliness and greed and
avarice and anger, which our very privileges
charge with a tenfold guilt,—delicate and self-
complacent offenders, men who know but do
not practise, heirs of all the ages who have
bartered our birthright, and declined our duty,
and sinned against light a thousand times,—
how stand we in the sight of God, in these
latter days, without a Saviour from our sins?

Is this an easy age, a careless age, a peaceful, secure, sin-free age for the inner life? On
every side, with growing knowledge, the shades
of the prison-house close around us.

The moralists tell us of ever-increasing obligations, duties, demands of personal and social
righteousness. The standard rises, but the inspiration sinks. Students of life tell us of the
permanence and power of evil, the taint of
blood, the corruption of nature, the force of
degeneration, the heavy fetters of heredity.

THE MESSAGE OF THE CROSS

We need a God with us to set us free. Philosophers tell us that there may be a God, but that he is certainly distant, impersonal, unknown, unknowable.

What an age for a divine Redeemer, a liberating God incarnate, a real atonement to deliver us from the coil of sin! Is there not a welcome in the world to-day for the Conqueror from Edom? Is there not a mission still in our inner life for the Son of God, who loved us and gave himself for us?

> "*The very God! think, Abib; dost thou think?*
> *So the All-great were the All-loving, too,—*
> *So through the thunder comes a human voice*
> *Saying, 'O heart I made, a heart beats here!*
> *Face my hands fashioned, see it in myself!*
> *Thou hast no power, nor mayest conceive of mine,*
> *But love I gave thee with myself to love,*
> And thou must love me who have died for thee!'"

www.ingramcontent.com/pod-product-compliance
Lightning Source LLC
Chambersburg PA
CBHW030238030726
47493CB00023B/135